Emily Edwards was born in the city of Coventry, United Kingdom, and grew to love literature through writing short stories and poetry at an early age. She gained an MA (2002) and BA (1999) in English and International History at university later in life. Writing is a passion that never decreases, and through this passion she challenges her readers to walk in the footsteps of her characters.

Other books by Emily Edwards:

THE RHIA BRYANT SERIES

The 'Art' of Deception (Book 1)

POETRY

The Shadow of Poppy (WW1 poetry)

Dedicated to Sarah, thank you for your patience.

Emily Edwards

The Double Edged Sword

Austin Macauley Publishers™
London • Cambridge • New York • Sharjah

A CIP catalogue record for this title is available from the British Library.

ISBN 9781398461017 (Paperback)
ISBN 9781398461024 (ePub e-book)

www.austinmacauley.com

First Published 2022
Austin Macauley Publishers Ltd®
1 Canada Square
Canary Wharf
London
E14 5AA

Question: *Can a deceiver be deceived?*
Answer: *Deception is the next move from arrogance.*

What is a Diary?
A diary can be a timepiece for each month of a year or, it can be the story within a story – the mystery that leads our footsteps from one life towards another.

A Double – Edged Sword
Metaphor –
Originated from the Arabic expression 'Sayf du Hadayn', meaning two sides of the same blade cut both ways.
Double Edged Swords- The Wookiee Warlord
Sith War Lord
Zha Boka
First known to England in the 15th Century.

The phrase can also represent the 'payback' of a deed.

Stolen Moments

Yours, I was in daytime hours.
When birds in unison sang.
Yours, I was through endless nights.
As the heat of passion sprang.

Snatching stolen moments.
As my beating heart awaits.
The sound of quickening footsteps.
And the rattling of a gate.

Lost in a world of shadows.
Where flesh the soul enslaved.
Sailing deep the murky water.
Dredging lusts consuming grave.

Praying for salvation.
From the pain of sweet deceit.
Drowning in the mire.
Of a love that is bittersweet.

Gone now, are the hours.
Of you and I entwined.
Faded pictures of a lifetime.
In my heart forever enshrined.

by Emily Edwards

Prelude
Brandenburg–Gordan Prison, Germany
December 2000

The man stared out from his tiny cell window onto the yard below. Deserted now, from the heavy rain that had suddenly drenched the single file row of prisoners walking around the concrete zone. Allowing his eyes to drift across the square the man imagined the pent-up anger of men shuffled back inside by the 'whack' of a stick, or abuse from the mouth of a guard. Grasping the iron bars covering the dirty panes his eyes followed the thrashing rain as it coursed like a river onto the windowsill outside. Labelled a political prisoner, he, plus his comrades were regarded as enemies of the state; savages to the people they had served. They were prisoners from the old East German regime: soldiers of a disposed army. His blonde hair fell forward as he rested his furrowed brow against the cold mesh latched between the bars. He sniggered, thought how the word "traitor" followed a kick of a boot, or the lash of a water hose.

"Payback," they would laugh.

Payback – These savages knew nothing about payback.

His hands, taut on the cage covering his window trembled with excitement as a faint rumble began to spread throughout the locked down cells. Tin mugs against metal bars. Fisted palms against old rattling doors. The low chant of "Freedom" rumbling from the mouths of confined men, cascading into a throbbing rhythm, weaving its way through the prison. The man quivered, his painful limbs convulsing with an overpowering delight. For a second day he would hear the reverberation of protest seeping along these corridors. A low, prolonged chanting, threatening those guards, whose loyalty wavered, with the masked conviction of retribution. From their mouths flowed the curse of the damned, held under the new state law, where men, such as they, should be punished.

“Why?” he mumbled. “Because they were loyal to a man that upheld a totalitarian dream”

The man spat on the floor, disregarding the ‘fool’ whose job it was to wash these cells: coughed as though his heart would burst from his chest. Suddenly hearing the scream “Stoppen” over a loudspeaker he knew those guards were losing patience; their fear shown through the guttural sound leaving their rough German throats. He breathed deep. Punishment was looming, more ‘rights’ confiscated. Flinging himself down upon the thin straw mattress his mind travelled to that commander these prisoners held in awe. No matter what fate lay within these walls, their obedience never faltered from this man of reputable authority. They would not be swayed to talk, whatever lay in wait for them in those rooms of interrogation. These guards, fools every one of them, stood as nothing compared to the Major, his mandate conquered all, even in this close guarded prison.

A low belly laugh triggered another coughing fit, creating spasms of wheezing, those moments when shortness of breath tore through the man’s body, leaving him panting and spluttering. It was his turn to curse. This illness had crept upon him as the days grew colder, and the nights longer, his prison cell dark and damp. Forcing his mind back to his previous introspection his heart slowed, replaced by a sensation of respect and fear. This commander German Intelligence sought was his father, an officer at the top of his game.

He sneered at the large bounty they offered for his capture.

His father, that elusive pedagogue, was far too clever to be caught. As far back as his memory allowed Stasi intelligence had ruled every waking hour: his childhood games, the family gatherings, his youthful yearnings. There was no room for play, only information and secrets his father gathered.

The man flipped onto his stomach, buried his head in the thin material of the pillow. His coughing might have ceased, but a sharp pain filtered itself across his chest, squeezing his lungs in the way a plumber would use his pincers. The man closed his eyes. Old memories had begun to haunt him, dragging him to a place he would rather forget – Hohenschonhausen, the old Stasi prison residing in the district of Lichtenberg, East Northern Berlin. Transformed by the East German secret police in 1951, this building previously known as Special Camp No 3, a prison and transfer centre for the Russians, was extended in the late 1950s by Stasi request. It became a hospital and interrogation centre, not recorded on the map of the day; stormed after the fall of the wall. This allowed all files to be burnt, leaving no statements apart from those who survived the regimes brutality. Using prisoner labour, a hospital wing, laboratory, and morgue were added, serving its own prisoners, staff, plus three other prisons. Along with the detention rooms, interrogation cells, exercise yards (dubbed by the prisoners as tiger cages) execution rooms, and a staff wing, this building became the backdrop to many a dissident or political activist's death. Information was gleaned by torture, but mainly by psychological persuasion through threats to family and friends, sexual deviances, and mental state. If these did not work, then waterboarding or water cells were called upon.

A cry escaped from the man's mouth as his mind trod the long corridors, the rancid smell of fear emanating with the dim light shining onto the closed doors, where 'pain' was a byword for men and women to suffer. He could still hear the screams, see the bleeding flesh, feel his own flinching body as blow after blow hammered down on an already unrepairable frame. His father had demanded his son's attendance, followed by a visit to the laboratory where specimens, bloodied and bruised, resided in sparkling dishes. Overlooked by Doctor Herbert Vogel with 28 Stasi staff, the 'pleasantries' of interrogation skills were 'soothed' away. His 'after school' activities transmitted into an adolescence of obedience. The son became his father's assistant, travelling to Stasi headquarters, meeting his father's commanders, learning the history of the regime. The service known as 'Staatssieherheitsdienst' – SSD – ministry for state security, was formed on 8th February 1950, overlooked by Wilhelm Zaisser, succeeded by Ernst Wollweber in 1957, later to be commanded by Erich Melke, once Zaisser's deputy, for the remaining period of Stasi rule. Then there was Marcus Wolfe, head of the HVA – Hauptverwaltung Aufklarung – Reconnaissance Administration – Foreign intelligence. These men, the man knew, had weighed heavily upon his father's daily commands. The motto rang out–

'Schild und Schwert der Parter' – 'Shield and Sword of the party'

Where was his father now?

The man thumped the pillow, rolled onto his back, eyes penetrating the dingy ceiling. It had taken ten years for German intelligence to track himself down, thanks to his clandestine role as a student at that English university, and later his immersion into the world of art.

His choking laugh penetrated his thoughts –

If they sought to arrest his father – It would be wiser to think again. He was a master in the field of deception. His dearest wish, to join his father before it was too late, before his body succumbed to fate.

The man jumped from the bed and wandered once more to the window.

Whilst the rattling of mugs had ceased, the rain was still thrashing itself against the glass, misting the panes where his comrades, with their downcast faces, now peered out in disgust, a dissembled army of forgotten men.

After the dismantling of the Berlin Wall his life had been taken over by the canvas and brush. He had found a small amount of freedom, if only with his joy of oils and brush. He had begged the guards for those tools, much to their humour, their sick, obscenities. They refused to acknowledge him. Refused to accept he was the profound painter sought by art lovers throughout the world.

How dare they – scabs of the earth.

The man swore, knew vaguely the fault lay with him.

Maybe he should not have tried to pass messages as he walked, even though shuffling was reality, and boredom the truth. He needed to be free. He yelped as he punched the wall with his clenched fist. Again, the sensation of coughing ripped at his throat as the blood oozing from his grazed knuckles made him wince, then laugh. Those costly hands trembled faster, refusing to stop. At least they had been insured. Heaven knew why. For a day such as this?

He thumped the wall for a second time, kicked the bed, his chest pumping out that rasping noise that signifies death.

--

The footsteps were sensed, and the turn of the key, way before the guards entered the cell. This effect was occurring more than he would like to admit of late; a sensing that led to confirmation.

"Sie," the voice barked, "Komm mit mir."

The guard was large, not only in height, but in girth, and the roughness in the 'you' and 'come with me' startled the man into leaving his window position and falling into line between two smaller guards. They marched from the cell in silence, a habit the man had found amusing on other occasions; almost as if they were children playing a game of trains. He wanted to ask questions, realised how futile that would be, for however many queries he had would fall onto deaf ears. These men believed strength was their password, therefore muteness was a command to follow. The man wondered if he was being transported to another prison deeper in the East. Many a rumour had reached him that this was a 'party' trick of the prison authorities, political prisoners hidden from sight. He sighed, if this occurred, his father would never find him. Yet, that man had once reassured him that if imprisonment became his son's fate, there would be no hiding place for those who locked him up.

Abruptly the guards came to a halt, turned right through a door into a spacious room of white painted walls, wooden blocked floor, large pictures hanging from the walls, and what the prisoner thought was the 'Piece De Resistance', large unnetted windows looking out onto a neat garden – a contradiction to this overcrowded penal system. The man stood still, looked around him, his mind wandering to whispers of 'reform' and how the guards tried. In various ways, to 'humour', a polite word for correct, the prisoner's thinking down the pathway of democracy.

'Try' the man thought, steeling his slight frame for onslaught.

Falling back the guards nodded for him to move forward. The man blinked, lowered his eyes to the bright ceiling light, then as quickly drew them up again to stare in disbelief. By the window that was *his* easel, *his* paints, and *his* canvas. Moving nearer he could see the canvas was not blank, as first thought, but a creative display of art recently bought by a museum for an unbelievable amount of money. His own secular impression of that phenomenon recorded as the Crux – the Southern Star: five celestial bodies gleaming in the night sky.

A tear ran down the man's cold thin cheek: a lonely tear for what may have been, not what he was experiencing now.

"Beautiful" the cultured tone spoke perfect English.

He swung round, his eyes still struggling to adjust to the bright light. Another figure had entered the room, his suit cut in the latest fashion, his shoes polished to resemble a mirror, and his greying hair combed across one side to represent the look of the day. To the man's amazement this figure of dignified fashion 'shooed' the guards away, then proceeded to squat on a stool placed in front of the easel.

"Ottmar Wilner," he said in a loud voice, offering his hand for shaking,

"I am visiting this prison on your behalf. I have passed this with the governor, and he realises what is wise for him."

The man stared into the startlingly blue eyes, let his words sink into his befuddled brain, then mouthed –

"Ottmar, – Vater?"

The visitor inclined his head, eyes scanning the door, fingers to mouth–

"Only English."

The man swallowed hard feeling that irritation in the throat which precedes his coughing. Trying to speak he was instantly stopped.

"Say nothing, just listen. What I must demand is important, hence why I speak to you in English. Nobody else must know. Since the fall of the Berlin Wall in 1989 your father has pursued another path..."

The visitor, weightier than at first presumed, continued his rhetoric, each word thrilling the feeble prisoner; those spurting lips moving as if his life depended on the transmission of his tale.

The man's thin lips twisted. At last, his father had a plan, the payback from years of waiting. This has got to be the beginning of freedom. His hands fell upon the paintbrushes grouped in a glass jar on a small table to the side of the easel. He fingered their silkiness, brushed the bristles across his hands. The visitor stood. Taking the man's shoulders within his hands he gently lowered him onto the stool.

"Paint," he whispered.

Reaching for another brush the man snarled through gritted teeth –

"Rache, Rache, Rache."

Frowning the visitor replied–

"Revenge, Revenge, Revenge."

Suburb of London
December 2000
Diary entry from Rhia Bryant

How this year had flown.

The wisdom of age would quote 'with golden wings', the young may state 'deluded happiness'. Now, whilst wisdom is priceless, the declaration of youth may be nearer to the truth. The frantic passing of this year, seen through the eyes of one whose delusions have crashed and burnt, are as follows:

No sooner had Jimmy and I climbed that mountain of happiness than we rolled back down.

Corollary?

Correct – a hundred percent.

The sweetness of our fusion was tinted from the beginning with shadows. One name continually 'popped' into daily conversations and nightly thoughts. In the manner of a bonfire night rocket a simple slip or stab of *that* name sent flames of wrath leaping from mouths that represented a crackling fire. Nights of passion turned into days of duress when that idiom 'walk on eggshells' became fact. Long summer days that began drenched in laughter fizzled into dusky hours of thoughtfulness as Jimmy sank into his own inner sanctuary. He nicknamed these periods of solitude 'work nests', I retaliated by labelling them the 'misery hour'. Neither mentioned our old pact. Neither dare tread the pathway of our past. We rolled, as aforementioned, through the leafy days of autumn, to the confrontation of this day.

Jimmy, whom I love, however I moan, is a workaholic. His position of senior curator at that museum of antiquities and paintings must receive the acknowledgement it deserves. His commitment to his position is truly admirable, sadly unlike myself, still incarcerated in the bank where my father is a director, on low pay and low status. Although I will add that pride may not be among my first admission when relaying how hard Jimmy strives, I do recognise his work ethic when it comes to his discovery of hidden gems. By that I do not mean jewels, but a painting within a painting.

I know, to those not from an 'arty' background it is a riddle.

I will explain –

Like most pathways in life the painter may become the genius of an adoring art world, or the creative master lost in the passage of time. It is true to say that most painters, past or present, fulfilled their wish to paint an inspiring portrait, a beautiful landscape, maybe that intriguing still life. However, if an instant dislike to their canvas arose these painters would cast their art aside, deciding to re-paint another subject over it, or pass it to a student for their use. Due to lifestyle, many of these painters were struggling for money, and a re-used canvas could be the solution. Known as hidden paintings, art from the brush of that original master becomes priceless. Even so, these 'hidden' paintings, according to Jimmy, can become an act of protection. A guise where the painter, in conjunction with their 'other' life, may conceal names or codes beneath their art; a collaboration with those who wish an oil to be an allurement: the means to draw a character into what maybe dubbed a 'spiders web'.

At the beginning of December Jimmy, who had been a visitor to the Paris art galleries more days than I thought fit, suddenly announced his removal to the sister gallery in Germany. Struggling to comprehend how this would affect my job, my flat, my way of life, the bombshell hit me when he further announced he was going alone.

"I am searching for a painting, Rhia, stolen from our museum only last week."

That was news to me.

Evidently, an exquisite watercolour of the cross in the southern hemisphere was removed one night under the noses of muscular guards.

"How?" I queried in astonishment.

"Goodness knows" he replied, continuing his exaltation of the painting.

'Five celestial bodies against a black sky. The Southern Cross, known simply in the Latin term as Crux, is the smallest of eighty-eight 'modern' constellations, yet the most distinctive. Easily visible from the southern hemisphere it may also be viewed near the tropical latitudes of the horizon of the northern hemisphere for a few hours at night during winter and spring. Contrary to belief the Crux is not opposite Ursa Major, which are both low in the sky, but exactly opposite Cassiopeia on the celestial sphere, meaning they cannot appear together at the same time.'

Pause-

'The Crux has one blue/white bright star known as Acrux, surrounded by four less bright stars – Mimosa, Gacrux, Imai, and Ginan, thought to be roughly ten to twenty million years old. The ancient Greeks recorded it as part of the constellation Centaurius. The Crux was forgotten, then re-discovered by

Europeans in the fifteenth to seventeenth century, 'Age of Discovery'. Contributed to the French astronomer Augustin Royer in 1679, other historians name Petrus Planais in 1613 as its new founder, later Jakob Bartsch in 1624'

Jimmy, hardly stopping to catch breath gabbled something about a masterpiece. Refusing to release the torrent of tears that had hovered daily when my partner was in Paris I groaned –

"How dare those fusty old codgers ask you to go to Germany alone. Those guards should be sacked."

My partner smiled "They swear they saw or heard nothing."

"Really," I returned "How convenient. What fool hired them?"

"I did" he whispered.

My mouth felt dry. Even so, it is strange how they saw or heard nothing.

"Sorry" I stuttered "Please..."

Jimmy's eyebrows arched –

"Forget it" he turned aside "I must find that painting. The museum believes it is important. Apart from the money paid, it has hidden elements."

Not that again.

Determined to lighten the moment I quipped–

"Who can be the ruddy painter – Gainsborough?"

I began to laugh – stopped – as Jimmy quickly spat–

"It appears your knowledge of art is as misinformed as your grasp of most things. The painter is Jules Dragner."

I stared at him, ignored his rudeness–

"Jules Dragner?"

"Yes" he said sarcastically "The nemesis of our arguments."

It is not often that words desert me, but my mouth had gone dry.

"I leave within the week," he stated firmly.

"Please don't go" I managed to stutter.

Jimmy threw me a glance, shook his head, then uttered those words my heart did not want to hear "I have to go."

Deep breath–

Shall I scream. Produce my best tantrum ever? Not a good vibe for a thirty something woman. I need charm, temptation, even seduction. If they do not work, nothing will. He had an urgency about him, a determination I had never seen before. Jimmy headed for the kitchen. Rooted to my spot I could hear the cupboard door open, hear the clink of glasses, sense him finding the wine.

“Celebration” he waved the bottle in his hand as he re-emerged “Germany and me.”

I would like to write that my defeat in this matter could be looked upon with honour, but this is me, Rhia Bryant, and I do not succumb without a fight. This was an emergency: a damsel trying hard to change her lover’s mind. So, this woman smiled–

“Let us toast” I said, stretching out the glass he had given me to be filled.

Jimmy eyed me cautiously. Taking hold of his free hand I whispered in his ear–

“Relax,”

and led him into the bedroom.

Two days later -

I lost the fight.

Four words that stand as a statement to my failure.

“How?” you may ask as I try not to stamp as a child.

I seriously tried everything. From the sweet alluring lover to the pragmatic friend. Whichever way I exercised my ‘charm’ Jimmy blocked it with his own version of reasoning. I was totally exhausted after half a bottle of wine, cavorting around an already crumpled bed, and implementing the most seductive voice my poor throat could handle,

NOTHING WORKED.

Over the past two days I had witnessed my dearest friend and lover enjoy our togetherness whilst throwing clothes into a suitcase with the speed of a cheetah. His continuous ranting of that ‘precious’ watercolour filled me with an anger I found hard to resist. Often, as I watched the stars flicker in a frost veiled sky, I turned to the body sleeping by my side, stroked the dark sweat streaked hair, and pleaded for him to stay. Naughty fate would not listen, she rolled her dice, demanded my Jimmy elsewhere, leaving me to contend with a past that refuses to melt away.

The day of parting dawned no differently to those Paris jaunts that Jimmy undertook. He was up with the lark, scuttering about from room to room, checking if everything for the journey was present and correct. I followed him around like that proverbial lost puppy. He thanked me, hugged me, swung me round the lounge, finally standing by the door, his lean frame cloistered in the warmth of a worsted wool overcoat.

"A gentleman," I muttered, suppressing the tears that were collecting.

"A traveller," he threw back.

The suitcase, propped by the sofa, glistened in the early morning sun, echoing the multi coloured fairy lights I had draped around the flat and deliberately switched on. Attached to the silver case handle the ticket displayed the letters Friedrichstrasse Sreet, 'GERMANY' in large black writing, delivering a cold sensation of dread; a disquiet one cannot explain.

"Ready," Jimmy warbled.

"Yes, I can see that."

He grasped my chin, turned my solemn face toward him and kissed me–

"There, do not fret. All will be sorted soon."

Those words again.

Picking up his suitcase Jimmy's hand rested on the door latch. Swirling to face me he commented –

"We have had fun Rhia?"

His eyes had misted over, confirming my suspicions that my partner did not wish to leave. Silently I cursed those guards.

"Hurry home!" I cried.

Jimmy opened the door. I made to step forward. He grinned and was gone.

--

I sat that night of Jimmy's departure watching the Christmas lights in the flats across the street flicker into life. Strings of sparkling colour welcoming this festive season, bidding the memories haunting my mind to recede back from where they had crawled. In my own dark flat (no lights required) I positioned my chair in front of the window, allowing me that unabridged view which a sullen heart requires. Jimmy had left me twelve hours ago. Hours, when my mind had forged every avenue that connected me to him. Waiting for news, any news, I had refused to go to work. Feigning a cold and pretending to be suffering from a headache I wallowed in the sympathy the receptionist at the bank poured upon me. Suggesting my message was relayed to the boss, my father, she continued her empathy, pausing only to gather her breath when a senior called her name. Wishing me the stereotypical 'Get Well Soon', she quickly replaced the phone. No sooner had the phone 'clicked' than my father rang.

"Rhia, what is wrong?"

How this man knows me.

"Jimmy," I moaned, trying not to blubber too much into the handpiece.

My father sighed.

"Yes, I have heard. Do not fret, all will be sorted."

These soothing words and perception of my plight guided my day.

The day passed in trivial pursuits, nodding, drinking – nothing. It was not until later that evening when acknowledging every tree dancing with multiple baubles and lights, and the frantic cavorting of small children in the fun filled rooms opposite that I realised my father's sentiment was parallel to Jimmy. Both had told me not to fret. Both had proclaimed 'it' (whatever *it* was) would be sorted. My two favourite men in the world had insisted 'all' would be fine. How can anything be fine when one travels the continent searching for a painting by the hand of a man who lied. No, my mind is clear. No matter what serenity overcame me with their comforting, the darkness of this room has brought thoughts I cannot guard against. As with the shadow of a hand, or a book left unfinished, my strange dilemma was taking shape.

Once more that earlier shivering I had experienced attacked me. Moving my chair nearer to the fire I rubbed my hand up and down my arm. There was a coldness in the room yet, that vibrant memory of heat. The familiar contradiction remembered from another night in 1989. How repressed mouths had flared. How anguish had mixed with expectation. I thought of that kiss, those hands, that…

I quickly flicked on every light possible. These thoughts were for the dark. Tonight, I would sleep with the bedside lamp on. The church clock struck midnight heralding what is known as the witching hour, creating an uneasy stillness around the street.

I had not heard from Jimmy.

True, there had been no promise, nonetheless… Restless I began to walk around the room. Across the street blinds and curtains began to close with the dimming of lights as exhausted adults found their way to bed. I yawned. Suddenly, my mobile phone began to buzz. Dashing to pick it up from its resting place by the fire, my eyes roamed over the text – It was Jimmy. Excitement filled my mind as I read–

'Arrived safe. Could not ring – Busy. I will ring New Year's Day… J x

"New Year's Day!" I screech. "That is three weeks away."

2001
Part One

January 2001

Monday 1st

I have decided to write a diary. A chronicle through a year of my life.

You may sigh when you read the date, for my life has a habit of rotating out of orbit on this day. A kind person would call it my 'Achilles Heel', I underline this day my 'Waterloo': the real nemesis to my troubles.

I must admit that my mother is appalled. She believes a diary, records of thoughts, pleasures, tragedies, and stories of a single woman, should never be read. In her opinion the whole memoir will be trivial: something a good married woman, that should be me, would not have the spare time to do. Simply not true. I know several married women at work who cannot wait for 'clocking off' time so they can write their diaries. They call it escapism from the routine.

With that said, I can assure you my diary will be frank (at times), uncensored, and certainly with that 'Rhia Bryant' spark of humour. From my own viewpoint it will be my reader who will add or subtract whatever they presume this woman has left out. Mind, it is important to remember that my diary is not an epistle, or for that matter, a statement of my likes or dislikes. It will be this thirty something woman's next step in her discovery of hidden truths; a path set out before my birth, yet prominent to my future revelations.

I will begin on this first day of a New Year, with Jimmy on a mission in Germany, and myself waiting for his call. I had just spent Christmas at the mercy of my mother. Herself, along with my beloved father arrived that festive morning armed with everything suitable to prepare a huge roast dinner, including my father's apron. We played Christmas songs, wore elf-like hats, drank numerous glasses of wine, before slumping on the sofa or chair to 'snooze' the afternoon away. To be honest it reminded me of my childhood – the three of us against the Christmas spirit. Concerned that her daughter would be falling apart by New Year over Jimmy's lack of communication she called every day with a list of shops to visit, or cafes to try out. By the last day of December my feet resembled a furnace, and my stomach an overloaded washtub.

So, you can imagine my horror on New Year's Eve, when my mother suggested declining father's annual dinner party; a gathering of staff appreciation, but secretly mother's celebration of all things 'swanky'. I must act fast. Bringing my most deceptive mask into play I delivered 'I am fine' speech. Reluctantly (emphasis on the reluctant) she finally agreed to go, leaving this down beat woman fighting the jaws of her subconscious predator, and a question I could not remove from my mind–

'Can a deceiver likewise be deceived?

--

Early Evening

Looking out the flat window I sense a wave of emotion shoot through me. Fairy lights are springing into life, dangling around panes already smeared with artificial snow, or draped across sills covered with holly. They sparkle, they flash, running one after another in their effort to bring New Year cheer. I laugh to myself, whisper Jimmy's name, before heading to the kitchen in the search for food. Surprisingly, the day had turned out mild, and any snow that had fallen over the past week had begun to thaw. The radio, always that crypt of information, had announced high temperatures for the first day of the year. I had listened with glee, crossing my fingers as though my life depended on my next wish, screamed with delight as they pronounced Europe had heavy snow. It was due to my excitement and the mild conditions that I had decided not to cook, grabbing a sandwich at lunchtime, and 'goodness knows what' now. Burying my head deep in the cupboard I emerged with a vintage bottle of wine; a present from my father many months back when Jimmy and myself were closer than a pair of squashed raspberries (I love this connection). Reaching for a corkscrew I release the bottle to breathe whilst I continue to seek for food. I think cold chicken, buttered crackers, a tub of coleslaw, or another sandwich. Discard them from my mind, grasp the nearest bag of crisps I can find.

Then it begins – Boom, boom, boom. Loud music, floating across the street, beating out its rhythm to an accompaniment of voices. Running into the lounge, bottle in one hand, crisps in the other, I fling open the window. The flat directly across from me has also flung wide the windows, turned up its CD player, and encouraged everyone within the street to join the party.

Boom, boom, the noise grew louder.

Singing, screeching, in or out of tune.

The fun had begun.

Lifting the bottle to my mouth I sip, feel the fire creep down my throat, took a longer sip. This is New Year's Day. I am alone –

Bah, who needs someone to have fun.

The room is streaming with the beams from a rotating disco ball; shimmery silver lighting up every corner making the demand for lights nil and void. Slowly my body starts to swing, hips gyrating with the music, head swirling in half circles to the beat, arms flying here, there, everywhere – Ohhh, wine trickles down my face. Caring nothing for my tangled hair, or the baggy jumper thrown over my silky pyjamas I raise my tempo, cavorting around the room with actions juxtaposed to a frenzied dog. I will not care. A woman must have fun.

Sip, sip, lights flashing, music thumping, squeals of delight – How the sound vibrates around the room. I pull open the bag of crisps, delve into its depth.

Louder beat – Boom, boom, boom.

Another swig of drink.

Another mouthful of crisps.

Munch, munch, move that body – round and round. My feet bang the floor harder as the beat grows wilder – Happy New Year!

Liquid splashes down my jumper as the wine carelessly misses my mouth: crisps float to the floor, creeping from my slippery fingers trying to slot them between my teeth.

A quick pause –

Ring, ring, consistent ringing – A shrill noise piercing the booming vibrations.

Go away – I refuse to register this extra sound in my brain, concentrate harder on my body. Boom, boom – Ring, ring – I gyrate around the room, sipping more wine, crunching the last of the crisps; head swinging in time with the throbbing of the music. Think tumultuous waves crashing upon rocks, that was me.

Suddenly I stop, listen, think – Was that the phone?

I fling my body toward the sofa, grab the handset as I land in a sea of cushions, shout-

"Hello"

A guffaw fills my ears, the high-pitched sound of mockery. Annoyed at this interruption to my 'party' I scream louder –

"What the hell do you want?"

Silence.

Just as I was about to slam the phone down thinking 'weirdo' a voice proclaims–

"Well, Rhia, if that is how you speak to me."

I fight with the cushions I have fallen into, my heart pumping faster than an old-fashioned bellow used for igniting fires.

"Jimmy!" I shriek.

Longer silence, then profound gabbling oozing from his end of the phone.

"A party?" he was saying "Just as well I am at my own."

"No, no."

I try to sit up, feel the lunge from my stomach, and the swing of my head. Jimmy was sighing–

"No to your party, or no to mine?"

Laughter again, this time in unison with his question.

Succeeding in pushing myself upward I gasp as the woozy feeling of not eating raises its ugly head.

"Where are you?" I mumble "Who are you with?"

There was a crackle down the phone; someone whispering in Jimmy's ear. Aware the 'boom, boom' from across the street was growing louder, accompanied by the screams of carousing revellers, I raise my tone, repeat my question–

"Where are you? Who's that?"

Jimmy clicked his teeth in that infuriating habit of his, a sure sign that he was nervous.

"My boss," came the belated reply, evidently answering me plus the person at his side. I could not believe my ears. Those fusty old creatures had left their museum to travel to Germany for the New Year. Wow, something important was going down. Head spinning, heart thumping, I managed to splutter–

"Is that good?"

Another drawn out silence, then more whispering. This distracting intervention was beginning to wear me down.

"For goodness' sake, how many more breaks in our conversation?"

Jimmy's teeth rattling was now competing with the 'boom, boom' from across the street.

"Cannot hear you," he suddenly returned. "Turn that bloody noise down."

Inside my temper flared. The movements of my earlier dancing had had a profound effect on my pyjamas. The elastic waistband was at war with my bloated stomach. I decided to hold my tongue.

In the most soothing voice, I inform him–

"It is not me. The flat across the road has a disco."

Jimmy's snap answer drove my resentment of being alone deeper–

"Whatever. Don't shout."

What is the matter with him? How dare he snap at me? How dare he think I would hold a party without him? How dare he be somewhere but in his hotel room? How dare– The heat inside me was bubbling up my throat. I struggled with my free hand to remove my jumper, a deed I should have considered when my dancing started, but crisps and wine kicked in. Thrashing around the sofa I pulled the heavy wool over my head. Calling down the phone for him to "Wait" I rush to close the window, banging it loud to make sure Jimmy could hear, rush back and splutter down the handset–

"Hello, Jimmy, p– please be there."

The phone whirred before his voice floated into my ear–

"What are you doing?"

"Shutting the window, lock out the majority of the boom."

He sneered. "Okay, that is your party finished."

It was not the way he said it, but the implication put upon it.

"Where are you?" I asked, my heart turning somersault as I waited for his answer. He hesitated, more teeth clicking.

"A drinking house not far from my hotel."

I froze.

There was only one drinking house to my knowledge within the vicinity of Friedrichstrasse Street, and surely the authorities had either closed or refurbished it. Dark haunting memories enclosed around me. There were no words. Vibrating black lines paraded in front of my eyes, punishing my stomach for the strong alcohol. Jimmy was talking, to me, to the person at his side, rambling on and on about a man, a journey, a painting, time, months, I must understand.

My groggy head refused to take it in.

His ranting stopped, started again, stopped; the wheels of an express train could not have moved faster. I felt sick. Memories of salacious lips danced around my mind: a large shape in a grey uniform leaning over me. I closed my eyes, commanded my stomach to cease rolling, begged Jimmy to repeat what he had said.

"Repeat myself. Do you listen to nothing?"

I flinched, pulled at the elastic in my pyjama trouser biting into my flesh, wriggled, then moaned as that waistband snapped.

"Damn," I exploded.

Jimmy was gushing "I have been allotted an assistant."

Forget the waistband.

At last. Those dull creatures that call themselves his 'bosses' have relented. Of course, that is why they are with him. It is their celebration. Jimmy cannot help where he has been taken, even if it is 'that' place.

Mentally I prepare to join in his euphoric joy, shout down the phone–

"I am ready (hic). About time. All the same you must hate that venue."

I could hear Jimmy's teeth (will he never stop it), I could sense his anxiety. Poor love.

My pyjamas resumed slipping, every movement, every twitch. I swear their sole mission was to slide to my knees, grasping my concentration away from Jimmy's exchange.

"He will be arriving tomorrow. I am so glad he can come to help at short notice. I have been told how good his tracking skills are."

From frozen to jelly.

"Who?" I screamed. "What are you talking about?"

"Thought so, too much wine."

His rebuke was spiteful.

"Who?" my voice imitated thunder, deafening my eardrums and crashing through my common sense.

"Your father," Jimmy pronounced with a giggle.

"Who?" I shouted again, laughing out loud.

"Your father," he repeated angrily "He will be joining me tomorrow. I have been advised he belongs to the best."

I swallowed hard, my temper threatening to choke me.

"My – my father. You are kidding me – Yes? I thought– " long deep breath-

"I thought you, me– " frustration growing "Who gave you this advice, Santa Claus?"

Jimmy began to click his teeth in rapid succession, ignoring my pleas for him to stop, my raging voice spilling out in a way the most blatant drinker would have foregone. Jimmy's tone was smooth –

"I have heard your father can discover the most hidden gems. Sorry, Rhia, it is agreed."

"Sorry?" I shouted "Sorry? *My* (emphasis on my) father is a bank director, you fool."

Jimmy's response was curt–

"I'm the fool? Oh, Rhia you know nothing."

His voice faded as the person at his side whispered again in his ear. I heard a meek "Yes", then heavy footsteps moving away. From outside my window the 'boom, boom' gathered volume, pounding out the latest rhythms, the flashing lights zooming across my nauseating frame. I called –

"Jimmy, tell me you are still there."

A husky tone answered my query –

"Hello Rhia, I am his boss. Jimmy has stepped aside for a drink."

I am confused, not sure what to think. How do I tell such a refined voice my father is just that – *my* father.

I hear Jimmy re-take the phone, apologise for my rudeness, then mutter –

"Get over yourself, Rhia. Everything is set. He will be here tomorrow."

"To meet your boss?"

Jimmy snorted –

"Not my boss. He will be on his way elsewhere."

"I still do not believe you. Probably a woman you have chosen to work with, but not me."

Jimmy grunted.

"Your choice, Rhia. Believe what you will."

In the background music was being played, a familiar tune I had heard before.

"Are they playing an anthem?" I queried.

"An anthem? Maybe?" came my partners answer, "I am in Germany."

A shiver swept through me.

"I have heard it before Jimmy, remember in 1989."

Jimmy was humming –

"Haven't we all? Let them get on with it I say. It does not worry me."

I paused, waited for the involuntary gag to pass.

“I swear it was that Stasi music, that night, in that pub.”

Jimmy let out a rasping sound.

“Come on, Rhia. I would not think so. They would not dare. Similar perhaps”

“Yes” I whispered.

Then, on a serious note he murmured –

“Anyway, Happy New Year girl. Let us hope you find what your heart desires. I am sure your father will.”

My father indeed. Oh Jimmy, you have fallen into that trap of choosing a colleague, so you lie – How could you?

I was mad. Even more so when oozing into the mouthpiece ‘I love you’ only to discover he had ended his call. He probably thought I would cause phone chaos. He probably thought right, yet mainly all I wished was to hear his voice, brush this nightmare parting away. I know when that painting is found we can forget the past. ‘Cast it to the Four Winds’ as the saying goes. Therefore, I should be there when it is recovered to dismiss the hand that yielded the oils for good. Replacing the handset on its base my hand shook. I took a long breath, felt the giddiness that accompanies nausea, hitched up the silk trousers and ran to the bathroom.

--

Late Entry

Believe me when I say that I feel ill. My head has rotated to such a degree that it honestly resembles a ball. My stomach, that this morning was plodding along on a few dry biscuits and an imperious attitude, now resembles the room of an old torture chamber; griping with pain, rumbling with wind. It has taken me two hours to clean a small bathroom, on my knees, moaning in agony.

I have heard the church clock strike the eleventh hour of the first day of a New Year. Popping my nose over the top of my duvet I watch the lights continue to flicker and judder across the street. The music, although softer and calmer was still playing, still rolling around as a forgotten wheel loosened from its mooring. In my state known as ‘post sorrow’ (an apt expression, I think, for my overindulgence) I command tonight’s phone call with Jimmy to play out in my mind. Naturally, my certainty had grown that he was tormenting me, fooling about over my father. How was I sure – No call from mother. Besides, let us be honest, how can a bank director find a painting? His art is in money, not oils or watercolours. No, it is a ploy on Jimmy's side to refuse my help. He thinks I would hinder him.

Well, just for your information my dearest lover and friend, my aptitude for poking about is nothing short of a genius.

Lord, I am cold. An aftermath no doubt, of my solitary binge. I hold my aching stomach, curl up in a ball, lonesome in this large bed. I visualise Jimmy in that bar, kiss the space on the bolster where his head would rest, think how we could have conquered this mission. Stretching my legs across the empty space I quiver, or should it be shudder, whatever. I discarded the pyjamas. They were cutting me in half, and irritating parts I do not wish to think about. Far too lazy to search for others I rolled under this quilted cover in T shirt and pants (not quite the graphic image my diary needs). At least I can move my legs without constriction.

Hiding myself from those flashing lights I try to consider what step I will take next. Jimmy's asking me to join him had been at the forefront of my mind since his departure. Cannot believe I must return to step one. Work at the dreary bank, live this solitary life, forget adventure, plus resign to the fact that mother will be here most days inquiring over my eating habits. Breathing in the musky smell of aftershave that has pervaded this bedroom since Jimmy's arrival I sense the sting of tears, an outpouring of anger and disappointment. I roll onto my side, envelope myself within the large duvet. With each tear I vow to sort this mess. My problem – I have no realistic solution.

Now, I must sleep, bid this evening's drama roll away as I wait to discover what another day can bring.

Remind me, diary, not to travel this pathway ever again.

Why does this woman imagine laughing faces?

Tuesday January 2nd

My ears register a sound, urgent and loud. I compare it to the demons of hell running around my head. Seriously, I knew it was the remnant of drinks that induced my ghosts, creating havoc between my dreams and reality. It had taken countless imaginary sheep jumping over countless imaginary fences to lull myself into sleep. To be forced to wake in circumstances like this was beyond funny. It was a nightmare.

Prising my eyes open I squint. Stretching my arms out in anticipation of Jimmy's embrace this woman falls into 'nothing'. Snatching my hand away from the empty space I stretch for the small clock positioned on the set of drawers next to the bed. Try to read the numbers, rub my eyes, try again. Slowly, realisation makes me gasp as I pair the small hand on the five, matched by the large hand on the twelve – Five o' clock.

Is this a joke?

Slamming the clock back on the drawers, mind cursing the hour, I turn over.

"Forget it" I tell myself "Most likely that woman from six rolling home from another party: her second in two days."

At least the room is dark, all lights from across the street have been switched off. I start to doze.

Loud thump, continual ringing –

I jump, feel that onset of fear when the mind settles on 'breaking wood'. My body trembles.

Shaken from that halfway sleep an expert would label 'dormant' I sit up and look around. Everything is in order: window shut, lights out, no voices. I jump again, glaring at the shine radiating from Jimmy's guitar, until I suddenly spot the moon sliding from behind a cloud outside the window, weaving its beams across the room, only to be hidden again seconds later. Another bang, more ringing, the screech of a wounded dog. I slip from the bed, my toes retracting upwards as they touch the cold wood boards. Finding the courage to put my feet to the floor, I fumble for the light, switch it on, switch it off, as I register the missing pyjamas, hastily recalling the curtains throughout the flat are open. Tiptoeing to the door, head bowed to relieve the pain, I grab the nearest dressing gown. Flinging it across my shivering frame I peep around the door. Nothing, the room is exactly how I left it.

For a reason I will not decipher my feet padded toward the telephone.

First thought – Ring Jimmy.

Picking up the receiver I rang his number, once, twice, three flaming times – Engaged. On the twentieth ring (no comment please) a voice floated into my ear. A voice that constantly repeats – 'This number is disconnected. Try again later'.

What!

How can his phone be disconnected – DISCONNECTED.

My temper flared. I slammed it down. Honestly, if that had been my mobile the poor thing would be grovelling on the ground.

Another 'Bang' reverberating around the room accompanied by the harsh trill of the doorbell. Panic. It was five o' clock on the morning of January 2nd, and not even the dawn chorus had taken place: meaning even a church mouse would be sleeping. The banging continued. Help – What shall I do?

Think hard, before this main door crashes inwards, and the perpetrator rushes in.

Try Jimmy once more.

Dismissed – Jimmy was evidently not speaking to me.

Idea – Call the local police station.

Dismissed – Calling the police would cause chaos, and besides this bloody dressing gown is not mine. I look a mess.

Think…

Creeping toward the main door I look through the tiny spy hole situated at the top of the door. Search the corridor outside. All clear. I begin to creep back to the bedroom upbraiding myself into how I could be this ridiculous. These flats have a night porter. No-one would pass his beady eye; no-one that is unless he knew them. By the sofa I paused, listening to a scratching noise up and down the door accompanied by the most dreadful squeaking sound.

Drastic thought – This interloper was known to the porter.

Got it, number six was sabotaging my rest. That woman had many such ploys to disturb her neighbours. Goodness knows why the porter did not report her. Money flashes into my mind. We will see about that, my father has heaps of it. I am Rhia Bryant, the daughter of a Bank Director, unafraid, and top of my game when it comes to the field of deceit. I will not join that foolish woman's game.

The scratching grows louder. What would Jimmy do? He would open the door and bid the woman 'Happy New Year' in not so friendly terms.

This is it!

I slide to the floor, my scream tearing through the room as the ring gets louder and longer.

"Remove your blasted finger from my bell push and get a life."

I imagine patting my back with a 'Well done, Rhia' ringing in my ears. The noise behind the door turned to moaning, the sound of a human in pain. My own nauseating pain I thought to be settling, came back, attacking me with vengeance, reaping its selfish grip throughout my inner gut. I shout–

"Fuck you, what do you want? Get your stupid ass back to bed."

A whimper, a howl, the taunting continued.

Sinking to the floor, tears welling up in already sore eyes I croaked –

"Please, get away from my door."

The scratching gathered speed, progressing to the rattling of the letterbox. Then, a name, my name – "Rhia". The sound compounds my angst, illuminating the foreboding behind my tears.

"G – go – a – way," I stutter.

"Please, Rhia."

A plea, spoken in a tiny cry.

Slowly I kneel, pull myself to my full height to re-search that spy hole yet again. This play acting would not stop until I decided to face the culprit. I hear my breathing, feel the constriction of my heart as I snatch the door backward and the transgressor falls into my lounge, distorted features glaring my way. I step back, anything to forestall the confrontation with the heap at my feet. I stare, feel slightly relieved as I confirm in my mind it is not the woman from number six playing her silly games. This person has a familiar air surrounding them. I continue to stare, go to speak, pause, before the sound that passes my lips rings around the room in abject horror–

"Mother."

Putting a dirty finger to her mouth she makes a hushing noise -

"Close the door – Now!" she barks.

Never, in my residency of this flat, has this main door been closed so fast. I almost fall over my own feet pulling the baggage that is my mother inside. She sprawls. Spreads her dirt ridden body across my clean wooden floor, fighting for breath. I kick the door with such ferocity that it wobbles from my pent-up anger. This woman on my floor has the cheek to lie, limbs sprawling, unconcerned to the fear she has caused me. Why should I care that her light blue tracksuit is smeared in mud, her mucky trainers marked in a way that signifies she has been crawling on the ground, a woolly hat plastered with what I can only describe to be grease, covering what surely must be a tangled mess of dyed red hair. Honestly, this woman noted for being queen of the moisturisers, now befits an advert for Halloween.

I was furious. It was five thirty, and I had spent the last half an hour cowing in fear.

Huddled against the doorpost she cries –

“Tell me no-one spotted me. It was bad enough that your concierge did.”

Speech deserted me. Ridiculous woman, I knew, without doubt the crazy female from number six would have recognised her. She, who took the brunt of my rage, would relish every moment of this extraordinary drama, waiting until I pass her in the corridor to speculate ‘How is your mother?’ whilst laughing heartily.

I stood like stone, recalling that biblical story from my childhood, and the predicament of Lot’s wife* as this figure of grimed in dirt began to crawl toward the fire. Assuring myself this nightmare would soon disappear, only for me to wake, and get dressed for work, I do not hear mother’s plea.

“Rhia” the voice has upped a notch “I am frozen, please turn the heat on high, my skin has suffered from the cold.”

I stare, hold my position, stare longer, move without question. Switching the fire to six, I catch my breath as she hauls herself onto the sofa, burying her filthy hat among my velveteen cushions.

“That is better” she sighs, closing her dirt smudged eyes.

Suddenly my cry of anger filtered around the room –

“Hell, what have you done? You look a bloody mess.”

Mother’s eyes opened a fraction. No tell-tale sign of rebuff.

“It is your Father.”

Statement – Said – Finished.

Pulling what I now understand to be Jimmy’s silky dressing gown tighter around my trembling body I query-

“Father? Was your play acting outside my door his fault as well? Five o’ clock mother.” I pause, “No, wait, it is sodding five thirty now, and you” another pause–

“*You!*” the scream became shrill “Are groping at my bloody door.”

An exhaustion I had never witnessed before settled across my mother’s face.

Running filthy hands through her tangled hair she looked upon my contorted features, those weary eyes stripped of her usual ‘snooty’ dominance.

“I am tired, Rhia. Yesterday after the bank lunch your father announced he was flying to Germany that evening. Jimmy needed his help. A painting had been stolen, and everything was not what it seemed, or something of the sort.

To me, he could not just ‘up’ and go. I threatened I would leave.”

“And– ” I stammered.

She shook her head, streams of dirt spilling across my cushions.

"I left."

"You left?"

"Yes. Do not sound so surprised. He took my credit cards, my garage keys, and what few notes I had in my purse."

I knew my eyes were bulging at this admission, and longed to quip 'Shame', but whispered–

"Oh, no."

"Oh, yes," she sighed.

"What now?"

I could sense the panic in my voice. Sense mother's reaction as she warmed her cold hands, the quick flip of her head as she removed her eyes from my searching gaze.

"I do not know. What concerns me has to be my credit card."

Lights were beginning to flicker on in the flats opposite; workers who craved a breakfast before setting out on their daily journey surveyed the street from behind frosty windows, eyes shuttered towards the creeping light of the day. Due to the spectacle lounging on my sofa, and the need for more light, I quickly drew the silky dark curtains, and switched on the light. The sight before me made my heart constrict. This was my fashionable mother, clothed in dirt, the sight of her hair not fit to be viewed in a mirror, cramped around my fire, grieving for what – A credit card.

Tossing her head, the grubby lips muttered–

"That is better I can see you now."

"See me? We need to sort you out."

Mother shifted awkwardly.

"That is true. First, phone your father, and ask him for my credit card. The man surely took it by mistake."

The seriousness upon her face triggered a sharp stifled giggle from me.

"Bloody credit card – There has got to be more. You look a mess. Really, mother what is going on?"

Mother flinched.

"Going on? I will tell you what is going on. I have no car or credit card. Your father has deserted me."

Always the drama.

"I do not understand" I spurted "This painting, your mess, father's flight, Jimmy's truth. I..."

Mother cut in–

"You knew?"

Her eyes hardened.

"No, yes. Oh hell, Jimmy told me when he called."

Mother became flustered.

"Everyone knew. How deceitful"

"I called him a liar."

"Poor Jimmy."

"I know."

"Anyhow, I need my credit card. We must visit your grandmother."

My mind reeled. This had got to be the jest of the New Year.

The words falling into the space between us complicated my mind further.

"Mattie?"

"Yes."

"Why?"

"I wish to."

"You?"

"Yes, why not?"

"You would not survive."

"Do not be rude, Rhia, I thought you would like to visit."

"I would. Why now?"

"No particular reason" she whimpered.

"Mattie would be shocked."

"Yes, and?"

"Not your scene mother."

"It could be."

"Never."

The questions into 'why' and 'how' shot back and forth.

Struggling to marry mother's predicament and Bhutan together I searched my mind for answers. This whole scenario was distinctively unbelievable. Mother had disagreed with my grandmother's move to the Himalayas. Her opinion of Mattie's 'reckless' jaunt to an 'impoverished village did not bode well with her snooty friends. So, for her to nigh on fall into my door, in this state, suggest we fly to Bhutan on a whim alerted my suspicion 'more': has my beloved father finally lost his patience, igniting mother to fly to a destination beyond her capacity to cope. Hearing the church clock chime six o' clock I make the excuse to prepare for work. There, with a modicum of peace I must somehow get hold of Jimmy and beg his forgiveness for doubting him.

As lightening forks across a grey laden sky mother's hand shoots out to grasp my own–

"Do not go to work, please. We have a lot to discuss. I must stay with you. I do not want to go back home."

Thunder bolt following the lightening.

The hand with its ragged nails grasped harder. A silent plea? I looked down into those penetrating eyes, felt the loss of reason, that powerful intimidation a rat discerns when it is backed into a corner.

I am trapped.

--

Midday

As the morning progressed mother had relaxed, no doubt content in her new role to be my flat companion. Her mood had calmed, although the cry for her credit card continued, spurring me to ring my father's mobile. Faced with that annoying sound of 'engaged' I automatically rung Jimmy's number. My main aim, apart from asking to speak to father, was my need to say 'sorry', to relate how down I was feeling, and to wish him a speedy return.

Honestly, I need not have bothered.

Neither answered, which threw me back into that attitude bordering on the spitting flames of Mount Merapi (an active volcano 28 miles north of the city of Yogyakarta in Indonesia). Like my own temper throughout my life, this volcano had erupted regularly since 1548*, and was noted as the silent demon. Unable to connect with my father, my mother would have to swallow her pride, and go 'cap in hand'* to the bank.

Placing two cups of coffee between the multitude of magazines adorning my snazzy, yet unpractical coffee table I look mother squarely in the face.

"You may have to forgo your credit card until Father returns; seek a loan from the bank."

Mother lifts her coffee to her lips, gulps the hot liquid, then winces before saying –

"Why, did *he* not answer?"

There was a catch in her tone, that emphasis on the word 'he'.

“Neither answered. I do not understand why.”

“I do,” came the growl. “Your father wishes us to melt into the background.”

She caught my startled eyes, and gabbled–

“On holiday I mean.”

That assertion uttered mother returned to her coffee, the sweet roasted smell pervading the warm room. Gazing at the hands of my colourful clock I mentally ‘click’ with each passing second. Any minute now the church clock would resound ‘midday’ over the busy street outside; people running here and there would not listen to its booming sound, or even consider that the morning of January 2nd of a New Year had passed in one swift move.

Wishing to steer our conversation away from Bhutan or anything to do with mother and I taking a holiday, I decided to quiz her into how she had ended up so dirty. Bad move.

“Garage creeping,’ she moaned. “Crawling the muddy ground, searching for anything that would lever a garage door. I ended up in a mound of dirt, or a thawed puddle. Oh, the shame, groping around in the dark. Afraid the neighbours would see me I crawled into the garden to contemplate my next move.”

The coffee cup was slammed into its saucer (mother hates mugs). A cry reverberated around the room, “Then, I lost my door key. Locked myself out.”

Possible, plausible, I thought, but why had she closed the front door?

Suddenly feeling pity for my cushions, I suggested she find comfort in a bath. Instantly my mother’s eyes lit up, her mouth producing a smear of a smile. Leading her into the bathroom I was unprepared for the complaining.

My products were cheap.

My towels were rough.

The water was too hot.

She had nothing to wear.

Complaint after complaint, until I soothed her angst with my only bottle of Parisian cologne, pouring it slowly into the water, and leaving her to ‘wallow’ in her sorrow for the revered credit card.

I switched on the radio; anything to hum along with. Heavy rain clouds were no longer threatening the world below, but had transformed into flurries of snow, only to transpire to sleet, splattering onto the ground in puddles of ice. Spotting the baggy top mother had thrown aside during the morning I stooped down to remove it from the floor to the wash pile. Lifting it up I could not help but notice the bulky pockets. Now, me being me, my curiosity could not be contained. I felt inside, pulled out crumpled paper, unfolded it, and read–

Mena,

Thank You for helping us once more. If you need assistance you know who, and you know where. With my love...

The name had been ripped off.

Held in that vacuum of intrigue my eyes skipped across the sloping handwriting; a woman I believe, one whom mother knows well and has assisted in her past.

Who?

Shall I text Jimmy? Ask him to tell father I need to talk. I reach for my phone, resting peacefully on the table, finger the letters, start to insert the letters that would say 'sorry', STOP – What if they laugh? It is only a note from a friend. Its meaning? – probably nothing. Hearing movement around the bathroom I hastily stuff the note back into the pocket, clear my phone, drop the top back onto the floor, then hurry into the bedroom to find mother fresh, if rather large, clothes.

--

Evening

Having removed the cushions and sprayed the sofa, the flat smelt of woodland pine: an aroma that I fooled myself reminded me of the countryside. 'Where' you may ask, 'in an urban melting pot such as this vastly populated suburb can the association with countryside be found?' I reply in earnest that 'a girl can dream.' Mother, refreshed from her bath made herself even more at home, curling up by the fire to toast her toes and doze. Refusing myself the luxury of napping, unable to settle my mind after reading that note, I eventually forced myself to watch the dusk weave its shadows across the room, where the flames of a roaring gas fire leapt tongues of fury against a black background of artificial coal. Churning over the message my brain tried to work out its content. Who wrote those words? What do they mean?

Again, me being me, dark answers of 'deceit', 'secrets', and 'lies' applied themselves to the ripped name prior to concluding 'I had discovered nothing'.

This ‘affair’ (no time to consider a more fitting word) was rattling my brain in the way chains ‘clang’ against metal poles, yet the thought that I could put mother on the ‘spot’, dangle the ‘bulge’ in her pocket before her face, demand an explanation, soon scurried away as an animal fleeing an adversary the moment the woman awoke.

“Hunger overtakes me, Rhia”

Mother’s face, bright red from the heat of the fire, held the request of a starving child. In that moment I knew my only way of discovering what that note, besides the mess of earlier, meant was to ‘play’ her game. Rustling up a sandwich, for this moment was of great importance, plus I could not be bothered to cook, I mention visiting her house. Colour drained from the blotchy face.

“We must visit without anyone knowing.”

“Why?” I laugh.

“The neighbours of course. They must not know your Father has gone.”

“Gone? The man is on a mission according to you.”

Her eyes narrowed.

“Whatever, neighbours talk.”

“To whom?”

“No more questions, Rhia. Let us eat and plan our holiday.”

Mother flipped her hand in the direction of those flat unappetising sandwiches.

Determined I would get my point through the barrier she was building I stated-

“I am sorry to disappoint you mother, but I do not wish to go to Bhutan at this moment. In fact, this woman wishes to follow up on that ‘lost’ painting, show Jimmy and father they will not search alone.”

I could not believe the scowl that settled on mother’s face.

“No, Rhia. No, no, no.”

“Why?” I shot her way.

“Your father does not agree with interference.”

I pull a face.

“Is that right? Well, Jimmy may be glad of my help, our help.”

“Our?” mother storms. “Our, I do not think so.”

“I do, if – if you want to live here.”

Cannot believe my mouth said that.

I waited for the coming storm, my skin tingling with anticipation.

"The contract for staying is I must agree to your plans to search for that, that painting?"

I breathe deeply "Correct."

"Rhia, that is unfair. You do not know how foolish you are being."

I could see no resentment in mother's eyes, just pity. Ignoring her I plough on–

"Thank you for that. Do you agree?"

She hesitates, rubs her hands together, holds my gaze–

"Not really, but against my will what can I say? I must stay with you. Your father…"

She chose her words "He would… will not be pleased."

I look away, follow the flames of the fire.

"Father is not here. Besides, if someone within his position can jump up and run to Jimmy, no idea what the hell to do, so can we."

My anger obvious. Mother glared.

"Can you not understand?" she said. "We tread this pathway full of consequences. Rhia, a lot is at stake – Bloody Hell."

I giggle, never have I heard my mother swear, a lifetime's social climbing discarded in one sentence.

Not once considering a word she had spoken I munch the stale cheese I had scrabbled around the fridge to find, its papery taste lingering on my tongue. Mother had given up eating, concentrating instead on the cascading sleet outside the window. I could sense she was fretting, knew this to be part of her 'getting her own way', also knew this time she would not win. I try to pacify her qualms–

"We will be fine, Mother. It is just a painting. Do not be so dramatic."

She shakes her head, glowers at me-

"You always were the stubborn child. Remember a painting is never just a painting, and most things are not what they seem."

Heaven alone knew what this woman meant. She was talking in riddles – Great – Wait until I speak with you, Father!

Wednesday January 3rd

The alarm, fixed from the day before, buzzed seven thirty. The continual clanging ripping through my sleep, dousing my dreams with its vibration. I had immersed myself in hot water and creamy soap as a prelude to the forthcoming night, before seeking bed in a state of caffeine euphemism. Mother and I had drunk far too much coffee, eighteen in all, allowing it to swamp our brains and tongues with numerous disgusting tales of how we would deal with Jimmy and Father on their return. In all honesty, our slip from sensibility to portraying drunken sops from an everyday drink is new to me. How was it possible? Too many bitter beans. Never again will I be told that wine stands aloft the drinking implements to cause dipsomania – Join the coffee crapulent (terrible word). Collapsing into bed both Mother and I had sunk under the strain of a banging head and a swirling stomach, myself for the second time within three days. As the church clock strikes the hour when birds in summer join in chorus, we finally meet oblivion, only to be woken an hour later.

I bang the clock face down onto the drawers by the bed, and stare round the room. Nothing has changed. Jimmy's guitar is still propped against the wall, toys and books amassed in a row on the windowsill. Yet, life has changed. Mother for one, work for another. The woman had begged me to phone the bank. Report I was sick, ask for leave. I had laughed: saw how serious her plea was, then wiped the smile from my sneering lips. Where did she think my money would come from? Father's allowance being a pittance compared with my money from that mausoleum. She must know Father believed in his only daughter providing for herself, often reminding me–

"Your position at the bank is not to be taken for granted, and inheritance is held, under your grandmother's firm control."

One too many I had 'poo-poohed' his scolding only to be 'docked' a few pounds.

Mother had argued, poured reason upon reason onto an already tired heart, intimidating my counter argument, until I gave in. I had phoned yesterday, just as the bank was closing, spoke to the receptionist, left a message for her to pass on.

The coward way you will say – I agree.

So, here I sit, clutching my rolling stomach, looking into the dubious abyss of the next few days, waiting to hear from whoever slips into Father's position until he returns, and counting my savings down to the last penny, praying lady luck will shine Mother's way, and her credit card materialises.

Tuesday January 16th

How do I write when my head is in a frenzy – '*Mother, Mother, Mother*'

Mother has been living with me for two weeks – TWO WEEKS.

Do wonder how this woman is coping. I will answer between gritted teeth – I AM NOT.

Please do not smile, certainly not in the manner of mild pity, displaying every sign of the paraphrase 'I told you so'. If you do, please take this warning as more than a threat–

"I will scream until the world falls apart."

She has rallied round from her 'absolute disaster' faster than a runaway train, organising my flat into an annexe of Buckingham Palace. Her new word as she rushes from room to room with a duster and pan in her hand is 'Charming'. Everything is bloody 'Charming'. Each room represents a perfumery, oozing out a certain smell as though it is being distilled in that space. I am declaring that this woman, my mother, has stepped straight out of a nightmare.

Take the kitchen for instance – Not one cup or mug is on display. Not one pot or jar. Nothing that indicates food or drink is prepared in this quarter. Chairs are tucked in tight, cutlery hidden away, bread, cereal, tea bags or coffee, closeted behind closed doors. I would go as far to say – Perish the thought if the toaster even 'winks' at me from the shelf above the worktop. Not one thing must be 'out of place'. To do so would summon anarchy.

Next the lounge, the focus of mess and pleasure through by-gone days has become that optimum of a Victorian drawing room. No more sofa and chairs at odd angles, both must be aligned, with papers neatly tucked away and the coffee table polished to that mirror image mother regards as correct. My poor cushions, happy no doubt in their habitat of creased and squashed, are washed on a weekly basis, straightened daily, and 'plumped' morning and afternoon. The curtains, dry cleaned yearly, are treated with the same hostility, grasped from the washer, and hung across the bath to dry.

The bathroom, with its unwanted cream bottles and empty tissue boxes, not forgetting old sponges lining the floor, has taken on a new outlook of prim and pristine. On entering this tiny sanctuary your eyes are dazzled by the shine emanating from the bath, sink, and toilet. They sparkle so brightly they spellbind an onlooker's mind. So much so, that I would not be surprised if anyone (me) were to run back out and search for a 'Take Care' sign outside the door. Especially as the floor has been scrubbed within an inch of a skating ring, and the mirror rubbed to the maxim that would easily compete with the Hall of Mirrors at the palace of Versailles in France*.

My bedroom, and I have saved this explanation until last, as according to mother, it deserved the largest transformation. It was stripped, tidied, cleaned, and moved; all in the hours of one day, accompanied by the beat of music from the nineteen sixties. Once sorted the pillows were plumped and cradled, the duvet shook and caressed, the windowsills cleared of their books and toys, boxing them and putting them to rest. Jimmy's guitar was another story – Mother moaned as she moved it, almost begged for it to be hidden in the wardrobe. I blatantly refused. Stood my ground until this dictatorial wind of cleanliness had passed me by and swept elsewhere. I replaced it at the bottom of the window, allowing it to recline, and view me as I slept: comfort in a roundabout way. For all Mother's foolishness I was secretly pleased at the tidiness I now moved in, although for everything else I have decided that somewhere within our past lives we travel through, I must have committed something wicked to be dealt this hand.

--

Afternoon.

Funny, the way an answer to my problem concerning Mother materialised out of the blue–

Mother had been cleaning, scrubbing, whatever she does to the bathroom when the letterbox clanged. Knowing it had got to be post I ran to the door. Letters always caused a thrill to sear through me, for although my flat was top floor, and post was delivered to the concierge downstairs, this kind man always carried out a daily 'post' round. Stooping to pick up the three long white envelopes, fallen in the arc of a fan, I noticed the top one had bold black writing. First thought – Interesting. Second thought – Lord, the bank is sacking me. Re-reading the name I noticed that what I had presumed was **'R Bryant'** was actually **'P Bryant'** then c/o before the address. Whoever this letter was from knew Mother was staying at my flat.

Tempted to rip it open and read its contents I called Mother from her cleaning.

"Letter for you, Mother. Shall I open it?"

Her face peered around the bathroom door, a large scowl illuminating her cosmetic free features.

"No," the snap was adamant. "I will deal with it."

I tried (honestly) to keep my tone level–

"Who knows you are here?"

Her aproned, yellow gloved form slipped further into the room.

"Your father of course, even if the man has refused to reply to those texts. This must be my credit card. Thank you."

She extended her hand for the bold written envelope gripped securely in my own. I relented. She had spoken the truth. We had sent text after text, to Jimmy and Father alike. We had received no replies, to the point that in further anger I had resumed phoning the hotel I believed was their hideout. Pouring insults onto the weary voiced receptionist I was staggered when my call was refused. Each call after that was cut off with an apology.

Casting my eyes across the thick white vellum I pressed in various places, turning to Mother upon finishing–

"There does not feel as if a credit card is hidden inside. This writing is not Father's."

Mother walked to where I stood, still gripping the envelope, staring at the writing.

"Yes" she said, removing her glove, then sliding the sheath from my grasp. "It appears so. Probably an old friend of your father. She said she would write."

Moving away from me she sat and tore the envelope apart.

"Savannah D' Mill," she whispered, as though the name burnt memories on her tongue.

"Who?" I queried.

Mother took a breath as if for support–

"Memories," she exhaled. "She knew your father when we were younger."

"His floozy," I blurted.

"Not at all. Savannah was a colleague."

I could see Mother would not tell more, therefore I needed to read the letter she had sent. Besides, it appeared to me, the writing in that letter corresponded with the note found in Mother's pocket.

Snatching the letter back (I know, that was rude) I read–

"My Dearest Mena,

How are things progressing at the flat? Hal said it would be 'difficult'.

Always the realist, and the sweetie. I am presuming the holiday was dismissed out of hand.

Never mind, I have someone who can help you in the search for the painting your daughter is determined to join. I have given him your number, he will phone. Please take care. As we know the spider does not always catch the fly, but – Oh Mena. Do not hesitate to get in touch. This must end. Savannah x"

I tossed the letter onto the sofa where Mother had sunk down, yellow gloves glinting in her lap.

"Who the hell does she think she is?" I cry.

"A friend."

Mother's whimper confirmed my thoughts 'This woman spells trouble.'

"Interfering cow" I cry louder.

Now, truth be known, at this moment in time this woman cares nothing about my father's flippant youth. Surely the past was the past, or so I thought, but if this woman thinks she can suddenly 'pop' up from nowhere to cajole Mother and me – Well, think again, lady.

"One day you may thank this woman for her help," Mother's soft lilt stoked my fire.

"Never!" I thundered. "You may bow to her, whoever she, or her dribbling helper maybe, but I will not."

"Rhia, the forceful. Will you ever change?"

A fleeting smile passed across mother's lips as she made her way back to the bathroom.

--

Evening

No sooner had the sun appeared later in the afternoon than darkness had settled. I detested this foreboding tell-tale sign of winter, enclosing the sky around us, allowing the creeping shadows of an over imaginative mind to steal away any sensibilities that the human brain may have possessed. I thought of that reference the Savannah woman had made towards the poem by Mary Howitt (1799-1888) 'The Spider and the Fly'* "How easy a spider can lure the poor fly to settle within its web–

'Will you walk into my parlour? said a spider to a fly'"*

What did she mean?

Mother had said no more where the letter was concerned, turning her full attention to concluding her tiresome cleaning, followed by roasting her toes by the fire, listening to soft classical music playing in the background. I was tinkering (so love that word. It is posh for dabbling) in the kitchen, grouping vegetables plus odds and ends together for our evening meal when I heard mother talking on the phone. Acknowledging her chatting as finally catching up with Father I hurried into the lounge.

"Phone call?" I mouthed.

Mother nodded, finished her conversation, then with a huge smile said –

"That was a Hans Parker, Savvy's man. He has invited us to meet up with him to discuss the painting. Evidently, he works at the museum with Jimmy, and belongs to Savannah's set."

"How boring," I quip. "Another social climber."

Her voice rose–

"This was your idea to 'help' with that painting. Your idea not to join your grandmother. Your idea to let your father see how 'inept' we will be. Your idea…"

I raise my hand–

"Stop" I demand "You have made your argument plain. We will meet him, heaven help us, anything for peace and quiet" I growl.

Mother closed her eyes, positioned her toes nearer to the leaping flames, and let the soothing music of the great composers soothe her mind. Somewhere deep within my mind the thought 'If ever I meet this woman' plagued my already depressing brooding, and for the first time since Jimmy's departure I felt alone; almost as if a great ocean had closed over my head, drowning me within its fathomless depths. The world was still rotating, mother was still by my side, good or bad, whilst all around me events were taking place without my control. I was being taken by the hand and led to that moment where destiny coincides with a truth I do not understand, or even sure this mind wishes to know.

Saturday January 20th

I sit at the kitchen table scooping small balls of rice corn onto my spoon, teasing them into my mouth, then popping them past my teeth as a coal trimmer would stoke coal into the furnaces of a ship. Today, mother and I have promised ourselves a visit to the family home. We set out the plan as follows –

Step One: Eat breakfast.

Although I believe my munching and crunching is the only breakfast eating taking place.

Step Two: Dress sensibly.

That is a laugh, as Mother has chosen an oversized jumper and an old pair of Jimmy's shrunken joggers. This, in her opinion will make her look what she calls 'incognito'; a disguise the neighbours will not recognise to be her. I say her outfit screams scruffy burglar. Therefore, she must not be surprised if the police come calling. Myself, I chose my oldest jeans, and a crumpled jacket thrown in the back of the wardrobe.

Step Three: Speak to no-one.

The truth is, in the district where Mother lives no neighbour would even acknowledge people dressed down to our level.

Step Four: Get in and out as fast as possible.

Question – Are we hiding for a purpose?

Mother came into the kitchen ready to depart on our mission, scarf wrapped around her neck and chin in the fashion of young kids hiding their face from a rough wind. Across her shoulder she had flung a spare holdall found in my bedroom, and numerous carrier bags tucked under her arm. I laughed, spilling the tiny pop corns from the spoon back into the dish.

"You look er – very incognito."

Mother's nose shot up into the air.

"Laugh all you like. I do not wish to be seen."

"Right," I spluttered the cereal now being shovelled at extra speed.

"What coat are you wearing?" her question caught me off guard.

I had not thought of my own disguise. This is our home. Why should we not visit?

"That worn anorak I suppose."

“The anorak you saved from your visit to Germany in 89?”

“Yes.”

Suddenly her eyes grew wider-

“No, Rhia, bad idea. Let me see– ”

What? now, she was being ridiculous.

Scraping the chair back from the table I pushed past Mother’s ‘yeti’ disguise to the bedroom where that old anorak lay waiting for me. Squeezing my jacket beneath the windproof material I swore. There was no doubt that I had added a few inches since that year. Grabbing an old woolly hat from the same trunk I pulled it down around my ears, hiding any strands of red hair from sight. Gathering my furry boots and old worn gloves, along with a pair of sunglasses, I marched back to the kitchen, and stood in front of mother.

“Good enough?” I ask.

Mother gave an irritated shrug.

“You can be really silly, Rhia. This whole business is serious.”

Part of me felt a teeny-weeny bit sorry for her as I followed her from the flat.

Outside we were greeted by a blast of cold air. Of late, the weather had been kind, holding its daily temperature at a warm 4.5 centigrade, delivering a monthly prospect of 12.5 centigrade. ‘Clammy’, one might call it after the snow in December, and the sleet at the turn of the year. Today it cannot select what element to throw at us poor unsuspecting humans. After a futile debate over walking or taking a bus, Mother claimed she must walk as ‘someone’ may see her, and tongues would start wagging, shattering her credibility as the wife of a top bank director within minutes. On my answer that those who lived around her would never grace the platform of a bus, she eyed me with distain, and continued her jaunt.

The journey to the house should have taken us exactly an hour but, Mother’s boots clicked and clacked in a slow procession of moans and groans, and my own brown suede furry things, drank the heavy downpour that had decided to plummet from the sky, causing me to squelch with every step. It was no surprise to me when halfway there the rain turned to sleet, slashing our faces with icy fingers, biting any feature not fortunate to be covered by a scarf; the large white shapes falling to earth, dissolving into small puddles of water. Miscalculating these small rivers of water led us to reach our destination in what must be dubbed ‘a sorry state’. I cannot describe the joy shown in two pair of eyes as we entered the street where the house stood. Head down, hearts racing, we progressed down the street like cats slinking back to their lair after a night of hunting. Each time the sound of a door or the creak of a window was heard, Mother jumped, grasped my arm, and almost ran to the house door, pulling me behind her. At last, we stood in front of that heavy door with its plaque displaying the names of those who lived there. Tutting at the darkening blur of the brass knocker, Mother opened the door for us to pass through.

Pleased at our entry into the world of subterfuge (arriving here without notice) Mother clapped her gloved hands together at the sight of a bulging post cage.

"My credit card" was her first squeal. Her second "Stay here, Rhia." Then an afterthought–

"Look for the card while I find my clothes and change – "Please".

No sooner had she spoken the last verb than she ran up the stairs, leaving me to unlatch the cage before diving into that mix of white, brown, and manilla post.

Untying the scarf and removing my hat I snap the cage lock holding the post and wait for the fall out. Envelopes fell everywhere. At my feet, across the floor, skimming here and there, joyous to be free. Sitting down with a bump, not bothering to remove the tight anorak, I began to flip through the mass that had fallen to the floor. Business letters, invitations, bank statements, family news, every conceivable communication but the letter I seek. I think of Mother's tantrum when she realises her precious card is not here. 'Try again' springs into my head as I turn the envelopes over. One, two, three – Nothing. Bored, I stop the sifting, look around me, absorb the expensive fittings and furniture surrounding me. Opulence, a word I try to remove myself from, yet here, standing bold in this hallway, is the reproduction of a King Louis IV table leaning against the wall, made more resplendent by the new white wing backed padded chair that had replaced Mother's old one. This really was a house that screamed 'money', my father's money.

Stretching my arms skywards I suddenly spot a group of letters caught in the bottom of the cage. Wriggling toward the door I stop and listen. Mother is humming to herself, a good sign that her mood is high. Reaching into the cage I yank the envelopes free, read the names, sense the thrill of Mother's name in black writing. This must be the card. I press it, turn it over, press it once more. I can feel something solid inside. Should I shout up the stairs or wait for her to join me. I chose the latter, mainly because my gaze had fallen onto an average sized envelope with typed frontage; my father's initials in large print – MR

HENRY BRYANT. It was not the name that stirred my curiosity. Many of father's mail came with capital letters. It was the fact it had no address. This letter had been hand delivered. The brown envelope was worn, almost as if it had been kept folded in a pocket until delivery. I swivelled it in my hand, pressing it as I had what I thought was mother's card. This inside was soft which meant only paper. I felt that urge to tear it open, pulled back knowing it was not mine. Shall I? Yes, no, yes, no, yes – an overpowering sensation overtook me. Rip it apart, look inside. I breath deep – Oh Lord, I have never been so disloyal. Stuffing the torn envelope deep into my anorak pocket I slowly unfold the thin paper to reveal–

TIME TO PAY HENRY BRYANT

I scowl at the paper in my hand, turn it over to find nothing written on the back, nothing to designate who sent it. What can it possibly mean?

Lost in the moment I was shocked to hear Mother's voice calling to me from the landing–

"Anything there, Rhia?"

The chirpy sound was incongruous to the heavy thumping of my heart.

"Yes, of course, I… I believe your card is here."

The "Thank goodness" wafted down the stairs, as the vibration of moving feet swam around my befuddled brain. 'What? Where? Who?' taunted my mind, vivid pictures of bank robbers racing across my imagination. I played with the thought of showing it to mother. Could I stand the continual muttering and fretting when she had digested the threat – No I could not. It had got to be some prank from a disgruntled customer. Who else would write such a thing? Thrusting it in the same pocket as the folded envelope I pretended to relax and sort through what mail was left.

"At last." she cooed reaching the bottom step "Where is it?"

Passing the bold written envelope to her with a forced iota of calm I watched as mother pressed it with joy –

"This is it," she almost sang. "This is it."

Tearing it open she held the card to her lips, kissed it with that adoration one would bestow on a favourite child, then danced around the hallway in unadulterated excitement.

Running upstairs to gather the packed hold-all and carrier bags Mother dragged them down the stairs, humming the same tune she had used earlier.

Placing her overflowing bags by the main door she scampered in and out of the rooms satisfying herself all was well. Unsure how two women, one determined not to travel by bus, would hobble through the icy sleet carrying bulging carrier bags and a hold-all I queried –

"Why not use a suitcase for your clothes?"

Mother stared, made the 'tutting' sound of impatience (becoming a habit?), then sighed as she answered–

"A suitcase, Rhia would tell the neighbours I am leaving. This empty house must already be a topic of gossip."

"Not if we called a taxi."

Mother released a tiny laugh –

"We cannot afford a taxi."

"The credit card" was my simple reply.

Excited eyes looked at me, the flicker of a mock smile penetrating her lips. Before my mouth could utter one more syllable the woman had shot back up the stairs, willing me to help her with the carrier bags and bulging hold-all.

It took five minutes to unpack those bags and fill a suitcase. I will not mention the clothes mother had chosen, apart from asking–

"How many cocktail dresses does a lodger, sorry – guest, need?"

In the end it came down to cramming it with 'tons' of frivolous nothings, and few essentials. Bouncing the case down the stairs to the hallway was an accomplishment of its own, only to be greeted by the ringing of the doorbell. We froze, both faces etched with our own sense of horror. Mother held her breath, the quick motion of a finger to her mouth. I stood still, my hand instantly finding that scrap of a letter stuffed inside my pocket.

Another knock, a call–

"Hello there," a pause. "Is that you, Mena?"

A rush of air left Mother's mouth. The defeat of a person caught in an act of concealment displayed in her eyes.

"Yes," she squeaked. "Is that you Olivia?"

By return – "It is. May I come in?"

The stylish voice of mother's neighbour vibrated in our ears.

Mrs Olivia Jones walked through the slightly opened door, head high, nose sniffing in that attitude noted with the detection skills of a police spaniel. This large woman dressed accordingly to her shape and size, radiated in a plain navy suit and boots, with tinges of red to match the large red glasses balanced on the end of her nose. Her hair, a mixture of ash blonde with brown streaks secured into a bun at the back of her head, then fanned out to frame her immaculate rouged cheeks and shiny red lips. All in all, she resembled the perfect social climbing diva.

To me – Another nosy parker.

A sharp stare took in the large suitcase standing by the door, mother's small fur jacket (the clothes she had arrived in – Gone, discarded to the bin) and the brown shiny boots, my outfit of deception, and the quiet 'eeriness' exuding generally throughout the house.

"Going away, Mena," she remarked in her haughty manner.

Mother was tongue tied, scrabbling over words to explain the scene before her.

"I… I…"

My turn–

"Forgive my mother, her throat is terribly sore. She has agreed to stay at my flat for a short while. My partner is away."

Mother nodded.

Mrs Olivia Jones snorted, the habit of a pompous virago–

"Oh, I see," this precocious woman spouted. "Jimmy has flown the nest."

Fists rolled into balls. I know where they *should* go.

"No," my cry rattled around the hallway.

Mrs Olivia Jones tossed her ridiculous fan of a head–

"Do not be ashamed. Young men these days have no priorities. You should have married him. Got the ring, got his money."

I was fuming. Three women pouting at each other and the space surrounding them. Casting a glance toward mother I move my head in the direction of the door, praying she would take the hint. At last, pretending to croak she whispered-

"I am sorry, Olivia, we must prepare to leave the house. If you would be so good to keep an eye to the place whilst I am away, I would be grateful. You have my phone number."

Mother put a hand to her mouth, the strains of a forced cough echoing around the quiet hall.

Mrs Olivia Jones twisted around and found the door latch, enjoying the snipe she flung mother's way.

"Oh, by the way, Mena, a scruffy looking person was at your door a day ago, posting what appeared to be a letter. Have you found it?"

Mother looked perplexed.

"Not yet. Nothing of importance I doubt. Thank you for telling me."

Mrs Olivia Jones cocked her head, sniffed down her nose: preliminary moves to her disappearing out of the door. I growled–

"That woman. She drives me to the edge of control. I would love to hit her."

Mother was searching through the post.

"A letter she said. Have you seen it?"

I so wanted to lie.

"No," caught Mother's critical stare. "Well, yes, here."

From my pocket I pulled the crumpled paper, handed it into Mother's waiting hand. She read it, took a deep breath, read it again, this time scrutinizing my face, then without uttering one word she removed her phone from the large handbag she had found and called a number. Within minutes a taxi drew up outside the door.

"We must go."

There was no explanation. No shared laughter at someone's silly prank. Only a quick glance across the hallway, and Mother almost 'shooing' me from my childhood home, to climb into a darkened window cab.

Thursday January 25th

Today I will put my hands up in the fashion of a cowboy's victim and shout 'The world has gone crazy'. From the moment we stepped from that blackened-out taxi to this moment, my life has been nothing but a round of frenzied action. Not one word concerning that threat over Father left Mother's lips. Instead, she entered the flat, rushed to the kitchen, and tore that eerie declamation into dozens of little pieces. She then declared we would 'shop' and sort out our meeting with Savannah D' Mill's man. There was no question of a discussion, or whether either of these solutions fell into line with my own thoughts. It appeared for the first time since I had flown the nest my plans would be her way; suddenly the boot of command had changed hands. She was dishing out ideas and orders, irrelevant of my disorientation at the world around me.

Credit card in hand we 'hit' the shops, designer named labels falling from rails and shelves into colour coded designated bags. The 'frenzied' rush through the smart boutique shops of our expanding suburb terminated when the silly plastic card, forever dangling between Mother's fingers, became stuck in a cash machine.

At last.

Mother handed me her bags (think of a stand overflowing with bags and coats), ignored the queue gathering behind us, and screamed at the man-made machine. Thumping it with her umbrella (another story) she managed to dislodge her precious card, but not before the screen glared 'No money'. Immediately Mother moved to the side to phone the bank, demand the new incumbent speak to her, lost her cool when answered by his secretary with information that the card had been capped until Father's return. Our running around the shops ended abruptly; believe me when I write that a bank appointment was swiftly agreed for the next day.

In tune with all this madness, the weather also lost control. Drizzle, heavier rain, sleet, snow, fog, frost, and to complicate matters dry and sunny, all in one day. My amazement grew as this ordinarily level-headed woman marched me into a bar, and with the few notes left in her purse, commanded the waitress to bring a bottle of red wine.

Friday January 26th

Arriving at the bank ten minutes before her appointment, Mother's inclination was to make the new incumbent aware that she was the wife of an important man. Duped into joining her by the promise that her word would secure an extension to my 'sabbatical' and extra funds, I followed as a sheep to the trough. My stomach as we passed through the doors of that vast mausoleum flipped and rumbled in rhythm to the beat of my heart. Mother, head held high, swaggering in the grey woollen coat and skirt, purchased yesterday, smiled in rapid succession at the many customers moving aside to let her pass. I followed, in what, for me, was quiet contemplation, tweaking the jacket of my black trouser suit every time someone looked my way.

Diary Note: Passing at least twenty imposing portraits of past directors, their grim faces assessing each customer who deigned to tread across those portals, I was amazed that Father's face was not among them. I had never noticed this 'hiccup' before. Suddenly feeling irritated that he had been cheated out of his ‘niche’ of fame, I vowed to bring the subject to light at a future staff meeting when I returned to work.

Reaching the reception desk Mother rang an old brass bell to summon whoever was manning the desk. From a door directly behind this varnished oak escritoire (great word for desk) a girl appeared, the largest grin covering a pair of pouting ruby red lips.

“Hello, can I help you?”

The hazel eyes joined the grin on her mouth, as her hand flew to the unruly chestnut hair straggling to be free from its elasticated band. Mother coughed, in that pretence way that shows her displeasure with someone’s attitude.

“Mr Richardson please” she demanded in her haughtiest voice possible.

The girl gaped.

“Wow, you must be Mrs Bryant. Nice to meet you ma-am.”

She bobbed a curtsy in the manner of a Japanese Saikeirei, the most respectful gesture to an honoured guest. I sniggered, felt the tiny kick as Mother’s heel touched my leg, and used the coughing trick instead.

“Ah,” the girl commented. “You must be Miss Bryant. Don’t you work here?”

Deflated comes to mind.

Nodding, I spotted the name ‘Fiona’ on the badge pinned to her white shirt. I pledged I would remember this embarrassment.

In her quandary at Mother’s presence, Fiona struggled with the buzzing intercom. She switched it on, cried “Hello”, switched it off by mistake, popping the button ‘up’ and ‘down’, all in her struggle to keep calm. After much flipping on and off the machine revealed a voice fraught with command–

“Conduct Mrs Bryant to my office *now* – Please.”

Fiona flustered, bobbed Mother another 45 degree ‘ojigi’, then pointed in the direction we would take. Following the girl in crocodile form I deliberately lowered my head as we passed the cashier section of blue suited, scraped back hair, bright red lipstick mouthed women speaking to customers in their predatory fashion to gain money. My wish for these women not to speak to me, meant I ridiculously bent my knees in the manner of a circus clown hiding from screaming children. For if the truth be known, however my father thought it ‘fit’ that I work here, these women considered me an enemy in their midst. What they must remember – I am the director’s daughter, and if I think I should disclose their gossip, I will.

Standing outside what I gathered was this interim boss's office, Fiona knocked and entered, calling out our names in the vein of a footman at a Georgian ball. Mr Richardson stood, proffered his hand toward mother, then flicked his wrist to bid Fiona to leave.

"My dear Mrs Bryant, how wonderful to see you."

His bespectacled eyes shrewdly glancing in my direction – "You too Miss Bryant."

Mother wasted no time.

"Good Morning Mr Richardson, I need to complain over my credit card."

The man smiled–

"Please call me Grayson."

I titter, Mother stares, I sit in the chair directed.

Mr Richardson flicked the intercom, commanded coffee, then returned to Mother's bleating.

"My good man, I am unable to survive without an ongoing card."

She paused to breath deep, then continued to ramble how she needed the card to 'open' certain doors, as she put it.

Imagine designer shops and restaurants, and you have nailed her gist. Absorbed in the large space that was my father's old office, I spotted a picture on the back wall of two smiling women – Mother in her younger day, and a dark haired svelte like character almost kissing the camera with their protruding pink lips. 'Fooling around' I thought before my attention was stolen by the door to his office opening, and Mr Richardson commanding "Come in."

Fiona slithered in, pushing the heavy door with her arm, a large tray supporting a coffee pot, cups, and various small biscuits balancing in her hands. She clattered her fancy goods down onto Mr Richardson's desk, again that impish grin, and waited to be dismissed, his hands promptly wafting her away for a second time.

"Thank you, Fi…"

"Fiona, Sir," the girl did not stop grinning.

"Yes, yes, that's it. Now go"

Fiona bobbed to Mother, then turning toward the door strode out.

Raising his eyes heavenward this draconian figure apologised for the girl's actions.

"Forgive the staff. A new girl. Started the same day as myself."

Mother smiled, dismissing his apology away with her need to discuss money. Scanning this room, that until New Year had been my father's bastion of command, an idea begins to formulate. Again, that question of 'Shall I?' slipping from my mind as fast as it entered. Not believing the sheer audacity of my thought I decided that here, within this office, I was secondary to Mother's needs. Elsewhere, I may summon my power of deceit to help my own 'sine qua non' – My specification.

Gripping my stomach, I started to wave my hand pretending to cool myself down.

"Excuse me, Mr Richardson, would you be so kind as to conclude business with my mother, I feel a little queasy."

Mother glanced my way, the dubious stare that signals disbelief.

I must act quick.

Mr Richardson paused his conversation, his hand on that infernal machine.

He pressed the buzzer, only too relieved, in my way of thinking, to have Mother to himself.

"No worry. If I have your permission Miss Bryant the Fiona girl will guide you to the staff toilet, although I am sure you know your way."

The sarcasm was clear.

I thanked him, pushed my chair back, and hurried to the door, leaving Mother to glower in rage. Outside, the 'girl' as her boss referred to her, was walking towards me, a look of pity settling across her cheeky features. She forged ahead, running at one point until we stood before a door marked 'Staff'.

Pushing the door open she ushered me to hurry inside, directing me to the first cubicle; a look of startled curiosity replacing the pity as she caught my downcast face suddenly change–

"That plan worked fine." I sighed.

This individual of cheek had grown pale.

"Do not worry. It was you I wished to speak to."

"Me?" those cheek filled lips quivered.

"Yes, I think you can help me."

"Me?" she muttered once more.

Moving from the grey door of the cubicle to the row of sinks lined up beneath the frosted glass windows, I cradled my bottom between the groove separating two bowls.

"As I have said, you can help me."

"Help you?" she whined. "How?"

My idea, that only a moment before had not even formulated completely, was now taking shape, granting my zealous mind the tool to discover what exactly was playing out around me. I began–

"From your post at the reception desk you greet most visitors to the bank. You may not know my father, but no doubt you have heard about him. Highly respected in this bank, he has up and left, for reasons I do not understand, to my partner, calling on the aid of a woman named Savannah D' Mill…"

I paused, maybe for effect, I would rather believe for my idea to bind together.

This kid, eighteen if a day, glared at me with surprised dismay.

"I wish information on whether this woman is a member of this bank, and if so," large breath, "you can report to me her details. Be brave, dish the dirt."

The kid's surprise was replaced with horror, her trembling hands a signature to my request.

"But, Miss Bryant, I am just a receptionist."

"Exactly," I threw back at her. "A good position to snoop."

Fiona started to argue – "If I refuse…"

I shook my head, the smirk of one in control stealing across my lips–

"No go: I will scream now and swear you cornered me for money."

The satisfaction in my eyes had got to equal any cat that stole the cream of the milk.

"I, I…" the ruby mouth could not communicate her distaste.

I sniggered "Well, Miss Fiona – I cannot remember your surname."

"Grubb," she whispered. "Fiona Grubb."

"Right, Miss Grubb, let us act like that name. I need any grubby truth you can find."

I cared not for the tears gathering in the girl's eyes. For me to find out exactly what Savannah D' Mill is to my father, and what she holds over Mother will mean that my idea has found its right conduit, and with that I will be well pleased.

I gazed at the kid's tardy shoes, and I knew she needed money, her job at this bank was important–

"Go, I will leave my phone number on your desk as I leave. Make sure your information is good. Contact me, remember my warning."

Fiona stifled a sob, rushed from the room as I closed a cubicle door, kicking it in triumph.

--

I stepped from the staff room, a woman pleased with herself. Deceit had not forsaken me. The brief intermission last year has only proved to me that a tool, mental or otherwise, cannot disappear unless its owner misplaces it, or the tool is taken away. What bothered me was the way my deceit slipped like butter from my tongue; the pleasure finding out about the D' Mill woman sat incongruously by the side of the small modicum of guilt I felt over the girl, who finds herself in a position of precarious loyalty.

On the other hand, it is wonderful that I, Rhia Bryant, may discover what hold this 'floozy' (to me that is what she remains) has over my mother, and 'yes' I will admit I cannot let Jimmy or that painting go. Those from a wiser mindset would pronounce this woman is caught in a time-warp where past and present fuse to reveal an insufferable headstrong female who cares for nobody or nothing but her own objectives.

True or False?

As this is my diary, I know an answer will not be forthcoming!

Mother met me by the reception desk. Her mood had swung full circle, the cherished card stuck to her fingers once more.

"Rhia, how do you feel?" she asked slightly dubious.

"Better, thank you," I replied, slipping my phone number into Fiona's pen holder.

"Good. I have sorted out both the credit card and a small increase for your allowance. I am afraid your wage reduces the longer you do not return to work."

Not waiting for my answer Mother popped the card into her grey patent bag and headed toward the door. From the corner of my eye, I noticed Fiona slinking from the door she first appeared from, her downtrodden expression a sign my threat had been taken seriously. A small qualm of guilt rushes through my mind, then I shrug my shoulders; that steely determination to help find the painting rising above this dungeon of red lipstick, and firm hold hairspray.

Wednesday January 31st

Last day of the month, and the crazy weather has brought snow; a thick dressing of ice that chilled my bones and depressed my mind. I tick Tuesday from the calendar, turning my attention to today – Wednesday. This is the day, according to the poem of days, when those children whose birth falls on this day are full of woe. Whether you believe this affirmation is purely down to how much flair and confidence you have in childish rhymes. For example: take my mother, a product of this woeful Wednesday, swimming to the brim of her life with panache, while many others born on this day, may find themselves to be doleful and weak. Whereas this poem has many variations and many superstitions, my belief in the life game can be viewed from one stance – Chance. Everything we do and say in this life has consequences our elders say, therefore, what we choose must be 'chance'.

Mother came breezing into the kitchen, letter in hand.

First thought – 'Father has put pen to paper at last.'

Second thought – 'No, Mother would be ranting more.'

"We must clean and buy cakes for Sunday," she was saying.

"Whatever for?" I questioned.

"Savannah is visiting. Gracing us with her presence"

"What?"

I sounded offended. I was offended. Mother flapped the letter my way –

"No need to worry. This woman and I have past connections. She is your father's secret friend"

Is that what they called a floozy in her day?

"We must present ourselves as knowledgeable," she continued.

"Knowledgeable?" I snapped. "We do not need her."

Mother flapped the letter more "Yes, we do," she returned with certainty.

Moving around the kitchen I found myself lost for words. My mother was fast becoming a far different specimen to the creature who thumped her fist onto the wood of my main door. Back then she was a Halloween Eve Banshee –

Mother outside my door,

Mother banging her head against the varnished wood, screaming in my ear,

Mother a jumbled mess,

Mother crying,

Mother pleading with me.

Now, she has transformed herself from jabbering jelly fish to fighting piranha.

Deep in thought I was surprised to feel her hand upon my shoulder.

"You have doubts about the painting, Rhia?"

As I swivelled the hand fell away.

"No, why should I? We must help Jimmy and Father to hurry home."

Folding Savannah D' Mill's letter she popped it down on the table.

"This whole business does not mean we have to get involved."

"Yes, it does," I snap again. "That painter must be forgotten for good."

Mother's eyes opened wide, surprised by the venom in my reply.

"This is personal. Please, Rhia, do not tread this pathway."

"Why not?" I cried, tears starting to form beneath my lashes.

"It is dangerous."

I laughed, laughed louder, the sound vibrating around the room. Mother hugged me.

I will re-write the words 'HUGGED ME'.

"Stubborn girl," her voice was soothing. "Always stubborn."

She let me go, headed for the kettle (the British antidote for problems – Tea), switched it on.

I dabbed my eyes, irritated at the pronunciation of 'girl' that forever preceded Mother's corrections or arguments. It is hard to face the fact that to certain people you remain a child.

"To help, we need help," her voice floated above the hiss of the kettle. "We must take Savannah on board as well."

What can I say to change her mind?

"Has this woman a hold over you?" I ask in spite.

"No," she answered, obviously on the defensive.

"Then why?"

"Strategy"

"Meaning what?" was my sarcastic bite.

Mother made the tea, poured it into the waiting mugs, handed it to me, before simply saying – "All will be told one day."

Argument closed.

--

Evening

The evening of the last day of January witnessed the thawing of the snow that had settled earlier in the day due to heavy showers of rain, and warmer air. This, to me, was proof that the year had begun on a topsy, turvy note. The conversation over the D' Mill woman Mother had begun at breakfast had not carried on. She refused to listen to my groans, and instead sulked throughout the day re-cleaning every room in the flat.

What did I write concerning 'Wednesday's child'?

Each time I raised my head from the magazine I had chosen to fabricate the word 'busy', Mother was on her phone, those manicured fingers tapping away messages to whoever she was in contact with. This piqued me, for I had not been involved, or even knew whom the recipient could be. Maybe it was Father, and Mother was lying to me when she said his whereabouts were hidden from her. Most probably though, it was that woman, poking her ugly nose deep into my own and Mother's affairs, demanding Mother's total obedience.

Head down, pretending to mind my own business, in that way all curious people view their opponent, under their eyelashes, I saw Mother press the 'send' button, then deposit the phone into a jumper pocket.

'Hide the thing,' I thought. 'No need to share', these thoughts running through my head as I tried to keep a tight rein on my temper. I jumped when Mother pronounced–

"Savannah will be with us Sunday afternoon February 4th around two. She has news."

"News? Of course."

Mother shot a glance that indicated impatience.

"For goodness sake, give her the space she deserves."

"Which is exactly?"

Mother sounded exasperated.

"Why is it always your way or no way?"

Heading for the bedroom she slammed the door, screamed at the top of her voice (how unladylike) before moaning (or that is what it sounded like) at Jimmy's guitar.

Returning to my magazine I decided those people who play chess would, at this very moment, move their queen around the board and declare 'Checkmate'.

February 2001

Saturday February 3rd

I am exasperated.

How many ways can a person shop?

This is my mother's solution for 'grumpy' therapy, trailing around countless clothes shops, dozens of shoe shops, various restaurants, and practically every cake shop in London. I put the blame firmly upon the business fraternity. If an agreement for overindulgent cakes had never been signed, then I would not be experiencing the pangs of one who has overeaten. Not only could this put my brain and feet on a pathway to collide, but my stomach on the road to despair. Presented with the largest choux bun I had ever seen this woman was a coward. I more than ate that bun, I purchased another, and – Well, we will not go there.

By midday mother's choice to wander around these dens of lavish 'goodies' was beginning to diminish; partly due to tiredness, partly an unrealistic excitement over the forthcoming visit of 'Father's friend'.

"It is a fact," she had spouted earlier, "that when you face life's depressive path, you shop."

Personally, I have never heard such a load of rubbish. Her assumption that Father's 'friend' will be a bearer of bad news tomorrow is just that – an assumption. For goodness' sake, this woman is no clairvoyant.

Arriving back at the flat to the chimes of our church clock we were confronted by the prying neighbour from number six on her way out.

"Ladies, you have a visitor waiting for you. Very smart."

Her bleached hair swung in time to her chuckling as she waved us 'goodbye'.

"Bloody woman," I hissed rudely, following Mother's rapid footsteps toward the lift.

Emerging from this enclosed space we were greeted by the most dulcet tone–

"Look at you. Shopaholic through and through. No wonder Hal needs my help."

The laughter made Mother look at her watch, concede our guest was a day early, then drop her parcels and fly into the open arms of Savannah D' Mill

I gape, my mouth falling open in the need to express myself, yet the words will not form. The voice belonged to the most immaculate dressed figure these eyes had ever encountered. From the top of her black hair, swept high in a pleated bun, to the navy tailored suit elegantly clinging to her beauty queen figure, highlighting the bronze shoes and nails, this woman was beautiful. I know beauty lies within the gaze of the beholder, but this 'creature' (better than floozy) was in a class of her own. No wonder my father was besotted. Just watching the smiling grey eyes scrutinizing the woman before her, and the peach parted lips trembling with joy, I was amazed at the serenity in her stance. This female was perfection (Oh diary, I hate her).

"Mena," the sincerity of the name rang out. "It is wonderful to speak with you again."

"Savannah," Mother returned. "Long time."

With that both women continued to grasp each other in the way long lost friends come together after years apart.

Suddenly those grey eyes settled on me. Drawing back from their hug the peach lips opened further–

"Is this Rhia?"

"Yes," Mother whispered.

"My, you remind me…" the sentence broke, the perfected nails glistening in the corridor light as she brushed what I thought was a stray tear from her eyes. Mother, taking hold of the woman's other hand, led her through the door she was opening (no-one would guess it was my flat), and placed her gently down upon the sofa.

"Make yourself comfortable Savannah. I will get a drink, then catch up."

Not bothering to see whether I had followed her: that word assumption being her password, she headed for the bedroom to deposit her bags. I closed the door.

Rushing to the fire to switch it on I sensed the woman's gaze studying my face.

"Warmth," I said, for the need to say something.

She nodded, flashed her beautiful even white teeth my way, before turning her attention to Mother's shout from the kitchen.

"Tea, coffee, wine, Savannah? You choose"

Those lips parted again "Wine, Mena, as always."

Mother giggled as I heard the glasses and bottle being retrieved from the cupboard.

"Here we are," Mother pronounced, the bottle clanging against the three glasses she held as she walked back to the sofa. Dropping my shopping treasures (sarcastic) onto the floor I settled into the chair. Mother poured the wine, sniggered as the clock struck the half hour, holding the glass aloft.

"To those days gone by."

Both women connected in a way I could not understand, their delight in one another's company plain.

I sat, sipping, moving my head from woman to woman, listening to the words 'Long time', 'Good job', 'The bank', 'Sweet memories' fly between the two. It was not until Jimmy's name was mentioned that I sat up and listened.

"Jimmy has one hell of a job to find that painting. No wonder he begged Hal to help" – Savannah's comment.

"Yes, but dangerous," Mother's reply.

"I really am doing my best to discover…" Savannah's sentence cut short once more, quick glance my way.

"I know you will," Mother sighed.

The silence that followed was heavy. My description, that of stifling air prior to a thunderstorm.

Mother was the first to speak – "Shall I get nibbles? Better to tell with a clear head"

Savannah nodded, her eyes travelling to mine.

This continuous scrutiny was beginning to rattle me. Why did this beautiful woman find me so fascinating? I will take a guess and say my unruly hair, or my ample frame compared to mothers, yet I know neither of those guesses would be correct. Deep down my senses told me her fascination was deeper than that.

"Do you miss Jimmy?" the question surprised me.

"Yes," I drained my glass.

"Never mind, you get used to being alone."

There was no pretension within her comment, just a fleeting memory behind her eyes. My brain scrabbled for a reply, anything that would make me look cool. There was no need, for Mother's return from the kitchen should have been heralded with a fanfare. Believe me when I write, my mother's idea for nibbles has always been that one step further than a 'nibble' should be. She held two large dishes filled with crisps, cobs, cheese, salad, and cake:

“Tuck in,” she chirped placing the dishes onto the table.

We sat, we ate, we refilled our glasses, you could almost dub it the ‘lull before the storm’.

Mother took a deep breath, a large gulp of wine–

“A day early Savannah?”

The woman’s dark head nodded, those white teeth biting into a sandwich. She swallowed –

“I thought it best to get our initial groundwork over.”

“True,” Mother murmured.

From my seat in the chair opposite this pair of ‘chums’ I could gather something was brewing. Something my mind wished to hide from.

Savannah lowered her plate to the table, steadied her glass in partnership.

“Your mother has told me you consider me to have been your father’s ‘floozy’.”

What? No, I cannot believe this – how could she?

“The truth is far more complicated than that.”

Those peach lips appeared to spring at me.

“We were partners in the Cold War – Intelligence. Our job was to deceive and retrieve. We were spies.”

Time to laugh – My father, this woman.

By choice, this woman gasped.

Childhood memories invaded my thoughts – A young girl on holiday – A beach house hidden among dunes – My father’s knowledge set against the Berlin Wall – Mother’s constant fussing – Their consistent silence regarding their younger years.

MEMORIES – HAUNTING MEMORIES.

Mother made to move toward me. I shrank back as tears ran down my face.

--

It is said a day has golden wings. This day, this harrowing day, has greeted this time in slow motion. Mother has made more tea, poured more wine; anything to appease my coldness. None of this has bearing on a heart, where trust of anything solid is falling apart. I sit in abject horror as this beautiful woman describes those frenetic days of shared deception, giving nothing away, skimming the surface, skating over the 'real' truth. All the time my mind is shrieking 'My parents have lied'.

I am in that black hole that overtakes a human being when the fabrication of their life falls apart.

Mother spoke softly to me, reaching desperately for a hand I snatched away. Nothing that either of these women could say would alleviate the dreadful torment inside me.

How could my father not tell me?

How could Mother not tell me?

I TRUSTED THEM.

Obviously, Jimmy knew before me. How? Heaven only knows. Thinking back to that New Year conversation I began to see the significance within Jimmy's insistence to put Father's help in front of mine.

Lord, I had been duped.

From the shadowy annuls of my mind I heard Mother's voice–

"You really need to listen to Savannah before we go searching for this painting."

Listen to that woman – That spy?

I tried to laugh – Nothing.

I focus on the taut mouth beside me, those green eyes, so like my own, yet they cannot hold the vibrancy mine must surely be holding at this moment. I drag my eyes from green to grey, watch as they flutter up and down as this 'spy' retrieves papers from her bag. The peach mouth begins to talk once more–

"At the end of 1999 Hal sent me this request to discover any information on a German citizen known as Jules Dragner. However hard I searched, or whichever of our past colleagues I contacted, nothing was forthcoming. No Jules Dragner came to light. For a reason I would rather keep to myself at this moment, I gave the name of one Major Emery Dreyer, a high-ranking intelligence officer within the Stasi regime. My reports went mad – news, concerning this man and his immediate family. His son, Kurt Dreyer, had been a student in London. Both father and son had disappeared after the fall of the Berlin Wall. Immediately my information was faxed to Hal carrying a query into 'digging' further. He confirmed 'Go Ahead'."

She paused for breath.

"These papers confirmed my beliefs. Relating to the capture of Jules Dragner, new master painter, Stasi soldier under the command of Major Emery

Dreyer, a man who will stop at nothing when inflicting pain upon his prisoners. Our research has also shown Dragner as this man's son. Passing these records on to your Father, surveillance began."

I read the details in front of me. Why all the fuss? This information is not new, not to me. I had discovered Kurt's past, the hard way. Had he not threatened me? I was pleased the brute was locked away. As far as I was concerned the German authorities could throw away the key – Forever.

A furrow had eased its way onto the brow of Savannah D' Mill–

"It is not the son we are concerned about," she paused. "Dragner will be the Spider in Emery's plan. This painting is to coerce. Yes, it holds names, ones in my view, that are sought by the German authorities, but the real reason for its loss is revenge. No one knows that better than your father. So, please Rhia, think before you head into the quarry. This game may be beyond your comprehension"

She fell silent.

How dare this woman sit in my flat and dictate to me? I do not care what her connection with my father unravelled. I do not care that their ridiculous partnership was strong. She has no right to consider bossing me – I do not care.

I let Jimmy's image spring to mind. He would not have regretted letting me help him. Three pair of eyes would have concluded the job faster, and besides, Savannah D' Mill, with her drivel about 'coerce' and 'revenge' is just scaremongering. I have come across those people before. For your information lady, I swear I will help him, even more now. This woman, beautiful she may be, can take her papers, and throw them in the bin for all I care. This admission has cemented my determination. Look at them, my mother and this 'spy', heads together, trying to plan my next move.

I say "NO" – No, no, no.

The need to scream wrenched at my throat, threatened to lacerate my mouth with its piercing force. Grappling for air I swallowed hard; anything to calm myself down. I knew if a sound escaped there would be no stopping it, and I must not show weakness. It was obvious both women were trying to frighten me, disengage me from my chosen path. Think again ladies – Emery who? I know nobody of that name.

--

Ten o' clock

Mother and I have spent the last three hours wandering aimlessly in and out of the four rooms of my flat in a processional sequence. Not one word was uttered, neither occupied the same space. The silence that had descended upon us, and the world outside these windows, was eerie: graveyard quiet. If one must be picky, as stated by those who choose to study 'human' nature, the only perceptible sound (to a mouse), could be the tiniest of shuffles from our furry slippers sliding across the floor. Each hour was noted by the church clock, and a quick glance toward the monstrosity hanging on the wall. Funny, I so loved that 'ball' clock, now the 'clicking' hands were driving me crazy.

Savannah D' Mill had left around six o' clock, a little worse for wear, this being her spy partner's favourite quote when someone has consumed more wine than they should. Gone, with those bloody papers stuffed back into her bag, and their revelations hidden away for what I hoped was forever. She had cheerily asked us to call her Savvy (think about that one), as my refusal to 'give up' the search for the painting meant she would be visiting on certain Sundays, according to herself and Mother's agreement (sod me). Together, they had planned our first meeting with her man, the date being February 14th.

At this point, cannot stop myself asking if this guy will turn out to be Cupid. If so, one 'splat' with his own arrow, and he will be taken down!

No sooner had she left than Mother had sunk down into the chair, head buried in her hands. I refused to get embroiled in her 'play-acting', so decided to change into my pyjamas. Changing into her own pyjamas Mother stood by the arm of the sofa.

"Rhia, this cannot continue. We wish to protect you."

"From whom?" I snarled.

"From yourself."

"Me?" I snarled louder. "Oh, I see, like my childhood."

"Unfair," Mother's remonstration was certainly worth applause.

"Unfair?" I return. "For whom? Father and yourself. Maybe the child you both lied to."

Mother began to cry. In my book, crocodile tears.

Savannah D' Mill had dropped her bombshell. I was that victim of deceit; that deceiver who evidently had been deceived. Get that (Oops slang diary) if you are in a better mood than me. I fixed my eyes on her face–

"I have had an idea that may lead us to the painting."

Mother's voice shook "Please, Rhia, think."

"I have, so when I say Germany I mean back to the beginning."

I could see Mother's argument forming.

"Germany?" she was almost panting. "Germany?"

"Yes, we will start at the beginning," I repeated.

"Ridiculous," she stormed, plumping the cushions with her screwed up hands.

"Ridiculous for whom, that stick like pencil that visited us, or you?"

Fury has no name.

Mother stood still, eyed me as a cat eyes a mouse–

"You," she says, all signs of argument dissolved.

I shrug.

"I am not playing your silly games, Goodnight Mother." and I bury myself among the cushions on the sofa.

My idea to sleep in the lounge was an easy option for I am beside myself with anger. Snuggling my head into the soft arm of the sofa I refuse to laugh at Mother's startled face.

"You are sleeping here?"

"Yes."

"The whole night?" Mother stumbles over her words.

"Yes"

"Germany?" her voice quivered.

"Yes."

"Oh, Rhia,"

"Please turn the light off on your way to bed," I said in the most snobbish tone found– "Goodnight."

Sunday February 4th

After dark comes light; a paraphrase to warm the bruised heart.

I had slept, surprisingly, solid through the night-time hours. On waking I found a cup of tea waiting for me, glowing in the light of the gas fire. Craning my neck to see the clock I registered it was seven o' clock. Trying to raise myself upwards I felt the pains of sleeping in a confined position attack me. My legs, my arms, my neck; aching limbs pressing me to stretch them to their utmost capability. I reached for the tea, let out one loud painful screech, slumped back and closed my eyes. Mother, running into the room, eased a pillow behind my back.

"If you had come to bed, Rhia."

Closing my mind to her disapproval I gently twisted this way and that until that precious mug of tea was in my hand. Sipping it slowly I caught Mother staring at me.

"Two heads?" I queried in scorn.

She smiled, placing her unbrushed head as near to my cheek as possible.

"Do not hold anger – Please. Your father and I love you."

The watery eyes found my pleading forgiveness. I continued to sip tea, breathe through my pain, and try to speak in a tolerant fashion.

By eight o' clock this painful frame was akin to the breast of a robin, reddened by the heat from the fire. Mother, whose plea, in her mind, had been accepted and removed from any future conversation, was in the bathroom applying 'her face' when the shrill ringing of my mobile brought her unfinished face bobbing around the door.

"Someone's early, who can it be?"

Thinking it may be Jimmy; not wishing her to know, I grabbed it from where it lay on the floor by the sofa, saying in the loudest voice possible –

"Oh, a company. I will soon deal with them."

Mother slid back into the room. Feeling the pain shoot up the back of my neck and along my arms I went to shriek – stopped – stifled the cry. Pressing the 'on' button I gasped "Yes," waiting in anticipation for Jimmy to speak.

That low crushing feeling when expectation dies rolled over me. A female was speaking. No, I will correct that last word, she was squeaking: a fox caught in a trap.

"Hello."

Quickly casting my eyes toward the door that hid Mother I repeated myself. The squeak sounded fraught, spilling over itself to convey the message–

"Miss Bryant, Fiona here. You said to call if I heard anything. Yesterday Mr Richardson was on the telephone during my appraisal. He mentioned the name Detdy – Etta Detdy when concerning your father. I do not know this name, or who he was talking with. Hope this will do. Bye."

The line went dead.

Gritting my teeth through my pain I sat up straight, my aching limbs a secondary consideration to that babbling girl. 'Hope this will do' – What the hell? One, without a doubt I had told her to text me, not ring, and two, her news made no sense. Had the girl never heard of customers, clients; whatever high profile bankers named those who sought loans. This information had no relativity to me. Immediately I text the number that had flashed on my screen 'Try Again' and left it at that.

Mother floated from the bathroom in a cloud of expensive perfume, her mouth, eyes, and lips defined by the most 'top shelf' cosmetics. Noticing I had eased my body upright she pointed to the room she had just vacated–

"I have run a bath for you. It will soothe your pains."

Offering me her arm she waited for me to stand. What else could I do? The bridge had been built. It was down to me to cross it, accept that she was sorry. Wobbling, I seized the hand extended my way.

"You dismissed that company?" Mother enquired.

"Oh yes," I said in conviction. "In an instant."

"Good" she declared, leading me into the lingering scent of the bathroom.

Saturday February 10th

Today is the first morning I wake with no pain. It has taken daily baths, and Mother's massaging to set my body right. It is a lesson I shall not repeat. Throughout our daily conversations (the human mind can only last so long without interaction of one kind or another) Mother repeatedly mentioned that approaching meeting with Savannah D' Mill's man. There had been no clue to his identity, nothing that could ease how fraught that meeting would be. Out of all the days in February, why had the 14th been chosen? Did Miss D' Mill believe the meaning of that day would help us to be more relaxed, accept whatever nonsense this man spouted? If that was her strategy – She will lose.

I declare to myself that February 14th is just a date, on a calendar, and the flowers and hearts are for those so disposed to taking the day seriously. Moreover, a more prominent matter has risen its head – the Fiona girl.

I should say 'Thank heaven she moved to texting, and not ringing', but her fixation on this Detdy woman has grown. In her book (her word, not mine) this female will turn out as an important factor in my father's disappearance. When I text back and asked where she had heard such nonsense, she replied that proof from old Richardson's telephone call lay in her grasp, also gossip was rife within the walls of that mausoleum.

What can I say – The girl is clawing at straws.

I am presuming the Richardson character must be sorting out my father's work. Anyway, my father has not disappeared. He is searching with Jimmy. Once more my kind heart (jest) chose to text back with 'Better next time'. The Grubb girl did not reply.

Mother is on her cleaning rampage: moving from room to room, covered from head to foot in green overalls with an old yellow headscarf to secure her hair. She reminds me of a cartoon character on a sea-side postcard. Trying to stay clear of her feather duster and rubber gloved hands I parade around the lounge pretending to tidy an odd magazine; maybe plump a cushion. Bending down to remove paper from the floor I jump as the doorbell is pushed with vigour. Hurrying to close the bedroom door on Mother's horrified face, I answer the continuous ring. That neighbour from number six, a woman I believe to be seriously intrusive grins at me, wiggling an envelope before my eyes.

"Ah, at home for once, Rhia," she stresses.

"Yes," I snap.

"May I come in. This letter is for you. I found it hidden within my post."

Blast. No getting out of this one. Cannot think of a good excuse fast enough.

Standing aside the woman floats pass me, her keen brown eyes skimming around the room.

"A letter, Katrina (for this is her name), what a surprise."

Her hands were patting the blonde hair she had sprayed into a sixties style beehive, her face contorting this way and that as she glared at my image.

"Busy?"

Those beady eyes whizzed around the room, her nose sniffing at the air.

"Place smells nice," she remarked, still waving the letter.

"Mother," I reply quickly, hoping to remove her as fast as possible.

"Letter," she slaps a white envelope to my hand.

"Thank you."

I suddenly realise this small expression is the first acknowledgement I have made toward this neighbour. Over the past year I have ran along the corridor, hidden in the lift, called her every name referring to a busybody, and generally disliked her.

The woman, Katrina Mallis, as I know her from her letter hole downstairs, moved into these flats the same day as myself. Along with her broad Liverpool accent and her mania to dress as a past hippie (much to Mother's irritation), she knew practically everything that occurred within these walls. I often think she should assist our wonderful concierge: where he turns a blind eye to certain 'mishaps', she would not miss a trick. Her gaze followed the white parchment as I slipped it between the pages of a magazine on the table.

"Not opening it?" she questioned swinging her skinny physique to look in the mirror,

"I noticed it had no stamp."

That was all the verification needed for me to know this woman had offered to bring it to my door from the concierge downstairs.

"Whoever posted it knew somehow it would get to me. I will open it later."

The woman glared again, her muddy pooled eyes lapping up the discomfort I felt.

"I am sorry to rush you," I spluttered. "The bank will be calling."

She grinned; that loathsome distain of one who knows I am lying. Her eyes travelled from the fluffy slippers to the faded jeans and oversized jumper. Katrina Mallis moved toward the door, gliding out the same way she had glided in.

Mother emerged from her retreat, unabashed laughter springing from her mouth.

"That woman is hilarious. A hippie my foot. Her clothes are more suited with a sixties disco, pink zigzags on a silky cream background"

Who cared? Her nosiness unnerved me.

"What was her ploy to visit?" she laughed.

"A letter mixed in her post for me."

"Important?"

"No mother, a bank statement."

WHY WAS I LYING?

Presuming she was content with my answer I strode through the room into the kitchen.

"Poor staff," she called "The wrong address."

"Yes," I answered.

There was no reason for me to lie, I did not even know who that letter was from. It was then I heard Mother softly reciting the lines of a poem; a hint to Savannah D' Mill's quip?

"Will you walk into my parlour said the Spider to the Fly*
Tis the prettiest little parlour that ever you did spy–
The way into my parlour is up a winding stair,
And I've many curious things to show when you are there –
'Oh no, no said the little Fly, 'to ask me is in vain,
For who goes up your winding stair can ne'er come down again'..."

The hand I had placed on the cupboard door began to tremble; an imaginary cold was wrapping itself around my heart. I shivered, slammed the partially opened door closed. This was ridiculous. It was nothing more than a poem: stanzas created from the imagination of an excellent versifier.

"Coffee?" I screeched at the top of my voice.

"Your pleasure," came her answer, as she continued to recite.

--

Evening

It is seven thirty, rain coursing into the drains at the speed of a supersonic jet, and my heart and mind disturbed to the point where this woman could scream.

The rain, that had started as a drizzle around mid-afternoon, had now decided to lash its way from the heavens onto the deserted streets below. I write 'deserted' mainly as an acknowledgement to the lack of humanity filling the street below my flat with their chatter and laughter. I do not mean the row of cars littering the kerb opposite while their occupants run to the corner shop for bread, or something similar, maybe visit a particular flat. From where I stood the headlights of these cars either twinkled in the scurry of pounding rain, or if the driver noticed my gaze, they instantly deflected their beam. Odd, but this was exact in the white car parked on the corner, whose driver appeared as if he (the figure looked male, to me) was there for a long haul. I finally concluded he was waiting for someone.

Turning from the window I suddenly remembered the letter I had slipped into the magazine. Forgotten during the afternoon due to Mother's determination to shop (am I sick of the credit card) it now drew me to its concealed hideaway.

Edging toward the table I smiled as I thought of our drenched bodies and numb limbs, the church clock striking six as we fell with our bags into the warmth of the flat. Hour and half later, cosy from the hottest bath I have dared immerse myself into, I listen for Mother's splashing as I draw that envelope into my grasp. Studying the writing I deduced it was exceedingly untidy, of no-one's hand I knew, and written in, what can only be described as a pen that had seen a 'better day'. So dear diary, you can imagine my surprise when I discover it is from Jimmy.

Hi,
Sorry I have not been in touch. Your father and I keep busy searching for the painting. Knowing you, I believe your determination will spur you on to help us. Therefore, I will say 'Thank you', and ask you to trust no-one that I, or your father have not passed, which is the reason I write. From what I gather, from your father's own lips, you will be meeting a man on the 14th February. As far as your father is concerned this man can be trusted completely.
Do what he suggests, not what you wish.
See you soon,
Yours Jimmy x x

Big, bold, nothing short of a command.

I could hear the clock ticking in the background as I studied the writing in front of me. This script was not like Jimmy; his style had always been larger with a quirk of the pen that encapsulated humour, if only to trail a dragon tail on the 'y', yet the phrasing would pass for his. I had known him write this way if he was in a rush, but afterwards he hated it. Immediately I grabbed my mobile, mother's splashing ignored, and rang Jimmy's number. Waiting for that recorded apology, and resolved to scream into the mouthpiece, I jumped as I heard heavy breathing and voices calling out assaulting my ear.

"Hello?" I queried. "Jimmy?"

"Yes," the voice responded.

"Are you– " deep breath, "busy?"

A crackling noise, the shout of another –

"Of course. This is work"

My mind registered impatience.

"What do you want, Rhia?"

"The letter," I said in bated breath.

"What about it?"

His breathing grew sharper as he called "Coming."

"Who is that?" I venture.

"Intelligence."

"Bad time?" I chuckle.

"You could say that."

"Sorry."

"As always."

What can I say?

Jimmy was clicking his teeth. I hated that habit.

"Maybe you should not have answered your phone."

I was hurt.

"Maybe not, now why the call?"

"You suggest I trust no-one but this guy we will meet."

"Right," Jimmy's voice rose. "Look, just follow my instructions – now."

Rising frustration on my part.

"Is my father there?"

"What?"

"My father?"

"No."

"Why not?"

"Busy, Rhia, b-u-s-y."

My heart was racing, my thoughts spiralling out of control.

"Why the rudeness?" I shout.

Nothing –

I scowl at this lame technology within my hand. The 'prize' of pioneering minds, the device to connect the world. More like the bane of society I believe. Fair enough, I have rung his number most days, but is that not what lovers do?

Mother had overheard my raised voice–

"Problem?"

Swirling to face her I saw the concern of one who had heard the scream of a frustrated mind.

"Sorry, I was angry. Phoned Jimmy, nothing doing."

"Again, never mind."

Mother consented to my lie, continued to rub the cream she had been using into her hands as I pushed this treacherous device into my pocket.

"Why this urgency?"

I smiled: anything to dissuade her from more questions.

"I miss him."

Mother moved to where I stood, patted my shoulder, let those scrutinizing eyes wash over me–

"Funny, I miss your father too. Still, this problem must be solved."

She had her credit card, for her the world was turning.

"The painting?" I ask, tongue in cheek.

She nods.

"In a way, remember Savannah's words 'Nothing is what it seems'."

For the first time my heart was confused, grappling with my place within this riddle. I knew my power of deception must be brought into play to its full potential if I was to help Jimmy and my father.

I will start with Savannah's man.

Brandenburg – Gorden Prison, Germany
February 2001

The man lay on his bed, the threadbare mattress allowing the strip of mesh that acted as a base to sag beneath the weight of his body. Snuggling, a habit from childhood, under the thin grey blanket, he shivered. The weather of late had not been kind to his aching limbs or rasping chest. The coughing had increased, bringing undue pressure to his breathing, especially since the new governor had taken over. His rules had made surviving seem impossible, for himself and the many young soldiers locked within these dark, damp cells. It was a stark change to that wonderful day in December 2000 when he discovered that the governor in command of this prison had been a loyal soldier to his father, their solidarity formed among the chink of brushes, and odour of paint. He remembered that day so vividly, feeling excitement grow as together they inspired the painting he had created. In the days that followed he waited for another call, further discussions, more relief to his mounting stress.

"Zero" the man spat; the spittle running down his chin to trickle along his scrawny neck. Now, he knew why. That governor, his one confidant in this hellhole, had been removed. Taken from these walls without ceremony or notice. Smuggled out during the night, and the new man in. He was loyal to the system: a spy for the state.

The new governor's laws instantly replaced the old rules, condemning him, a famous painter, to confining measures.

One: No communication with other prisoners.

Two: Implementing stricter compulsory exercise he will participate in or find himself dragged out.

Three: All meals alone.

Four: No writing implements, he may try to smuggle letters to party members uncaptured.

Five: If a guard is apprehended breaking 'rule four' he will receive the severest punishment.

Six: This prisoner is not allowed extra rations.

The man had complained, lacerated the guards in German and English, all in vain.

In the following weeks extra guards had been allotted to his block. Men whose wide girth would have halted any siege that may have been planned. They were cruel: frequently jostling with the younger inmates which lead to savage beatings and hours of confinement in small dark holes known as cupboard cells. The cramped conditions of these holes were an insult to the name 'brush cupboards' given to them by their laughing jailors. They were neither clean, nor odour free. Too small to stand up in, the small latrine could not cope with the hours, maybe days they were not emptied, making hygiene a forgotten pleasure. He cradled his shivering body.

"Oh yes, these dogs will pay. When my father is back in charge these guards will face the consequences of their actions."

He thought of what interrogation *his* governor suffered. Whatever information he gave these 'puppets' it would be minute. The man sneered, tried to laugh out loud, rasping as that laugh turned to coughing: surging pains raging through his chest, tearing through his muscles and bones, gripping his pulsating limbs until even the task of resting became an arduous task.

The man turned onto his side, forced himself to breathe slower. He willed the pains to recede, vanish into the cold air.

"Hallo," came the distinctive sound of a German voice.

The man slid onto his back once more, looked into the cheery eyes of a young guard.

"Franz," he choked, trying to pull himself into a sitting position.

The young man stared at this prisoner who had been kind to him when caught weeping outside his cell. He knew who this man was. His beautiful paintings, his clever mind. Accepting the proffered hand of the young guard the man slipped upwards, knowing how this boy's sensitive nature hated the severe handling of the prisoners. With that in mind he had used him. As the women he seduced, he captivated the young guard's mind; an old trick instilled into him by his father. In the way of all people who fell at the feet of idolatry, this young guard longed to please his idol, so whatever the man asked, Franz complied. Today, it was pen and paper, tomorrow it could be food.

“Ausblenden,” the young mouth whispered as he passed his wares.

The man nodded his thanks, instantly doing the guards bidding to ‘hide’ the paper beneath his mattress.

“Spaziergang.”

The soft brown eyes searched the ice blue irises of his prisoner, gently easing him from the bed to walk.

--

How he hated that ‘hour’. The painful trotting, stumbling almost as he dragged his feet, holding tightly to Franz’s arm. How those dogs laughed, pushing these two fools, the young inexperienced guard, and the rasping, wasted painter, out into the rain. He had returned soaked, with only a quick rub down from his blanket. Squatting on the mattress the man rubbed his wet hands, praying his clothes would dry quick, and his cold, shivering form would soon dry out. Rotating around that wet concrete he had concentrated on the jeering mouths, longing to see how quickly it took to bruise those flapping orifices. He juxtaposed himself to a wild horse, subdued, waiting patiently to bite the hand of its trainer – that time will come.

Rising slowly from the iron bed the man slumped toward the window, anything, to try and ease the spiralling grating sound within him. Scanning the skyline, he watched the clouds chasing each other, spilling their tears onto a wet, dreary world below. Following those translucent drops downward he spotted a van, back doors wide, guards patrolling the barren vicinity. This van was here to carry another prisoner to his destination. Franz had already informed him over how many of these former soldiers were disappearing. Many brought before the judiciary and given harder or lengthier sentences, moved deeper into Eastern territory for safe keeping. Their guilt, according to whichever judge supervised their trial, recorded their crimes as fanatical idolisation: an excuse when torturing their fellow citizens. The man clenched his fists–

“Not true,” he gasped. “It was obedience.”

“Obedience,” he murmured again as a voice cut through the rain, loud and clear–

“Schild und Schwert der Parter” – The Shield and Sword of the Party.

He listened as the soldier in line for transportation called the party motto.

He knew this soldier from old. He was a student under his father's instruction, an honoured captain. They would prise nothing from him.

"Why can't my feeble bones understand the need for revenge."

He rattled the bars at his window, accepting the black depression descending upon him. It would not be difficult to succumb to these pains, to float away, let oblivion ease his mind. Yet, he was his father's son, and their plan must succeed. For all his life he had been told revenge will be sweet, the perpetrator will pay. He stopped thinking, breathed deep as another grating cough threatened to disable him. It was in these moments of dark melancholy his mind travelled to another time, another revenge. This pathway he *must* tread, seek the tears of that red-haired seductress. The man laughed out loud; a cackle that represents a definitive line: the malicious sound of one who seeks victory.

--

The sun was struggling to compete with that heavy overcast sky as the young guard unlocked the man's cell to walk him to the visitor room. No words were spoken as the soft footfall of rubber soles squeaked on the freshly scrubbed tiled floor. Every now and again the young boy, smart in his uniform of grey, nodded instructions. His prisoner acknowledged, not in the way of his usual discourtesy, but more menial; a sign that collaboration was taking place; a paper passed hand to hand, lay hidden within the folds of the young guard's shirt until such a time that he could commit it to memory and flush the paper down the staff toilet. This guard knew the hardest part would be when he finished his duty, the search that always took place. He must keep his face bland, no tell-tale signs of guilt.

A door swung open, and the man entered a room. White walls gave him an impression of a clinical vibe more than visitor room, especially as the rows of tables were painted in the same sparkling colour, flanked by two white chairs. The heavily barred windows were slightly open, allowing a freshness that follows a morning of rain to filter through. Walking further the man suddenly lost that fresh air permeating the room, leaving him to digest the rancid aroma of dirt and decay. Lead to a table the man sat, accepted the forlorn glance from his young guard as chains were bound around his legs and that of the chair. Mouthing 'sorry' he nodded in compliance to the deceit he must perform, stood up, saluted the senior guard on visitor duty, and marched away.

Settling down, the man's eyes searched the tubular light above him, blinking as it flickered a warning of malfunction. Around the room a bevy of guards were gathering to stand and 'listen' into conversations. No-one could escape. No-one could pass messages to the visiting people. He stretched his aching legs as far as the chains would allow. A whistle sounded, and a door opened at the back of the room. To the shout of a guard, prisoners were paraded to tables down the far side wall. Free from chains they sat with their heads bowed, and their hands folded into their laps. The man stared, cold eyes paying attention to the faces of these skulking traitors. Each visiting day men, such as these, were paraded into the room, and allowed freedom of movement to speak with their visitors. They had been 'persuaded' to forgo their loyalty to the old regime for extra rations, softer commands, lenient sentences. Bile filled his mouth. He had served with these men, played as a boy with their sons and daughters.

"You are dead men," he snarled under his breath in German.

They in turn, never looked his way.

Several of the prisoners herded into the room at the same time as himself began to thump their tables.

"Traitor," they were crying, pointing two fingers at the bowed heads.

The man's eyes did not falter from their faces that showed fear.

"Fools," he flung their way, his disgust palatable.

The men sank lower in their seats, the guards moving closer to their prey.

'Fools,' he thought again as his lips parted in a smirk. They had grabbed that proverbial carrot offered in a promise to circumvent the stick. Chosen betrayal. One day his father would hunt them down. No hiding place would cover their perfidy. Do shrink away, for your hours are marked. Hearing the creak of the large steel gate that fronts the prison the man knew visitors would be pouring in. This day, he was excited. The messages the young guard had carried back and forth spoke of an accomplice, trained within his father's employ, engaged when the heart was low and the mind malicious. Today he, the son of this great officer would meet him.

The man whispered, "Mitarbeiter," in German.

He whispered again in English "Collaboration."

Suddenly the room exploded with noise. Those prisoners thumping tables were shouting louder, arms waving, and growling at the men still viewing the floor. The guards rapped sticks down onto hands already sore from past beatings, the word "ruhig" (quiet) booming out across their heads. A moments' disorder followed where the rattling of chains and muffled words petered away, then – a guard blew his whistle. All prisoners knew if he blew it twice there would be no visiting today, and no food until tomorrow.

Silence descended.

"One, two, three," the deep resonance of a German accent flowed around the room. On the count of four another guard blew his whistle, and the doors, locked from outside, clanged wide. Bodies poured in, mothers, daughters, sisters, all crying, some with outstretched arms to welcome their loved one. A few stepped over the threshold with fear in their gaze, others looked around, quickly walking toward the table they sought.

The man craned his neck, those once chiselled features seeking the face he craved. Behind the crowd a hand was waving, a head bobbing, a glance denoting love, yet pity. He stretched his head higher, waved back, straining to see if she had a companion. She stood alone. His heart restricted, hope began to fade. Had his previous letters not arrived at their destination? Was the boy playing him? The man sighed low, heard his mother's call. He focused on her moving frame, the slow laborious trudge, the sinking of the shoulders. Reaching his table her grey head twisted in the direction of the door, beckoned to the figure loitering there.

The man's eyes lit up, joy illuminating his pallid features. A figure was moving his way, dark head bobbing as it moved between the tables. He signalled to the guard, whispered something about family and 'a long way', asking for another chair to be brought. The guard moaned, signalled his senior, gave the request. Verging on the side of refusal, the woman sought the guard's hand, slipped some notes within his palm, appreciated the change taking place. The senior guard nodded to his junior, waited for the chair, and marched away. The man nodded his thanks, scanned his visitor's bewildered eyes.

"You came," he whispered in English.

"My orders are to notify you that the plan is under control."

His visitor had spoken in a voice so soft that he hardly could hear him. Yet, he did, and it was his words that thrilled him, uplifted his spirit, let optimism play its part.

"How sure can you be?" he mouthed, looking around him, pleading inwardly that no guard heard.

"Very," said his visitor.

"Sehr," his mother repeated.

"Gut," he broke off before whispering, "die Falle ist gesetzt."
For the first time that day the man genuinely smiled, "The trap is set."

Part Two

February 14th

St Valentine Day 2001

Typical, this specific Valentine's Day happens to fall on a Wednesday, and what is recorded over this certain day of the week?

Woden – Germanic mythological God was called upon before war. He was known as a shapeshifter due to the belief he could move between worlds. The day Wednesday was named after him, and often referred to as 'Woden's Day'.

Ash Wednesday – the beginning of Lent. Taken from an ancient Jewish tradition of fasting and penitence; human mortality is observed with a cross of ashes placed on the forehead.

Spy Wednesday – named by Christians as the day Judas betrayed Jesus.

Wednesdays Child – being full of woe, that fortune telling song of the days of the week.

No doubt then, this evening when we meet Savvy's 'man' it will be a complete disaster, woe from the start, and woe to finish.

For the last week I have been wishing, praying, whatever word may cover 'stop', to refuse this invitation I did not want in the first place. I woke this morning to find the weather is not on my side. No rain, no snow, just dry. Terribly unhelpful, as I cannot use that as an excuse. Waiting for our concierge to deliver the mail I tried imagining how a hen must feel waiting for her eggs to hatch. Hearing the letterbox 'ping' around midday I run to gather the mail. This has got to be Savannah D' Mill informing us this meeting is really cancelled.

"Why not the phone?" I hear you say.

I must scream, "I do not know. I just want this farce terminated."

Turning my thoughts to the 'day' I rummaged through the envelopes for a note, for a card from my lost lover, being Valentine's Day. There were no notes, no cards, only bills. I moaned at the top of my voice.

Mother, a green gungy mask spread across her face rushed into the lounge.

"Whatever is the matter? Have you seen a letter from the bank?"

My head shook from side to side.

"Blow," came her exasperated answer. "I need to talk to that Richardson fellow."

My irritated comment "More money?"

The green mask cracked as her exasperation grew–

"Not exactly that…"

"Stop lying mother," I wailed. "Stop spending."

Mother's eyes narrowed, creasing the gunge into tiny splits –

"Spending? Nobody would be spending if we had visited Mattie."

Here we go again.

'Get over it," I ranted. "Fuck, I hate this day, I wanted a bloody card."

Mother's slits opened into bulging orbs–

"Is that the reason for your mood, a silly expensive practise?"

Diary, I doodle, a grizzly face  a heart that is hurt  a snapping crocodile 

All these represent me today.

I sulk for the rest of the morning. Nothing spurred me from my despondency, not Mother's need for another bank meeting, not my own need to find something suitable for this stupid meeting which Savannah D' Mill had informed Mother would be at a restaurant on the evening of the 14th. Asked which restaurant Mother just laughed and told me to 'Wait and see'. By lunch time my mood had sunk to a level far beyond the black depths of a dusty coal mine, crashing into that bottomless pit where heartbroken creatures live. In this desperate wallowing you can envisage the depth of my gloom when a text came through from the Grubb girl.

"Hello, Miss Bryant,

I have found nothing more to report, apart from the Detdy name. Oh, and Savannah D' Mill was in Mr Richardson's office yesterday discussing that same name. I had to deliver the file. F"

Is this girl toying with my patience in the same way she plays around with her text font? Maybe she really thinks her boss was discussing that name to be polite, on the other hand, the girl could have heard more than she tells me. Why would a former colleague show interest in a client? Has this client, whose name, forgive me pointing this out, spells 'Teddy' when unravelled, a connection to the painting, the bank, and my father's 'spying' days? For the first time that morning

I put the missing Valentine card to the back of my mind. I text back, none too polite–

'Stop mucking about and find more – or else.'

I received no reply.

--

Afternoon

A bowl of sugary puffs and two pieces of toast at lunchtime, sprinkled with extra sugar eased my mood, a little. Mother complained about my eating habits, of which I snubbed her. I had not heard back from FG, and yes I was getting to that stand where any form of showdown would harm her more than me. The rate she was moving I would find nothing out, and Jimmy will not think twice when he gloats over me. Today has proved that – not one thought to my aching heart. It appears, and I hate to write this, that I must butter Mother up and accept help from Savvy's man – 'accepter gracieusement' as the French say. Either way, I will play the game – Best man wins, or woman in this instance.

Afternoon crept slowly toward evening with Mother rushing in and out each room with a dress over her arm, a drink in her hand, and the largest smile possible. I pondered on that smile while choosing my own non-descriptive garment.

Is it worth considering that my social climbing Mother could be hiding further secrets? That her 'genuine' friendship with the D' Mill woman screams 'conspiratorial' to something in my father's past, and this painting is a by-product of this 'something'?

As this hypothesis flew in and out of my mind, Mother's twirling figure came into view, the symbol of elegance. Her calf length navy taffeta dress highlighted the tiny waist, rippling over underskirts of the same colour, adorned by a navy tailored bolero. Vibrant red heeled shoes matched her hand-held bag. Patting the neatly sprayed bun at the nape of her neck, she focused on the black suited female beside her.

"Trouser suit again," she groaned.

I blinked, settled my eyes on the bright red patent clutch bag as I retaliated firmly–

"This is a business meeting, nothing more."

Mother winced as I added, "The guy probably will not look at us twice."

Her withering gaze said it all. Mother did not get dressed up for no-one to notice!

--

The 'Amour' *

Evening of February 14th.

It is often written that 'fate' takes a hand in a situation when you least expect it.

You can imagine my face when the taxi pulled up outside this building with large red letters 'Amour' carved above the door; rendering Mother and myself to skitter from the taxi like the mice being chased by the farmer's wife. Embarrassed by the grin imprinted across the doorman's mouth we hurried through the double glass doors. Greeted by an overdressed French butler (our waiter) amid a cloud of dangling red hearts and glistening chandeliers, I really did consider suggesting we should go home. Mother, ignoring my blushes, urged me to follow as our waiter lead us through various sized round tables, draped with flowing red tablecloths, and situated around a polished wooden floor, which I presumed was for dancing. In the middle of this floor stood a small dais where four violinists and a pianist sat playing soft romantic music. The atmosphere was buzzing due to parties of six, four, or two, clustered at their given table chatting, laughing, or to Mother's disgust, canoodling.

"Time and a place," she commented as our waiter moved on.

For my heart, still pining for a Valentine card, this scene clearly signalled purgatory.

It was impossible to guess why Savannah D' Mill would choose such a place, especially on this particular night. The woman either had a sick sense of humour, or she was reminding Mother of another time and another place. Not specifically looking for the stranger we were meeting I caught sight of a figure rising. Instantly motion left my body as every muscle tightened, and that sinking feeling of isolation gripped my heart. The shadow waving to us across the table was resurrecting an impression: a depiction of another era, another effigy.

Impossible. This could not be true.

Mother, who had continued to walk forward, had left me gasping for air, my feet invisibly screwed to the floor. Dark undercurrents were seizing my limbs, submerging each thought with emotions of 'what if' and 'why not'. I felt myself falling, attacked by the sensuality of past charm. Light was fading. A hand took my arm–

"This way, Miss."

Through the thick mist I heard the quiet voice break through the vapour of my disbelief, as he gently steered my sagging body toward a table where I dropped down onto the seat offered. No sooner had I sat than a figure lurched my way–

"Miss Bryant, how wonderful to meet you. My name is Hans Parker."

A hand extended my way. Bypassing the common gesture of welcome I raise my head, slowly lifting my eyes up the tall, lean body to the face, catching my breath as I stared into eyes of deep blue. A moment to pause, time for a tiny flutter of relief to shoot through me; to recognise these sapphire pools were not hedonistic like those of my ghostly nemesis, but calm, and genuinely pleased to see me. Accompanied by a fine chiselled nose that could have jumped out of any oil painting, brought me to the broadest smile radiating from full lips, decrying my imaginings of a guileless persona. Dark brown hair tumbled across his gaze granting him the characteristics of a young boy; belying his real age, which was easily five years senior to myself, Jimmy, or *'him'*. On closer inspection this was not that image from my past, even if from afar something had screamed *'Kurt'*. How ridiculous of me to consider this man a candidate from my past. I will accept that the tall, lean frame bears a resemblance to my former lover, even an odd gesture, but I must give the D' Mill woman a little credit. Would she, a former spy herself, thrust an enemy of the new German republic upon us? Whatever was I thinking? I swallowed hard, the thought darting into my mind – 'Even if this man has similar features'.

His excitement filled the space between us–

"I was just telling your mother ours will be the discovery of a lifetime."

Breathing deep I realised Mother was kicking my foot for me to speak.

"Apologies," I started. "I thought..." stopped, took another breath "It was nothing – Good to meet you Mr Parker."

This time my hand extended to his, quivering as he squeezed my fingers in a surprising grasp. "Call me Hans, please."

I remove my hand, rub the still quivering fingers, concede to let the music, and the wine, carry my mind back into my own introspection, once more mulling over the ground I had just trod.

"Savannah told me you both are determined to seek the painting Jimmy and your father hunt."

This impeccably English voice disturbed my concerns.

"She has asked me to help. My knowledge within the art world goes back to my childhood. I was weaned on paints."

He laughed, the clarity of this sound reverberating around my head.

"Can either of you tell me *why* you wish to join this hunt?"

Mother looked at me with indignation and annoyance.

"Rhia's wish. It seems I must follow."

Not true Mother, especially the last part.

Hans was nodding, digesting Mother's statement as he ran his eyes over my downcast face.

"Why?"

Irritated at his persistence, my next sentence flew from my mouth unchecked–

"I will not let Jimmy crow over me. It should have been me with him, not Father. Spy or not, I am sick of being second best, told lies, and being pushed aside. This woman needs to put the past to bed (inappropriate word), while letting her talent for deception manifest itself."

Spoken with resentment, a covetous mind on the rampage.

Mother was incensed, Hans smiled–

"Well, that certainly has told us," he sighed.

"Rude," Mother sipped her drink in that socially inclined manner of pretending I had not spoken which made my confusion over this night and this man beside me descend into an emotive war within myself.

Pointing out the slinky singer readying herself to perform. I was furious as I behold their giggling and their benign conversation. It was as if (how I hate that word) 'a brush had swept my comments under a carpet', an idiom for embarrassment.

"I do believe we should start at the beginning, in Germany," I snarl.

Two heads rotate my way.

"Germany. Whatever for?" Hans Parker sounded amazed.

"Where the painting was commissioned," I snapped back.

"She has mentioned this journey before. Not a good idea," Mother said flippantly.

"Agreed," he replied.

“But…” I stumbled.

Mother, playing with the stem of her glass waved my interjection away as if she were batting a fly from humming around her head.

“No ‘but’, Rhia, the suggestion is foolish.”

I look at the man between Mother and myself, saw him nod, and set myself for battle.

For if anything is certain within this meeting, this plan is ‘my way’ or ‘no way’.

“You do whatever you please, but this woman is going to Germany.”

A fleeting smile danced once more across Hans Parker’s lips.

“Determined woman,” he quipped. “I like that.”

Mother’s eyes clouded over. My thought– “Pretentious prig.”

The waiter murmured “Bon Appetite”, as he placed our meals in front of us. The poached salmon with its glazed potatoes and vegetables smelt delicious. To be honest, I was so hungry I could not wait to tuck in. This proved harder than it seemed due to the warbling notes of a woman dressed in a sparkling white dress, roaming the tables, stopping now and again to serenade any couple she could find in her dusky Caribbean voice. Brushing past our table her perfume filled our nostrils with an aroma of jasmine, as she stopped to dangle her arms around Hans’s neck; bright red nails slid provocatively across his chest. After a moment, her tone became huskier, and she slipped those nails upwards, halting at his lips to steal a hurried kiss. Passing to the next table the song grew more passionate: the woman’s actions more daring. I caught Hans looking my way. I turned away, took another gulp of wine, and set about the meal before me.

--

“Dance?”

His question penetrated my silence. I had seen no reason to continue talking for I had aired what needed to be said. Mother had set about her salmon with her usual approach of picking and sorting in what she considered was a genteel fashion. I called it ‘messing’. Hans had eaten his with gusto, leaving me to eat the last bean sprout and petite pois. Realising the question was posed at me and catching Mother’s insistent glare to accept, I rose from my seat. I hated dancing, unless it was cavorting around the lounge swinging a bottle, whilst pretending to know every move. On the square floor he pulled me toward him. I stiffened.

"Relax," he laughed. "I have eaten my meal."

I smiled (actually, it could be called a smirk) as we moved deeper into the centre. The music was a waltz: this rotating on the spot awakened my mind to another memory, Jimmy and I smooching in a deserted park, a celebration of togetherness. Hans pulled me nearer, the heat of his hand burning through my jacket, my body trembling when he began to whisper, his breath tickling my ear, disturbing any equilibrium I had mustered.

"Germany," the tone was soft. "Why?"

"The..." I breathed deeply. "Because the clues are there."

"How do you know?"

"Trust me, I – I do."

"Really?" was his only answer as the music intensified, and he held me tighter.

The floor became more crowded, and Hans laid his cheek against mine, his faint odour of cologne rousing another memory I thought forgotten. Looking across his shoulder I counted the couples locked in a tight embrace, shuffling around this space; lost in a world only known to lovers; emotional vibes pouring from silent mouths. If this waltz had been slow, the dance that followed was hectic. Arms were thrown upward, hips gyrating to a beat, tongues wagging in time to the pulsating resonance.

"Savvy warned me how obstinate you are. Your father's daughter"

Hans moved around me with the movement of a matador taunting a bull. To the spectators clapping from the surrounding tables those dancers brave enough to remain on the floor appeared engrossed in each other – Not I.

"Did she now?" I sounded angry.

"Don't worry," he gasped for breath. "Savvy likes you. You remind her of 'Hal'. Will not be persuaded from her decision."

I could hear the playful mockery in his voice.

"At least that is correct. I will not be moved. If that is your plan, forget it."

Hans moved his head to scan my face.

"I have no plan just yet. I follow orders."

"Savanah D' Mill's orders no doubt," I slam his way.

Again, that enigmatic smile.

"Well, tell her this, I will still go."

With that I rudely walked from the floor.

Our dessert must be described as a tower of cream, with raspberries and blueberries hidden in the centre, built up in what I had always considered a 'sundae' glass where the long-handled spoon acts as a fishing rod. I threw it in the sea of cream and glorified at the catch, letting my taste buds savour the fruits succulent tang. Mother had regained her decorum by chatting pleasantly on everything but the topic of Germany. Hans, laughing at a dob of cream spattering his nose, surprised me further.

My displeased attitude had not moved him to bite. To show his 'true metal' as Jimmy would joke. Instead, in a calm manner he recounted how he had met Savannah D' Mill through art, and how he soon slipped into calling her 'Savvy'.

"Is that so? Whatever," I mumbled, still scooping the cream and fruit onto my tongue.

He leant toward Mother, raising his voice to be heard.

"Rhia is determined to visit Germany."

Mother shook her head–

"Always the 'I want' child, never the 'I give'."

That was unfair. Could she not see, it was that ridiculous painting, which I knew was imperative to find, that drove me to return.

Mother downed her drink in one go, surveyed her surroundings, let out a sound of exasperation before saying–

"We must go with her, but I know her father will not be pleased."

Hans looked sympathetic.

"Yes, we must go. Yet, I am sure there will be a way to distract her."

I glanced from face to face. This was not the social climbing woman I knew. That woman would care nothing about a painting. Her main priority would be to retrieve her full monthly pay, and her banker husband. As for our 'man' – I was perplexed. The way he had used the term 'distract' sent a shiver coursing through me. Who the hell did he think he was? My eyes wandered from the newly clad singer, re-dressed in pink, eyes awash with lovestruck words, to Mother's furious face. Jimmy had warned me not to trust anyone but this man. What did he mean? I raised my spoon to tease my palate with the remains of my cream 'bomb' when I notice the warbling pink dress moving between the tables.

'Not again,' I inwardly cry as my spoon is plunged between my teeth.

Sunday February 18th

Four days have passed since Mother and I met Hans. Four days when my already unsettled mind has scrutinized his looks, his voice, his movements – Him. I have tried to put this guy from my mind. Arguing with myself that Savvy's man was just that – Savvy's man, and yes, diary, I could not be bothered to keep writing that 'elongated' posh name. I have scrutinized his offer to help with searching for that painting. Asked myself if his motive was truly on behalf of Jimmy, and nothing to do with the way he kept looking at me. Then, annoyed at myself for thinking such nonsense this female mind provided me with a ray of light: the man did not concentrate wholly in my direction. As a matter of fact, after my refusal to dance with him again after that singing canary had wound her arms once more around his neck, his attention reverted to Mother. That was it, the man was being friendly, due to those orders he mentioned. This woman would be satisfied with her verdict, until nightfall encompasses that offensive where thought and torment merge. No matter what I did, how I spoke to myself, or how I pleaded with the gods of my implausible perspectives, nothing changed. I could not move his face from my mind. It would be easier on my conscious if I could say the frosty nights and mild days had sent my thoughts into a lather more than this man, but I cannot, and they have not. He stalks my mind as a leopard stalks its prey; enticing me to think nothing is afoot, then 'wham' I am caught.

Ahhh, my pen leaked…

Diary please, pay no heed to my blathering.

--

Mother is cleaning and hoovering yet again, in her expectation that our spy would keep her promise to visit. I am counting on it. In a roundabout way I need her intervention between Mother and myself over Germany, if only to smooth the rough road this visit will create. If Savvy books our hotel, plane tickets etc, then mother might be more persuasive. Maybe she thinks our trip will be dangerous. Why? I cannot imagine. What I do know is Mother's notion of fear is anything that removes her from the social graces of designer shopping and luxuriant bathing: remember her expedition along the Great Wall of China? Her connection with an 'ordinary' life has got to be tenuous, causing me to wonder however she met my father, heaven only knows.

Midday, and the bell buzzes loud. Almost stumbling over herself to get to the door Mother greets our guest with a radiant "Hello". Savvy stepped into the room, a muffled figure swathed in a padded coat and furry hat.

"Forgive me looking ridiculous, but my plane landed an hour ago, and once I had cleared customs I came straight here."

Everything, no doubt being the 'tittle tattle' she had to report.

Removing the heavy coat and flinging her furry hat onto the sofa she flopped down, throwing the huge bag she carried onto the floor beside her.

"Boy, I am tired."

"Tired?" I sniggered, from my position by the window. "You have sat all morning."

Mother raced into the kitchen, raced back out with the coffee she quickly prepared.

"Thanks," our guest spurted, trying to sip the hot drink. "How are you both?"

Obviously dismissing my snipe.

Mother scowled, passed a hurried glance my way, before placing herself in the chair opposite the sofa.

"A good question" she began "My ridiculous daughter has sworn to travel to Germany"

Another slurp, another 'ouch'.

Considering this action to be Savvy's descent into horror, Mother's voice rose an extra pitch–

"She wants her own mother and your man, to be her minions, obedient and willing."

Oh Lord, this was pure theatre. When did I demand their allegiance? Savvy looked past Mother to where I sat–

"A reason?" she questioned.

"I have this feeling it was commissioned there," I refused my voice to shake.

Savvy nodded, swishing the remains of her coffee around her cup before drinking it in one go.

"Exactly what Hans told me," she sighed. "Before his addition of stubborn, and not moving."

Mother's 'grin', that is what I will call it, expanded.

"True," was her input. "I knew you would not agree. She can be headstrong, like her father I suppose, moving into unknown territory before thinking."

Headstrong would be my last claim toward my father.

Savvy exhaled, smiled my way, waited for Mother to finish before exclaiming–

"The last two days have been spent in Germany, sorting out your accommodation, and gathering information that may help."

Who shall be in the laughing seat now, Mother?

"You agree to this foolhardy plan?"

The woman on the sofa flapped her hand up and down; a process of cooling her now overheated body, her exhausted voice resounding around the room–

"Do not be surprised, Mena. Hans informed me how insistent Rhia was to visit the old haunt. He, like yourself, did not agree, but honestly, how could I stop her?"

Mother's deflation was that of a balloon, fast, wheezy, and instantly flat. How my heart wanted to jump for joy. This quick-witted spy was beginning to walk in my shoes.

Oh diary, please do not judge me so, every woman has the right to change her mind.

Savvy looked at the woman in the chair–

"Mena, that painting must be found. If your daughter believes she will uncover information that will help Hal, then so be it."

"But – you know…" Mother began.

Savvy let the hand drop "I know nothing, Mena. Stop fretting – Trust."

Both women fell silent. I had not uttered one word, too busy gathering their rhetoric, sifting through their innuendos, mentally laying out their implication of 'go' or 'stay' as many de-coders would have tried in the last war: it was time to 'join the party' (cool phrase).

"I need to visit Germany, not only to lay old ghosts, but to thank a certain woman for her assistance when Jimmy and I needed it."

Start at the beginning and scrape memories away.

The climate within the room on this Sunday afternoon could only be registered as frosty. These two friends, congenial before this conversation, were hurling toward a tipping point. Holding a hand up for silence Savvy had delved into that bag at her feet, bringing out a stream of paperwork.

"See," Mother screamed. "Danger."

I laughed "A home visit is dangerous?"

There was no doubt that Mother was growing angrier by the moment, noted especially when she cried out–

"In this instance, yes."

Savvy flashed what I believed to be a warning Mother's way–

"Stop worrying, Mena."

Mother stood, her intention, as stated, was to make more coffee.

"Please sit, dear friend," Savvy gently asked as she placed a manilla folder on her lap.

"This document," she exhaled, "contains the past atrocities of one Major Emery Dreyer, an Intelligence officer of high degree within the Stasi regime, listing his control over the men and women who served under his bullish oppression, and labelling his actions toward prisoners as 'murder'. His interrogation skills were deviant to say the least. Whereabouts of this officer – Unknown – His son, the painter Jules Dragner, formerly Kurt Dreyer, is being held in Brandenburg–Gorden Prison."

She passed the document to Mother, whose face had turned ashen.

The clock ticking on the wall reminded me how the countdown for a race begins – One, two, three. For the second time since the New Year, that harsh sound of a man's voice floated through my mind, evoking the fear that had gripped my heart back in '89'. I had not seen his face, nor the stance of his body as fear had held my limbs against the wall, but his presence was sinister.

"How can we go?" mother whimpered "You…"

Savvy cut her off, "My German colleagues inform me he does not visit the home. They have waited for him day and night to return, with no luck. A quick visit from you may stir his curiosity, willing him to expose himself. I have my doubts. Hans will accompany you to the country, although not to the house."

"Oh," I mutter, surprising myself.

Savvy frowns–

"He will trail the museums. I think it better that way."

Pleased to have been granted my wish; mind, I would have gone anyway, there was one question that was pressing to be asked –

"Do you both know this man?"

Mother gasped. Savvy smiled –

"Us," they quipped in unison. "What made you think that?"

"Words, actions, curiosity"

Three words that covered it all.

There was a lot of shaking heads, on mother's part especially, as Savvy spoke with earnest –

"Within my work his name has always been there, but know him, why would I? Your mother is secondary to my findings, a passer-by you may call her."

Mother was conceding, "Yes, that is right."

As they spoke my eyes fastened onto theirs, mothers twitching, Savvy's revealing nothing.

"Did father know him, in his spy days?" I ventured.

Savvy replied in the same calm manner as earlier –

"He knew about him. Pathways cross."

I was struck by the contradiction in her answer.

With that memory of 89 still uppermost in my mind I was just about to continue my 'digging' when Mother clapped her hands–

"Well, it appears we shall visit Germany whatever I say. With that concluded let talk of this man cease. Savannah has told us her colleagues guard the house. Let us eat, enjoy what is left of this afternoon, pray your father is home soon. I need money."

Typical, this woman never changes!

On her command I followed her into the kitchen, my eager probing resigned to the shadows of the dreary afternoon, snuffed out by whatever directive was thrown in my direction concerning sandwiches, cakes and more coffee. Our tray complete, I had decided to rest the subject until a day in the future, for mother had moved on to what she called 'important items' such as clothes and shoes. Striding back into the lounge, we were greeted by the gentle snoring of one sleeping spy.

Thursday February 22nd

At bingo they evidently shout '22, two little ducks'. My shout towards this day is "Can we please skip it – I am bloody tired".

Reason? Unbelievable.

Throughout the night, from Wednesday evening to this Thursday morning, I have received spasmodic texts from the creature 'Fiona'. In sympathy with me you, the reader, who finds themselves lucky enough to read this diary, may ask 'How', and even venture to step a little further by inquiring 'What for?' Your concern would be gratefully received before my poor weary throat croaks, "The Detdy woman."

Can you believe this?

Luckily for me Mother had retired to bed early complaining of a dreadful headache: another 'strop' over Germany. I had decided to sit in the lounge and read. If I had known I would be there for the next 'goodness knows how many hours' I would have put my pyjamas on, found a blanket, and snuggled down, this time sitting up.

At nine thirty exactly those mobile texts began bleeping their way through my phone. The first, relaying itself to me in the form of an essay: I swear nigh on five hundred words into how she found herself locked inside the staff toilet at the bank.

Please no laughing, this is deadly serious.

Apparently, wishing to get what she dubbed her part in my snooping 'over and done with' she had made herself return to the bank when her boss and her colleagues had left for home. Enthralling the cleaning staff and the security guard with sweet talk over a folder she had left in her boss's office, those chatting women and besotted man had invited her in. Once in old Richardson's office she had 'picked' the lock of his drawer (who would have thought she had it in her), and retrieved the dossier needed.

At this point in the text my head was spinning, literally, considering '*what*' this girl's family chose to do for a living.

Running through the document before her she photographed each page (two) with her mobile. Finishing, she returned it to the drawer, re-locking it in the same way she had opened it. Suddenly, the girl heard feet coming her way. Grabbing the first empty folder she could find Fiona headed toward the door just in time to nod a quick 'thanks' to the security guy, and hurry in the direction of the main doors.

That complete, you and I would have scampered home.

Not this girl.

Ignoring the clock above the cashier desk she suddenly realised it was imperative to relieve her bladder. This she did, not bothering to panic upon hearing the slamming of doors, until turning the handle on the staff room door to discover the guard had locked it. Fear gripped her, for she knew everywhere would be plunged into darkness within minutes, apart from two security lights in the reception area.

Panic set in.

Her first thought – Scream. Second thought – No-one would hear her.

That is when she began texting me every five minutes to plead for me to come to her rescue.

Trying not to howl at the girl's dilemma, plus guilt creeping in over the length she had lowered herself to be free from my threat, I gently told her this request was impossible. My father had never allowed me to know the key holder, plus I must not be caught in stealing confidential information.

Honestly, you would have thought the heavens had caved in.

Her texts became more raucous as the wording took a turn into unladylike language. I demanded she stayed there until morning, think of an excuse to tell whoever found her; lastly reassuring her at least the heat was kept on. Slipping the phone back down on the table I returned to my book. Three sentences in, and the buzzing of my phone told me this night was just beginning.

Midnight, and my poor brain was equal to a wobbling jelly.

The texts began chasing one another in volume, number, and sarcasm. I tried to calm the girl down, made the small joke now and again, even tried to persuade her to sleep. No, the tumult of ten texts in ten minutes bombarded my screen. She then tried using the speaker mode, presumably shouting at her end. Thank heaven that did not work, for the kid's tears would have driven me to distraction. Realistically I could have switched my phone off, but underneath my madness there was slight contrition that all her problems were down to me. Could it be my threats, my insistence for her to seek out something, anything from my father's past that drove her to this end. I suggested she text me the photos she had taken, then delete them from hers. Not quite the easy task I had presumed. Her phone was old, so therefore pictures took six attempts and lots of 'text' moaning. I received the blurry images at one thirty complete.

Four o' clock, and my eyelids were rapidly drooping.

Reading the same excuses for her boss; her explanation that she had used the toilet, washed her hands, sipped water from the cold tap, and whatever else the girl found to do.

Six o' clock, my head was running havoc.

I had read, re-read every excuse this world has on offer for female's locked in a toilet. On my part, I had consistently text back how good her excuses sounded, and maybe when found she could ask to be sent home (with my wish to fall off the planet).

Diary, I will suggest the way to the moon and back if I can get this girl out of my face.

Seven thirty I was ready to murder the hand at the end of each text.

It took this sweet hearted woman (you have guessed, one huge lie) another half an hour to leave this night of horror behind.

Eight o'clock, and Mother was moving.

This had got to be my lead. The next text flew to Fiona in the way of someone throwing a bottle to the ground, harsh, broken, and straight to the point. I told her to smarten herself up in readiness to face the curiosity of Richardson; get ready with as many wiles she could muster, after all she was a female, put a few extra delectable words, and sent it.

At last, my phone fell silent.

--

Afternoon

It was two fifteen in the afternoon, and Mother had left for a hair appointment. Her excuse, to look her best in Germany. I remind myself how against the visit Mother was, deciding her outing is an excuse to chat to Savvy. This woman is aggrieved and tired, only being allowed to catnap through the morning as mother's incessant gabbling disturbed my rest. I had fallen onto the newly made bed at eight thirty, trying at least to 'snooze' while mother slammed through the flat, remonstrating her horror, and my inconsiderate behaviour. I ask her "Has she never been so tired", only to sustain a bombardment of groans over the bed, my lazy attitude, sleeping in the chair, and whatever else crossed her mind. This bleating carried on until the main door closed, and the shriek of "Back soon" disturbed me further.

Decision– Give sleep up.

I glared at my phone. The two blurry files, just readable if I strain my eyes, Fiona had text to me winking in my in-box. My fingers fumbled over the buttons, daring myself to click them open. What will I find? As a child the sheer excitement at finding a 'surprise' package my father had hidden was electrifying, my mind and body experienced that inquisitiveness hard to contain. That feeling was coursing through me now. I clicked–

Page One:

Under strict supervision of Henry Bryant.

Other informants – Savannah D' Mill, Philomena Bryant, and at this specific time, one Grayson Richardson.

In small print underneath – This document has been re-typed by Savannah D' Mill who will likewise discuss with her associates any change of plan.

Page Two:

Miss Etta Detdy – German citizen, linked to (writing blacked out), and in hiding.

No contact only under strict supervision.

No contact with Henry Bryant's daughter – Rhia Bryant.

Secrets Act of 1969.

Once more in small print was a warning of what would occur if any other body apart from those hereby mentioned read the contents.

The pages swam before me.

My head was scrambling to try and cipher through the meanings of what I had read. Secrets, nationality, demands, what can it all mean? Mother's name, mine, Savannah, even old Richardson from the bank? I do not understand. The woman in hiding, who can she really be? What have I got Fiona Grubb into? I must erase these files. Pressing the delete button I clear my phone, text Fiona–

'Delete those files you sent me– Now. Do not speak of them or contact me before I contact you. This is imperative'

No sooner had I 'sent' the message than one came back to me –

'At home. They believed my excuse, I think. Deleted those files – Why?

I will wait for your call. Thanks for spending night with me. F'

Idiotic girl. Seriously, if she does not stop messing with her font I will…

I grabbed the pillow, screamed as loud as I could, then grasped Jimmy's guitar, and hugged it toward me.

"Please come home, Jimmy. Something is not right. I need you."

Laying down, guitar in my arms, I floated into that oblivion I craved, yet not into those beloved arms of my partner, but into the bewitching smile of a man called Hans.

Monday February 26th

Berlin, Germany.

England disappeared from my sight covered in the thick grey clouds of a February morning. Drizzling patches of rain had floated past my porthole window, highlighting the dark despair of a choppy channel, and the receding cliffs of Dover. My heart, already heavy at the thought of returning to the habitat that had been a prelude to those consequences of my past life, held me prisoner, making this shuddering iron bird a talisman of events yet to come. Confronted by various forms of facial activity, from those who felt the swoop of the plane's dipping and diving as the rain lashed and the wind blew, to those whose stomachs edged nearer to an overworked mouth as they chewed away at whatever the trolley had on offer, leaving those few who demonstrated the reality of fear by clutching onto another person's arm, or the sides of their seat. My doubt into whether this journey would turn out to be the brilliant idea first thought struck me earlier on entering the airport. From the moment we had walked through the gaping doors a parody of porters, rumbling trolleys, and screeching loudspeakers had silenced our own communication altogether. Hans had been waiting, suitcase by his side, the tell-tale signs of disapproval etched across his face. After checking in we had wandered from seat to seat, read magazines, gave small insipid smiles, then obeyed the collective call to board our plane. Forming what schoolchildren know as a crocodile line we edged our way out into the wet morning, and across the tarmac.

I noticed mother's tension as the plane swooped through the dark sky, and she snuggled deeper into the fur collared coat wrapped around her. Snow had been forecast for Germany, and what those travellers of a sunnier disposition than I would hail as 'magical', to my mind conveyed disquietude. Was this really the right path, returning to walk old ground? Maybe Mother, for once, could be right, and this visit would prove to be nothing if not a ridiculous farce, for what can Kurt's mother, the wife of a bullying husband, and the mother of a malicious son, tell me. Yet, the feeling to call upon her was strong. It had gathered strength as I read those files FG had posted to me; a premonition that Etta Detdy was somehow linked to this woman. I had struggled with a connection between my father and this woman, but it now appeared he was her 'handler' (an expression

I heard from a film). Alarmed at this knowledge it was impossible to stop myself sending a text to Jimmy.

'Guess what, my father is the 'handler' (cool phrase) of a woman called Etta Detdy. Please do not tell him I have found this out. Lots of love Rhia xx'

Five minutes later he replied–

'Clever you. How?'

Back I wrote– 'Never mind.'

His comment– 'They say the fledgling comes home to roost.'

I laugh, text him– 'Cheeky. Hurry home xxx'

No reply. I will accept how busy the man is.

It was only now as the plane began its descent into Tempelhof Airport that I realised this journey must hold some clues. It was that scenario I had been taught as a child – To discover the end, one must start at the beginning. To that I answer, painting here we come. I smiled as the tension on Mother's face drained away, and Hans let go the frown he had carried since boarding. Hearing the screech of wheels, accompanied by the judder of the plane's body confirmed my hopes – We had landed safely on solid ground. Peering through the small window our eyes took in the heavy stream of snow, and the large neon sign –

'Berlin Welcomes You, *City Of Memories'*

--

Tempelhof Airport, used in WW2 by Nazi forces, was designated at one time, to be the largest airport in the world. Designed by Ernst Sagebiel, and built between 1936-1941, it was considered modern for that era. A special feature was its gate stretching 380 metres in length and 40 metres wide, complimenting the huge reception building flanked by two office wings and a 'check in' area; a vast space my brain had not appreciated on my last visit, and would have loved to do so this time. Feeling Hans eyes on my face I smile back at him, as under an ink-painted sky we slowly follow our fellow travellers into the building, past two burly custom guards standing behind long desks, and out into the bustling avenue of waiting taxis. Our porter, a boy of hardly seventeen, sprang to our aid the moment we had cleared customs, hailed a black shiny cab, and deposited our suitcases in the boot. Crunching through the newly settled snow we climbed inside: three pensive humans lost in their innermost thoughts.

Winding in and out the busy cosmopolitan streets our taxi pulled up outside an average looking hotel with beige painted walls and large brown doors. Nothing spectacular was my instant thought. The journey, although pleasant, had been fraught by emotions I found hard to translate. I understood the stress of this city: to think of my past was to think of Berlin. Yet, that invisible strand of electricity passing from the man sitting by my side held me within its grip. Only the driver making small talk concerning his beloved city prompted a response from our sealed lips. I had never known Mother to be this quiet, usually Father or myself would speak louder; an effort to 'shut her up'. Tired by our lack of communication the driver began to sing, under his breath at first, then out loud, the words lost within his language, but from his raunchy voice probably an insult we deserved.

Opening the doors for us to vacate his car, the driver whispered his thanks before beckoning to another young boy (it appears youth is the by-word) to carry our suitcases inside. Nodding, the boy led the way into a small lobby.

"At last." Mother sighed, attempting not to hide her displeasure.

"Safe," interposed Hans, finally allowing a smile to light up his face.

The woman behind the reception desk smiled back, her deep blue eyes twinkling into his.

"Bad journey, sir?" spoken in perfect English.

Hans inclined his head.

"The snow has been steadily falling since daybreak."

Handing over his passport Hans mumbled something about the cold and commented how fretful the flight had been. The woman flashed her white manicured nails, locking them around his tiny book, flipping through the pages in the way an avid reader would scan the latest novel. Annoyance swept over me. This receptionist was flirting – I will repeat the declaration – *She* was flirting with our man, and I had no notion into why it riled me. However, who did she think she was, and how dare she seduce him; those heavy painted eyes, hidden beneath the fringe of red dyed hair. I coughed, pushing my own passport across the desk toward her.

"Miss Bryant," I said, ignoring the smirk passing across her shining pink lips.

The woman continued checking Hans' passport, fluttering her eyes as if they were peacock feathers.

"All correct, sir," she cooed. "Enjoy your stay," and she pushed the book seductively (if that is possible) toward him.

He moved to my left, not once removing his eyes from my face. Mother began to drum her fingers on the wooden counter, a sure sign that tiredness and boredom were beginning to surface. I snatched my woolly hat from my head, freeing the mass of red hair confined beneath it. Curl upon curl tumbled onto my shoulders in a fury of unspoken irascibility toward this amorous woman. Glancing at Mother I tilt my chin upwards; using the glance that signals superiority. The woman runs her eyes over the small tasteless picture stuck inside my passport and the stamps of past journeys. I lift my chin higher. She, the receptionist of this inconsequential hotel, wriggles her nose –

"Miss Bryant, you have visited our country before. In 89, a few years past."

"Yes," I hiss holding out my hand for my passport.

"A troubled time," she continues. "Were you visiting or otherwise?"

What did she mean? I stumbled over my words–

"I, I was a visitor of sorts."

"Ah," she answered looking from Mother to myself, then smiling sweetly at Hans–

"You marched to the wall."

I stared, she meant I was an activist.

Hans stepped forward, folding an arm around my shoulders.

"Problem?" he queried.

I felt the tremor at his touch, recognised the woman's resignation at the same time.

"No, sir"

She handed me the small book. I snatched it, waited for Mother, then we swaggered in the way a Swan postures when it has snatched the largest bread thrown into the pond, toward the boy with his finger on the lift button.

Stopping on the second floor, the boy, whose job it was to show us our rooms, ceased talking. His attempt at broken English was not only painful for us, but incited Hans to show off his linguistic skill in the German tongue.

"Showing off" I whispered to Mother.

The boy, laughing aloud at Hans's German phrases opened three doors.

"Madam, this is your room," he pointed Mother toward No 32.

"Sir, this is your room," directing Hans into No 30.

"Miss," he looked my way, a cheeky smile lighting up his face, "this is your room, No 31"

Depositing our cases in each room the young boy tipped his cap, dipped his head with thanks toward Hans for whatever sum he had given him, and returned downstairs. Mother gave a slight yawn–

"That journey tired me. I will ask for tea to be brought to my room. Take a long bath and meet you both at dinner."

My mouth whispered "Fine," as my heart lurched in abandoned excitement.

--

I stepped into room 31 with steps motivated by a passion I could not control; an emotion, I must now admit had grown throughout the day. To try and explain it would render me dishonourable. I feel as the proverb states 'A stone that gathers no moss'*, which in Brewers Dictionary of Phrase and Fable 1546, meant a person that never stands still. My eyes travel to the dim light of late afternoon streaming through the long windows, draped either side by heavy brocade curtains. This room was not comparable to my last visit to this city. That was an ordinary bedroom, in an ordinary house. Here, the word 'plush' would not do justice to the furniture in this room. Even Mother, in her dissatisfied mood, had got to be enchanted by her surroundings: her social hierarchy mind shouting 'yes' to these beautiful French objects. It would not be fabrication to state this hotel was a misconception of what I had first thought on arrival; it belonged to that world of chicanery.

I ran my fingers across the smooth top of the dressing table, down the sculptured front, and along the curved legs. My admiration grew as I fell upon the embroidered bedding, enclosed by matching brocade curtains as the windows, the silver ornate headboard gleaming in that hazy yellowish sky. An armoire set against the wall across from the bed drew my eyes to a door. I acknowledged this was not an en-suite, for that was across the room, and the door was open. A dressing room I pondered or, I could not contain that thrill as I stepped across the thick plum carpet and twisted the handle. It was dark, yet movement could be heard, and images of a room furnished as my own filled every sense that was awakening inside me. Wanton, (oh diary, that is the word that fits) I venture further into the darkness, sigh as hands slip across my eyes, throw me deeper into darkness. A husky voice purrs in my ear–

"Guess who."

I struggle to twist round, that silent knowledge of caution slipping, feel hands running up and down my arms. Suddenly Hans's face closes in on my own, the warmth of his breath fanning my surprised eyes, the softness of his lips caressing my cheeks, my ears, my neck.

"I…" he begins.

I pull apart, stumble to the door between our rooms, mind demanding refuge.

"This room leads from my own," I gasp. "The boy was mistaken if he thought…"

I willed myself to stem the tumult of fervour growing in the pit of my stomach.

"No mistake," he whispered.

A simple statement, an invitation.

I thought of his fluency in the boy's native tongue, the struggle within my own translation of his narrative, the boys mischievous grin, and somehow, those words rung true. I closed my eyes, the faint hope that upon re-opening he would not be there; a lie within a lie – I was among a jostling crowd, Kurt's blue eyes boring into my own, lips awash with sensuality, arms inviting, beckoning me, calling me, the savagery of remembrance causing my breathing to become difficult.

Clutching onto the doorframe I struggle for composure, my emotions conspiring with the lust of a past memory. Hearing a door lock being turned, and feet moving stealthily back across the floor I was about to fall when arms embraced me. Warmth penetrated my trembling limbs as lips, soft and tempting found my own. From afar I heard the words "Oh, no," creep up my throat, as desire pushed me willingly into hands already unbuttoning my coat.

--

I stir from the sopor of passion, my gaze settling on the lights falling across the bed. Realising my nakedness, I touch the body reclining by my side, feel the softness of skin, the heat of straddled legs. He stirs, mutters a name, my name, hauls his body onto mine, recreating that earlier frantic rollercoaster of nurtured yearnings; relighting an ardour I was powerless to sever.

--

A bell rings, winding its way into the crevices of my mind. I listen, hear the sound again, consider what meaning it can hold for me. Reverberating around my head I realise that bell must be the summons for dinner. The light moving its way slowly up the bed was a neon sign flashing on and off in the street outside, calling to me, warning me– It was time to meet Mother. Scrambling from the body stretched across mine, the soft film of sweat pressing us together, I announce–

"I must go, Mother will be waiting."

He moves, his eyes skimming my panic-stricken face. Thought fenced with thought, emotion with emotion, allowing the chill of realisation to fill me with shame. Jimmy crept into my mind, those brown eyes accusing, saddened by my failing. Running his forefinger across the tattoos on my breast Hans sensed my withdrawal–

"Will you not stay?"

"No, I am already late."

I sit up, catch my breath as the coldness of his nose burrows into my stomach, and the softness of his lips roamed its white expanse. I feel the thrill of his touch.

Pulling away I leap from the bed, snatch up my clothes.

"I will see you downstairs," then an afterthought. "Mother must not know."

His eyes follow my move to the interconnecting door–

"No worry, I will not be there."

My hand falters as I turn the handle–

"You are not joining us?"

"I will send an apology. I have an appointment."

"An appointment?"

"I must go."

"You wished me to stay here with you?"

"Then I would have cancelled."

There is a saying – 'Confusion reigns', and at this moment that is me.

From the depths of my mind, I recall two bodies on top of a bed arching and crying out as if those moments of arousal had been their last: the thirst for passion drowning every other consideration, exploring the known, yet unknown. I sink between the labyrinth in my mind, and the complexity of my past, hear a whisper of gratification–

"Until the next time."

I close the connecting door.

Tuesday February 27th

It was eight thirty on Tuesday morning. I knew that not only because the travel clock glowed in the emerging light, but also the clamour of voices could be heard from the street below. My meeting with Mother the previous evening had been strained, which my excuse of travel exhaustion I am praying covers my lie, but also my own guilt. Hans' apology had been delivered to Mother by the cheeky young boy, alleviating any explanation from me. Although Mother was shocked by his absence, first evening and manners, after a slight moan she joined me wholeheartedly in sorting through our plan for today. Of this, I thank those lucky stars, who for once stand firmly by my side. For let us not pretend, my fall from 'grace' can be summarised as a beguiled young woman that had no clue to what she was doing. As the call sounded for last orders from the hotel bar we shuffled back to our rooms, Mother expressing her satisfaction at its lush interior, myself craving for that bath to rid my mind of contrition.

Stepping from the heavily scented bath I surveyed myself in the tall mirror situated on the wall above the bath. How those black markings accused me, twisting my fragile excuses to nothing. Primary guilt was being compounded by my need to place the blame for our passion solely with Hans; it was he who enticed me to stay, he who lured me into his web. I reached for the towel, hid those accusing markings from sight. Pulling my tangled hair into the strictest bun I dare, the tears of deceit well up. Hans had kissed these strands, tweaked them through his fingers as he whispered my name. Not bothering to stem the tears I pulled the bath plug, find my pyjamas, rush to the door that led into Hans room, and secured the lock.

--

Mid-Morning

"Stoppen," the voice rang out.

Halting at the end of a cul-de-sac of three storey white boarded houses the driver beamed in the direction of Mother and myself. Suddenly aware this was the stop I had asked for in my schoolgirl German I rose from the seat, indicating mother to do the same.

"Danke," I said, passing the beaming man, and stepped down into the snow.

Watching the bus pull away Mother shivered.

"I did say this was not going to be a good idea. Between riding on a bus and suffering the cold from the snow."

She paused to rub her hands together, a gesture aimed directly at me–

"I do believe Rhia, your reasons are totally selfish."

Moans that fell on 'deaf ears'.

From the first steps we took I could see the years had witnessed changes, some subtle, many portraying a grotesque picture with ugly extensions that neither suited the buildings nor added to the 'finesse' that in the past heralded 'status', whatever that status maybe. Walking slowly through the recently fallen snow I led Mother to the far end of these buildings, her ridiculous ankle suede boots squelching with every step. Wavering before heading up the path I took a deep breath, ignored Mother's comment to 'Let us return to the warmth of the hotel', and marched forward, terminating in front of an eagle door knocker, still claiming to the world this was an important house, its glass beady eyes staring straight at me. I lifted the knocker and let it fall. The clanging sound, remembered from my last visit, penetrated what I recall was the long hallway. Rubbing my hands together I followed the clouds above slowly turning from a dingy white to mucky grey, filigree flakes of snow deciding to whirl for the second time this morning, threatening to settle their particles of lace throughout an already frozen city. I rang again, the reverberating 'clang' ringing louder and longer.

"Nobody is in," Mother bit, clapping her hands together. "Let us go."

Annoyed that I must surrender to her demand I seethe, "The bus it is then."

Now whether it was that flash of satisfaction in Mother's eyes that severed my willingness to comply to her wishes; maybe my own determination not to give in – whatever it was a sudden inertia rooted me to the spot. It was then I heard the shuffle, slowly, deliberate, moving down the hallway.

"Mother," I called "Someone is in."

The door opened, a fraction, just enough for a body to be seen. It was a woman, her penetrating gaze throwing distain over the two women shivering outside. I noticed her eyes first, deep set in their shadowed sockets, carefully roaming over us, before the curtain of eyelashes hid her pale blue irises from sight. Next, I notice the thinning grey hair brushed back into what I presumed was a neat plait, not the strict bun she had worn on my last visit, and certainly not as healthy looking as I remember. Her skin was crumpled, yellow in colour, with lines chiselled from her eyes to her mouth, whilst the thin lips trembled, almost as if they were continuously mumbling; whispers no doubt of a bullish husband, and a capricious son. Her body, in contrast to the haggard face was round, large breasts weighing down onto her expansive waist, met by ballooned hips that would not seem out of place in a comic cartoon. The knuckled hands, skin rough from what I guessed was constant cleaning, showed chewed nails and bitten quicks. While the flash of terror in her eyes when she opened the door could not be denied, she was certainly a woman of two halves.

"Ja," she snapped, poking her scrawny face a little further round the door.

I searched for that radiant smile from our first meeting. It had disappeared.

Mother's face held astonishment, disapproval; the disappointment of one cosmetically perfected woman to this ghostlike creature. Stumbling over my words I venture "Hello," followed by, "do you remember me?" in my poor German tongue.

A frown spreads across her brow, and a memory of her poor English filled my mind.

"Rhia," I tried again, "1989."

Her pupils dilated as memories fought to control her thinking.

"Natalia?" she mumbled, shaking her head. "Nein, nein."

Mother was flapping in the way of a frightened hen.

"Rhia," I offered again.

Her dull eyes moved up and down my frozen body, before "Ah, ja."

Had she remembered me?

"My mother," I stuttered, touching Mother's arm.

"Ja," she repeated. "Es tut mir leid – E-en-glish – Schwach."

Mother stared. I rummaged through the German I had doodled through at school. If only… Never mind, I believe she was apologising for her poor English.

"89," I spouted. "I want to say thank you – Danke"

I said it slowly, praying she would understand. Her face clouded over, and I knew whatever happened I could expect a long day.

At last, the door was opened wider, her knuckled hand beckoning us in. Brushing snow from our coats we stepped into the hallway, Mother scanning the drab passageway. It had not improved in eleven years. If truth be told it resembled that saying – 'Worse for wear', totally neglected. I took in the faded paint on the doors, how threadbare the stair carpet looked, and furniture that if I was honest, was only fit for a dustbin. I could see the photo gallery still lined the stairs, although the mesmerising number of family photos had been removed, including the saluting man and boy I knew now to be Kurt and his father. In their place lots of small watercolours of sea scenes, woodland scenes, city scenes, anything that could argue 'family despot' was no longer on show.

Entering the room at the back of the house I registered again that nothing was the same. The room was basically empty apart from two frayed armchairs either side the grate where a few logs burnt, and an old stained wooden table in the middle of a tattered carpet. This house, that in '89 had been 'grandeur' itself, was nothing more than a rundown hovel.

"Sitzen Bitte," the woman was saying.

I directed mother's gaze to the worn chairs– "We must sit," I whispered.

Scowling at the torn material and ill-fitting covers mother edged herself down. Moving slowly to the remaining seat I sat and instantly warmed my hands from the meagre heat the logs were bestowing. Removing her coat Mother began to rub her legs, trying with her gloved hands to circulate the blood the cold had removed.

"Thank you," she sighed. "It is cold outside."

"Should have worn trousers," I gloated in a subdued voice.

The woman ran her gaze over us, sniffed, and offered to remove our coats.

Struggling with the easiest of English words Kurt's Mother made gestures toward the kitchen. I nodded, mouthed "Please", arguing with the thought that his mother's English had been a trifle better eleven years ago. Heading into what I presumed was still the kitchen the woman began to mutter: that infuriating mumbling she had greeted us with.

"Mir wurde gesagt dass du kommen kannst."

Words falling from her lips as water from a fountain, continuous and frenetic.

Mother nudged my foot. I shook my head, leant nearer the fire, whispered low–

"I think it is something about she was told we may come."

"Think?" Mother shot back at me "I told you this was a bad idea."

Not again – I shrugged my shoulders.

"How do I know? My translation is not brilliant. Perhaps your friend visited?"

"No," Mother was adamant.

"How do…"

I stopped, the tray preceding the woman's rotunda form was large, too big for the three mugs of tea, and a plate holding six plain biscuits. Clashing it down on the nearby table she passed one mug, then another, the word "T-ea" flowing from her mouth with frustration.

Finding a high back wooden chair the woman sat, sipping the tea she had made, eyeing us in mutual curiosity. Mother, not one to keep her nosiness to herself, asked–

"You (hand gestures from herself to Kurt's mother) knew we were coming."

The woman squinted, creased the wizen forehead, looked my way–

"Sie," I indicated to herself, "wusste," I struggled, "wir waren kommen."

The best I could do.

The woman cast her head from my anguished frown to Mother's indignant pose.

"Ah," she said. "Ja, anderer mann, charmant."

"Another man?" I queried slowly "Charming?"

The woman nodded vigorously.

"Who? Wer, wer?" I tried again, trying to communicate, failing miserably.

Expressing the word in a gesture I was beginning to feel as if I had been thrown into the lap of an alien. Then she laughed. Heaven knows why, for the deep throated roar demonstrated more sneer than joy.

"Neine, neine, zwei wochen, alter mann. Fragen, fragen, fragen."

Mother let out a sound of exasperation for me to translate.

"I think she mentioned two weeks ago, and something about an older man."

No way was I telling her, what I believed to be this woman's last three words 'Question, question, question,' snarled through clenched teeth.

We paused to eat a biscuit, drink a little tea. I foolishly think Mother's probing is at an end – Wrong.

"Your (pointing toward Kurt's mother) husband (pointing at wedding ring, mouthing 'man') is he at home?"

I cannot believe this. Apart from Mother mentioning *that* man, the barking dog who filled me with terror, I need help with my German. I will forget last night if only Hans could be here. Promise never again to let myself be led by another's yearning. I will bury my guilt once and for all – I will enter a convent – Please, if only Hans could be here. Fury is building. Is this what Jimmy meant when he told me not to trust anyone?

It took our hostess a good five minutes to master mother's actions and words; her features changing as she grasped its meaning.

"Ich habe ihnen gesagt dass ich den sohn meines sohnes vergessan habe, class ich geschieden bin."

The woman was struggling to keep calm, I was struggling to translate this irate response.

Rising from her chair she rushed into the kitchen. Mother extended her hands.

"What is wrong?"

"I was supposed to speak."

"It was only a question."

"Exactly. She answered your bloody question by sidestepping around it."

"No need to swear."

"For goodness' sake, Mother, I believe the man who visited went down that route."

"What route?"

"Husband."

"And?" she pushed.

"Evidently they are divorced mother – Why?"

This is ridiculous, what has any of this got to do with *my* mother.

"Curiosity," she answered: a reason not forthcoming.

We drank the remains of our tea.

The strained face showed not a shadow of emotion as the woman reappeared with more tea. To me, she was either a brilliant actor, or the fear of that man held her to ransom. Searching through my mind for something to say when a voice cuts into my thoughts –

Pointing to the painting above the fireplace Mother smiled and commented –

"Won- der- ful dep- ic- tion"

I glare, the woman's eyes soften, evidently understanding Mother's remark.

"Ja, Sohn," she says in Mother's direction.

I glare harder.

"Pardon?" Mother asks.

"Son," I cry. "Her son is a painter."

"Yes, I know," was Mother's haughty admission.

Everything was getting out of control. In her hurry to put things right Mother unleashed another 'faux pas'–

"How proud you must be."

She indicated toward the woman by bouncing her fists up and down on her chest.

"Rhia (pointing my way) was his friend. Shame the relationship ended. She may have saved him."

Diary, can you imagine how I feel? I need out.

Standing up I desperately ask–

"Toilette, ja" confusion mixing languages.

The woman's lips twitched at the sides as she rose from her chair and said- "Ja," indicating I follow her out into the hallway, where she directed me upstairs. I thanked her, relieved to disappear, if only for a few moments, and begin my ascent, passing that gallery of paintings, wondering what I can do to shut Mother up. It was then I made this promise to myself – From this moment I must snoop alone. If I need help, I will consult Hans, tell Jimmy (if available), leave mother to Savannah D' Mill.

--

Standing outside the bathroom I am mindful that each bedroom door had been thrown open. 'Strange' filtered through my mind, as upon my last visit these rooms were closed to prying eyes, the master bedroom especially. This time, curiosity was willing me to probe. Daring to tiptoe further I creep into the main room. Space greeted my eyes, no furniture, no curtains, no carpet – Nothing but empty space. It was obvious this room was unoccupied, which led my mind to push me back along the corridor to the room Jimmy had used, and once more – Nothing. This left the bedroom I had occupied back then; the room that had witnessed the birth of my sexual stirrings. It too was empty, the prelude to that night long ago standing desolate, eerily alone in the gathering afternoon. It was hard to believe how this empty chamber suddenly became the banality of my youth.

Creeping back to the bathroom door I could not stop myself wondering where Kurt's mother slept. Catching sight of the narrow attic stairs I ruled that upper floor from my solitary debate, pondering over our hostess's girth, and the steep incline. Deep in thought the voice calling up the stairs did not penetrate my brain until it began to shriek in panic -

"Rhia, are you alright? Do you need help?"

Mother!

My mind in a flurry, too many questions penetrating my brain, I deduce an answer must be given.

"I am fine. Just about to reapply my lipstick"

I twisted the door handle, made sure Mother heard the door open. She will think I was already in the bathroom.

"Hurry up, it is snowing outside," she called, relaying her impatience to leave.

"Give me five minutes," I called back, thinking. 'What has snow got to do with anything?'

Lowering myself onto the closed lid of the toilet, I consider the possibilities confronting me. The fabrication of this house is disturbing. Almost as if it has been set up in a hurry; emanating an ambience that is challenging my sanity. Hearing Mother's high-pitched inquiries over 'this' painting, or 'that' plant outside the window I decide to wash my face, and apply the lipstick promised.

I splash cold water eagerly over my eyes. rubbing in anguish, scrubbing in hope that the sights around me will fade; the water stinging my eyes, my forgotten mascara clumping together. I grasp for the towel I had noticed on the bath and pat my face dry. I pat again, move the towel up and down, trying effortlessly to loosen my sealed eyes, all the time water splashing around the basin. Groping around I feel for something to help – Nothing. I groan, reach for another towel also spotted on a peg by the mirror over the bath. Not caring it was a silly place to put a mirror I gave one swift pull, felt the roughness, heard the 'crash. I vigorously rubbed my stinging eyes. Easing my eyelids open I stared in horror at the mess in the bath, shards of glass looking up at me, twinkling in the drab light. Trepidation held me fast as I heard feet stomping up the stairs-

"Stimmt etwas nicht?"

The sound penetrated the locked door, asking, I am sure, 'Is anything wrong?'.

"Neine," I called, "fein, fein." please let that be 'fine'.

The feet retreated as another call made me jump.

"Rhia, what has happened?"

Mother was displeased.

"I am fine," I repeat the lie. "I bumped into the bath. Be down in a moment."

"Hurry up," she barked.

"I will."

Those small acorns of fibs are popping into my mind. What comes next – Huge grown oaks of lies?

Scooping the shattered pieces into the black smudged towels I stuffed the towels behind a lose bath panel. Many months later I would laugh at this for the panel was not lose, it had been unscrewed. Withdrawing my hand from the dusty hollow I felt a small piece of cardboard, laying on the floor. Presuming it was a rough drawing for a watercolour lining the stair wall, I plucked it from the mess. About to turn it over I read the writing scribbled on the back –

My Beloved Sons – Hans and Kurt.

I knew those names, and this was no rough drawing.

Defined in startling monochrome this photograph was the lover I had dismissed, and the lover of the previous evening, snuggled in the arms of a woman that looked nothing like our hostess downstairs.

Indignation burnt deep within me. Tears braced my eyes as the heat of embarrassment clawed its way through me. I looked again at the smiling young men, eyes blazing with merriment toward the hand holding the camera. Panic was gathering inside me, the grasping angst that I was being played.

1) My father was a spy.
2) My mother and his past colleague share tete et tetes.
3) Hans, it seems, is that painter's brother.

What, or who can I trust?

I sense the bile rising, swallow hard, determined not to show weakness. Hiding the photograph in my waistband I tuck my jumper over it, return to the question of the woman downstairs. I am a hundred percent certain that the woman talking or fooling my Mother into believing she cannot understand her, is not the woman I met in '89, which means my conjecture must be correct – This house had been used as an illusion; a decoy to cover the path of that painting, and that woman was a fraud.

--

As I walk back into that room I had left easily half an hour ago, I heard Mother talking. Leaning against the window pointing to various plants in the garden, she was reeling off their names in childlike English, while the woman by her side nodded her head as the pretender I had decided she was. It took a moment or two for both women to realise they had been joined by another presence–

"At last." mother sighed "We… I, thought you were sick."

"I am, Mother, we must go."

Mother exhaled, obviously annoyed.

"Go? I was just beginning to chat with our hostess," she looked at me meaningfully.

The woman agreed followed by an expressive "Krank, armes madechen"– sick, poor girl. Hastily my eyes scrabble the room. Evidence had been there. This room, this house, this woman. Suddenly terrified without reason I snapped–

"I must go."

Startled at the callous edge to my demand Mother tried to mollify my outburst.

"Calm, child, we cannot be so rude."

Rude? I will show her bloody rude.

"Child? I must leave," I grip my stomach.

With a hunch of the shoulders Mother smiles at the woman beside her–

"I will say 'thank you' for us both," her hands expressing her words in ridiculous movements. The woman managed a thin grin.

Handing us our coats from across the back of the chairs our hostess gabbled-

"Ja, danke," hurrying us out into the hall, and toward the door.

By the stairs Mother stopped, pointed to the watercolours lining the wall–

"Jules Dragner – T-h-e p-a-i-n-t-e-r"

My stomach lurched – This crazy woman never gives up.

The woman's eyes grew cold.

"Gehen, Sie wenn sie nur wussten"

Her tone could easily have matched any witch in a fairy story.

I could see Mother was puzzled. I racked my brain for translation. 'Go' came to mind, along with 'If only you knew'. I dismissed my thoughts, this translation cannot be correct, what relevance could these words possibly have to the painting. Never one to forget her manners, Mother took the woman's hand in her own, squeezed it saying–

"Take care."

Take care? That is not what I am thinking.

Opening the main door Mother and I step out into the snow. I feel the cloak of deception shrink away with the knowledge that whatever is occurring here has not concluded, and the past is rising its ugly head once more.

"Schande," pause "verrater," the woman shouts at me.

The smirk dancing across her lips brought a terrifying chill to my already shaking limbs. Who was this woman to smirk at me? What had she said, 'Shame'– stop – 'Traitor' –

What did she mean?

Oh Lord, why did I not listen to my language teacher?

--

Evening

The choice to remain in my room for a light supper was simple. A wish to see no-one, talk to no-one, and basically try and work this 'mess' out. I had locked that door leading from my bedroom into 'his'; too guilt ridden to tag him with a name, more than ashamed that lightning has struck me twice. My tortured mind seeks a respite from the torment hounding me, yet where can I hide? I text Jimmy, railing over the photograph I had discovered, demanding his reason for his insistence to 'trust' Hans. I received no reply, evidently not surprised at any trap I had fallen into, plus being more than pleased he chose father to help him, not me. Suddenly I could hear movement along the corridor; an instant presumption on my part that Mother and Hans had finished their meal and heading into their rooms. I was not a person who lived in a fool's paradise with the belief that Mother would keep her visit to herself. Oh no, they would have mulled it over, Hans's sympathising, much to Mother's gratitude. I had decided against mentioning the photograph to her, mainly for that reason that Mother blabbed everything. I kept up the sickness ruse, hence why I find myself cocooned in this bed, trying to hate that self-satisfied gargoyle (do not care that it lowers the diction of this diary, that is precisely how I see him), yet failing miserably. I lower the light on my bedside table, hold my breath, pray they would think me asleep. Tomorrow we travel home, the conception of this 'mess' tantalisingly near in the form of the man in that connecting room. Can I admit to myself, if nobody else, that curiosity and jealousy led me down this pathway, or will I still believe that Jimmy's refusal to seek my help validated my intervention, ignoring Mother's pleas to leave the country, and trailing her in my wake? Sliding down the bed, I seek the warmth of the duvet, pull it around me tight, command it to comfort my cold body.

--

I wake, it is dark. The light on my bedside table glimmers low. I am desperate to drink the water in the jug, hiding behind the lamp, sparkling in that glimmer. I pour a glassful, let the tepid liquid run down my throat, wishing it to drown the dreams I had woken from. An image of that kid, pleading to keep her position at the bank had stepped into the forefront of my mind. The large ruby lips refusing her any form of pardon if she walked away from my proposal, threatening; pommelling her brain what would happen if she refused. I swallowed more water – Those lips were mine.

A name compounded my brooding, swirling around my head, ambushing any hurdle my mind cleared by sitting up and cooling myself down – Etta Detdy. The 'teddy' woman, Father's little secret and D' Mill's charge. What is her role within all this? How does this painting involve her? I let my eyes travel to that interconnecting door, imagine the handle turning, the flutter of sensuality building inside. Could this journey accentuate new strands to this mystery, that when brought together they form a whole?

I lift my diary from the bedside table, turn the page to where I had ceased writing. In capital letters I pen –

PAINTING, WOMAN, FATHER, MOTHER, SAVANNAH D' MILL, AND HANS???

I switch the lamp off, the lights from the traffic in the street below shining through the window, whose curtains I had not bothered to close. My ears strain for sounds from the connecting room – Silence. I plead for my mind to cease probing, craving for sleep. Our plane leaves at eleven thirty in the morning, leaving this country behind, suppressing the nightmare I had encountered.

Tuesday February 28th

Goodbye, Germany, there can be no further revelations you hold.

'Famous last words' my mother would quote.

I push this thought aside.

At last, the snow had eased, and due to the ploughs working overnight, our return flight was on time. I had not slept, instead moving up and down the bed in panic, drinking water at a speed of a person stranded in the desert, finally crawling toward that oasis would do. So, it was no surprise that once seated on the plane my eyes closed, and I drifted into thankful oblivion. It was not until I heard Mother's voice informing me the giant bird had landed that I realised our homeland had greeted us with comparative calm. Apart from a slight change within the temperature, where pockets of sun upon a covering of snow glinted as glitter on a Christmas card, everyone's face held joy instead of the relief of harassed travellers.

Upon trawling our way past custom officials searching most bags that passed their desk, I wished for nothing more than to part company with Hans. Preparing myself to say 'goodbye', no time like the present to break our friendship, those pesty butterflies attacked me with a thrill of excitement as he gazed into my eyes. I was mad, with myself, with Hans, with life. It is obvious this reaction is just that; the reaction of a silly girl who walked this planet a decade ago, that fantasist long buried. Ignoring his entreaty, I marched out the main door muttering something about a taxi.

"Rhia, slow down. My feet do not have wheels attached to them."

Mother's call boomed in my ear.

"Keep up," I snapped casting around for an empty car.

"She speaks," the husky tone vibrated my mind.

I glared, *he* smiled, Mother frowned. Glimpsing a hand waving Hans stated–

"I believe that's my lift."

Detecting the surprise settling in mother's eyes he added. "A meeting."

"Savannah's man," I quipped, emotionally wrought, and if truth be known in a terrible flummox over my erratic thoughts.

"Rhia, that is unfriendly."

"So?" I flung in Mother's direction, bypassing the facetious smile of Hans wish 'to meet soon'. Mother tried to raise her best smile. I spat "Goodbye to you," hurrying to a taxi that screeched to a halt.

Sitting in the back of that taxi, watching the black sleek car carrying Hans to Savannah D' Mill navigate through the busy carpark, I thought of the black and white photograph tucked away in my suitcase. What had the woman I believed now to be a fraud, sneered on our parting–

"Schande – verrater."

Had she guessed I would find that snap of the brothers. Had those smiling profiles been planted? 'Shame and Traitor' mingled among those words – Shame for who, Traitor toward whom?

Oh, Jimmy, the man you told me to trust has betrayed me.

Post Note

What can I do to cease the conflict between my heart and my mind?

From this platform where I stand my heart throws down the challenge for my mind to seek a resolution to how I feel.

March 2001

Sunday 4th

By the third month into this diary, I honestly believed my report would contain a positive declaration into English weather.

"Warm sunny days," would be my claim. "The summer looks positive."

Forget it. Nature has different ideas.

In fact, it is cool and stormy, the wind so high that trees should consider themselves nature's 'predators', for I swear all the daffodil and crocus heads have been blown from their natural habitat to decorate the compost heaps. I will compare these winds with the hurricanes that sweep the Caribbean Islands.

Exaggerating? – A fraction.

On the positive side we should be grateful we reside this side of the Atlantic, and not America, where thunderstorms have been chasing one another on a daily occurrence. Even so, this small country of ours is gripped within the claws of an 'ephialtes' (a swanky word for nightmare – love it) due to the largest outbreak of foot and mouth disease throughout its population of livestock for many a year. Cumbria has recorded 843 cases alone. What began in pigs has quickly spread to sheep and cattle, bringing a ban from the U.S. government on exported meat from England.

Breathe…

It does not stop there. The horror mounts. Gossip is leaking out of Hollywood that the guild of American writers will go on strike. This could mean screenwriters, even directors, and heaven forbid, producers. Our cinemas will close – Yes, close, apart from an odd British film.

Question: How will I survive?

Answer: With everything else playing around my head, how can I tell, and although I cannot spare time for visiting the cinema, that is not the point.

Other news…

These four days since returning from Germany Mother has been unusually quiet. The humming has stopped as she cleans and dusts, the long chats, saved especially for the evenings, have declined to 'Yes, please' and 'No, thank you', and she has taken to 'retiring' early. Here, I will grasp another pause, for that 'whirlwind' I have dubbed my mind is gathering speed, recounting every move she has made since her arrival at New Year, and whilst I have vowed to 'go along' with her silly antics, I have made this pledge to myself – Find out what my mother 'gets up to' during the spare hours she is supposed to be sleeping, and myself watching television. I do not pretend that I have not grown fanatically suspicious. Moreover, since discovering my father's background, and that visit and photograph of recent days.

Therefore, I write, shrouded in the hope that my diary might deliver a clearer insight into Jimmy's warning to 'trust' nobody apart from the man who knowingly enticed this woman into his bed. Those words pulsate continuously around my head as I plead to the page before me to smooth the stony pathway I tread.

Speak to me, diary, please.

--

One o' clock, and Mother has been bolstering the cushions as she does, avoiding this moping figure slumped in the chair. At last, the knock we have been waiting upon. Rushing to the door in her usual hectic manner Mother flings it open, laughs out loud. Staggering through the door one windswept Savannah D' Mill, dark hair streaming down across her face in a tangled mess that could equal any rampaged bird's nest. She begins to peel off the mud splashed coat, raging over her 'poor' clothes, moaning about the 'disgusting' weather, shivering as a cat whose master has 'chucked' it outside to face the elements, and fend for itself, which I have got to add this 'spy' knows nothing about. Noticing the lack of trousers on the silk laden legs I forced myself from the chair to the airing cupboard for a towel.

"Here, rub your legs" I snigger.

Taking the towel her hazel gaze ran over my simpering contours, as she rubbed the dirty splodges from her tight bound legs.

Mother, still chuckling, hurried to the kitchen in the hope that coffee would retrieve this woman's equanimity (what else?).

"How much longer must we live through weather such as this?" Savvy moaned.

My head twisted in the direction of the window, still raining, still blowing, the heavens raging.

"You know what they say?" I pronounced. "Heaven is angry with the world below."

Weary eyes looked up from her rubbing– "New one to me."

Coffee arrived amongst a tray of sandwiches and cakes (mother's offering for every ailment), the steaming liquid tipping the mugs' edge, no doubt trying to escape. Savvy folded the towel onto the floor, took her mug, sipping and blowing simultaneously.

"I need this," her voice trembled.

That is not new.

"Germany's snow or English rain and wind? Which do I dislike the most?"

"Germany's snow," Mother stated.

"This wind and rain?" I replied in a hurry, not wishing to bring that subject to the forefront just yet.

Savvy tried her best to look surprised "You did not enjoy your visit Mena?"

I made to protest, failed miserably.

Mother rolled her eyes "Rhia, came down ill."

"Ah," the sipping mouth sighed. "Tell me what happened."

Clever, I thought. That is a sure sign this woman knows 'something'.

"Your mother informed me how weird the situation was."

I am correct diary, as always.

I placed my mug on the tray. Confirmation hit me – Mother's early bedtime had been spent phoning or texting. Jimmy's warning 'trust no-one' scuttled through my mind; rats scampering along the sewer pipes searching for nibbles, anything that is an appetizer for their hunger: their pathetic secret society.

Anger took hold.

Passion bubbled inside me. It will be more than a pleasure to throw into this cauldron of secrets that photo. Watch the horror run through their eyes as the world of 'faith' in *her* man crashes to the ground.

Oh, dear Miss D' Mill, is Hans Parker a 'bad' choice?

I run into the bedroom, run back out, photograph in hand, literally chucking it toward the woman still trying to create warmth in her chilled limbs. This was damming evidence. Whatever was going on between these two women, I had now gained the upper ground. Savvy fingered the photo, blew what I will call an exasperated wheeze, before turning it over to read the scrawled hand, then passing it to Mother.

"I know," she said quietly.

Train – Running away – My mind on board?

"What," I thundered.

"I know who his mother is."

I looked at Mother. She nodded her head.

"You knew," I screamed, "before we visited that house."

Mother nodded again.

"Great," hard to catch my breath. "How many lies surround me?"

Fury knows no depth, so it is quoted.

Mother sank further back into the chair, looked pleadingly at the woman sitting opposite – "Tell her, Savannah, please."

I stood in the heightened silence, not one fibre of my raging body could have sat if I had wanted it too. The restrained quiet paralleled a tomb; that eerie stillness which clothes a body put to rest. What explanation could that slick mouth offer. I waited. Savannah D' Mill (yes, at this moment my pen is returning to her full name) gathered her breath, breaking the silence, eyeing Mother with the conspiratorial knowledge shared–

"Hans Parker..." she began, "is the son of Ametti Dreyer, and the nephew of Emery Dreyer, half sibling to Kurt Dreyer i.e.: Jules Dragner, the painter. His father is Ernst Dreyer, younger brother of Ametti's husband. When Emery found out his young wife had secretly been seeing his brother he locked his wife away, and banished Ernst to the East. On finding Ametti pregnant, Emery demanded the child to be brought up by his older sister Alys who lived in England with a man called 'Parker'. She doted on the child."

She took a deep breath, scanned my face for the slightest emotion, continued–

"It became obvious the two brothers hated each other. Not wishing to recount past intelligence, and not wishing to be dramatic, it must suffice to say the brothers fought, and Emery killed his younger brother."

An involuntary gasp left my throat.

Taking a folder from her bag Savvy placed it on the table–

"I met Hans Parker at an intelligence recruiting day, wary, unsure, scared. He was offering to work for us, against his aunt, against his brother, even against his uncle. Throughout his childhood he had been indoctrinated into the Stasi system. For us, the chance to work an agent on both sides proved alluring. I hired him, trained him, and introduced him to the world of spying.

Hence, when Hal contacted me, my thoughts turned to Hans. I agreed if I could use this man. Your mother agreed."

Both women looked contrite.

My eyes sweep across the brown folder.

"The painting must be found. Colleagues in Germany seek those names."

I stared at their bent heads, two faces red from the fire, two minds battling with the right and wrong of this information parted.

"Rhia, have you nothing to say?" Mother queries.

I shrug my shoulders.

"I am lost, for words. I suppose this must change things."

"Change?" Savvy sounded surprised. "Nothing has changed. If you do not wish to continue the search, please follow your mother's advice."

"Yes," Mother sighs. "Mattie, here we come."

Deep in my mind I could hear Jimmy's insistent to trust Hans. I hesitated, could see mother's grin; victorious, irritating. Damn you Jimmy, this was information I would have been better not knowing. Yet, why does my brain insist there has to be more?

In that instant my decision was made–

"No," I exclaimed. "Bring it on."

Mother let her head fall backwards onto the sofa.

"Has anyone told you how infuriating you can be?"

Savvy looked from mother to me.

"More coffee?" she said with a self-satisfied beam.

--

Mid Afternoon

Coffee had indeed been our saviour, along with the cream cheese sandwiches and bite sized raspberry muffins. Busy eating and drinking we had no time for petty arguments, instead discussing the 'pros' and 'cons' of our recent trip to Germany (amicably would you believe). It was interesting to discover that Mother had gleaned how old Kurt's mother was, and that her life had been 'turned upside down' by what she called a family tragedy. Interesting I think, especially as I still hold fast to my presumption the woman was not *her,* and Mother could not speak the language. My interest grew further as Mother recounted how she had not been 'taken in', allocating her grumblings to memory for later scrutiny: a first for a woman who can gossip at the 'drop of a hat'. Anyhow, in Mother's view, that woman had an axe to grind, and was more than determined to be part of whatever this 'family' was grinding.

"Of course," she pleaded, her eyes finding Savvy, "they would never succeed."

Our spy supported this conviction.

At three o' clock Savvy's phone buzzed: a consistent noise that sent its receiver practically into delirium.

"I have been informed that an 'Art Fair' is to be held at Tatters Place* on Saturday March 17th at six pm. Lately modernized the hall is not far from here.

Hans's aunt, a lover of fine art, will be visiting, and has secured him two tickets.

"That will be you and him, Rhia."

Opening my mouth in objection the sound died as Mother jumped in–

"Is that wise, Savannah?"

"Most certainly," she mumbled as the last of her muffin disappeared between her lips.

"You know…" Mother urged.

"I do."

"What if…"

Another muffin found refuge between those immaculate nails.

"Rhia said 'bring it on' so that is exactly what I am doing."

I could sense Mother's concern.

"We do not know who will be there."

"Correct, Mena, so no need for me to say, we need as many 'spies' as possible."

Mother defused as a balloon losing wind.

"I have requested you a ticket, so make the most of your entry, play the game.

You will be supported by my people in various forms of disguises. I cannot implement how important recovering the 'Crux' is."

Three muffins and four coffees downed in rotation and this woman can still think work.

Mother bobbed her head in numbed agreement. I wanted to scream, grab the two heads now in deep conversation over raspberries in baking, and demand a 'get out' clause to the art fair. I cannot go, cannot pretend to be Hans's partner, my guilt will drown me. I must refuse. Finding my voice, the sound emitting from my throat was weak–

"Saturday the 17th is a tricky day for me…"

Both stopped talking, both looked my way.

"Tricky?" it was a duet of sound.

"Yes," I faltered. "I have promised a girlfriend to celebrate Saint Patricks Day."

"Girlfriend?" Mother questioned.

"Oh, dear," Savvy followed.

Both heads shook with disbelief.

I began to walk toward the bathroom.

"Rhia," came the command. "You asked me to 'bring it on', is that no longer the case?"

Savvy's accusatory tone was heralded by mother's "Just so," their rhythm of talking heightened to joyful gabbling.

Help – as those readers who participated in my formative years know, this woman cannot allow a challenge to be thrown down, knowing it is impossible not to stoop and pick it up. My body, pleaded with me to go forward; float into the bathroom, the kitchen, the bedroom, anywhere to renew my strength of will, and for one fleeting moment I tried. My downfall: the cackling coven huddled across the table. I replayed every excuse my mind had grasped while Savvy was setting out her invitations – I replayed them – hesitated – then dismissed them as worthless. Turning around, I walked straight up to them, banished any warning bells ringing in my head, and declared–

"I will find the Crux, whatever it takes."

Thursday March 8th

Eight am in the morning, and it is time to stand up and be counted. Shout out loud that this woman is turning into a duck. The rain is constant, flowing down the streets, bubbling across the pavements due to blocked, overworked drains. The storm, at intervals throughout the night, had considered itself to be in a similar mood to my own – Pensive: a brief relaxation then 'boom' off we go for another round. Between this drab weather and my own sullen disposition, I must correct any former claim to humour as my heart is connecting with my 'messed up' brain and tumbling around my body at a pace this woman cannot keep up with.

Laying the predicament over Hans and this art fair aside, for one moment at least, I try to listen to the various upbeat voices on the radio proclaiming International Women's Day: a day that heralds the deeds, issues, complaints or otherwise the female gender need to bring to the surface. This day, for those born with an activist nature shines a light on the ongoing fight for equality with our male counterparts. I listen, think 'This is me', before falling on my own sword in my plight over that painting. In my claustrophobic dungeon, for that is what I have named my morbid state, I crunch my toast, hear my mobile ring, glance at the name flashing across the screen, note the Grubb girl, and switch it to silence. Two more bites, a swig of tea, then the name shoots across the screen once more. I let it vibrate, munching faster than a thrashing crocodile before realising this girl was not going to stop. Grateful that Mother had popped to the shop I pressed the speak button.

"Hello," I growl between munching and swallowing.

"Miss Bryant?" the voice was timid.

"Yes."

"I have news."

Not again, bound to be something trivial; superficial nonsense to try and extract herself from my grip.

"News?"

Let it float over me, that was the panacea.

Excitement had entered her voice, causing her to gabble–

"I have found – Oh, Miss Bryant I have found…"

"Stop," toast bits fly from my mouth. "Slowly" I say brushing up any overspill with my hand.

"Miss Detdy," she expresses the name slowly.

"Yes, and…"

I have stopped munching.

"I was sent to clear out your father's cupboard and…" her voice grew louder–

“And,” excitement was growing, “I have found a paper tucked inside this old book,” another squeal of elation. “I know what you said about deleting the last text, and I did, but things are getting spookier.”

My mug, halfway to my lips, was put down with a bang. This girl is trying my patience.

Grappling with her childish diction, and her excitability my brain refused to store what she had been saying–

“What cupboard?” I demanded.

“I told you, your father’s old store cupboard where Mr Richardson thought it to be full of old bank programmes and dusty out of date accounts. He was wrong.”

“And?”

She was like the wasp who could not make its mind up whether to sting or not.

“I found this paper snuggled in a page marked ‘Miscellaneous’.”

I was itching to shout ‘Get on with it’, or ‘Are you still locked in the cupboard?’

Remember the staff toilet?

Instead, I put on the snootiest voice possible, and asked–

“Where have you put that paper?”

“I have posted it to you.”

The girl was evidently pleased with herself.

“You have posted a paper from my father’s cupboard to me?”

“Yes,” she said in triumph.

“Was it not possible to tell me?”

“Too spooky”

Seriously, if she mouths that word for a third time I will…

I heard the click of the door. Mother had returned from her sojourn to the shop. Quickly I sneered down the phone –

“I must go. We must meet. When I have read the paper. I will contact you, bye.”

I clicked the ‘off’ button and placed the phone face down on the table. In all fairness my hasty ‘Goodbye’ had been rude. An ‘uncalled for dismissal’ my father would say, but I really do not care, wishing, just this once, to be back in that supercilious mausoleum.

Friday March 9th

It arrived today. A long brown envelope with a first-class stamp. Mother eyed it with displeasure as she stooped to retrieve the post.

"For you, Rhia"

It is hard to relate the knots gripping my stomach.

"Oh, that must be from that old school friend I told you about."

First thought in my head.

"Thought we could meet up soon as, since cancelling Saint Patricks Day."

Mother twisted the sleeve this way and that, finally nodded and passed it to me, her attention absorbed by her neighbour's monthly report of the family house.

"Right," she squeezed through a firm set mouth.

I made the pretence of using the bathroom, locking the door, and sitting atop the toilet.

At this point dear diary, one may ask 'why' is the bathroom my hub of discovery?

I can only shrug, and say it is my porthole to privacy: my step into the board game detective?

There was no hesitation opening the envelope, removing the yellowing paper hidden inside. Immediately I saw it was a document – An official document, signed by whoever was head of intelligence back in 1969.

> This Document declares that one Alina Dreyer, East German citizen, will forthwith be known as Etta Detdy.
>
> Guy Billington, new alias Henry Bryant is sole contact.
>
> Other subsidiary contact – Helena Crevelle, new alias Savannah D' Mill
>
> Whereabouts – Secret Location.
>
> Signed

The paper was signed by a squiggle, the usual unreadable format of intelligencers, according to my way of thinking. My head was reeling, the black dots before my eyes jumping to the tune of my rabid thoughts. My father, the man I had known and loved all my life, was – Oh Lord – two people. Savannah

D' Mill – the same, while this Detdy woman belongs to *his* family. Hell, does Mother know all this? Is she in collusion?

I turn the tap, hear the crashing sound of water rushing into the sink, force my fist into my mouth so the low dark scream can only be heard by me.

"Rhia?"

That voice through a door.

Louder – "Rhia?"

Is that really my name?

"Hello," I whimper.

"Whatever is wrong?"

Is this where the truth is unwound like a skean of wool?

"I feel sick."

"Whatever for?"

I am tempted, yet still the cold hand of reason holds me back.

"Headache," I lie, wiping the tears from my pale cheeks.

"Is that it?"

Is that it? Mother, I am collapsing inside. I have nothing solid to hold onto.

I think of Fiona, that silly young girl, weaving her way through this minefield of duplicity. My heart restricts. I register cold ice within my veins: a forerunner maybe for whatever lies in wait. I shiver, think how morbid my thoughts are becoming, tell myself to 'man up' to these discoveries, not allow them to drag me beneath the mire. I throw water onto my stinging eyes, blink a lot, dab them dry. Without a shadow of doubt an explanation will await me, somewhere. My chief priority is to get in contact with Jimmy, tell him about this paper, ask his advice, demand I speak to my father. Mother is still rattling away outside the door: her concern nothing but 'sweet talk' in my ear.

"Coming," I call, sense her returning to whatever she was doing.

Gazing in the mirror I swear *his i*mage stands behind me, those blue eyes laughing, tormenting, waving his bloody paints my way. This is my very own Pandora's Box; that mythical jar or 'pithos' as the Greeks called it, a gift to Pandora, who swore never to open it. Curiosity overcame her, and as she opened the jar out flew the troubles of the world, one after another.

This is Greek mythology, yet does it remind you of someone?

I turn from the mirror, and hurry from the room.

Saturday March 17th

Saint Patricks Day.

Officially on the world's calendar this day is for the Irish. To acknowledge their culture, visit their churches, and celebrate. The presence of a Romano-British Christian missionary to the shores of Ireland in the 5th century A.D. began a long association of patron saint and culture. This man, Maewyn Succat, later to be named Padraig, or Saint Patrick by Pope Celestine, would be celebrated on this day by Irish communities around the world. The need to wear green, visit church, bake soda bread, and socialise by drinking has long since been accepted as tradition.

Mother, in her usual quandary over 'what to wear' has decided to light up the art fair in a lime green suit. Now, while this colour shows off her paler skin and reddish hair (dyed or not) she will, in my view, be the obvious choice for unwanted attention. Myself however – I will enter that hall in a black trouser suit, of course, what else, heedless to the snide on how 'smart' this woman looks, even the petty jokes that I am in mourning. All this will be taken in my stride compared to the nervousness I feel accompanying Hans. Such as was proved yesterday when my phone kept buzzing. Thinking it was Fiona, and not yet quite ready to meet up with her, I let it buzz. Not a good idea. It buzzed and buzzed, until I picked the dratted thing up, and to my surprise saw Hans's number.

Finger balancing on the speak button I went to press it, drew back, hovered again, refused to press, then told myself not to be ridiculous.

"Hello," I in the way a dog snaps a new-comers hand.

"Hey," came his reply. "Ready for Saturday?"

I lied. What else could I do?

"Yes."

"Great, I will call for you both at seven o' clock."

"Right," I answered.

"All okay?" his voice sounded tired.

"Yes, why not?"

"Nothing, just thought…"

"No," that 'snap' was loud.

"Fine," he replied.

The 'click', followed by silence told me our conversation was over.

The day glides by as I listen to the calibration of the hands of the clock, five, four, three, two, one. At the seventh hour the doorbell rings. Glancing at my image greeting me from the bedroom mirror I mutter "Here we go," to the guitar by the wall, imagine Jimmy's reply of "Go for it", and inhale with self-righteous pity. My hair alone will have tongues wagging. Tied in a bun, yet seductively creeping from its holding to hang in those natural curls around my shoulders; a fire burning with indignation.

"Hans's here" Mother calls

Slowly I stepped into the lounge, force myself to smile in the direction of the smartly clad figure by the door, then saying nothing walk past Mother, gaze, past the mocking grin of the man by the door, and out into the corridor.

--

Tatters Place*

The journey to Tatters Place took exactly half an hour, through winding backstreets until our arrival at the newly furbished hall on the outskirts of town. Once known for its relationship to various groups and societies, it had closed a year ago due to lack of funds. As with many of these old buildings the financiers who buy them create different representations to its previous life. This was certainly the case with Tatters Place: a beacon to the modernisation of this area. Large glass windows, wood panelled frontage, and contemporary décor heralding a new era and wealthier patrons. Tonight, it was this building's debut into the art world.

Dodging the rain, and many umbrellas, we entered the hall through double fronted doors to be greeted by a waiter sporting a red waistcoat over his whiter than white shirt, and black trousers. Offering us a glass of red or white wine he pointed to the reception desk and a youth handing out pamphlets. Making our way across, lost in admiration, Hans suddenly waved to a woman standing at the far end of the hall underneath an arc of flowers. Beckoning her over his introduction was one filled with pride–

"Rhia, Mena, may I introduce my aunt, Alys Parker."

We stiffened at the name, yet the figure heading in our direction instantly dismissed any thought I held concerning that family in Germany. She was beautiful. Her brown hair, cut in the new short swept aside style drew attention to the delicately outlined face, where bluish green eyes reciprocated the pride of the man who had called her. The woman's slim figure dazzled in the bright green off-shoulder cocktail dress, matched by a pair of green satin evening shoes.

"Wonderful to meet you at last. I have been told so much about you both."

The musical voice held not a hint of German, and the smile transformed her face from radiant to alluring: the features of a woman used to admiration.

Mother greeted her warmly, commenting on the colour they both wore. Hearing the tinkling chuckle my hand found hers (I do not know why), and grasping it with a nervous breathlessness I neither understood nor control I ventured–

"Hello, wonderful to meet you."

Her fingers wrapped around mine, her eyes penetrating my own–

"Lovely to meet you, my dear."

For a reason too baffling for me to clarify Mother's spider poem floated through my mind. Letting my hand drop she focused her attention on Hans.

"I am excited you came. Hopefully, Hans mentioned we have the famous collector of art, Count Reinbach here. I must introduce you. Anything you wish to know, please ask him."

Picking up on the quizzical look we were both displaying she pretended to scold the man beside her–

"Oh, no, you have not mentioned him. Dear, Hans, you naughty boy."

Hans raised his eyebrows, winked at me with a cheeky grin, before following his aunt through the mingling crowd.

To say this building had emerged from downtrodden to classy would be the most wicked understatement I could make. Every part had been stripped down to the foundations, later re-built, re-fashioned and re-designed in this millennium's pioneering manner. It was startingly magnificent. Each painting had been given its own special place, fixed to the white painted walls, where they shimmered in the small strip lighting angled above them, illuminating the beauty of what arty people call 'the hand of the painter'. Sadly, for me, I was surrounded by oil and watercolour splashes and a crowd of nattering people. The words–

"Count, I would like you to meet my beloved nephew, and his guests."

–shook me from my musing.

I heard the 'click' of the shoes, and the most expressive, handsome face peered into ours. Hans was the first to speak –

"Sir, an honour indeed."

Again the 'click'.

Fascinated by this man's demeanour my gaze took in the charm of his smile, the penetration from those startling blue eyes as he bowed his white head over my hand. Rising, I was entranced to notice the small white beard around his chin: an apt partner to his full, yet sensitive lips. My gaze fell down the tall slim body detecting a degree of tautness; a strength that somehow resisted the softness of his voice–

"Delighted," he was saying, a dash of a foreign accent obvious.

Mother was captivated, her smile lighting her face–

"An honour," she was gushing, not bothering to hide her veneration.

"Your accent is..."

"Austrian," he laughed, taking her hand within his own, and brushing his lips across the back.

Alys Parker took his arm, leading him toward the group of paintings she had been viewing upon our arrival. We trailed in her path. It was here, surrounded by expectant faces and anticipated minds that Count Reinbach's knowledge was superior. Each brush stroke came under his scrutiny; the subject of those paintings mulled over in a way that bored me, yet delighted others; the lilting tones in his voice holding onlookers in rapture. Moving slowly along groups of paintings, drink in hand, we stop in front of a collection of watercolours. It was here the Count pointed to the sweep of the sky, and the prominent detail in the landscapes. He praised these painters for their articulate judgement when viewing the land around them, the capacity these painters were willing to go to for their art. The zeal in his voice heightened as he glanced over one specific canvas–

"A favourite canvas among art collectors such as myself. Inspire me with the knowledge you may have of this beautiful landscape, and where it portrays?"

There was a buzz of chatting, many animated in their pondering, before a young woman in the group excitedly called out "Jules Dragner, and France."

My heart dived to my stomach.

Taking larger sips of my wine, gulps in fact, I heard "Correct", grasped another voice calling, "Parisian Barley Field", and sunk to the depth of my gloom when a third voice asks – "When will this painter's latest rendition show?" The Count smiled, flashing white teeth that almost matched his beard and hair, shook his head, and looked longingly at the painting–

"My dear, you certainly know Dragner's paintings. His painting of the Southern Cross constellation has been stolen, and connoisseurs cannot wait until the painting is found."

Another mouthful of wine, the thought 'Ditto' racing through my mind. Turning to a young girl at his side the Count directed his next remark her way–

"Now, my dear art lovers, I must pass you onto dear Florentine here. She will talk you through the remaining paintings."

He broke from the group, took Alys's arm once more, then led us all towards a set of chairs at the far end of the room.

Sitting, the Count expelled a loud groan–

"This business of Dragner's painting is worrying. I am asked countless times if, or when it will be found. What us art connoisseurs are doing about it. I have no answer."

He looked at us, that mist signifying frustration gathering around those soporific eyes.

Alys patted his arm, signalled to the waiter to bring more drinks. This hall was crowded, genuine people whose love for art overflowed into the very air around us. I shifted in my chair, felt that compulsion to say something–

"Maybe those who stole the painting did it for a reason more sinister than a love for art."

All eyes turned my way. Hans patted my hand–

"I think those who stole the painting, Rhia, knew exactly what they were doing.

Their plan was devastation upon an artist's career, and the world of art in general"

The Count agreed, as did Alys, whilst Mother sat in silence.

The waiter arrived with our drinks, bowed low, gave me the quick smile that accompanies a mutual warmth, saw Hans's disapproval, emptied his tray, and hurried away.

"Too familiar," Hans spiked.

"Friendly," I commented.

"Presumptuous," Alys stated, slightly annoyed.

"Carefree," mother added.

"A sacking offence," the Count murmured.

For goodness' sake, the boy smiled.

Settling down we chatted about 'art'; the love for it, the money it gained, the sheer hard work of painter and brush. I say chatted: Count Reinbach was vibrant, his enthusiasm relentless, a desire that would have filled any person with similar leaning to 'throw caution to the wind' and follow his ecstasy over a brushful of paint.

My mind a sop with artists' names, their birthplace, their work, how many of their canvases had been exhibited, even the day they died, was compounded when he began his eulogy of modern painters with their emotional outpourings, and modernist squiggles. I longed to scream – Stop, my poor brain overwhelmed and assaulted from French Impressionists to modern contemporary. I have nothing inside when it comes to swooning over a portrait or landscape, not even a fruit bowl. By ten thirty Count Reinbach stood, those fascinating eyes wandering over each person in turn–

"This evening has been perfect. It is my honour to meet you. I thank Alys for this opportunity and hope we may meet again soon."

"You too," we chorused.

As he walked away it was impossible not to think that a light had been switched off.

"A wonderful man," Alys was saying. "Hans darling, let's get together soon."

Hans leaned over to kiss his aunt's cheek; her love for him striking and transparent.

"That would be wonderful, but for now it is time to wish you farewell."

She smiled, took his hand, and squeezed it hard. Addressing Mother and I she quickly added–

"I was so pleased to have met you – until the next time."

She rose from the chair to join a group of art enthusiasts hunched around a canvas.

Leaving the hall and its paintings behind Hans led us across the road from the building to the slot where an attendant had parked his car. All was quiet, except, and I do write this with a grain of humour, a car was parked at least six or seven cars away with its sidelights on, and a man with dark glasses in the driver's seat. It is important to mention the word humour, especially as my mind ran riot with images of spies. I was becoming obsessed. Climbing into the car we launched into more 'thanks' than our driver could deal with, and although this pleased him, I must admit Hans was quiet. There was no small talk, no mimicking or joke relating to our evening; a smile now and then, as if absorbed deep within his own ponderings. We sped down deserted streets, careered around corners, two wheels I swear, then with a jolt pulled up outside the flat.

"Sorry, I must fly."

The voice was serious, the eyes switching between the view in the rear mirror, and his scrambling passengers.

"Be in touch," he flung as we closed the doors, rushing off at top speed.

Stepping into the porch of the flats entrance I caught the sight of a low, white sports car pull away from the kerb at the end of the street.

Sunday March 25th

I have been thinking, whilst parading up and down in front of my bedroom mirror, linked together by an inward scrutinization to work out where my crazy emotions are going, and how I present myself to the world. Like the alphabet being taught to children I must start with the 'a' word, yet immediately jump to 'c' for confused. My mind will not let me grasp why the truth of my life (if indeed this spy thing is everything) has emerged now, just as Jimmy and I were 'bobbing along' happily, as my grandmother would say. Why Hans fell into my lap as a gift from the gods.

Lord, why should I think that?

I must say, Diary, you absorb all my rambling thoughts, yet are not too keen to administer formation when it is needed.

Why do I find myself ignoring Hans's connection to *that* family, ignoring my fear and dislike? Hidden deep inside me, the black melancholy that surfaces when I allow myself to think. Society would label it 'insecurity', blame my childhood, a need to surround myself with never ending adoration.

I step away from the mirror, close my eyes at the figure glaring back at me, run my fingers up and down Jimmy's lonesome guitar. I need to speak with him. Reassure myself I am searching for this painting on his, and my father's behalf. The sooner I get them home, the sooner my jumbled mind will understand my past. I ring his number, wait, tension building. A click, the sound of voices, then a whisper–

"Rhia, what is the matter?"

“Jimmy?”

A sigh, “Yes.”

“I had to ring.”

“Why?”

Louder voices.

“I need to speak to you.”

“Why?”

Temper rising.

“I don’t know who to trust,” I blurt out.

No sympathy.

“I have told you that guy, what’s his name, Hans. Now please, your father and I are busy.”

The connection dies.

I can hear Mother humming and splashing water in the bathroom. It is Sunday, and her ritual for welcoming Savvy is in full swing. I consider Jimmy’s irritation on answering his phone. Wonder what I had interrupted. Contemplate whether I really am taking everything as serious as I should. Hearing Jimmy’s voice, no matter how irritated or subdued, has fired my guilt over Germany. Silently I mouth ‘sorry’, promise to be honest with him when the painting is found, then wrap myself in the knowledge that both men are busy, and maybe my need to call is selfish.

--

Three o’ clock

I had walked from the bedroom at one o’ clock, mind jangling with determination, only to find Mother puffing in aggravation, and a full coffee pot steaming on the tray on the table.

“Late,” she moans. “Misses last Sunday, then late.”

I pout, unsure what to add to her tiny tirade, but hoping my downcast mouth might cause her to laugh. It did not. Mother is so punctual, to the point of arriving at a venue well in advance. In her eyes Savvy’s late showing was flame to the fire. We drank the coffee, felt the ‘zip’ of the caffeine laden liquid burst forth through the nonsense we were speaking. Nothing made sense, and if someone pressed me to the contents of that exchange, I would shake my head and admit I cannot remember a thing.

When the woman arrived at our door, three o' clock exactly, the scowl that Mother had worn expanded into the largest moan escaping one person's lips.

"Savannah D' Mill, what time do you call this?"

The woman glided in, smiling as if she had just won the big prize from the National Lottery everybody is rushing to play.

"Sorry. My plane has landed but an hour ago, so I came straight here."

Mother's eyes widened –

"Plane? You did not say you were travelling."

Savvy chucked her coat across the chair, as usual, then sat down in a rush to sketch out her latest mission.

"I was unable to let you both know of my latest jaunt, hence my disappearing act. Intelligence had a green light on the whereabouts of Emery Dreyer. Flew me to Germany to interact with colleagues there; hoping our agents could pick up on his trail."

Mother sniffed, "And, did you?"

"Sadly, we lost that trail somewhere outside Berlin. Our agents turned eyes upon London, but nothing"

"So, you lost him?"

Mother's tone was marked with irony.

Kicking her trendy ankle boots off Savvy sighed –

"That we did."

I quickly offered to brew tea, complaining that Mother and I had drunk an over amount of coffee, and joking our stomachs would hold no more. Savvy agreed, anything in her viewpoint that was wet, tasteful, and gave her a shot of energy. Hearing their back, and forth gossip as I moved around the kitchen I wondered if Kurt's father had chosen London for his destination. To wonder 'why' was beyond my reckoning. There was nothing in this country he could possibly want, or no-one he needed to see – Unless – the name blasted into my head in the same way a creative thought flashes through the mind – Etta Detdy.

Gathering everything I need onto the tray I head back into the lounge. Mother and Savvy were deep in conversation: witches over their cauldron. I longed to mention the Detdy name, filter out of that 'spy' mind that was gossiping and giggling away, what relevance that woman had to my father, let alone herself. So, nobody was more taken aback than myself when I opened my mouth, and nothing, apart from a "Tea" squeak, came forth. Both women ceased their dialogue, stared in my direction, and queried “Pardon?”. Lowering the tray onto the table my next move was to try and cover up my blunder–

“Look, I have made tea.”

Amused, Mother shot a glance toward Savvy, which she then reciprocated.

“Is that it?” Mother asked.

I nodded. Pouring tea Mother continued her inane chatting to Savvy, whose gaze held nothing but curiosity my way. Wishing not to be the centre of her interest I mumbled something about Germany and reports into Emery Dreyer’s disappearance.

“What are the German authorities doing to find this Emery man?”

“Everything,” came her determined answer. “The man uses disguise like a chameleon. He can integrate with a crowd, and we would not know.”

“That good.”

The remark was flippant.

“That good, Rhia.”

Deep in thought I moved to the window, push it open, and wave to the delivery boy entering the flats.

He had parked his van directly outside the flat steps causing several pedestrians to move into the gutter if they wished to pass it. Thinking how this white vehicle would appreciate a good hosing down, my eyes wander along the street, counting the people scurrying here and there, busy in their everyday routine. How ordinary this street is, far to humdrum for a ‘spy’s daughter. I chuckle, catch the delivery boy leaving, notice how he jumps into the cab, before he revs it up, and zooms down the street. My eyes follow the mucky cab as he careers around the bend, leaving me to contemplate the low white body of a sports car ticking over on the corner. I could see the driver, decided he had to be short, for his head was barely higher than the steering wheel. The dark glasses covering his wandering gaze hid his potential subject matter. It was impossible for me to say exactly where he was looking. Even so, fear washed over me. Only eight days ago this car had trailed us from the car park after our visit to that Art Fair, pulling up as we had been dropped off at the flat, then speeding away from the kerb as Hans hurried to leave.

Noting that Savvy and Mother were still discussing the whereabouts of one Emery Dreyer, my panic began to mount. What if this car – No cannot be – Why would that man be interested in us? I am beginning to feel an urgency in the air;

a clear message that was prompting me to think deeper. While the painting of the 'Crux' was important, is it the real reason Jimmy hired my father above me?

I exhale, hearing the 'zinging' noise scatter around me. I glare toward the two heads, still deep in collaboration, and say a silent 'thank you' for not disturbing their discourse. If I had Mother would have wanted to know 'why' I was fretting, and that suggestion to 'fly away' would have surfaced once more. I continue to roll Jimmy's name through my mind. It is becoming clear to me, that my partner is privy to something apart from finding a painting. They all know something. Could it be my father's past? Could it be – and here my breath comes quicker – a connection to *that* family? I quiver, mumble "Oh, no", look out into the street in hope those gossiping women did not hear me, and spluttered "It has gone."

Savvy was speaking to me–

"Rhia, what is wrong?"

Should I say – Maybe – Not sure – When all is said and done…

"Nothing is wrong." I gabble.

"What has gone?" she queried further.

Excuse my brain shouts – Think.

"Oh that. I was waiting for the delivery boy so I could wave. Silly me"

"Mmmm," was her only reply.

I hurry into the kitchen, run the water, pick up my mobile phone, find Fiona Grubb's number–

Meet me at Postman's Park, London, Sunday 1st April, Noon.

Information invaluable – R.B.

Friday March 30th

Two Lines –

I know something is not as it should be.

Mother keeps mumbling that bloody poem!

April 2001

April Fool's Day

Sunday 1st

This day has long since been regarded as a national date to torment the population with many myths gathering across the centuries into 'how' or 'why'?

As far back as 1539 the Flemish poet Eduard de Dene highlighted how a nobleman, on this day, sent his servants on foolish errands. In the Netherlands it was attributed to the Dutch victory at Brielle in 1572 where the Spanish Duke Alvarez de Toledo was defeated. The most likely source for the origin of this day could be in 1582 when the Julian calendar was exchanged for the Gregorian calendar, and anyone who forgot the change, trying to celebrate past ceremonies on this day, were teased as 'April Fools'.

--

Postman's Park London

Lying north of Saint Paul's Cathedral, and bordered by the streets Little Britain, Aldersgate, Saint Martins, Le Grand, and King Edwards Street, this green belt among a metropolitan city stands in honour of 'nature between the fumes', an oasis in the heart of hustle and bustle. Created from the burial grounds of Saint Botolph's, Aldersgate in 1880, the park was expanded over the coming years incorporating the burial grounds of Christ Church, Greyfriars, and Saint Leonards, Foster Lane. Saint Botolph's had been granted all assets pertaining to the former Cluniac Priory and Hospital during the dissolution of the monasteries in the sixteenth century, therefore making this area known for its wealth. This park is also the site where several memorials are noted such as the notification that John and Charles Wesley conducted their evangelical conversions here, and the memorials of fifty-two ceramic tablets holding the names of sixty-two 'heroes' who gave their own lives whilst saving others, erected in 1900 by

George Frederick Watts; the bones of ancestors lie beneath the feet that tread this park. Overlooked by the large Grecian building of the General Post Office this park invites workers, and shoppers of all ages to sit and enjoy their lunchtime sandwiches and drinks, hence my idea to meet Fiona at noon among the throng of Sunday shoppers. Annoying as it was, my text to the Grubb girl was not answered until this morning, then only a quick 'Noon is fine', and nothing more. Honestly, I will repeat, the girl is a complete misery. She should be pleased, for I have changed her life. Can the girl not understand her role within my 'snoop' is key to my research. Not only that, our 'togetherness' has saved her from the drudgery of that mausoleum.

As I make my way across the park, I think of the lies I told Mother just to get this far. Boy, question after question had been fired at me.

"Going out?", "Who with?", "Am I not invited?", "Do I need to tell Savannah?" Really…

"A school friend," I had said casually. "A girl I have not seen for ages."

Her mouth formed into that usual pout–

"Oh, you… Never mind"

I quickly add–

"She has invited me to meet for a drink and catch up."

"Today?"

"Yes" I fire back, not wishing to get involved in her prying game. "Only day she has free" I finish.

"Goodness, what is her job?"

Catch question- Mind whirling–

"Bank manager," the lie runs as water from a fountain.

She sighs, "Good Job. Please, pay my respects to…"

"Julie," I stumble, "Julie Predence."

Where did that come from? Mother continued her Sunday routine, the word 'pretence' edging its way past those downturned lips. I hurry to get ready.

Surprised just 'how' crowded the park appears I cannot help but wonder why the population's fashion desire has not been sated during the week. Generations of both genders are gathered here, sitting, talking, eating their sandwiches, and drinking whatever beverage they had fought through a crowd to obtain, bags and boxes at their feet. I could not help but consider 'how empty' the suburbs must be today, as I think of the women back home, drinking coffee while planning their perfidious moves. Watching the clouds above me, I think how grateful I am it is dry, for in my rush to leave the flat I had slipped my feet into bright orange pumps to match my ankle length jeans and heavy knit jumper. My only rain covering being a short cream raincoat.

'Satsuma,' Jimmy would have joked, and we would have laughed.

I push his face to the back of my mind as my eyes catch the petite figure scrunched up on the bench, trying hard to look insignificant, compelling many walking in her direction to view her with extra curiosity.

I hurry over, greet her with an enforced smile, sit beside her–

"Hello" I say, trying not to burst out laughing at her large cape.

The figure turns my way, her small face a speck within the large cowl hood.

"Miss Bryant, I should not be here," her eyes flicker quickly around the crowded park. Stifling an angry retort my mind turns to my immediate need.

"I need more searching on the Detdy woman. You need to 'up' your game."

Here I write– If looks could kill. The girl breathes deep-

"This is blackmail."

I stare – She has mouthed that word, the one word I was trying to shun. It makes me feel dirty. I must get this connection out of her mind.

"No, Fiona (I say the name soothingly) I would never blackmail you."

She gave me that look teenagers use when they have no faith in what you say.

"Miss Bryant, you sit in your ivory castle looking down your nose at the likes of me, then demand us to fall in with your schemes. I have told no-one. I could, but then my job would be finished. Is that not blackmail?"

I follow those clouds, white, pink, grey, floating over our heads in a menacing manner, the girl beside me bordering on the hysterical. I had to produce something, quick.

"Fiona, I too feel sorry you have been involved" lay it on– "This could be the last time. What you have found is-er- brilliant, but I need added information.

For instance: an address. Why has the Detdy woman been kept a secret from me?"

Pleased at my smooth talking I take her hand, forget the people around us.

The girl sniffed, rubbed her nose with paper from her pocket, those hazel eyes boring into mine.

"You? Why is everything about you?"

She glared at me.

"The last paper I uncovered told you about her. Your father's informant."

Her voice had risen.

“Quiet,” I snapped. “No-one must hear us.”

“Hear us?” the girl’s voice rasped. “You need to hear yourself.”

How dare this chit of a girl speak to me, Rhia Bryant in this way. Holding the rising indignation in check I ask–

“Anything else?”

The girl scrutinized the crowds, shrinking further into herself as a couple with a child came near, causing Fiona to cover her face with her hands. I tried not to laugh out loud, queried if she thought they were spies from the bank. After five minutes of this nonsense my hand dropped hers.

“For goodness’ sake, pull yourself together. Just tell me.”

Her eyes widened, studying me with disgust. For the first time since our ‘collusion’ began I shrunk from her gaze, as she spluttered–

“When your text came through there was nothing to tell, so…” here she caught her breath “I began to pop in and out Mr Richardson’s office with excuses to dust and tidy paperwork etc. Tuesday past he had Savannah D’ Mill in his office. She had not long returned from Germany. They were discussing something of importance when I barged in with coffee. Had I known she was there, you bet.

Yes, I got told off, and yes, he was mad, but I caught the name Etta Detdy and the city of Coventry. Just a snippet”

Her eyes lowered, “This is it Miss Bryant. Any good or not, I am done.”

Her teenage ‘twang’ resounding in my ear the girl stood up, gave me that moue deployed by most of her age, then nodded her head, and walked away.

I sat there, dazed at her expediency. Around me the park was getting busier, the buzzing sound of conversations ringing in my ears. The city Fiona had mentioned was beyond the jurisdiction of my knowledge. I remember father mentioning this city’s Cathedral; something relating to new and old, side by side. How I wish he were here.

Can this city be the clue to the Detdy woman? My throat restricted, suddenly felt dry; the gritty dry of someone struggling to comprehend the world about her. On my way into this green belt, I had noticed a small café. It was but a short walk from this bench; a place to contemplate Fiona’s finding, and my own emotional mess.

--

The small café reminded me of a scene in a play, square wooden tables covered by old-fashioned oil cloths, white crock mugs, and a glass fronted counter. Counting myself lucky to find a spare table pushed up a corner by the window I gave my order for a cheese sandwich and tea. Settling into the chair I stared out the window, not onto the busy street, but lost in a void of my own creation. Deep in thought I did not hear the voice low at my side.

"Hello, it is Miss Bryant, am I right?"

Surprised at the figure bending down, almost whispering in my ear, I stumbled over my words, the cheese mouthful nearly losing its hold on my tongue.

"Yes."

The man, who now came into view, looked familiar, white hair, white beard, shining blue eyes. My surprise matched his inquisitive gaze.

"Count Reinbach?"

He smiled, the twinkling eyes glancing from the table to the counter.

"That is correct. I saw you through the window as I passed. Thought 'ah, tea'. Would you mind if I join you?"

Swallowing the bread and cheese that I had nearly choked on I bade him sit down.

"I am sorry, I was deep in thought."

"Fine," he said, "I believe the saying is 'A penny for them'."

His accent made the phrase sound quite funny; a release from the drama displayed by Fiona.

"Nothing important. A silly girl having a teenage strop."

He smiled again, thanked the woman carrying his tea to the table, answering my statement with the sympathy he considered it worth –

"Ah, young girls. How rebellious they can be."

For the first time this morning I laughed with bona fide joy.

The Count drank his tea in small gulps, blowing it around the mug in his insistence that the 'beverage' was hot. Every time he muttered the word I laughed, astonished how easily we had settled into the diversion of one another's company.

"How long are you staying in the city?" I ask, still diminishing my sandwich.

He groaned, "As long as it takes the museums to find that painting of Dragners'"

I stopped eating, took hold of my tea; anything to cover up my rapidly beating heart.

"My apologies, I am boring you. Life becomes governed by art, sad to say. It rules everything else. I have a buyer waiting to collect this masterpiece. Until it is found," a shrug. "What can I do?"

I collect my thoughts, slow my heart by taking a deep breath, raise the slightest smile–

"How frustrating for you. My partner and my father are searching for the painting. I feel I must do my bit to help them."

He grinned as he lifted his mug to drink more tea.

"I do believe half of all art lovers must be doing the same. They search too. You are not alone."

He called for extra tea.

"Allow me. You have saved an older man from his own company."

"A pleasure," I reply, giggling as a young girl on her first date.

We drink.

Two more teas, an in-depth conversation on the comical side of art, and it was two thirty before I knew it. Count Reinbach was an interesting man, our exchange dealing with his childhood in Austria, my childhood in a London suburb, and my up and down relationship with Jimmy. He was interested, I was fascinated. Not once did he say anything reproving. Nothing to make me nervous or concerned that I had only recently been introduced to him. He was the man with the perfect manners. Finishing his tea, the Count rose, pulling the raincoat he had nigh but dumped across the chair onto his lean frame.

"I am sorry to leave you, Miss Bryant, work calls. I hope to see you soon."

His eyes never lost their sparkle.

"I thank you, Count, for an informative conversation. Please call me Rhia"

Honestly, he bowed.

"It has been more than interesting, Rhia, I thank you. Beg you to take care."

He left as quickly as he arrived.

I stared through the window, this time following the crowds jostling along the street, straining to maybe glance what direction the Count had taken. There was no sight of him. Puff, he had gone, leaving me strangely bereaved; astonished how easy it was to talk to him. On hindsight I would comment that this meeting was the medicine required after Fiona. I thought of Mother and Savvy, chatting away, still putting the 'spy' world right. Wait until I tell them of my unexpected encounter. Their response will be worth savouring. Mother will be so jealous. Pushing the chair away from the table my mind turns to home. No point hurrying for a bus, those trilling women will be suspicious and nosy if I appear early. I will wander around a shop or two, have that quiet look around I have been promising myself for ages. Solitude, within my head, to work out my next step for my teenage snooper. I allow my face to hold the broadest grin ever, ignoring the snipes from other diners. There remains nothing in this world that can match the vibrant elation of being pleased with one-self.

Oh yes, I can honestly say, this woman is no April fool.

Thursday April 12th

Maundy Thursday

April holds so many important dates within the calendar. For instance: April Fool's Day, Maundy Thursday, Good Friday, and Easter Sunday.

Today is Maundy Thursday, a day of servitude and repentance. Known in Germany as Grundonnerstag, where green vegetables and salad become the dish of the day, including spinach. In England, our observance leans to the traditional. The Monarch gives alms to the poor, or those chosen from a list of elderly citizens' Church congregations, and choirs scatter after an evening service to represent the scattering of the disciples in the Garden of Gethsemane. While Friday becomes a day for thought and prayers, and Sunday, in the Christian calendar, the celebration for the risen Christ, and lots of chocolate eggs.

My repentance today means I have been considering the world in general. That is to say: my life. As a tumble dryer whirls the clothes my mind has pondered 'this way and that' in my ordeal to deal with 'life', seen through my eyes. I have been given three options as I see it–

One: Hans – Savvy's agent, and in my mind, a good actor. I will team him with my teenage snooper – Yes, I know I promised to 'go it alone', but surely it would be halving the burden if I 'play' one, and 'use' the girl.

What?

For goodness' sake, cannot people change their mind?

I know he belongs, loosely or not, to *that* family, and his aunt certainly has closer ties. Sometimes one must dance with the devil to extract the truth, and I do like his company, in an erroneous way.

“Caution,” the word rings in my head.

Let me state here and now that ‘caution’ is not my ‘by word’, but ‘action’ certainly is, and I will not forget who his half-brother is.

Two: Fiona Grubb – For the way she spoke to me, let alone anything else, her card is marked. Essential usage.

Three: Count Reinbach – the most charming man this woman has ever met. A mind that knows art in the way a reptile can shed old and new skin. That man will sniff a lost painting out if it was buried at the bottom of a rubbish tip. I am excited. I find myself drawn towards him. Those bewitching eyes that mollify and tease my stressed mind. His common sense will uncover that dratted painting far more quickly than Savvy’s slow deliberate searching, or Father and Jimmy.

I have forever been considered a ‘girl/woman’ who follows her head, more than her heart, and at this moment my head is screaming ‘trust this man’. If truth be known what else can I do? In the last few days, since our park meeting, I have texted Fiona so many times until my poor fingers were sore from pressing her number. The fool is playing ‘hide and seek’. Not funny, as she will realise when she reads my last text. I have veiled it in a slight threat.

I pause writing to consider my deed – Screw my nose up and add – She wishes to retain her job.

Last, but not least on this critical day of decisions I have sent text messages to Jimmy and my father. My message reads simply–

‘Still searching for painting. Do not worry, I have met someone with knowledge within that art world; a man of integrity and class’

How crazy is this–

I have called, or texted their mobiles every week, almost every day, heard nothing, then one sentence threw both into disorientation.

Father wrote – Take care my precious girl. The wheel is turning.

Honestly, what is he jabbering about, but who cares I know my father has answered me because the text came from his phone.

I reply – Instead of telling me, get yourself home, please.

No answer.

Jimmy’s was encouraging – That sounds good. Maybe we can find the thing and come home.

Wow, I cannot believe my luck. Today has proved one thing – Mother and Savvy sit on the periphery of my search.

Sunday April 15th

Easter Day

I feel sick.

So many chocolate eggs devoured within a limited time zone. Rich dark chocolate, festooned with candy roses, delivered on Saturday by a beaming concierge with the morning post. Dismissing the white typed envelopes to the coffee table, Mother and I unpacked our parcels of eggs. Two packages each, bundled in brown paper, sellotaped down, with names written by hand. I tore the outer casing from the large box, addressed to me in large letters: a huge multi – flowered creation displayed in an ornate box with a card that read–

'Enjoy, be in touch soon. Love Hans'

My smaller box contained a basket of dark, milk, and white chocolate eggs, wrapped in iridescent paper of various colours. Beautiful to look at, and delicious to eat I would say. The card from Mattie was full of love and concern for my stomach if I munched through them all at once.

Oh boy, if only I had taken notice.

Mother had similar boxes. A large egg from Hans with a card wishing her well, and a basket from Mattie, edged with letters from the alphabet. I laughed, asked if it was a coded message, then corrected myself by the strongest reproval.

Anyway, by lunchtime today I had consumed my large and half my chocolate eggs.

Reason – the need for something sweet to bolster my courage when I tell Savvy and my mother their plan is 'yuk', and I will occupy the driving seat from now on.

It is one o' clock, and I cannot believe the lavish 'picnic' Mother has prepared for our usual Sunday guest. Savannah D' Mill has been visiting us, an off/on routine for the past three and half months, mainly on the pretext that Father wishes her to keep those beautiful eyes fastened upon us, or should I say 'fastened on me' – an intelligence afterthought toward a wayward daughter. Looking at the kitchen table stacked with tiny hors d' oeuvres (starter food to you and me), and fancy finger sandwiches, tiny muffin cakes, and a bottle of wine, my stomach creaks. How can I traverse my way through this field of food without being ill, especially as Mother is showing no sympathy, plumping up those blasted cushions as though any minute now royalty will stand in our lounge, commending us on a comfy headrest. Therefore, you can imagine my horror when the phone rang, and a voice apologised that 'Miss D' Mill' was unable to visit.

"Not again." Mother slammed the phone back on its holder.

First thought: Thank Heaven, we can slum out more.

Second thought: Hell, that food, that chocolate – Help.

Five minutes after the call Mother received a text from the absent Miss D' Mill.

"Excuses?" I ask sarcastically.

"Yes and no," she remarks, running her thumb up and down the phone face.

"Where has she disappeared to this time," I croaked.

The eggs were threatening to chase my stomach in circles.

"An urgent call to Germany."

"Again?" my query was scathing.

--

Four o' clock, and with the final remains of Mother's 'picnic' either crammed into quick freeze tubs, or in the gaping mouth of the waste bin, we throw ourselves onto the sofa to sort out the post from yesterday. Outside the window the church bells had rung out before lapsing into a quiet period for contemplation. We held our glass of wine, no point in clearing everything away, wished each other 'Happy Easter', and tore away the various envelopes from their inner partners.

"The bank," Mother sighed. "Richardson wishes to see me."

This is ongoing. Take care Mother.

"When?" I ask unfolding another typed written letter.

"A.S.A.P, he writes. Another correction meeting" she moans.

"Authority gone wild," I splutter. "Silly so… man."

Mother was frowning, I was thinking. This was my opportunity to confront Fiona. I would be the last person she would expect to see.

"Book an early appointment. I can wait for you, then we can shop."

Mother's face brightened. Brushing my letter aside, prominent news of an offer I may find interesting, I swirl the liquid in my glass.

Oh, this drink is sweet.

Friday April 20th

Eight thirty am, standing in the foyer of the bank, Mother waiting for Mr Richardson to begin their interview, myself keeping an eye to the whereabouts of my young receptionist. Within these walls business is playing out as usual; the cashiers lining up behind their glass panels, fixing their set smile, last minute pat to their hair sprayed buns. The managers and advisers setting up their offices, waiting their early morning clients, making sure their mugs are brimming with their favourite drink of coffee or tea. The doors will soon open for the public; inviting those few gathering outside to commence transactions, ready themselves for good or disappointing financial news. Fiona stands behind her desk, earphones on, pen in hand, allowing her gaze to fall on the customers waiting for the commanding word 'Enter'. I keep my gaze secured to that desk, wonder if my teenage sleuth is fretting over my presence. The bell rings – Nine o' clock. Mother is escorted to Richardson's office door as the people hurry through the doors. I sit and wait.

Fiona greets, Fiona directs, Fiona listens, pointing her consumers to the correct personal, or cashier. This continues, until looking my way the young girl acknowledges my waiting. Slowly she moves in my direction.

"Miss Bryant, you wish to speak with someone?"

Silly girl, I am neither here for business, nor to be treated as a customer.

"Yes, you," my reply is simple, the boredom of waiting obvious.

Searching left and right, noting there are no eyes watching her, she lowers herself beside me–

"I thought…" she began.

I raised my hand, slightly, halting the question before her mouth could form the words.

"Well, I need further information," I whisper.

The pale face loses the set smile.

"But," a sigh. "But…" she begins again. "We finished in that park."

"You may have thought just that, but I need an address."

Robespierre could not have been more adamant.

"What?" the sound was wrenched from her throat.

"An address," I repeat, patience thinning.

Tears beneath her lashes. She moved uncomfortably, rushing up to her desk to direct another customer in their required enquiry.

For a few moments she did not move. Her thoughts, to my mind, in that place many academics call 'contemplation'. Suddenly, swiftly Fiona rushed back to me, her voice low; veiled with a hint of a threat–

"What if I refuse you?"

I do not believe what I am hearing.

"Refuse me?"

"Yeh," she said, the cockiness of youth displayed across her features.

I longed to laugh, spit in venom that it was 'me' who held the reigns.

"No go area"

Please tell me this was more the girl's way of speaking: the common assault of our English tongue to Mother's way of thinking. Fiona sank back down on the seat, twisted her hands together in her lap–

"What you ask me will be impossible. Old Richardson dislikes me"

"Bah, you can do this, and will."

I really was intimidating.

"Please, Miss Bryant, why the urgency? Why me?"

The cry came from the heart. It left me cold.

The buzz of voices and movement grew louder. Fiona spent the next ten minutes back and forth to her desk, sorting queries, soothing, in her down to earth manner, anxieties and stress of the collective public. Returning to me she nodded, this assent assuring me the girl would 'do the job'.

"Good," I muttered.

"Good?" she moaned. "My mam always tells me we must pay for hurting others."

Did the girl mean me?

The next half hour I sat twiddling my thumbs Fiona deliberately refusing to speak. I smiled when a customer joked with her, chuckled at a child that rapped her desk, and waved as a delivery boy winked at her – All for nothing. My truculent informer spurned every act of spurious kindness I made.

Thank goodness for the mobile phone keeping us in touch with the 'sane' world. The melody I had set for messages rang out, growing louder as my inpatient cell phone bopped and sang at high speed. Embarrassed I switched it to read, my heart leaping as the words danced before my eyes.

'Rhia, please meet me, May 1st, at the Millennium Dome. We need to talk.

Clear the air. Savvy passed it – H'.

My main thought should have been –

'At last, this guy must confess. Own up to those people he knows, and who his brother is'.

This was not the case.

I let go Fiona's grumbles, forgot the threats we both made, delighting in this message. Oh, Diary, I must hold up my hands, confess that idiom–

"While the cat's away, the mice will play."

–fits me perfectly.

Mother's release from Mr Richardson's office broke no remark from me concerning her visit, or extra money. Nothing passed between us until we stepped outside the bank, mother smiling broadly, and asking–

"Shop?"

Brandenburg – Gorden Prison
Germany April 2001

The smile playing across his thin lips held personal satisfaction for the man returning to his cell. It had been a dreary, wet day; one out of many this year that nature had deigned fit to bestow on the world. First, the rains of January, followed by the snow of February, rain returning throughout March, and finally April's showery downpours. Miserable weather that consumed the body and mind, feeding the complaints of the prisoners, and the anger of the guards. Summoned to the governor's office mid-afternoon with the notification that he had been granted a personal phone call surprised him. He knew calls directed through the governor's office were reportedly political; high status callers, or as those manning the prison cells often mimicked 'An officer', 'Public figure', or in less humorous terms 'Men or women with money.'

On walking into the room, flanked, as usual, on either side by large burly guards, the man could see from the fearful look on the governor's face this caller held high rank of one form or another. Instantly the guards were dismissed, the room fell silent, and the governor's mobile phone handed to him, more with reverence than command. The prisoner knew this action to be strange, for personal possessions were not as a rule permitted to be shared. Holding the phone to his ear the man listened to three words the caller spoke, the hot solitary tear leaving his eye to travel over his cheek. Returning the phone to the governor's outstretched hand he bowed his head in gratitude, then readied himself to walk from the room. It was then the smile had sealed itself across his lips. The man had been waiting for the call, knowing that sooner or later he would be summoned. He believed the promise, passed to him on that occasion when the dark-haired man had visited. Three words 'It had begun' rang in his ear: words that gave him hope, spoken in English, meaning a beginning to an end. Freedom was evolving… Wait, he could not think that far ahead. This place gave no credence to a brighter future.

Back in his cell the cries of other inmates could not disturb him, he must not allow them too. The merry-go-round was turning. How long that rotation would take he did not know, but however long, he would wait. Accept the cold brutality that these 'so called' men of integrity held as their right. Brutality such as yesterday when four of their burliest slammed into his cell pushing the young man he colluded with to the ground. Shouting, they pulled the cell apart, exchanging glances while keeping the grovelling form prostrate beneath their boots. The more they found nothing, the more they kicked and punched him, splitting his lip, breaking his teeth. The letters they sought had been sneaked out the night before, hidden in socks and down trousers. Not ideal in the man's opinion, but any way out is better than no way out. Again, a fist: followed by abuse from a mouth running amok. The man registered whose hand and whose mouth caused the pain, assigning it to his memory to be dealt with in a future time. Throwing the boy against the wall they dragged him from the cell, ordering the man to clear the mess up, before slamming the door closed.

Today, he would sit on his straw mattress, pleased at his effort to straighten the cell. Today, he cared nothing for their indiscriminate mouths. His concern, that phone call. The 'plan', stirring in the world; tentacles of hope that would bring to conclusion a past that tore his family apart.

May 2001

Tuesday May 1st

May Day

This day is a celebration of Spring.

Although the metrological Spring is noted in March, the festivities of 'May Day' adhere to the history of the British Isles. It is understood that in the nineteenth century, the day of May 1st was celebrated as an International Workers Day, or Labor Rights Day, many workers dressing in their finest to dance, drink, eat, sing, and be merry.

The Celts saw this day as the most important day of the year called The Festival of Beltane; a day that divided the year in half. Symbolic fires were lit amid a celebration of life and fertility.

Roman times worshiped this day as Floralia Day for the goddess of flowers. As time passed the Celts Beltane and the Roman's flower festival eventually fused together. Over the past one hundred years a Maypole has become the main feature of this day. Its origin unknown, this pole, mainly adorned with ribbons of every colour, entices rural villagers, especially the young, to take a ribbon and dance around it.

It may be called Spring's individual gala.

--

I believe we are living in a goldfish bowl!

The rain has not one thought of stopping, the chill cutting through us in the form of an artic wind. Many would accuse this woman of fictional license. Maybe they would be right, but even so, it is May, and the chill is that of a March wind, not the gentle breeze known to late Spring. I feel sorry for any May Queen festivities. If I had been asked for an opinion, there would have been no question into my answer–

"Run, hide, I wish to be Queen in June".

Anyway, today I am meeting Hans at the Millennium Dome, and sad to say I resemble that Highland rambler, i.e.: wool trousers, thick jumper, anorak, gloves, scarf, and a hat. On the plus side my lips are shining with a new ruby lipstick, and my eyes look sultry dressed in smoky grey eye shadow. Pushing my coiled hair beneath the woolly pull down, I pick up my umbrella, and plod through the lounge. Mother, while trusting Savvy's seal of approval for the meeting, still holds dubious tendencies to my meeting him alone.

Her comment – "How do you know where he will take you?"

My answer – "The Millennium Dome, Mother. Do not worry I am armed with a weapon."

Brandishing the telescopic brolly in the air, she snorted , bid me 'Take care' then absorbed herself in reading, or pretending to read a magazine.

I head toward that giant landmark.

--

Millennium Dome

Situated on the Greenwich Peninsula, this massive structure, designed by Richard Rogers, and completed in 1999 for the new millennium era, has a glass fibre coated fabric roof that stands fifty-two metres high in the middle; one metre for each week of the year according to the news when it was built. The symmetry of this canopy is interrupted in the centre to house the ventilation shaft from the Blackwell Tunnel: an important feature no doubt, especially when you consider the twelve 100 high yellow support towers surrounding it. Apart from these twelve towers which represent each month of the year, they also signify the numbers on a clock face portrayed by Greenwich Mean Time. The circumference of these poles measures 365 metres, another representation for each day of the year. When brought together in one building, all these references to months, weeks and days highlights the third millennium, and the passing of age.

Although opened to the public on 31st December 1999 as part of the festivities, this building is now closed due to the Flying Squad and the Metropolitan Police foiling an attempted robbery of the 'De Beers' diamonds that were on display at the end of the year 2000. Among the £350 million diamonds inside the Dome was the flawless 'Millennium Star' diamond, weighing 203.4 carats. It was known to those who deal with these gems as the most perfect blue diamond: an observation to its priceless value.

Question: Can you believe this gang, or any gang, would try and ram the part of the Dome known as the 'Money Zone' with an earthmover, secured as it was by electronics and plodding police people?

No?

My thought exactly.

The nearer I get to this awesome building the louder I can hear the River Thames lapping in the background. Closed this iconic dome may be, but the grounds and area surrounding this monument to time, remains as busy as the first days and months it opened. Gathering speed, heart flipping up and down within my chest, I spot Hans, standing by a post, gazing at the milling crowds around him. I wave, notice he is not looking my way, and hurry forward. Approaching him I spot a man lingering in the trees a little further to my right. Trying to behave normal (if this word can ever fit my actions) I spot a camera in his hand; the whirring sound tells me this man is videoing around him. While most people mulling around this part of London can be deemed 'tourists', this man is not filming the magnificent structure before him but the those faces close to him. Displaying a nonchalant grin and a cigarette dangling from his mouth he nods my way. What troubled me was the constant moving of that mouth, which I decided was not to balance his cigarette, neither to speak to a companion. Overdosed on the 'spy' thing, I tapped Hans on the arm as I hurried past him saying through clenched teeth– "Follow me."

Surprised at the severity oozing from a muffled woolly jumper, yet realising that jumper was me, Hans stepped into line.

Darting behind a bush I raise my fingers to my lips, make sure we are not in view of the crowd, then release a large sigh. The man had not moved. He was still moving his camera, still smoking the cigarette, without a doubt enjoying the few rays of sun peeping through the waterfilled clouds, and whatever other shifty behaviour he was immersed in. Hans's astonishment transferred itself to his lips–

"Whatever is the matter?"

"Keep your voice down, I thought a man back there was following you."

"Me?" Hans smiled. "What for?"

I gaze through my leafy hide-out, search for the loitering figure, note he had met a woman by the river. Withdrawing my face from the bush I peer into his smiling eyes–

"Evidently he was just a tourist. See, the guy with the dark sunglasses and the camera."

Hans let out a laugh–

"Him? That chap asked me for a light. Told me he was waiting for a friend. I had no reason not to believe him," he paused. "Look, a woman has met him."

If for nothing else but to please him I peered out from the bush. It was evident this couple were more than friends, leaving me to fight down any embarrassment I may feel. Guiding me from the bush onto the pathway we began to walk toward the Dome.

"Let us find somewhere to sit" he was saying, smiling as I consistently looked over my shoulder.

I followed, head bowed, agitation at my imagination getting the better of me.

Coming upon an outdoor café Hans asked me to sit, ordered two cans of pop, then complaining how cold they were sat opposite me. I drank eagerly, feeling the refreshing liquid bathing my throat with its vibrant taste.

"Right, Miss Rhia Bryant, ask away."

I could sense the tension, which triggered my own uncertainty into what I wished to hear.

"You do not seem troubled over what I may ask. Is that due to conceit or shame?"

Hans lowered his can, held my eyes with his own–

"Neither. I hoped you would understand that I would not treat you bad."

Is that it?

"Hell, I found out in Germany, the night after we…" I inhaled the largest breath possible, "that you and that, that painter," another large breath "are brothers."

Hans took a large gulp of pop and ran it around his mouth. His expression hard to decode. Eventually – five minutes – ten, probably a couple of seconds–

"I am his sibling through his mother, and sad to say his cousin through my father."

Matter of fact.

People were beginning to congregate, talking loudly, sitting on whatever chairs were free.

"Repeat," I whispered.

"My father was the brother of Emery Dreyer. His wife, Ametti, was having an affair"

"An affair?"

"Yes."

"With her husband's brother?"

"Yes, but you know all this from Savvy."

Thoughts, bad or otherwise ran around my head–

"And, if I had not found out. You…"

I could not finish my question.

He moved his hand across the table toward mine. I moved mine away.

"Savannah told me to come clean with you. Rhia…please"

His plea left me trembling with humiliation, at my memories, at a yearning that was stripping my mind of common sense.

I delve deeper, no room to think, no room to feel anything.

"You have been brought up by your aunt. She belongs to…"

My mouth is dry.

"Emery Dreyer's family," he concludes.

I began to move from the table, spilling my drink in my hurry to leave. Tears, for whatever reason spilt down my cheeks. The faster I tried to move, the more my legs would not work. Hans caught up with me, placed a hand on my arm. I flinched.

"Please, Rhia, I do not belong to them."

Should I laugh? Should I scream – 'You do belong to them'.

The world, as I knew it, was spinning out of control, and my heart knew why. The bare facts told their own story. I had cheated on Jimmy. I trusted no-one. I was the miserable child of a past spy, and at the core, please hold no scepticism over this, for I am certain, sits the figure that is Etta Detdy.

I ran, as fast as the weight I was carrying allowed me, my ears vibrating from the panting exhaling from my mouth. Hearing *his* feet at my back, *his* voice begging me to "Slow down" I tried to run faster, felt the burn in my chest, stopped. As the figure behind me caught up I threw at him–

"You are the same, a liar, a cheat, a – a turncoat."

Words were falling from my tongue in rapid succession, slashing the air around us. Hans was shaking his head, a seriousness I had not encountered before hovering around his eyes.

"I tell you the truth, Rhia. Savvy told you I am working to bring these people to justice. True, they are my family, but they believe a cause that is abhorrent to me."

Strong emotion gripped me–

"How can I trust you?"

"Because today I have proven you can."

The tension firing its way through me sparked the next question that flew between us.

"It appears you play both sides of the coin. A dangerous game, and a duplicate nature. I fear for my father and Jimmy, for you must know I love Jimmy."

I felt the need of verbalized protection.

Hans turned his head to the side, pretended, I am sure, to watch the mingling crowds. When his answer came the slight took me by surprise–

"Do you?"

"Meaning?"

"Meaning, Rhia, that night in Germany."

"A mistake," I cry. "I do love Jimmy."

Somewhere deep inside me that question of guilt must be tackled, and my lax attitude to the phrase 'out of sight, out of mind' challenged. Without looking at me Hans began to walk away. I meekly shadowed him: part of me disturbed by his inquiry. Deep in thought I did not notice the man with the sunglasses swinging his camera whilst laughing with his female friend.

--

The Café by the River

We strolled, eyes not moving from the free-flowing river; my feet pit-pattering in his wake. Neither spoke. I, for one, had not a clue what to say, or even how I should act. In all this 'awkward silence' it had taken a few minutes for my mind to latch onto the reappearance of the couple trailing behind us, every now and then stopping so he could 'click' that wretched camera. They laughed, nodded at the passing tourists, portraying that impression of a happy couple, deeply in love, content with the world. I dubbed it false. Hans did not re-act to their sudden appearance. However, without a word, grabbing my wrist, Hans pulled me down a concealed set of stone steps. At the bottom, a little further along the stony pathway, tucked out of sight of the tourists above, was a building nestled into the walls overhanging greenery. Not saying a word, but looking behind him, he drew me to the most sheltered spot against the wall. Waiting for a few minutes, hand across his mouth to convey we must not speak, he listened to the footsteps above us. Hearing the rush of feet, a voice muttering 'Verdammt' in an accent I knew to be German, we huddled together until the sound of feet moving away allowed Hans to almost drag me through an old gate door, and motion me to sit.

"You suspected," I said, a tiny bit pleased with myself for registering the tail first.

"I did," was his simple reply.

"I am presuming the 'damn' was because he lost us."

"It was."

Images of that low white sports car wrapped around my mind.

Fascinated by this dark 'garage', with its water urn and its taciturn hostess I ventured to ask–

"Who can they be?"

He shrugged, leaving the question to hang between us, beckoning the woman sitting at a small table near the back wall to bring two drinks.

"Sorry, more drinks, better stay here for an hour or so."

Scanning the dimly lit area I asked– "What is this place?"

Hans smiled, thanking the tiny thin woman who had appeared with the coffee, whilst watching my face with almost childish glee.

"It belongs to Savvy's lot. A hidden gem, unknown to those not in the game.

From outside the place resembles a disused shed full of rubbish."

Now, there is a surprise.

Hans stirred his coffee, hesitated on his next exchange–

"Rhia, you must start to take this hunt for the painting serious. I have so many doubts. Your mother for instance, knows more than she pretends. Savannah D' Mill may be my boss, but do I trust her when imparting knowledge? – not sure.

Is it possible she is holding information back?"

His face had grown serious.

"Such as?" I stumbled, stirring the milky substance before me.

He moved nearer to me–

"Well, a day or two ago I heard Savannah on the phone. Not strange you will comment, until you hear the rest. She was whispering in code to someone called Rufus.

I have never heard her speak of this person in all our dealings together, and catching my gaze she replaced the phone, fast."

His eyes moved to the woman sitting quietly in the seat she had returned to. Contented she was immersed in her magazine he whispered–

"Have you heard of this name?"

I rotate my spoon around the mug, hearing the 'clank' as steel touches the ceramic sides. I shake my head–

"I have never heard this name. Who do you think it maybe?"

His voice was low–

"I believe it is someone, an undercover agent, protecting someone."

I swear an electric bolt passed through me.

Casting a quick eye toward the woman by the wall I try to suppress an urge rising within me, try and fail–

"Hans can I really trust you?"

He smiled, "After Germany. Do you need to ask?"

Please, not that again.

"Forget Germany, can we not just work together if possible, for Jimmy rates your trust."

His eyes clouded.

"Trust me? Oh Rhia, you know you can. I actually…"

I must stop him. Cannot hear the conclusion of his sentence. My hand shoots out, covering his mouth, and stopping his flow.

"No more admissions. They are not real, why would they be?"

"Because…"

"No nothing," I hiss. "If we cannot form a working partnership, I will leave now."

For a moment Hans assumed an appearance of deflation, then, just as quickly sprang into the man Mother and I had first met.

For the first time since this business had started, I was beginning to take control.

"I will give you my professional self completely," he said.

"Good. Jimmy will be pleased."

Jimmy will not know. I could not possibly tell him what I cannot explain to myself.

"Do you know the name Etta Detdy?"

There, said it.

Hans's brow crumpled, "Etta Detdy?" He stressed the 'Etta', before rolling the surname around his tongue, frowned, shook his head, closed his eyes, re-opened them.

"No, should I?"

"Me neither, but Savvy knows her."

"Really?" his eyes took on an alertness I had not seen on previous occasions.

I thought of Fiona and laughed, suddenly lowering the sound as I remembered our position.

"I have someone on it."

"Who?" his interest heightened.

"No-one who may be given a second thought."

He made some comical gesture, pretended to groan–

"Share."

It was then, something I cannot explain, refused me to voice her name. Hans pressed his case, almost to the point of begging, I declined – End of discussion.

Emerging from the dim light into the brightness of the day I focused on the Thames. These lapping waters where Queens had been borne to their death, and Lords to the punishment of a King's fickle notion, yet a safe port to those fleeing the Great Fire of London in 1666. I would accept Jimmy's acknowledgement that the man accompanying me today could be trusted, unlike my parents, beloved or not. Now Hans and I were in a platonic relationship our aim would be to discover the 'truth' behind the missing painting. There was no need for names, no need for Hans to meet Fiona, she was but a small cog in a larger wheel. Once everything was settled Jimmy and my father would come home. One to my open arms, another to the questioning that years of deceit merit. Deep in thought I did not hear Hans say 'Thank you' to the woman darting in and out of the hidden premises, or the muffled music in my pocket that denotes a recorded phone message. Instead, I grasped his hand, as together we climbed back the way we had trod earlier.

--

Later that Evening

Arriving home as the church clock struck seven o' clock I was amazed to smell the spicy odour of a tomato pasta bake. Reclining on the sofa, glass of wine to hand, Mother glared as a wolf scrutinizing its prey.

"I was beginning to worry."

Basking in the past two hours of convivial conversation and laughter at which Hans and myself had finally secured, I was not about to enter the Gladiator's arena to fight; certainly not with a woman that had already downed half a bottle of wine. Flinging my coat across the chair I make my apology–

"Sorry, bus was late."

"Is that it?" she mumbled, splashing the drink onto my beautiful velveteen cushions.

"Yes. Pasta smells good."

"So, the thing should. I have been cooking it for an hour."

The glass wobbled as she drew herself upwards.

I have got to level with you here – Mother does not allow herself to fall into a state like this unless a new problem, or an on-going problem warrants her attention. From past experience I know one must tread carefully if the blast from the ship's horn, otherwise Mother's temper, is not to blow at full speed.

"Shall I dish that inviting pasta?"

Indulge her.

Mother stirs, totters toward the kitchen, slams her glass down on the table, points to the white envelope laying there.

"From old Richardson, blast him" she croaks.

I smile, say nothing, but cannot believe how like Fiona she sounds (Mother would hate that). I lift the letter, read the date franked in the right-hand corner– April 27th. As calm as possible I say-

"Why did you not mention this letter yesterday?"

"Why?" she screeched.

"It may concern something important. You have not even opened it!"

I pulled it apart, read the letter inside, laughed out loud.

"He wants you to inspect the bank's papers. What a feeble excuse to get you to his side."

I laugh louder and add, "If ever there was one."

Mother scowls.

"Silly man, does he think your father has ran away?"

Good thought: 'No'

Bad thought: 'Why not?'

Mother had managed to lift the pasta from the oven, place it on the table, then pour it (somehow) onto the plates she had found on the draining board.

“What date has the commander insisted upon?” her bleary eyes matching the floppiness of the form pulling out a chair to sit on.

“Thursday 10th” I said, eyeing the brown hardened edges of my tomato bake.

“A week,” she stated, spooning a heap of pasta into her lipstick smudged mouth.

“A week” I sighed, knowing she would demand my presence.

We settled on munching our way through overcooked pasta, Mother too busy concentrating all her effort to balance her food with the wine to stop and think what her daughter had been planning. Maybe, and I write this in a tentative fashion, if we had discussed my day events the future could have panned out differently: that is on the conception that I relayed ‘everything’ to her, especially as I was teetering on the trust word.

Hearing the music playing from my phone I realised it was still in my coat pocket.

“Is that the radio?” Mother asked, her mouth chomping pasta.

Now, while it was funny to see my socially climbing mother in that mood of ‘tipsy’ behaviour, I could not, and would not, sit here to poke fun at her expense. I made my way into the lounge, sought my coat, still unremoved from the arm of a chair, felt in the pocket, and produced my phone. Bringing up the text the name ‘Fiona Grubb’ ran before my eyes. ‘Great’ I mused as my fingers tapped the ‘read’ button.

‘Did you get my voice mail? Have not heard from you?’

Calming my irritation over her text play, I think voice mail?

Fingers pushing buttons at a speed the wind would envy I listened to the squeak of the girl’s voice–

“Miss Bryant, must, will say it again, *must*, talk to you. Pick a day. This *must* be the last time.”

Three ‘musts’ – How lucky am I?

I switch the voice mail off, considering ‘What now?’

“Rhia,” the sound crashes from the kitchen.

I rush back in, stifle my laugh as I spot Mother on the floor, pasta covering her moaning face as she kicks the chair she slipped from. Hastily I text Fiona back–

‘Thursday 10th’ at bank’

then crawl on all fours to where Mother lies in a flurry of tomato pasta.

Thursday May 10th

The bank is frantic this morning, customers rushing through the doors in vast numbers. Mother and I sit, in our space opposite the reception desk, scanning this busy world with avid interest. The past week had procured for us days of relentless hibernation due to the wet weather having not the slightest idea when to stop. Sleepless nights when Mother's concern over not being able to contact Father drove her, and myself, to distraction as consistent ringing brought no relief. Savvy, who had not appeared for two Sundays, much to Mother's angst, left that woman groaning and grumbling to such an extent that I thought at one stage Mother would leave this painting hunt to me whilst she boarded a plane for Bhutan.

Now, that would have been worth being a pack pony for a day!

Within our front row stalls, I mean these seats in the bank, I try to count the 'ants', people to normal minds, running in and out. Please show no surprise to my stab at humour. It has crept upon me due to being far calmer thanks to continuous funny faces sent via my phone from Hans Parker. His way, according to the guy himself, of enlightening my mood, encouraging me to laugh with him. Sitting here my head zooms left to right, almost in that image of a spectator at a tennis match. Suddenly, I begin to giggle, nod my head toward the man heading our way. Mr Richardson, adorned in the most lavish of suits, hair slicked back, and the largest of smiles one can imagine. Looking at this man instantly reminded me of a shark; those fierce carnivores seeking a shoal of fish to devour. I nudge Mother's arm. The quick twist of her head in his direction, then back my way, tells me this lady is set for war. I wish him 'Luck', for as my father could advise him, never think Mother is an easy victim, her tongue will sting, and her teeth will bite.

Accepting the 'sharks' greeting, a generous "Good morning" for Mother who stands to walk to his office, and a sarcastic "Work awaits you" for me, I deny Mother's supplication to follow her, not wishing to draw on my past excuse of the toilet break once my snoop arrives with coffee. Shaking the resplendent fascinator atop her sprayed hair Mother vanishes around the corner, and into Mr Richardson's office. I sit, alone, uncomfortable, gazing in the direction of the staff room. Can it be that my 'agent', a kindness on my part to call her this, and not something more derogatory, is not in work? That I do not believe, especially as this job is her lifeline (her words not mine), yet her desk is abandoned. I wait… five, ten, fifteen minutes, finding myself willing the girl whose job it is to run in and out of each office with trays of liquid redemption, in her task of alleviating boredom, to suddenly appear. She does not.

Sensitive to my concern the prim woman that had finally arrived to staff the reception desk slowly walked my way, backside wiggling, air of self-importance preceding each step.

"Miss Bryant, can I help you?" the voice sounded a little strained.

Throwing her a look that indicated 'I am important', she completely ignored it.

"I was hoping to speak to Fiona Grubb" I managed to say, deliberately forgetting the 'please', so this woman understood my position.

I wait for her response. Nothing, in fact her attitude sharpens.

"Fiona? Oh, the dizzy kid who should be running this desk."

"Yes," I answer, strangely annoyed at the woman's remark.

"Ah, she (scathing tone) has been scheduled to wash up for the day."

She has got to be joking. The look upon my face must have said it all.

Without hesitation the woman moves, wiggles that backside quickly across the polished floor, through a door at the far end of this mausoleum. After a wait of another five minutes, she returns with the Grubb girl peeling yellow rubber gloves from her hands.

"Apologies Miss Bryant, I disturbed her in the middle of a sink full of suds. Fiona, pass those gloves to me. When Miss Bryant has spoken to you do not forget to collect them, silly girl."

The woman wiggles her way back to the desk, thrusting her head toward the ceiling with an arrogance known only to those who believe they are far above someone of lower rank.

I will not insult this diary with the words crossing my mind.

I patted the chair beside me. Fiona lowered herself, watching the tiny security camera slowly brushing a lens across the reception area. Catching my glare toward the clicking beady eye the girl retorted –

"We will be picked up."

I could tell she was fearful.

"Tell them I was enquiring into your placement here."

She snorted "You think they care. No, I believe they are suspicious of me."

"How?" I scoffed.

"Since this," she whispered back. "Not sure whether I was spotted."

The hand nearest to my thigh pushed a piece of paper in my direction. I instantly sat on it, pretended to read the girls palm (do not ask!) "What is this?"

"Her address" she whipped her hand from mine, looked around her as if the walls had miraculously grown ears – "The Detdy woman supposedly lives there."

"What?" I could not believe what I was hearing "Why did you write the thing down?"

Fiona winced "For you."

"For me, do you think I am thick?"

"No," she stuttered "I did not want to forget it. I thought you would be pleased."

"Pleased?" pause. "I am, but you do such stupid things."

Fiona flinched, let her sulky face show her displeasure.

At this point in my diary, I must question why teenagers believe they have been dealt the most undesirable card in a pack of thirty-two. Because they do, their retorts follow this belief, as I was about to find out.

"Tell me, Miss Bryant, why are you such a snotty cow?"

The shock on my face was enough for her to run to the reception desk, grab her gloves, and head to the staff room. The sight of my mouth gaping open as a goldfish in a bowl brought the wiggling backside scurrying from the desk.

"Whatever is the matter Miss Bryant?" she screwed her eyes in Fiona's direction.

"Really, has that girl upset you?"

I glared, heard the faint rustle of paper beneath my thigh.

"Err, no, nothing of the sort. Our conversation was work, just work. I am cold."

"As long as the silly girl has not upset you."

"Not at all," I force myself to smile.

"I tell you, that girl thinks herself far above her position, gliding in and out the boss's office with coffee. Maybe she thinks that will bring her promotion."

The woman leans my way–

"I say dream on, girl, I am first in line."

The woman flapped her hands in the way a park keeper would 'swoosh' the birds from a pond. Her disgust with the girl was blatantly obvious; suddenly her condescending attitude toward me hidden beneath the contempt of gossip.

Struggling not to show my blatant dislike I managed another withering grin as she whispered in my ear–

"Between you and me, Miss Bryant, that young lady will be gone soon."

"Why?" the question flew from my mouth, if only to get her overbearing smug expression and wiggling backside back behind that desk.

"Funny business," she said in a hushed voice. "Constantly taking coffee to the boss. I am sure woman to woman you will understand."

She twitched the side of her nose. It hit me, that sudden realisation. This woman believed the kid and old Richardson… I stifled the laugh gripping my stomach, forced the most serious look I could find–

"Really. Oh dear, wait until my father returns."

"Exactly," the woman mouths, standing upright, and moving her swaying backside back to her den of spite.

I settle into my chair, my fingers trailing down my thigh, relocating the paper beneath, warm to the touch, causing excitement to course through my veins.

--

The way Mother walked from Richardson's office you would presume the world was crashing in on the beloved human population it took such great care to deny and divide. In truth, Mother's feet stormed more than walked, flames of conceptualized fire roaring from her nostrils. Having removed the paper from under my thigh I found myself ordered abruptly from the chair. That alone told me a monumental argument had taken place. The wiggling backside rushed to the door, almost curtsied in her hurry to hold the door open.

"Out of my way."

Mother's command rung through the bank, eclipsing the chattering noise from customers and the gibbering of screaming children. This was not good. Something had seriously gone wrong.

Outside the rain had ceased, allowing a watery sun to blink on those chattels below. I took a deep breath, my own excitement pushed to the back of my mind. How could I approach whatever had occurred in that office remembering my own resistance to accompany Mother into what now I must label 'the lion's den'.

It was easy to see that small refusal was a 'bone of contention' within itself. Bracing myself for the most imperious onslaught I was shocked, as we walked along the street to a café on the corner, to hear Mother laugh.

"That will shock the slimy weasel into knowing exactly where he stands."

"He cast his eyes over you?" my query was hardly audible.

"What?" she sighed. "Oh Rhia, wrong conclusion as usual."

This annoyed me, for concern (mainly that refusal to accompany her into the man's office) had outweighed any other conclusion I may have made.

"You were snorting fire."

"Great, I am equal to those fictional dragons of your childhood."

Yes, but the comparable distinction suited my description.

Holding open the café door Mother slid in, her disgust at the overpopulated eatery plain. Noticing a table by the window I quickly sat down (I love windows) pulling a 'shame' face at a small child heading the same way. Mother 'plonked' herself on the chair opposite me, still chuckling, still amused at whatever had occurred in that man's office. Catching the waitress's eye, her hand expressed the need for liquid.

"That man," evident she was referring to Richardson, "presumed to tell me, Henry Bryant's wife, what to do."

She cocked her head on one side, presumably the sign of importance.

"Fool, I will relay any orders given to me, not him to me."

Confusion grew. What orders? Surely this meeting was about money?

I perceive myself to be facing the same situation mice find themselves in when enticed by a cheese cube, dash for it, only to discover the cheese is fake: a delusion of the real product.

I watch Mother's self-satisfied expression, edge carefully, then ask–

"I thought this call to the bank concerned our finances."

Mother abandoned the quiet laugh, re-modelled her features to display a more serious tone.

"Yes, yes it was. Indeed, that is what I meant," she thought before continuing–

"That man will never command me," extra breath, "where your father's money, or anything is concerned."

Her head whipped round toward the window as the waitress laid the coffee down on the table.

I sat in silence moving the froth covering the dark brown liquid to the edge of my cup. It is time to find humour!

"I will look like those coffee beans."

Flat – try something else.

"Maybe I was wrong not coming into his office with you."

My turn to pretend to laugh.

"Why do you say that?" she expostulates. "It was easier on my own."

"Your face did not motion that when I refused."

Mother made some sort of noise that I took for a cough, "I was startled, that's all."

Still peering out the window she brushed my comment away, convincing me that her journey to the bank this morning had absolutely nothing to do with money.

Deciding to leave that subject 'aside' for another time, I pleasantly tripped my tongue round a variety of nonsense to which Mother would find equally endearing. She was just about to get into a lengthy discourse pertaining to certain designs, and their creators, when she suddenly trilled–

"There is Count Reinbach, heading toward the bank."

Pointing across the street in the direction of a grey suited man carrying a briefcase toward the bank.

"He must have business with Richardson," her voice trailed off.

"How brilliant," my admiration was evident, "someone such as he should choose a small provincial bank whilst he is here not a large metropolitan one."

Her green eyes widened– "Why?"

Honestly, this woman must know the 'in' and 'out' of everyone's business.

"Shall we wait for the Count to finish, then call him over? I like him Mother."

A look of horror played across her face-

"No, Rhia, how beneath us to shout. Leave the poor man to his deeds."

Idea foiled.

I thought to argue, to remind her how clever this man was when it came to art, and how exceedingly charming he spoke. Yet it appeared her attention had been taken by something else.

"Mother, what are you staring at?"

"That car," she answered. "Look, over there Why would he park there?"

Across the road a white sports car had promptly motored to a standstill, parked on double yellow lines without a thought. Apart from being a traffic road ‘sin’, those lines that had been introduced in the 1960 traffic road act, were to stop vehicles parking and causing congestion or accidents in certain busy areas. I felt my stomach constrict as I stare toward this sleek car. Why was this car trailing us, or to pinpoint another aspect – could it now be trailing the Count? I do not understand.

“Can you believe it,” mother was saying. “The driver will get booked.”

Most customers were nodding. Her next admission surprised even me.

“Rhia, does that car belong to Count Reinbach? Is it here to collect him? Someone must advise him about our traffic laws.”

I shook my head, the frown of disbelief edging my brow.

The tables around us were agreeing, raising their tea, coffee, even glasses of pop in Mother’s direction, at which this woman was basking in their regard. She laughed, dipped her head in thanks, drained her cup.

“Perfect specimen of a car all the same.”

Her voice penetrated my silence.

“I doubt it is the Count’s car.”

“Why?” her favourite word again.

“I don’t know.”

How weak my response sounded among the jubilation of Mother’s declaration.

No sooner had I breathed my rejection of Mother’s statement and the Count emerged from the bank, minus his briefcase, and wearing dark sunglasses. He headed toward the car, spoke to the bespectacled driver, then climbed into the back seat.

I sank into deep despair.

Sunday May 20th

How many ways can you count the ten days that have passed since my initial shock over that white sports car? These days have given me headaches, tension, hours of endless fathoming, and I suppose it is only right to pen, an inkling of joy. The headaches and tension can be clumped together, and you will not be surprised when I mention two names – Mother and Fiona. Yes, those wiry advocates in my life. Mrs and Miss Gloom and Doom I shall call them; their antics unsurprisingly always unclear, and their secrets mounting by the day. I have begun to believe that double trouble haunts me. Where one problem springs up, another may follow. Anyway, for interest of information I will report on these predicaments–

Mother – Certainly found it her duty to inform Savannah (who was around once more), of Count Reinbach and his relaxed attitude toward this country's traffic laws. She, in her turn informed Hans, mainly in my opinion, so his aunt could warn the Count before the police decided to do it for her. Did I agree? Yes, in a roundabout manner, although I thought we should have called him over, and told him ourselves, besides I needed to know about his connection to that car, which may not even be the car across my street, but the same design and colour.

Breathe–

Next – Fiona Grubb, and would it startle the readers of this diary if I reported this girl was on the telephone blubbering out her woes relating to her job? Moaning she wanted 'out' my father's bank, and 'into' a sister bank. Honestly, who did she think I was – Houdini? Besides, I have not sifted out the information she gave me, so to be honest that girl is going nowhere.

Please, do not give me that look that connects me to the wicked stepsister in the fairy story. I am positively being kind to her.

Inkling of joy – Savannah has informed us that Han's information on his 'so called' family and their colleagues will most certainly lead her in the right direction, and eventual arrest of those members who so far escaped the German authority. She cannot praise him enough, and therefore neither can I. This warms my heart– Platonically of course.

I will move on–

According to Fiona's snooping, Etta Detdy resides in Coventry: a city of which I have no knowledge. The address on the paper reads –

'14, Provost Gardens, Memorial Park, Coventry'*.

I have never heard of a Memorial Park, let alone the gardens mentioned.

Wondering how I will get there gave me two nights of whispering into Jimmy's guitar (please, do not utter a word) while Mother purred through slumber as a cat who had been overfed. That was until 'joy' entered my despairing life. Henceforth, my inkling of joy. Out of the blue Hans rang, a subdued excitement in his voice. Our conversation was as follows–

"Hi, Rhia, speaking at last" – anybody would think we had not spoken for years.

"Good to hear you" – restrained.

"My aunt has invited yourself and Mena to her Midsummer Ball in Coventry."

"Coventry," my appellation rang down the phone.

"Yes," he crooned. "Why, do you know it?"

Collect breath, slowly, slowly–

"No, but it sounds very posh."

"Maybe," he faltered. "Say you will come. She will send out invitations."

"Come," the word rushed from my lips, then controlling myself. "Thank you."

"Cool, great, oh, Lord, I cannot wait to see you."

"Me too."

What am I saying?

Hans hesitated, gabbled the next sentence: a flurry of words that signify the depth of thought he had procured to get to this point–

"Rhia, (here we go) I know our promise was to be working colleagues,"

I could hear the rush of his breath–

"Can we meet?"

I felt the stab of guilt trickle through me, the fight beginning deep inside.

"Sorry, I am being unfair. Please, forgive me."

"Why not?" I said softly.

Hans hesitated again, let the pause between us say more than our lips ever could.

"Really? I will plan something," his voice was low.

"Accepted," I mumbled.

The 'Goodbyes' were continuous, as was the self-reproach.

Wednesday May 23rd

I watched the hands of the clock meet at the number twelve, relaxing in the newly acquainted sun lending its beams to a very dull flat. I had opened every window wide, stretched out as a lion cub on the hottest piece of grass it could find (for me the sofa) enjoying the peace this beautiful morning had granted me. Mother had obtained a cancellation spot for her hair, did not think twice when taking it, and left me to my own devices, which was to do nothing.

At first when I hear the mobile ring my peaceful thoughts switch to the Grubb girl, then jump, faster than a hare scampering to Hans. Excitement impossible to control swept over me–

"Hello,"

I breathed deep, determined to refuse my mind leeway into my building emotions.

"Hi to you,"

The voice penetrated my indulgent fantasies.

"Jimmy?"

I sat upright, heart fluttering up and down in the way of a trapped butterfly.

"Who else?"

He laughed, I panicked.

"No-one silly"

The conviction was not there.

I could hear the teeth rattling. That nervous disposition when something was amiss.

"What is wrong?"

Full attention.

He laughed– "Nothing. Your father and I need you to do something for us."

Solemn will be the word I will use to describe his mood. A part of Jimmy I was unfamiliar with.

"Anything. Can I speak to my father?"

The teeth rattle more. This is unlike Jimmy to be so disturbed. I knew something was wrong whatever he said.

"Sorry, sweetheart, he is really busy. A very clever man"

The sigh that left my throat was pronounced, an exhalation of breath that announced my deprivation. Jimmy was speaking–

"Have patience, Rhia, all will be settled. Now, to this task we need. Have you met a Count Reinbach? The man is an expert on art. A man your father and I believe could help us in the search for the painting. He has contact with buyers, knows many an artist, it would help us immensely if you could involve him in the search, but please not your mother or that woman that claims she knows your father,"

The name passed my lips in a flurry of disbelief.

"Savannah D' Mill?"

He let out a whistle –

“That’s her.”

I was astounded.

Moving to the window I found the hottest spot in the sun’s rays; anywhere to still the sensation of ice running through my veins.

“Father wrote to her, got her to keep an eye on us,” I spluttered.

“Did he? Evidently, from our chat last night that woman betrayed him on his last mission in Germany to a Major working in the Stasi.”

My world was growing darker–

“What? I saw the letter she wrote to him indicating her to help us.”

“You thought it was him who wrote that letter.”

The pain of subterfuge was staring me in the face.

“What?” forcing that word through my lips I cried, “Hans Parker?”

“He belongs with us,” a pause, then, “trust him.”

I shivered. Did not my grandmother say mortals collect only the sorrows they can bear. Really Mattie, I am afraid in my case that is far from the truth, unless I have stepped into a parallel universe where the secrets of life play on a continuous theme.

Jimmy was humming something indistinct.

“Mother will not be pleased” I sigh.

Further teeth chatting, pushing my nerves to cry out in pain–

“Ignore her, tell her nothing, your father will sort it out when he comes home.”

This is the guy who times past reprimanded me for speaking rude to my mother, now frowning on her every deed.

“Listen, Rhia, we are near the last stretch of the search I promise you. Soon you will be with me. I can hold you. Now, any information you find, let me know. Yes?”

Talk gabble. He could not have said it any quicker if he was imitating the London bound express train.

“I will,” the return was low, then, “I love you.”

Jimmy clicked his teeth, blew a funny kind of kiss before that standard cut off tone.

I stood in silence, the shivering of my body paramount to the confusion of my brain. Had Savannah D’ Mill wheedled her way into my life with Mother’s approval, and on a more serious note – Was Hans Parker aware of her guileful plan?

--

Afternoon

Savannah D' Mill's Surprise Visit.

In she glides with the demeanour of a bombastic mother hen; eyes blazing rockets, ruby penned mouth ready to discharge. the pink floral dress, worn on her lissom figure, an advert for this beautiful May afternoon. Mother, whose rush from the hairdressers etched on her red cheeks, had crashed through the door demanding we tidy the room for a surprise visit from the D' Mill woman.

So, here we stand, both awaiting this arrival in different ways.

"Savannah," Mother preens. "You grace this flat with your presence."

Both women burst into laughter, raise their hand, and give that accustomed 'high five' they find so hilarious. I nod, neither extending my hand, saying 'Hello', or doing any of those perfunctory habits people do when greeting each other. The woman overlooks my snub, instead flouncing to the window to search the street below.

"Something wrong?" Mother inquires, joining her friend leaning across the sill.

She nodded "I must report a tail."

"A tail? Where? Who?"

Mother was alarmed, followed the finger discreetly pointing in the direction of the corner.

"There."

Pretending to chat in a normal manner Savvy removed her phone from a pocket hidden by the folds of her billowing dress and typed in a string of numbers.

"That should sort it," she said, heading back into the room to sit. "Two minutes and my colleagues will be here – Boom, tail gone."

She released that tinkling laugh I had once found so fascinating.

Wafting the pink creation to spread across the seat of the chair her red mouth asked – "Now, you two, what have you been up too?"

Mother's hurry to speak first would have been hilarious if I had not begun to suffer a panic of conscious. What had Jimmy said– These women could not be trusted.

"Oh, this and that. Mainly the bank."

Mother pouted her lips, pretended to cry. They laughed (their antics are boring me).

"You, Rhia?" her eyes moved my way.

I shook my head. Words that before today would have poured into the room to meet this woman's questioning were gathering in my throat, but now in the form of a bonfire rocket. Jimmy had warned me to share nothing.

"You are very quiet, Rhia"

I tried to act flippant, worried as I was over Jimmy's revelation. If left to me, would this be the moment to counterattack, throw the names 'Guy and Helena' into the ring, witness the shock of horror, or simply ask 'Why are you both lying?"

Yet, if I brought my knowledge into play my liaison with the Grubb girl would be finished, for Savannah D' Mill would exploit me to find out my source, and the girl would be taken away, and interrogated.

Dramatic? Possibly.

I need to lie. Be resilient in my answers.

Slowly, with a conviction I did not feel I answered-

"Small headache. Nothing to worry about. Any news?"

"About what?" she asked, her stare never wavering.

"Whatever you have come here to tell us."

Savvy patted down her pretty dress (yes diary, I feel deliberately sarcastic), eyed Mother and myself as if any moment she would crush us under her shoe, before starting what I will call her disquisition.

"The past few weeks have been spent sorting out historic assignments your father and I served together. At various locations I found people willing to say more now than back then."

'Betrayal' my mind screams.

"Although I am not willing to disclose those missions, they are tied in with the painting we search for."

'Pinch of salt' I silently mumble.

"Now, as you already know your father wished me to keep an eye to your activities…"

I smile. She turned to face me–

"Hal understood your determination, to the point that if he was here, his main concern would be to warn you, that painting is bait for a deeper movement: a ghost from the past. Something that occurred within a past assignment."

Your unscrupulous behaviour I muse.

Mother, who up to this moment had not joined in, heaven only knew why, edged her way to balance on the arm of the chair-

"You are worried?" spoke quietly to her friend.

"A hundred times over," our guest replies.

The women turn their faces toward each other, anguish spreading across their fine features–

"That man?" Mother's voice was hoarse.

Savvy nodded, fear creeping into those beautiful eyes.

"Henry will be…" Mother's question diminishes as a tear is stifled.

Savvy takes her hand as I quip–

"The man you would exchange tomorrow for your credit card."

Honestly, if looks could kill.

Mother brushed past me, hurrying into the kitchen where the kettle was filled, and clicked 'on'.

"You do not understand," Savannah D' Mill snapped.

"I understand this," my pitch was high. "You both treat me as a child."

"Then, do not act as one."

How dare she – How bloody dare she.

I glare, eyes for eyes. Deep inside me that force named spite was growing. How much did these two women know about Etta Detdy, and could she be the reason for Jimmy asking father to help him over me; the solitary piece within a jigsaw, once found, that completes the whole picture.

"I have discovered information," I state, not once removing my gaze from hers.

"Information?" Mother repeated, swaggering from the kitchen.

"What information?" Savvy asked not removing her exploration of my resentful stare. I stretch my palms out signalling my reluctance to co-operate.

"Nothing really, just that the painting may have been re-painted."

They shot each other a look–

"Who told you that?" they simultaneously chirped.

"Oh, you know, *my* source."

"Who can that be?"

I had vexed Savannah D' Mill.

"Not sure," I hastily spouted. "Someone on my travels."

Both women reminded me how a flapping hen would act – Okay, Mother was the person spilling questions, running to collect tea, and fretting over no biscuits, whilst the spy among us locked onto my agitation with another shake of her head.

"Rhia, you are treading dangerous ground. My extra visit today is a warning. Please take care. Any information you gain pass my way."

It was my turn to laugh. A double request in two days.

Now, the game begins.

Part Three

Brandenburg-Gorden Prison, Germany

The grave smile on the sullen cheeks gave the man's worn pallid face resemblance to those ghostly skeleton masks created for parties of a sinister nature. It had been many a month since his tired mouth had broken into anything as near the smile that was playing on his lips today. Not even a visit from his young comrade had moved him to feel half of the pleasure he was experiencing at this moment. The plan was in motion. The painting he had 'renewed' was resting in the wings for its 'Grande' reception. How did he know this? His mother on visiting day, or should he say the ghost of the woman she once was, had given him the thumbs up. No words, for who needed words when actions completed the task. The stupid guards had thought she was signalling their help: their embarrassment was raw when she lied over a 'twitch'. The man inwardly laughed all the way back to his cell. His only regret – his absence from the room the painting will finally be displayed. He would give his chance of freedom, anything to be in that room when those snobbish jackasses come face to face with his creation. The noise certain people will make as their ignominy will be plain to the world filled him with delight. Can his poor emancipated body take such delirium?

Conjuring up that image he had painted helped him repel the disgust felt toward his incarceration. Time within these walls grew longer, cold seeping into his bones, movement restricted. The man winces with pain as the smile broadens, his mind recalling how those brushes caressed the nude he was painting, graphic in every detail, an expression of lust and hate. This game he had played since his youth was part of the larger plot; a plot that he, a soldier of that old regime would follow with his life. That red-haired minx, immortalised in paint would lead to the larger prize, the like that her fantasising brain was unable to comprehend. The man sniggered, holding his stomach from the pains of hunger, the pains of loathing. He would succeed where his father had failed, ingenious as that man was. They would work together to retrieve what they had lost. He, the son that loved him, would be the password for unlocking the crux of his father's revenge.

The man rubbed his arms and legs, willing the pains to cease. He swore these pains had grown worse since his cell had been searched, spending extra hours locked up. The solitary walk, when the weather permitted, hardly alleviating the sword piercing his heart. He thought of his comrades. How sick he felt at the dwindling body of the faithful, the majority being transported further afield, while the few changed sides. How he would like to confront those turncoats, witness their fall from grace when his father had finished with them. Mind, and here he must admit, there was an odd moment when freedom, bought by a change of regime, was tempting. The man moved to that small window, let his gaze search the boundary that rolled beyond this place. He must not think like this, be tempted so, his father would lambaste him with his own bare hands.

The yelps that accompany abuse filled his ears. Another comrade fighting removal. The large, well fed frames of the guards swam before his eyes. How they tried appeasement, forced the non-resistance position upon their prisoner with the help of a stick. He could feel the fear, acknowledge the pleas as they were dragged past his cell. The man spluttered a long low growl, the smile vanishing. These dogs, who had the cheek to call themselves guards denounced their prisoner's family; took the love shown for that family and pressed it underfoot into the ground. He had been taught love was a discipline, an order within a family. Was that not why his uncle died, ignoring the family order? If only he was stronger. He would show all usurpers where they belonged.

Moving from the dirt ridden window he slumped toward the cell door to hold the rusted iron grilles, praying they would keep him upright. He strained his eyes along the dimly lit corridor, heard the expletives of comrades left behind. One voice in particular rung in his ears. The last time he heard it was the day he changed his painting. This prisoner was, at one time, his father's batman – Ottmar. How was he locked up within these walls? His father had him covered, unless… The man's smile returned. Those fools had imparted how a faithful servant had 'vomited the truth': they were relating to Ottmar. His 'truth' was lies; deliberate, calculated, pre-planned lies. This man would never betray his father. In another life the two men would have been brothers, true brothers, not like the spineless man who had held that appellation. With each curse the man heard the swift movement of a boot, or the thump of a fist.

"Keep heart and faith," Ottmar was calling in English.

"Shield and Sword," he croaked back.

The guards kicked the doors hard in a bid to silence their prattle.

Damn them to hell.

The man thumped the wall, a recurring habit day after day, his knuckles holding testament by the scars they carried, his swollen fingers misshapen and sore. In his mind, the man imagined those digits writing interrogation forms, abusive documents where these guards could be brought down under his father's justice for the traitors they were. He knew many had spied for the West when the wall was in place, holding both sides to ransom with their information. On the wall being felled these men grovelled, begged for sanctuary, accepted a pardon that placed them in jeopardy from a regime on the run. The man was aware his father knew everything about these men, their families, their friends, even their whereabouts. The second croak that left his throat was more painful, stretching his lungs to their full capacity. He knew his moment was drawing near: the sweetness of revenge within sight.

--

The first day of June had settled over the prison with a warmth the man welcomed. Penetrating the window of his cell, the sun had cast its rays onto his bed, and for the first time this year his body had responded to heat. Stretching his stiffened limbs to the capacity of his pain the man indulged in a satisfied smile, forcing his mind to wander.

At precisely ten o'clock this morning the governor of this prison had commanded the guards to bring him to his office, where he received the news he was to be moved. At first, on entering that tightly secured room, he was convinced it was 'bad news'. News that would hurl his world and his plans crashing to the ground. The man was unsure how he would react if he had been told of his father's capture; thrown into a prison deep in the East, or worse, they had executed him. The pain of holding his breath had torn at his lungs, causing him to cough until he believed those lungs would burst. It was not until the room had been cleared, and the governor had collected his thoughts that he pronounced the reason for this exchange. He, the prisoner this governor had selected, was being moved, deep within the depths of East Germany, now re-unified with the West. The governor had assured him all would be well, for he had been informed, this prison was where his father's plan really began. 'Say nothing' he had been told, for the shadows hold those who might betray him. The man knew this to be true, for had his young guard not been betrayed. How, that was beyond him, as each passing of a letter, or slipping one back, had been completed in secret, or so he thought. He had been taken away screaming in agony.

Easing himself from his bed he stumbled to that window, the square mucked lined glass that was his view of the yard below. His gaze focused on the men below, sweating from the beating sun that had replaced that consistent rain, crawling with a despondency that filled him with anger. Many he recalled in uniform, stalwart in their commitment; handsome young men who held high his father's principles. He let out a howl, the call of a lone wolf, heralding his pack to him, chilling the hearts of those men whose guardianship he hated. Likewise, for the last time, he slammed his fist into the wall. Once, twice, the third, breaking the skin, a trail of his blood staining the bricks, leaving his mark. He cursed his own foolishness for doubting, as the howl turned to a scream, and the guards rushed in to lock him down. They transferred him to the detention cell, his wrists bound together, his arm the means to sedate him.

--

The days ebbed and flowed, staggered on in monotonous boredom. He was fed, washed, and monitored by a hulk of a guard, who showed little respect, and less patience when questioning him. His disbelief that the governor would allow this treatment was verified upon being told he had been sacked, taken into custody for questioning. The man who had taken his place was no sympathizer of the abandoned force. Their quest– information, of which he refused, and they relentless of his ills, conducted endless interrogations. He held his tongue, revealed nothing. Fools, he belonged to the best, and his training was something he was never likely to forget. After a week, which to the man implied a lifetime, they removed the hulk, and replaced him with another guard, younger than himself. Releasing the wrist ties the guard had thrown him emollient for the lacerations, and tablets for the pain. Standing over him, watching as the trembling mouth swallowed the pain relief, his captor planted an odd kick of his boot, or twitch of his stick, pummelling the man's bleating frame with his fists of steel. Unmoved by the silent tears streaming from the prisoner's eyes, and the deep cough hacking the thin body, this onslaught continued as days turned into weeks and desperation filled the tortured mind of the victim often to be found scrambling around the floor.

By the second week in June, the heat robbing the small amount of sanity the man clung too, he heard the boots of an approaching travel corp. He knew from the quickness of their step, and the rapid breathing, they had come to remove him. Nothing these guards had bombarded him with had worked in their favour. The beatings, the savagery of their words, their useless taunts of mockery, all had been in vain. Swinging the door open with a 'thud' the men approached the figure sprawled across the floor. Kicking him they shouted–

"Steh auf, bewegan" – Get up – Move.

Not waiting for him to comply, they dragged him to his feet, pulling, pushing the limp frame in the direction of the door. Down the corridor they heaved his body, not listening to the man's pleas, out into a courtyard, and the blazing heat of the sun. Screwing up his eyes, he bowed his head, felt the sensation of mucous slowly drip from his nose, streaming across his lips and chin, dropping to the earth in globules of snot.

The doors of a van opened, and he was thrown. No ceremony, no care. His head bounced on the floor, staggering the light hurting his eyes. He felt the manacles on his hands and feet snap into place, restraining any movement apart from his aching head. In the yard beyond the van doors a raucous was taking place. Unfocused as his eyes were, they disclosed several soldiers gathering around a dark-haired man, grasping what he assumed was money.

"Dort," his head nodded, whispering 'There' to the guards sitting either side him.

"Wer ist das?" – Who is that?

The guards laughed – "Bruder"

He stared, forcing his red rimmed eyes to focus better. They had said 'Brother'.

"Bruder?" the man echoed.

"Ya," they agreed. "Madchen, rote Haare."

The man stared, as a guard closed one van door.

"Witz," they laughed again.

The man did not laugh.

Closing the second door the words 'Girl, red hair' whirled inside his head, then 'Joke' followed by their contemptuous laughter. The van sprang into life, moving at a speed that would frighten any ordinary motorist. The guards were laughing, counting their money, looking his way, and nodding their heads. They had been paid to move him, paid to carry him East. That carried his father's signature. His brother, the willing servant. However, the joke, that was a different matter. He had made Hans promise not to touch her. The man drew a painful gasp, held onto the seat they had strapped him onto, as the vehicle upped its speed.

Waiting for the laughter to subside he tried to relax – Impossible.

He may be weak, his body wracked with pain, but there was a determination in his thinly veiled voice –

"I will kill you Hans – Believe me."

June 2001

Wednesday 6th June

Will you believe me when I say the flat is in an uproar.

Mother is complaining, whining would fit my description better, that she has nothing to wear. Reason: Alys Parker's invitation to her Midsummer Ball – white fluted card, silver writing, small delicate silver bows of ribbon attached to the edges, and an extra card to reply. They are sitting on the coffee table gleaming up at us with the probing eye that would match an Elizabethan spy master (cannot help myself), and for Mother this invitation has become such a 'big' deal. I will point out social climbing. If she announces one more time that many a person there will hail from the art world, and we may discover a lead to Dragner's Crux, I will scream; besides her itchy buying fingers are on the move, searching for something new to wear. I suggested she sort out an old gown, worn in the past for Father's gatherings. Anyone would think I had scurried her name, let alone made her feel tardy.

Oh boy, let me sit in the naughty corner.

For my own outfit I considered various trouser suits I own. Anything really, but it must hide my own art, and decrease the weight I seem to have gained. It is obvious I have been snacking, too many Easter eggs, too many cakes. I blame this on Father and Jimmy. Their fault my life has spun out of orbit. I need extra vitality to handle the shocks and orders Jimmy especially keeps plying me with, and if that means cakes and chocolate, so be it. Well, that is my excuse. Seriously, in future months I must lean my mind toward a short diet. Naturally one that does not deprive me too much. How would I cope?

Anyway – Trouser suit + Mother = not in agreement. When mentioned she let out a wail you would expect from the mouth of a petulant toddler, gasping that I belong to the 'social disgrace' group; everything from flouting convention to disregarding Alys Parker's feelings.

Talk duplicity.

It appears she revels in it. Not enough to conceal Father's past, or her intrigue with his faithless partner, she is stepping into *their* world as a magnet – But for what? All I know is I must play this game to the best of my ability. Mother must never guess Jimmy is fully aware of their deception.

We set a date to scour the shops for 'gowns' – Wednesday 13th. Great. Wish me luck.

One week to change Mother's mind.

Wednesday 13th June

Did I truly write that I had one week to change Mother's mind about scouring the shops for a new dress?

No luck!

So, my motto will be – Do not step on cracked paving slabs, do not walk under a ladder, and do not stare at a black cat. It is the thirteenth after all.

Oh, Diary, what is wrong with me?

The number thirteen is no more related to bad luck than any other number. Besides, it is a Wednesday not a Friday. Truthfully, I have far greater concerns than a superstition. Mother has gone crazy, and I mean craz-zz-zy. If these feet walk past, or into, just one more dress shop I will faint. My heels hurt from the low strappy sandals I have worn (why miss a fantastic sunny day), my back aches from slopping around, scrambling through row upon row of 'gowns', and finding nothing; not to mention my poor stomach, held to ransom with oodles of coffee, packets of biscuits, tiers of cakes, and, to top it all, in that order, prawn sandwiches for lunch. Let the word 'nauseous' run through your mind, and you have the whole picture. Now, while your humour may think of this woman sinking to her knees in food and drink, your heart needs to think of the many dresses Mother has held up for me to wear. Red flowing chiffon, blue low back silk, black sequined figure huggers. Spare one small moment to consider my generous curves in these garments of splendour, and do not utter a word, or snigger, I know my limits. Yet, if Mother believes that stuffing oneself without thought, and shopping until a person 'flags' is the perfect answer for impressing someone, can I realistically say it is my duty to question her judgement?

Around three thirty on this miserable day, two sad faced, overfed women, emerge from the latest 'upper class' franchise. Settling on no purchase for herself or her daughter, Mother had turned her attention away from colours, and more towards the concern of how little flesh I should display. Fair enough, I could understand her worry, it was probably irrelevant to mine, yet to be reminded every two minutes was equivalent to a wet fish being rubbed into my face. In other words, I felt it to be downright insulting. However, my mother was an ace when it came to 'stropping', as those wide-eyed assistants in the last boutique had just discovered. Gathering her jacket and handbag in a storm of protest she had crashed out onto the street in what I can enigmatically document as a thunder cloud raring to 'clap'.

Heading homeward with no purchase?

I watched as Mother strode forward, my spirit collapsing into a puddle on the ground. It was then an idea, wonderful to my way of thinking, entered my head.

"Shall we look for a quiet café, far from the beaten track, to enjoy a last drink before the journey home?"

Mother scowled, "This is not an expedition Rhia."

Wrong Mother, that is exactly what it is – a peregrination (cool word, means meandering journey). Let us go that step further and write, a tiring peregrination, mmmm, cool.

Mother patted her hair, fussed over her suit, reapplied her lipstick would you believe, pursed her mouth in a perfect 'O', before commanding me to "Lead on".

Stepping into an alleyway (always a bad omen for me) we tread carefully over dirt and stones until we reach a row of shops awaiting to welcome us. This is part of the East End of London, vibrant, busy: overflowing with curiosity. Trailing down these back streets was not accepted with grace on Mother's part. Her consistent grumbles into 'who may see her' and 'no large designer shops' halted my process in front of a retail outlet that had become dear to my heart: a charity shop.

"I have found many an item of clothing here, Mother, at a price within my budget."

Mother's face crumpled, shot back into place with sheer horror, hardly allowing those shinning lips an opening to mutter "Here?"

"Here," I said hiding the sly grin dancing around my own mouth.

She moved closer to my side, tittering words of–

“They sell used clothes. Nothing I could possibly want.”

The slim figure started to retrace her steps–

“Follow me, I am sure there must be an acceptable coffee shop somewhere.”

I ran after her, touched her elbow, requested she gave the shop a chance, for my sake. Mother sighed –

“Honestly, I know you find this comical, and yes, I will accept your witticism as a slap at my pride, but I can assure you we will find nothing for such a grand evening.”

“No harm in looking then,” I threw back.

With protest leaving her throat at the rate of nautical knots we stepped warily through the door to the sound of a clanging bell.

--

Mimicking the slave who had been led into the lion’s den Mother eyed the rails of clothes before her. Different sizes and colours hung in rows of their tag price, winking at us to ‘delve’ in and rummage through them. Holding her stiff body at least a metre from the rail Mother picked through the dresses as if problems, of whatever form, could transmit themselves onto her hands.

If only I had a camera with me to store this moment for perpetuity – the social snobbery anchoring itself to every part of her body, the fornication of pretending to look whilst wishing in her heart to be traversed elsewhere, the discomfort of being seen through the window – I could continue.

I glanced her way, caught the manicured hand brush the suit she was wearing, a repetition of her former condescension. How could I even think this woman, embedded in her haughty social world could recognise the joy of entering a charity shop and discovering a ‘treasure’; that rare find that would set the wearer apart.

I noticed the slight movement toward the door, made apparent by a couple also leaving the shop, hands gripping the bags of clothes they had just purchased. Almost running to the counter tucked into the corner of the shop I let my fist bang down onto the flat round bell. Surprised at the noise Mother turned. From behind a curtain that led to an outer room an assistant crept. She was small; a jolly woman possessing the broadest smile to melt the hardest heart.

“May I help you?” spoken in the broadest Jamaican accent I had ever heard.

I followed the fitted black skirt upward to a bright yellow t shirt, stretching the thin cotton material across her large bosom, up to the folds of her double chin, stopping at the welcoming beam on her mouth. Older than first supposed I noticed tiny lines inching their way around the warm brown eyes, framed by her brown curly hair, offset by a puckered pink mouth, and sparkling white teeth.

"My mother," I stammered. "She needs an exclusive dress."

The woman shot a glance toward the door, brought her attention back to me–

"Size twelve, on the rail dear, over there," the head nodded in the direction of the dresses.

Mother sniffed, "Come, Rhia, I have seen nothing to my taste."

The large brown eyes glowed–

"You find nothin', ma'am. I could sort you a gem."

"A gem?" Mother gasped. "Among these?"

"That I could."

The woman walked around the counter to the rail marked size '12', scrambled among the dresses, and produced a damask glory of bright green.

Mother shrieked, "Never."

I could sense tension growing as I oozed–

"Wonderful. Do you have that in my size please?"

Mother, who by now had stepped a trifle nearer to the counter laughed out loud –

"Do not be silly, Rhia, you will resemble a sprout."

Furious, fuming, flabbergasted – I shall certainly buy it now if the woman has it in my size.

"Yes," the deep voice rang out. "Size '16' I presume," she chuckled.

"Correct," I whisper, "I will buy it."

Handing me the garment as she passed in a torrent of 'tuts' and eau-de-cologne, the woman edged her body behind the counter once more. Out the corner of my eye I could see Mother about to make some barbed comment, pausing only to let the robust assistant claim–

"I have something Madam (sarcastic emphasis) may be interested in."

Darting behind the curtain the woman returned a moment later smothered in the folds of a huge white sheet. Eyes glowing in the dark face, her white teeth shining in the rays from the afternoon sun, she started to remove the cover. Swivelling the dress in her hand, the woman raised her face toward Mother, those features adorned with an almost paradisiacal smile. Displayed in all its glory was a low backed strappy black silk and georgette gown, studded with crystals and tiny pearls.

"Madam may wish to try on?"

I had never in my life been witness to my Mother's confusion for words. Staring at the beautiful creation twinkling before us it was apparent how snobbery was attacking this new desire within her, an argument between mind and the heart. The silence lasted five minutes, when her rankled voice rang around the shop.

"I do not think so," Mother hesitated to state her point. "It is second hand."

A sound of disbelief wheezed from my throat in convoluted spasms. Mother eyed the assistant, who had no qualms of eyeing her back.

'Battleground' here we come.

Holding the gown in front of her our assistant spoke first–

"Exactly," she pressed. "It is second hand, but if it were new, Madam (again the emphasis) may not have been able to buy it."

Wow, I like her.

I felt the previous gathering of thunder in Mother's demeanour rolling around as she suppressed the backlash rising. The woman once more uses that radiant smile as a shield–

"If Madam looks inside, the label will reveal the name 'Vionnet'. This wonderful gown was designed by Madeleine Vionnet, the French designer born 1876 – 1975. It is true her fashion house closed in 1914 due to World War 1, but it re-opened afterwards, enabling her to join the leading designers of Paris.

Again in 1939 she was forced to close, bringing about her retirement in 1940.

Famous for her designs cut on the bias, Vionnet dresses are a 'gem' if discovered, such as this one. They are gold dust."

The brown eyes continued to twinkle; this lady certainly knew her designers and their history. Edging Mother out of the dispute, knowing exactly what she was doing, the woman twisted the gown this way and that, an enticement amid a day of bemusement.

I registered Mother's incapability to speak for a second time, her arms dangling at her side as our assistant led her to a 'cubby hole' behind the curtain. Hearing the shuffling of feet, plus the gasps of what I hoped were real appreciation I waited in uncertainty.

How can ten minutes drag to give the belief of an hour?

Suddenly they emerged, and the words 'vision of beauty' crowd into my mind. The gown, cut on the bias to highlight the nipped in waist and fitted bodice, cascaded over Mother's figure; the sparkling crystals and pearls rippling in the way a waterfall gushes into a river, the black silk and georgette material unifying mother's shape. My eyes ran down the long semi cathedral train at the back, glowing with jewels.

"Beautiful," I was choked with emotion. "I am sure this gown is worth all your gratitude."

Running her hands down the length of the encrusted gown mother reverted to her former self.

"I will give you fifty pounds."

The woman, whose eyes and lips had risen with triumphal glee blinked, saw the horror cross my face, and replied in an undertone filled with pride–

"I believe Madam knows the gown is worth far more."

Swords drawn.

I stood, unable to move, the hanger of that green dress sweating in the palm of my hand, amazed at the fire simmering in the woman's eyes.

"Sixty pounds," Mother heaved.

"Please, Madam, it is a Vionnet. It will not leave the hanger for such a puny amount."

'Victoire' I think the French would say.

Mother was 'spitting coal'. I know this is a slang expression, but at this moment I really do not care.

"One hundred and fifty." Mother's tone matched the small ball her fingers had curled into.

This time the woman mouthed 'Higher.'

I could not believe this.

"One hundred and eighty." Mother's aggressive lips snapped.

I cannot write how excited I felt.

'Mother', cannot contain myself, was fighting within herself. This was a charity shop find, yet that stubborn heart was in a duel with the snobbery displayed in her daily life. Believe me, this was one show I would not have missed for the world, and dishonourable you may call me, but my feet stood firmly in our Jamaican assistant's court.

"Two hundred," my brave warrior added.

"Pardon me," Mother gasped. "This, this is a second-hand shop."

The woman raised her brow, brought it together in a scowl.

"So?" those white teeth rattled.

"So?" Mother threw down the gauntlet.

This was fencing on a grand scale, inflaming emotions both women were concealing. Think suffragettes, and I will applaud.

Time to step in.

'A referee?' you will query

I must submit to the question because what is obvious from my perspective is – Mr Richardson (note my politeness) is going to pull his hair out whatever occurs today, for Mother will have that famous 'melt down' if she does not get this gown.

In truth – I am in a 'no win' situation.

Moving further forward, not crossing the counter boundary, I speak directly to Mother.

"This lady appears to know her fashion. Instead of playing cat and mouse we should pay the respectable price."

Turning to the assistant I find myself inquiring–

"Have you gloves and headdress to match please?"

The fight in her eyes dies a little–

"Yes, long black gloves, and a crystal encrusted feathered headdress.

They match perfectly."

I smile, "Brilliant."

"Three hundred?" the woman cheekily suggests.

I have seen my mother startled, but never like this.

"Three Hundred," she whimpers. "It is a charity shop."

I let out an over exaggerated wheeze, place the green dress on the counter.

"Of course, Mother I forgot. We will leave it."

I began to walk away, the woman not quite caught up with my plan sighs at her loss, Mother's confused face scanning my retreating back.

"Stop, Rhia," an agitated catch in her demand. "I will agree the gown is beautiful," a rasping noise. "It is second hand, but if I must pay…" another objectional note in her voice. "What about the bank?"

I twirled round, "I am sure you can talk old Richardson to help out, " eyes twinkling.

Mother made the sound of irritation, "You win."

The woman moved quickly, not one for allowing a good sale to pass her by.

"Shall I pack both gowns?"

Mother conceded defeat. Within minutes my dress was layered in tissue then bagged. As we patiently waited for Mother to change that beaming smile expressed a 'Thank you' at which I reciprocated back.

Battle Won.

Victory to the East End I record.

--

Stepping outside the shop I filled my lungs with the wonderful breeze that had decided to bestow itself upon us flagging humans. Inside the closeted shop air had been minimal, with no air conditioner, or doors left open. We had easily spent an hour arguing over a gown that Mother now carried in the way a security guard would transport a money case from a van to the bank, tentative, possessive, certainly with the vibe of 'if you dare' running through her determined eyes. The woman, whose large smile had not left her face during the few moments it took her to fold and pack the gown into a box, bagging it not in a charity bag, but finding a huge white carrier bag and tying the handles together with a maroon ribbon, thanked us profusely, much to Mother's dismay, and although the money given had scarcely honoured the designer's name, the woman herself was satisfied. Nevertheless, it was good to be free from the claustrophobic atmosphere.

As we trod slowly across the sun-drenched pavement the feeling easing its way into my heart is genuine pleasure: mainly for Mother's significant find, and secondly for 'getting up her nose' with my own purchase of that green (sprout) dress. If this sensation was not enough to last me throughout the rest of this day, you can imagine the thrill that flowed through me when a voice I had come to recognise called my name. Shielding our eyes from the sun I smiled as Count Reinbach crossed the road to greet us.

"Ladies, how wonderful to meet you here."

Mother smiles, I gush, "What are you doing around here?"

"Looking for art," he laughs.

"Not many of those shops or galleries in these parts," Mother sighed, a return to her high and mighty attitude.

"Oh dear," the Count looked contrite. "I thought they may have the hidden gem."

“Not here,” I laugh. “Unless you believe the painting has fallen into the hands of East End pirates.”

The Count eyed my smirking face, laughed out loud, and added–

“Not at all, it does not matter, I have met you both.”

Searching up and down the street I could see no white car waiting or parked, so concluded the man was on foot, enjoying the sun, and truthfully hunting for art. Anyway, as I have already penned, how did I know if the car spotted often sitting at the corner of our street was not just another version of the same brand? This man could never be deceptive. His eyes were pools to his soul, open and honest. Raising my hand to brush hair from my eyes I said-

“Actually, I am glad we have met you. We may need your help.”

His features showed surprise.

“My help? Anything, my dear. A friend of Alys and Hans is a friend of mine.”

The velvet sound caused my heart to skip. Mother was becoming restless.

“It is really warm, are we ‘up’ for a drink?” I motioned toward a café further along the street.

“ ‘Up’ for a drink?” his face screwed up with confused lines.

Mother shook her head–

“I apologise for my daughter, she presumes everyone speaks her language.

Would you care to join us for a drink?”

The Count agreed, I seethed.

We found a small wine bar around the corner from where we had stood. Through the inviting frontage was a passageway into a garden where tables and benches had been scattered throughout. We chose the nearest with an umbrella. Sitting down, Mother laying the precious gown on the seat between us (mine was laid on the grass at my feet) she motioned to a waitress hovering to collect orders. Our thirst was great, so long cold drinks of lime laced with soda were agreed by all. The Count removed his sunglasses, admiring the beds of flowers.

“I do believe your country to be stunning. Its scenery, women and art inspire me.”

The sincerity in his tone soothed my troubled mind. Ignoring Mother’s implied hand on my knee, no doubt to slow down, I ploughed straight in.

“Count Reinbach, we need to find this painting of Dragner’s Crux. Can you snoop for us?”

His eyes fixed on mine, creating tingles I cannot explain. Mother said nothing.

"My dear Rhia," his gaze fell on Mother, "I am a connoisseur of art, not a 'snoop' as you call it."

Mother wriggled in her seat. I felt the pain of embarrassment grip my throat.

"I do believe my daughter is asking, 'Will you help us find this painting?'"

The Count raised those penetrating eyes; icy blue globes devouring our own.

"For you, Mena, is that not right, and you Rhia, I will leave nothing unturned."

I squeezed Mother's hand laying on my knee.

"Thank you," I gulped. "You will not regret it."

"No," he said, "I will not."

His attention reverted to the flowers, the weather, the joy of meeting us. I sat fascinated, entranced by this man, and indubitably his love for art.

What is the saying – 'One can swim in another's eyes-'

That is true, for I could have drowned in his.

Sunday June 17th
Evening

There is a saying that when 'one door closes, another opens' – I find these words awesome, not only because I believe them to be true, but also they stand for my life, whether that second door is good or bad. Another saying which I must admit shadows my days equal to that turn of phrase already mentioned is – 'You wait ages for a bus, then three turn up at once'. Today, both phrases became applicable, metaphorically speaking. A quick call from Jimmy left me with a feeling of loneliness, after the guy informed me there was 'no way' himself or my father (latter seems to have fallen off the planet) would be home before Christmas. I found this ridiculous and downright infuriating. How can I get my life together when the person who holds all my answers, by that I mean my father, is searching his way through another country, ignoring my complaints of mother's invasion into my home; and for a reason unknown, avoiding every chance to speak to the daughter who needs his advice?

Door closed.

Mind, it was good to hear Jimmy speaking even if he fled after fifteen minutes. I suppose there had been time for me to tell him I loved him, notwithstanding his phone line crackling and breaking up on return of his reply, yet if I could follow my endearments, I would be down that wire, wrapped in his arms, passion aflame. Wherever they are staying the communication needs to be sorted.

Release guilt That is better–

I must own up to moments during our chat when Hans's image pummelled my brain, that night in February still haunting me. Guess it always will. However, no sooner had I replaced the phone than my mobile rang again. It was Count Reinbach using the number written down for him at the end of our drink session. He called to inform Mother and myself that he had stumbled across the most important clue where the missing painting was concerned. Due to his busy schedule, plus our invitation to Alys's Midsummer Ball, would we consider it rude to discuss it then, and not now? Seriously? Impatience came first, then the humility of how kind that man was, so we (Okay just me) agreed.

Result – Door open.

Mother and I spent the rest of that afternoon waiting in a fluster of plumped cushions and small cupcakes for our mediator to ring the bell.

I write 'No show – No call.'

The surprising fact – cakes and kettle waiting patiently for a beloved hand to seize them, while Mother stands ready with an imaginary ruler for the gorging child (me) to dare pick one up and pop it into my mouth. I was amazed, after all her work, that Mother was so compliant to Savvy's absence. Did she know? Had this been planned? What act of mistrust was being forged now? These questions, and more, rolled over and over in my mind, enticing me to puff and groan, until eventually I was given the 'green' light to at least demolish four small cakes – For my mental state you must understand. Just as I was about to devour another I heard–

"Hello – Do not worry Savannah, we more than discern your problem. Take care. We will see you in July."

July? That means the woman is burrowing her nose deep into spy territory.

"Savannah," Mother said in the most unruffled manner. "She cannot visit today."

"Really, Mother, the woman is a nightmare. Can you not see that?"

"She works hard, and you must not de-cry her. You have no idea."

Door closed.

Noting the buzzing emitting from my own phone I snatched it up with the reluctance of one who was tired of answering–

"Yes," the cry was loud.

A whimper of a cry. Lord, it was the Grubb girl. Picking up on mother creeping I jumped to my feet, and pointed toward the bathroom–

"Must go."

Kicking the bathroom door closed I snarled–

"What the hell are you calling me for?"

Another whimper–

"Oh, Miss Bryant, do not be mad. I have news."

Senses alert–

"News? What news. You gave me that address. I presumed…"

"Dangerous thing to pre… whatever."

Cheeky kid. Why does this girl annoy me?

"Miss Bryant, are you there – Are you there?"

"Yes," I fling. "Where bloody else?"

I could hear the tremor at the back of her throat.

"I overheard old…" she corrected herself "Mr Richardson speaking. Actually, he was whispering on his mobile," she took a breath.

Bad things were running through my mind.

"To whoever was on the other end," – whispering – "Discussing our woman Etta Detdy"

She stopped talking to gather breath, allowing space for me to leap in.

I screeched, knowing her answer before she gabbled it–

"Just exactly how did you hear?"

"Well, I was in his office cupboard, the walk in one"

For goodness' sake – "Why?"

"Well, I was supposed to be tidying. He must have forgotten me."

Her third long breath. 'That's easy' I thought, and if the 'well' word is used one more time… "And?" I said through clenched teeth.

"Ah," she continued. "Well, (scream) that is it. He muffled something about Etta Detdy. She's that painter's aunt."

"What?"

"The painter. You know, for goodness' sake, I have told you."

Everything this girl came out with held my sensibilities to ransom.

Not wishing to tell this little chit more than I believed she was worthy to know–

"Maybe," turning the sink tap on, fast.

"Well, old Richardson shut the cupboard door."

"On you?"

"Well yes, who else?"

Keep calm, remember her age–

"Is that it?"

The poor girl stuttered – "Yes, I heard no more."

Gently, my kind of gently, I probe–

"Do you suspect Richardson may think you heard him?"

Fiona made that sound I believe dogs use when an offender backs them into a corner; a whining noise, filled with alarm.

"I dunno, Miss B, I dunno. I had papers round me when the door was opened."

More panic –

"I need a switch, Miss B. One day he *will* catch me, then I will swing."

Miss B – Miss B? I could hear the water slapping around the sink, sense the electricity collecting within me. I steadied my voice, spoke with command=

"You will be fine. Just keep your eyes and ears engaged."

There was a lull; a lapse when the head knows more will follow, and the mind prepares itself for the onslaught.

"No, Miss B," the trill acts as a skittle through my mind. "You do not know what's it like here. No-one likes me. They think I am knocking off the boss."

Mother would faint at this girl's terminology. My thoughts are seeking an escape route, spinning out of control: names and places chasing each other in their determination to torment, yet elude me – Aunt – Dragner – Painting – Father – What does it all mean?

"Miss B?" the girl is spluttering, moaning, crying in unison with that hammer and anvil in my head.

I speak–

"Fiona," hard, unrelenting. "Please, get yourself together."

"They think…" she went to say again.

"I care not what those silly women think. We must keep going. Do you hear me?"

Her sniffling passed, and the moaning ceased in her hurry to believe me. I had no reason, at this moment, to suspend that trust by informing her I was lying to her; promoting staff around the system was beyond my power and changing that wiggling backside's damning thoughts were beyond my capability. I could almost feel the rigidity leave the young girl's body, her gushing reply almost consuming me within its grateful yearning–

"Thank you, Miss B… How can I repay you?"

"Eyes and ears," I gush.

"Yes, but…"

'No more,' my banging head pleaded. I need to sieve through this information in the way nineteenth century gold diggers used a mesh bottom pan.

"Goodbye."

My termination of the call was abrupt, no doubt leaving my young snoop gaping down the purring receiver, forcing me to lean over the rushing water to turn the tap off.

"Welcome to my world, Fiona," I murmur. "Bus Number One" and left the bathroom.

No sooner had I stepped into the lounge than Mother's hurried figure rushed toward me, arms flapping as though she was ready to take flight.

"Thank goodness, Rhia, at last."

She pushed her mobile phone into my hand–

"Take this I need the bathroom. It is Hans. He was unable to get through on your phone, so he rang mine."

I grasped the device, held it to my ear saying, "I was busy."

"Chatting," he laughed.

"Yes," I hissed. "Do not tell mother."

"Why?"

"Jimmy," first name to mind.

"Right, is that good?"

Did I sense doubt, or maybe jealousy?

"You sound peeved" was his next comment.

I inhaled as deep as possible, releasing the pent-up emotions building inside me.

"I am," was my quipped answer.

"May I ask 'Why?'"

"Jimmy's absence for one, information received for another."

No criticism or opinion.

"Go on."

"Evidently that Etta Detdy I told you about is Dragner's aunt," a quick intake of breath. "Oh Lord, Hans that makes her your aunt."

The buzzing on Hans's end of the phone was so loud I thought the connection had broken.

"Hans?" I called "Hans?"

His voice –

"Sorry, I was searching through notes I had discovered about the Dreyer family. Nothing concerning an Etta Detdy. Where is this information coming from?"

Fiona's mumbling coursed through my mind. What is it the sages say –

'*A problem shared, is a problem halved'*.

If I name Fiona, the girl no longer remains my private 'spy'. No, as before the whereabouts of my informant stays with me.

Hans' voice had changed slightly, a fluctuation in his meaning–

"I have an aunt Rhia, and as you have seen, the woman is nothing like they impart. Whoever is giving you this information is fooling you. Please – who is this person?"

The words 'tug of war' enters my head. Yes, the kid drives me to distraction, but for a reason I cannot even explain to myself I must keep her secret.

"An old colleague from uni."

His sigh said it all – You lie.

An awkward silence followed, until Hans mumbled–

"I need your trust, Rhia."

"I know."

"Well?"

Jimmy had begged me to trust this guy, and I do, besides what else I try not to feel, yet I find myself suspicious of everyone. What is waiting for me within the shadows of this hunt? That key my father has thrown away, and I, his daughter, intend to find. An unexplained flutter wound its way through me. Hans was talking–

"I must go. It is impossible to meet with you just now. Trust me with this latest information. I will sort it. One day I will explain. Oh, my aunt's Ball, I will collect you both at ten o' clock on the morning of the 23rd. Agreed?"

I could tell he was upset. Trust had been found wanting.

My retort was an automatic "Yes."

Click – Gone.

I place Mother's phone down on the table, begin to move toward the bedroom mumbling "Bus Number two."

Waiting for Mother's emergence from the bathroom I noticed a text message highlighted on my own phone. Pressing the screen, I was surprised to read Father's name–

'Hello, my beautiful girl. I am in your debt for whatever you discover, please–'

About time, yet strange.

It is as though something else caught his attention, and the text was sent before he finished what he wished to say. Also, that is not his usual text font, father has never been that fussy. Let me see, I scrolled through the fonts, stopped when my eyes fell on Berlin Sans, giggled as I thought of his implication. He was reminding me of '89' and that trip to the wall. He knows I will help him.

A voice floated into my ear – Mother's voice-

"Was Hans arranging our journey to his aunts?"

I jump.

"Yes, Mother"

"Why so jumpy?"

"You crept up on me."

"Hardly."

She 'tuts' at the suggestion.

"Anything else?"

"No, should there be?"

Mother thought for a second.

"You sounded ruffled."

Eavesdropping.

"Ummm, Bus Number Three," I say without thinking.

"Pardon?" the puzzled face scowls my way.

"Oh, nothing," I say in haste. "Just silly nonsense."

Mother grunted as she retrieved her phone from the table, headed into the kitchen flinging that monotonous word "Coffee?" I think of Mother's puzzlement and my own hurry to say 'nothing'; a word with strategic cost when linked to certain situations. Funny, how a flippant assertion, like the nothing and nonsense just used, could turn out to be the most damning understatement of the year.

Saturday June 23rd

Midsummer Day

Dear Diary, I have known years when this country's weather has resembled a rollercoaster in fast motion, for example: it rains, the sun comes out, it rains, thunder descends on us, and finally we have snow in spring. All this, our stoic population has dealt with in their spirit to 'Carry on, we're British' frame of mind, even though I am certain we have suffered the rains of the Amazon, such as now, at the middle of the year, when girls should be parading flimsy summer wear, and boys scurrying here and there in shorts, we find ourselves in a game called 'Find the sun, if you can'. For explanation I will offer the topsy-turvy weather of the first six months of this year: Rain, snow, wind, rain, rain, and more rain, abetted by sun, hot sun, rain, and today patchy cloud and sunny spells. For goodness' sake, I am sick of thick jeans, woolly jumpers, and eating to lift my mood. I have no doubt that I, Rhia Bryant, must be the only female not prepared to succumb to a summer dress. Astrologers are telling us that the planet Mars is in biennial retrograde. This fiery planet is moving backward, whatever that may mean. Can this be the cause for our weather and lives spinning out of orbit?

Worth a thought.

Delving into my computer yesterday I discovered that Midsummer Eve, was recorded in the early church as a prelude to prayer: a Christian observance for the following day (today) known as Saint John's Day, in honour of the martyr Saint John the Baptist. Originally noted as a holiday, this day was centred around the summer solstice, where feasts and celebrations were held to herald the earth's forthcoming hot days. Oh dear, 2001 has perished, or been forgotten.

I will resist further grumbles over the weather. It cannot change the pattern of my life, and I must prepare myself for Alys Parker's Midsummer Ball.

--

Coventry

The three church spires of Coventry loomed before me like candles on a child's birthday cake. These veritable statues of history, St Michael's standing 295ft, Holy Trinity at 237ft, and the octagonal steeple of Christ Church, the smallest at 230ft, invite many a potential visitor to discover their story. St Michael's would become known eventually as the city's cathedral, suffering devastating bombing in the second world war, spearheading the design of a new cathedral by Basil Spence and Arup to be re-built side by side with the ruins of the old cathedral, the foundation stone laid by Elizabeth II in 1956, and consecrated in 1962. The old and the new stand together as holy ground and an inspiration for a city's rise from the ashes. Holy Trinity also came through the blitz of the war, but due to the vigilant effort of the priest in charge Reverend Grahame Clitheroe, his son and curate, who slept within the church with hydrants and ladders, they defended the building from bombs, with the small loss of two windows and various cosmetic damage. The latter, a remnant of Grey Friars Monastery, demolished in the reformation of 1539, completes the triangle. These spires stand as resilience shown by this city throughout its history: symbols of unity and peace.

Hans had collected us, complete with our gowns and overnight bag. Evidently, according to our 'chauffeur' this ball, with its arty guests and free flowing champagne continues into the early hours of the next day, highlighting Alys's offer for us to 'stay'.

It is impossible to put my thoughts down on paper, suffice to say excited, yet apprehensive. We had zoomed down the motorway in a long sleek jazzy sports car, the wind in our hair, and the lamentable sun on our backs. Our companion steered this car at a speed I would rather not mention, as my mind was too busy praying the police were nowhere to be seen. It was a relief to see those spires, only to realise Hans was driving the car onto what was known as the Coventry inner ring road. We journeyed along several roads until my eyes caught the sign that announced Baginton. Instantly, Hans began to explain–

"This village was built around an old manor, a recording going as far back as the doomsday book under the name Badechitone. It was ruled over by a Lord, and in conjunction with most small villages Baginton was, and still is, noted for its public house– The Baginton Oak. Dating back 500 years, this ale house, like so many, maintains a myth. Our pub concerns a boy called Elliot who sat under an oak tree to make great decisions in his life. Therefore, what better name could a drinking house own, than the myth of this small village?"

Finishing his chronicle, Hans let out a wheeze of satisfaction. To me, pride had invaded every word of his narrative, yet it was obvious to me that Baginton village was extending its borders, and although I would still put it in my list of 'quaint', a typical English village where nothing happens, and the slow wheel of life turns at a measured pace, I decide not to call it 'small'.

Shooting up a driveway the car rasped to a sudden halt outside the most impressive house I could imagine.

"Welcome to my home" Hans said jumping from the car and calling his aunt.

Slowly Mother and I eased our aching limbs from the car, the tension of speed plus the forthcoming unknown had rendered both into that state many would tag 'mute'; as opposed to the woman who flew from the door and into the waiting arms of her nephew.

"Ladies," she tweeted. "Has naughty Hans drove too fast?"

Their muffled laughter irritated me.

I am sure the sight before her was a spectacle to behold, with Mother's perfectly moisturized face speckled with dust, and my carefully tied back hair tumbling across my face in strands of red fire. Our hostess disconnected herself from Hans engulfing arms–

"You look exhausted" she remarked "Follow me. Nothing a soothing bath and rest will not sort."

Mother thanked her, as together we stepped into the large sparkling hall.

Set out over three floors, this house was exemplary of that era known as 'Art Deco'. The striking black ornaments set against the pristine white walls and furniture, presented a backdrop for any painter struggling to find inspiration. The purity of the white venetian blinds against the crystal cut chandeliers took my breath away. This renowned art and design movement had overtaken Europe, Britain, and America by storm from the nineteen twenties to nineteen forty. Every house that was noted 'exclusive' displayed the fashion known as monochrome. Originating in France around 1910, the style quickly captured the hearts of fashion followers and art lovers throughout the world. I could imagine how Mother's gown would fit into this era, the gems sparkling along the charcoal carpet of the white staircase. How beautiful and stunning she would look. A momentary stirring pulled at my heart. Whatever Jimmy had found out about my mother, she was exactly that, 'my mother' and the moment she would descend these stairs I would find it hard to breath.

Hans, arms bulging with the bags and gowns we had piled into the car began to ascend those stairs.

"This way" he called, his voice that of a young boy showing off his ancestral home. We followed, Mother chatting to Alys who wandered behind us in the mode of an incumbent Duchess showing us around her mansion. Opening a door Hans signalled me to follow, while Alys drew Mother through a door already ajar.

"Your room, Rhia" Hans stated, dropping my overnight bag and gown onto the bed.

I could not believe my eyes. It was a replica of my room in that German hotel; its only difference was the colour scheme.

"The bathroom," he nodded to a door in the far wall.

I sped across the soft black carpet, turned the handle, exhuming a sigh of relief as the white appliances met my gaze. Kicking my shoes off I drag my cold toes through the warm pile, catching Hans' snigger as he watched my face relax.

"I know what you thought," he quipped. "Don't worry, there is no connecting door."

I sat on the bed, tracing the white patterned duvet with my fingers.

"Sorry."

Still holding Mother's gown and suitcase he bent and kissed my cheek.

"Trust, Rhia."

Saying no more he walked from the room, closing the door, and leaving me with a complexity of emotion.

--

Afternoon

How long I had spent reclining in the scent of bubbled water came as a shock when I finally pulled my body from the cooled bath, my poor skin on the brink of resembling a prune. Reaching for one of the large black bath towels reclining on a stool nearby I heaved myself out, and onto the mat covering the tiles. I swear this room is a replication of Versailles Hall of Mirrors – Wherever I turn a mirror greets me, therefore this woman must close her eyes in despair; an alluring clad female may aspire to such meticulous inspection, this prune-like creature will not. Throwing on a dressing gown I discover hanging on a rail by the door I walk into the bedroom, still pushing my toes deep into the succulent carpet. Someone had placed a tray with a sandwich and a pot of coffee by the bed. 'Thoughtful' was my instant thought, then a deeper, more curious disquiet of whom it might be, my gaze falling on a note peeking out from below the plate. Removing it I unfold it to read:

'Sandwich, my dear. No rush, we will meet at six in the garden. Alys'.

Disappointment gripped my mind. I had thought, hoped if I was honest, that we may have chatted sooner, her opinion on that painting one factor I came. My mind whirls around 'one', forcing any emotional torment to creep away.

I fold the note, drink my coffee, pick up a sandwich, and wander to the bedroom window. From here the reason Alys would wish her guests to meet in the garden was plain. Rolling lawns, herbaceous borders, roses creeping over arches, meandering their way through trees, pale buds entwining with full blown heads, inviting the dark colours of summer clematis to kiss their petals. Dotted here and there benches had been placed under weeping maples: secluded arbours where people can sit and talk. Honestly. I could go on, until my eyes roamed across the vast space toward a bench tucked beneath an arbour where pale pink roses cascaded down the wrought iron framework. I could see two figures deep in conversation, their heads barely an inch apart. Using my hands to shield the glare from the sun I tried hard to focus on the couple before me, finally settling on our hostess and a younger man, not her nephew. There was an intensity around them: electricity, vibes, whatever makes a woman grip a man's hand as if she feared to let him go. He, in return, sat upright, his head the only part of his body to be dipped in her direction. It appeared they were arguing. I stared harder, the crusts of my sandwich forming a barrier between my teeth and my tongue, that insatiable curiosity of mine squandering any prudence that may have stifled the squeal I uttered as another man came into view. I blinked, recast my eyes in their direction. I knew that man. He was the 'slob' who frightened me that night the Berlin Wall came down in 1989. Trepidation rushed through me. I was sure Savvy had told us all colleagues of Emery Dreyer had been imprisoned, so how… plus how did this woman, Hans's aunt, know him?

Hearing my squeal, the younger man stood, all eyes observing the part of the house my bedroom window was situated in. Alys waved in my direction.

'Act normal' my brain advised.

‘What is normal?’ my over excited heart flung back.

I was transfixed.

Peeping round the curtain I noticed the ‘slob’ staring my way. The younger man, twitching his large dark sunglasses, cast what I presumed, was an angry glance to the woman beside him. I could see – I must be wrong, but Alys is crying.

‘Shall I step forward and wave?’ ran through my mind.

Confused and frightened I nearly strangle myself in the rush to tighten the dressing gown further, that man’s beady eyes sprinting through my head. Emerging slowly into the sunlight I raise my hand, breath heavily as Alys and *him* acknowledge my action. The young man, without a doubt in a temper, flings his glasses into his hostess’s hands, and stormed off, the ‘slob’ racing after him. I was so busy thinking how, why, and who, my mind running around in the way of that legendary ‘headless chicken’ that it was not until I stumbled back to the bathroom that the identity of the younger man occurred to me. His hair, his features – I knew them. This time my heart not only skipped a beat – Oh, Diary, it pained in a way I could not begin to describe. That face belonged to Jimmy.

--

Evening

They say the mirror never lies – Take it from one who knows, it does.

I stand here, glaring into those mirrors strategically placed around this bathroom, and laugh at my own reflection. Wrapped in the green damask gown I had insisted buying I truly resemble the ‘sprout’ mother had warned. This ‘gown’ highlighted the weight I had gained, and the whey colour of my skin. My skin, I blame firmly on the shock I had faced earlier, and the continuous worry of ‘why’ my partner, whom I believed to be with my father, was here, in this house, mingling with the likes of that ‘slob’. I could mutter “Undercover”, but that would be stepping too far into the detective novel. It had taken me the power of Cleopatra (69-30 BC), the last Pharaoh of Ptolemaic Egypt, regarded for her super intelligence, (always like to show my history degree was not wasted), not to throw my clothes on and run downstairs to confront him. After a quick period of ‘Should I’ or ‘Shouldn’t I’ the thought entered my head that Jimmy could be here on father’s command, and that if (that small inconsiderate conjunction) the ‘slob’ saw I knew Jimmy, all would be lost, whatever ‘lost’ was. That is ‘if’ (please) it was Jimmy at all, for no sooner had I spotted his face, I close my eyes. On opening them the trio had disappeared – Whoosh, gone, leaving me disoriented.

There were several options I could have taken. For instance, to sneak from my room to Mother's, explain my dilemma, then ask her opinion. She may have been horrified, or simply told me to stop being silly. Asked 'why' (as always) should Jimmy be here? I may splutter "How the heck do I know", only for Mother to advise that our curiosity is put to our hostess. I would have to refuse for had not Jimmy told me not to trust her and voicing my worry could be part of her plan.

Next option – Hans. He may have been able to help my dilemma, even ask his aunt outright, better for him to venture down that road, than Mother.

In the end I reluctantly decide that the rule of 'mouth close, ears open' may get me further. So here this woman stands, presiding over the judgement of one problem, and almost hysterical over another, with nothing else for it but to keep a low profile, and find out if father *has* sent my partner here.

My heart must surely break into guilt filled pieces.

--

It had been no exaggeration how magnificent Mother would look among the setting of this Art Deco house. She descended the stairs at five minutes past six in a triumph of exuberant sighs. The gown was stunning, the shimmering tail fan lapping each step in the way an ocean laps the shore. Slowly, with the determined steps of one who knows she has captured her audience, this woman made her way out into the garden. I was amazed. In all my thirty years I had not realised how beautiful my mother was: a glistening night sky among the flamboyant women around her, all inundating her with compliments.

"Wonderful," Hans whispered in my ear. "Yourself too."

Feeling his breath upon my face I turned–

"Mother looks wonderful, and you are a liar."

His brow held a humorous scowl–

"Liar? Never, your gown is… different."

I took a deep breath–

"Different? Yes, and makes that small green vegetable look far more appetising?"

This time he threw back his head and laughed, something unreadable hovering around his eyes.

"Trust me, I love the taste."

Almost a murmur, yet instantly my fingers entwined the flowing strands of my hair I had shown no mercy with, brushing until they shone: passion and anger surging through my veins.

Steering me from mother's 'Grande Entree', we sauntered around the lawn, his hand resting in the small of my back.

"Close your eyes," he whispered again, this time his breath warming my ear.

The movement of being propelled up steps, through a door to be greeted with music filled my senses with an overwhelming desire to know exactly where Hans had led me.

"Open your eyes," he said with what amounted to swelling satisfaction.

My eyes shot open. I gasped, as the fairy tale ballroom surrounded us. In what was once the servant's kitchen, situated to the East part of the house the cut glass chandeliers glimmered in the mirrored walls, bouncing sparkling light onto the polished wooden floor. Coloured lights glinted in the four corners of the large room where figures depicting mythical tales inspired and delighted. Couples pivoting around the room to the small band at the far end of the room, laughed as their reflection in the mirrors doubled the dancers, and the magnitude of the room.

The illusion before me held me stunned with its beauty.

"Smoke and mirrors," a voice said behind me.

The deep sound caused me to flinch, my hand jumping out to take hold of Hans.

"Alys," my escort whispered.

"Go, Hans, find the Count. Rhia and I need to wallow in this fairy tale for a moment or two longer."

No sooner had he vanished than Alys walked further into the room.

Slipping her arm through mine she purred–

"I have left your mother to the compliments she deserves. Wonderful gown.

Outshines my simple creation by far."

The silver slinky gown twinkled beneath the lights.

"I see you like my fairy tale setting," she sighed her free hand pointing to the dancers still pirouetting around the room. "In this life that word may cover many things."

My voice faltered "Like? I think that word diminishes its beauty."

Alys's smile was wistful–

"I must apologise that my husband is not here. He has been called away.

Business, always business. My stand in host, the brilliant Count Reinbach"

Her eyes sought the approaching figure.

"Rhia loves my fairy tale setting," she cooed as he gave us that bow I find so comical.

"That is because her life has that feeling of unreality. Correct, Miss Bryant?"

I tried not to show surprise, for this man's perception outweighed his ingenuity toward art. Hans, who had accompanied the Count from the garden, called a waiter.

Drinks in hand we toasted Alys, this afternoon's exploits wiped from my mind.

"Dear Alys, you have such creativity, unlike us smaller mortals" the Count laughed.

Alys pretended to look sad–

"My dear Count," she scolded. "This young woman beside me has creativity in her blood."

I took it she was being kind over my gown and cringed.

"Beauty is in the eye of the beholder," the older man quoted with sincerity, his eyes conveying more than his mouth was prepared to speak.

"How true," Alys replied taking her drink and the Count's arm in one swoop.

In jovial conversation she steered him back out into the garden among her guests. The warmth from the hand on my shoulder causing me to flinch.

"Penny for them?" the voice mumbled.

Hans's face, barely a breath from my own, was staring at me, concern sweeping across his worried glare.

"Embarrassment of a very bad purchase," I lied, Jimmy's face threatening my sanity. I ran my hand down the green brocade dress–

"Bought in temper, worn in regret. It is heavy and warm."

"You look beautiful," Hans said.

I do believe he meant it.

For a second time he called over the waiter, whispered something in the young man's ear, whose blonde head nodded in assent, before turning to me–

"Shall we dance?"

Irrespective that my dancing was hopeless, and the clouds of this afternoon rapping at my thoughts, I agreed. Hans led me through the arched doorway and positioned us between the cacophony of dancers already engrossed in the soft lilting music.

"My aunt and the Count seem very fond of you."

His comment fell in time to the band's tempo. The faster we twirled, the faster he spoke.

"I know."

"My aunt would have loved a daughter."

I was lost for words. The happy family he was promoting was not the family Savannah D' Mill had mentioned.

"You and your aunt are close, but the family…"

Hans stiffened.

"She would never," he spluttered, then louder, much louder–

"Heaven help me, Rhia, surely that is obvious?"

Everyone was looking. I stood there: an island adrift in this sea of dancers, my gown a beacon to those rotating around me.

Hans was fuming. Snatching my arm, we forced a way through the mirage of gowns and dress suits, out into the hallway. Steering in and out of the gossiping women, many pointing towards the garden, probably tittle-tattling over the woman in that exquisite dress. Bored looking men, holding drinks in one hand, cigarettes in another, waiting for their partners to command them to duty. Almost running down a corridor to the back of the house, we came to a door marked 'Private' and stopped. Letting my hand drop Hans looked around. Content no-one was watching or following us he removed a key from his pocket and unlocked the door. Pushing me through the door he quietly closed it, re-locked it, and switched on a light. The room was small, a square boxed cupboard with one window shuttered by a black canvas awning. In the middle of this cramped space was a huge crate, covered by a white flimsy sheet.

I began to panic–

"What the hell. I thought you worked for the D' Mill woman. Let me out, now."

The fear building inside my throat exploded. His voice was raw–

"Do not worry, I am not about to ravish you," his anger was undisguised. "You, are such a simpleton that you cannot tell who you can trust, and who you cannot."

His pain was stark.

"My aunt took me when my mother would not keep me. Never did she fill my brain with their ideology. She has become my mother, not Ametti Dreyer. I think you should thank her more than criticise her, and to be really point blank, if you do not trust her, then trust me," he was struggling for breath.

The redness of his face frightened me.

"Stop your search for that bloody painting. After all, it is your moronic stupidity, driving you, and…" another deep breath, "and it will be your downfall. You must admit, Rhia, the word 'Numpty' suits you fine."

Temper or not I could not believe what I was hearing.

'Numpty' he had said– 'Numpty', the word Jimmy threw at me that night in Berlin. How did he – Where did he – 'Downfall' he said, Who the hell – This guy is Savvy's aid, her chosen messenger – He was *delivered* to me – although I was quite capable to snoop on my own. Well, I will tell him exactly what I think–

"Stop searching? Are you mad? Jimmy insisted I trust you. Evidently, he must be wrong too. How dare you call me a numpty. The last time that was thrown my way this woman showed exactly what she was made from. Savvy said…" I hesitated. "What is going on?"

Torment I cannot describe was clawing at my brain. Paraded in front of those dancers, struggling with my tears, locked against my will in nothing more than a box. Hans, the heat from his temper subsiding, went to put his arm around my waist. I took a step back–

"Forget it, I will scream."

He smiled–

"It is soundproofed, my friend. As I have already told you my intentions are honest. I have brought you here for a reason, but first, you will hear me out."

My fire balloon collapses.

Hurrying to the door he listened, waited. Satisfied, he returned to where I was standing.

"Be quiet" his instruction was formidable.

I could hear my heart pumping, the heavy material of my gown weighing me down.

"Do not panic," his tone was softer, "I was making sure we had not been seen."

"Would it matter?" I muttered.

"My aunt had to dismiss her gardener this afternoon after knowing him a long time. A fellow I called 'Jimmy's double', who was caught stealing the petty cash. If she knew I was about to show you her second upset of the day, it would break her heart."

Hans gave me no leeway for any questions, no sharing what I had seen.

"I want to show you something," there was an edge to his voice–

He moved to the covered easel.

"A Dragner painting, sent to my aunt from Germany. My uncle found it, in a gallery. Thought she would like it. Heaven knows why. My aunt loathes it.

What is about to confront you may change your mind about continuing the search."

He yanked the cover away.

The sound from my throat was a combination of pain and disgust. The painter had left nothing for an observer's imagination –

Portrayed on a bed of richly painted covers a nude reposed, stretched as a cat submitting to a rapacious hand. One arm had been positioned above the head whilst the other was draped across the fold of her stomach, the hand pointing downward to a sliver of silk resting between the crossed legs: an implication of a secret love affair, or unequivocal enticement. Full bodied, with round curvaceous hips and large breasts, the nude lay with a tantalizing smile across her ruby red lips, her green eyes beguiling those who look upon this oil to join her. The highlight of the painting, which set it apart from any previous portraits this artist had undertaken was the flaming red hair streaming over the shoulders to lay within an inch of a bright pink nipple. The depiction of a sultry, pleasurable plaything, smouldering lascivious hunger.

It was ME.

The cry reverberated around the room as a hand flew to my mouth. The word mortification had no bearing on my humiliation. I groped for something to hold onto, another hand: anything solid to diminish this torment. To liken the swathes of this heavy gown to a whirlpool, dragging at my body, pulling me down into that pit of mire would be straightforward, the truth is my shame had caught up with me: paint thrown onto a canvas, displaying the pitfalls of my youth. Was this a warning? What would my father say? As the sensation of an unguarded hatred and desire permeated around me, the man at my side spoke–

"I would not have put you through this, but it is important to presume he has another copy out there. This one may be the 'Crux', yet who knows."

I shuddered.

"Do you believe this disgusting image covers the canvas Jimmy and my father search for?"

"I do. It would be his mindset."

"What can I do?" the supplication left my mouth faster than I could breathe.

"If you continue, you must promise me that my aunt and myself will have your complete faith. We need your trust."

I shiver, think of everything Savvy told us, fight within myself over Jimmy's command, ultimately succumb to my insatiable curiosity–

"I need to know the truth," my voice sounds broken. "I promise."

"Good" he said.

My heart sinks.

Hans covers the painting over, the pure white sheet an antithesis to that ignominy beneath it.

"Please say my mother has not seen this?" I plead.

Hans shakes his head–

"Do not worry, my aunt will not display it. The main reason the Count has taken my uncle's place. He would have expected it to be shown."

The pain in my eyes preceded my query–

"Has the Count been privy to this abomination?"

I searched the face before me.

"No, Rhia, he has not. Only my aunt, myself and you, and my uncle."

The room spun. I clutched the man beside me–

"Please, promise me nobody will view it – Please Hans."

A lop-sided grin settled around his lips as he kissed the flowing tears one by one.

"I promise, my sweet friend. Say those words – you trust me."

I clung to him, returned his kiss: deep down a stirring.

"I do. My secrets are your secrets."

--

We creep from that room secured in our promise to trust. Hiding the shameful painting back in its crate, our companionship had forestalled further alarm on my part. The incident in the garden I had overseen had been explained, apart from that 'slob', and concerned with our immediate problem he had slipped from my mind. Stepping our way through the spinning figures of the Viennese Waltz we headed toward the doors leading to the garden where Mother, Alys, and the Count were congregating on the terrace.

"No waltzing?" the Count asks as we join them.

"Too dizzy," Hans remarked.

"I see," the man smiled, soft waves of his accent igniting that delirium his presence created.

"We thought to walk in the garden," Hans announced, eager to find seclusion.

"At the bottom of the garden there waits a bench surrounded by bushes. You will not be seen," the Count laughed expressing his meaning.

"Stop tormenting them E – Ellis," Alys appeared flustered.

That was the first time she had used the Count's name. How 'English' I thought for a Count from Austria: a moniker from his ancestors, or a parental quirk for something 'unusual'. Whatever his name the man had my vote for his alluring characteristics. I noticed the flash of reproval sent Alys's way as he downed the remains of his drink, clicked his heels, and offered his arm to Mother, who still preening, allowed him to lead her into the throng of twirling bodies.

Consigning Alys's deflated figure to the appraisal of a potbellied guest, whose curiosity over her roses was inclined to focus rather subtlety on his hostess far more than the wonderful aromatic flowers around him, we wandered through the fairy lit garden. Partly listening to the vivid description of its creation I let my mind wander to the man we had left.

"Count Reinbach is an upstanding man."

My comment was genuinely felt. Hans sat me down on a bench.

"Yes, if only we could all be that fine."

The sarcasm I took for jealousy was not lost upon me.

"You do not really agree?"

"Of course. It is just – Oh Rhia, please think again about what you are doing."

For the first time since *that night*, I took hold of his face within my hands–

"Do not worry so, this female comes well prepared. I have an address for the woman I mentioned before."

A tiny movement in Hans body informed me of an interest he denied.

"Etta Detdy? For goodness' sake, Rhia."

Kicking my shoes off I scrambled my feet onto the bench, covered them with the folds of this heavy gown: reverting to teenage years and the ploy of remorse.

At least three minutes past before Hans let out an expression of frustration.

"How do you know?" he lowered his tone.

"Contact. It is obvious she knows my father."

"That's it," his abruptness exclamation surprised me.

I let out a moan. "That's it. Is that all you have got to say?"

Disregarding my query Hans began his cross examination.

"Who is telling you this?"

That familiar tetchiness invaded my mind–

"Not telling me – I am asking them."

"Who?"

"Please do not ask me. Trust me"

The sudden lurch forward almost tippled me from the seat. It was in that moment of movement I could feel that old familiar confusion rising within me. I could picture Savvy reading from her paper – 'Alys Parker is Ametti Dreyers sister, aunt to Hans, but also to Kurt Dreyer (alias Jules Dragner)'. For that reason alone, can I really trust Hans?

Hans grabbed my shoulders–

"Listen to me, that painting is proof that Kurt, Dragner, whatever handle he wishes to be known by, is out for revenge. Because I…"

Hans let his hands drop, looked around us–

"Did you hear that?"

My eyes searched the bushes, "No, what is the matter with you?"

"I heard a noise."

"Again?"

I began to laugh.

"Quiet" his tone was serious.

My stomach lurched at the drama in his voice. What had my companion been about to say? I knew something had to be said to ease the tension–

"Right, you must not breathe a word. Promise me."

Hans's head flew up and down in what I presumed was a promise.

"My confidant is from my father's bank."

"His bank?"

"Yes, and do not ask me the name. I will not say."

"Man or woman?"

"Does it matter?"

"No."

The hesitation on his ‘no’ concerned me. Will he relate this conversation back to Savvy? I could not tell, but at least Fiona had no worry, and she could continue to spy for me.

I stretch my hand out to the edgy man before me, still eying those bushes as if the demons from hell were readying to jump out at us–

“What are you not telling me?” I ask.

“I have said, I heard something.”

“And?”

My impatience was clicking in–

“As you say, but that is not what I mean.”

I gave him that look, the stare that signifies ‘more’. Pulling his eyes away from those bushes he almost mumbled–

“I also cannot reveal the source, but I believe your father knew her, Etta Detdy. Abducted her when he was younger.”

I caught my breath.

“Abducted. That is ridiculous. What fool told you this?”

This time the laughter would not come.

“Who?” I demanded.

I could hear my own irritation.

“Be quiet, please. This garden has ears.”

The man has turned pale. My displeasure was plain.

“I cannot tell you.”

“Right, that decides it. I *will* visit the Detdy woman. If you join me that is up to you. Tell no-one, and I mean no-one.”

I shuffled from the seat, rammed my feet into the shoes I had scattered onto the ground.

Hans frowned, turned his gaze back to those wretched bushes.

“There will be consequences.”

I could hear the catch in his voice.

“So?”

“Me,” he said, suddenly on a lighter note.

This time a noise from behind the bush made Hans scramble to his feet, while the gentle rustle of leaves, and the tread of feet made my own heart skip a beat.

“Found you,” the Count drew aside the thick branches.

“Count,” I sighed.

“I have sought, if that is even the correct word, Rhia out for the dance.”

"Yes," I was gabbling. "Almost right."

"Good."

He glanced at Hans, swiftly held out his arm for me to hold and led the way back to the house. Hans said nothing: a compliance that showed respect, but grated on my sinking heart, all the time wondering how much this imposing man had overheard.

--

One dance led into two, then three, and four: a constant soliloquy from the Count on the fascination of hidden art. I tried hard to listen, believe me, in-between my head spinning from the constant rotation of the dance, plus an overpowering sensation of the Count's proximity. His theory into how many great names in art hid paintings for the sake of money or convenience became what I shall call, a predicament of spin – catch a word – spin – catch a word – the nausea in my stomach consistently threatening my sanity. Finally, and I thank heaven for this, the Count directed me into the hallway, sat me on a chair, and plied me with a glass of champagne.

"I must leave you, my dear. I have various art pieces I must discuss with Alys. Our dances have been a pleasure. Till we meet again, my friend."

He kissed my hand and left to find our hostess.

My head, in the throes of a pirouetting ballerina, encouraged me wildly to drink my champagne straight back. I did, in one go, and employ any reader who has even a small notion to try it themselves, please – do not. I will use the vernacular mother would hate – Do not be a bloody fool –

My world spun out of balance, women scurrying about in the method of a film director's take of a busy shopping day. Men coughing and spluttering over the glasses in their hands. The waiters Alys had hired for the evening, laughing to many a course joke this woman could neither hear nor relate too: for me this scene came straight from a horror movie.

I decided to call a waiter and inquire what year this champagne was bottled. Why? I thought it may have fermented, especially as everyone was cavorting around me, prolific in their actions of a Victorian brothel. Suddenly, a distorted face loomed above me – a female, red lips moving up and down like those of a bawd.

Did I shout 'no', or was my head bursting from the bubbles popping in my brain? Another face, this one was male. He was talking, directing the female, whose face now grew long and dark, to hoist my body upwards. Then a wizard, white beard, white hair, eyes that pierced my soul.

I must fight.

Take that – I fling my hand at someone's nose – Ah, blood over his chin.

Good, Rhia, again. Ouch, my hands are being held tight. I am moving, up, up, up.

Bhutan women carrying me like the last time to find their 'anchor mother'. Will my grandmother materialize? Who knows – Must not let this happen – I must find Etta Detdy – get Fiona, the Grubb kid will help me. What now – Calls for me to kick.

Here we go –

I am falling down a pit –

Blackness –

Ahhhh.

July 2001

Sunday July 1st

Oh Diary,

How sad I feel.

I belong to that group who start a diary, find themselves revealing their inner emotions, then refuse to write. My riposte: literally this diary has taken on the guise of a mirror; it has allowed me to view myself as I really am; that side of myself no-one else must see.

What did Alys say about those mirrors lining her ballroom – 'Smoke and Mirrors'.

How true, for what looks innocent may turn out to be nothing of the sort.

Today I need to write, catch up on the story I cruelly abandoned after the night of Alys's Midsummer Ball. For this, I will apologise. My lack of understanding into the 'whatever' or 'what happened' scenario that caused my 'hiccup' that night. Evidently, according to Mother I had drunk the champagne too quickly, and unbeknown to her I had probably been downing the bubbly concoction all evening. I promise that was not true. Hans, on the other hand, offered an explanation more sinister; my drink had been 'laced'. Whichever it was, and I have my own suspicion, it completely took me down the road of delusion, to the degree that Mother and Hans stayed in my room all night, listening to my gabbling, and trying to deduce what I was saying. According to Mother I was spouting names in the style designated to the man, or woman who calls bingo numbers, fast and furious. I can only plead in the way a child pleads to be forgiven over an unexpected remark, plead that Fiona's name was not mentioned, especially as the Count and Alys carried me to my room. What would they have thought?

After breakfast in my room the following morning Hans drove back to London, assuring me that Alys had overlooked my 'faux pas' in hitting the waiter that came to my aid, for the Count swore he had never laughed so much for a long time. Nevertheless, the waiter, whose bloody nose shone like the brightest lighthouse beacon, marched from the house with disgust. Whoever he was, may the man or boy forgive me. I felt sad not to have the chance to say 'farewell' to the Count or Alys, whose presence had been required at an art conference in Germany, but as Hans stipulated, when they returned another 'get together' was high on their list.

⊥

Well, dear Diary, here we stand, back to the present day. It is Sunday, and we know what that means, if that certain lady bothers to turn up. Even if she cannot, which has been often, we have the sun; a blazing orb we can compare with a furnace, to such an extent that Mother's choice of a flimsy, daring, 'look at me' dress said it all, whilst my blue cotton three quarter sleeved loose shift covered my tattoos and everything else. Besides, I had never heard Mother so chatty. Mainly rubbish, but now and again she dropped a hint that we should visit the house, look in on the neighbours, and collect what will turn out to be mountains of post. Agreeing, if that was the way to halt this flood of badgering, we settled on a date the following week. Satisfied she flicked the kettle switch to ready herself for our guest and her desperate need for coffee. Humming, then stopping in that sudden way that warns a person they are not going to like what they hear, she intonated –

"Who would 'F' be Rhia?"

Eyes wide, throat dry.

"Rhia," Mother repeats. "Did you hear my question?"

I am flustered.

"Yes, I heard you, and I was thinking. 'F', do not know anybody with an 'F' initial."

I feel uncomfortable.

"I meant to ask you after the ball. You kept repeating a name, but I was far too concerned to hear it properly."

Relief.

"Maybe it was the swear word?"

I giggled, anything to dissuade her.

"Maybe."

Mother's answer was lost as her ears pricked on hearing the bell ring.

I started toward the flat door –

"There was that girl at the bank" she began again "Grubb I believe. Her name started with an 'F' I believe. Fin, Flo, Fiona, that was it."

"Was it?" I returned, opening the door.

Savannah D' Mill entered the flat as a sprinter to the finish line.

"Have I got news for you both" she gushed, hurrying to her usual seat.

Mother handed out the mugs of steaming coffee, settled down to partake in this woman's gossip. Savvy, shimmering in a peach organza dress and jacket, looked from Mother to me, then brought her gaze back to rest on Mother's face.

"We have heard Hal's bank have sacked a female for snooping."

The gasp I made echoed around the room.

"Who?" Mother demanded, her mug wobbling by her lower lip.

I waited with bated breath.

"A cleaner," Savvy pronounced. "She was rummaging through personal files."

I gulped my coffee, anything to hide my emotions.

"A cleaner, whatever for?" Mother was asking.

Tension was growing. Savvy let the coffee swirl around her mouth, swallowed it with a sigh of delight.

"Her excuse was she knew nothing of their accusations, and was this a joke?"

Mother shook her head "Who caught her?"

Savvy began to chuckle. She was obviously revelling in this tale–

"Will you both believe me when I tell you a junior reported her? A girl with the name Grubb. Do you not find that funny?"

I literally drank my coffee straight down.

My insistence to re-fresh the coffee pot was readily accepted. In my hurry to get to the kitchen I dropped the pot 'Clang', heard Mother groan, swooped it up, and banged the kettle on for affect. Removing my phone from the pocket in my dress, I hastily sent Fiona Grubb a text –

'What the hell are you doing over the cleaning woman?'.

Waiting for the reply seemed a lifetime, the hissing kettle piling on the pressure. Hearing the chatter from the lounge warned me that however funny Savvy thought this announcement to be, that part of her 'snooping' brain would not let it go. At last, my silent phone vibrated –

'Hello, Miss Bryant, it is a busy day. I am in Richardson's cupboard sorting files I need.'

I text back 'What the hell have you been up to?'

Another pause–

'You have heard. How?' she replied.

Please, not multi fonts.

'Forget how' I wrote.

'It was her or me Miss, and if it had been me that would have meant you.'

What!

'We must meet' was my next text.

'Okay, when?'

This is driving me mad…

'How the heck…'

Pause, from her–

'Next Wednesday, yeah, where?'

'At the bank, no suspicion'

'Blimey, you're brave.'

Head, coffee pot, sure you can get the gist.

'See you. Oh, what bloody time, forgot to ask.'

Wow, two the same.

'Two'

'Bye'

Phone switched off, hidden in pocket.

I head into the lounge, pot in hand. I smile.

"Here we go."

Savvy and Mother pull back from their in-depth discussion to look my way.

"That Grubb girl's name," Mother begins. "Can you remember if it was Fiona?"

I try to seem surprised, answer in the most casual way possible.

"I would not know."

Mother was insistent–

"Yes, I believe she told us at our very first visit."

I tried to look unconcerned–

"Cannot remember," I continue to lie.

I could sense that ambience of irritation building. Mother was rattled at me–

"She brought us coffee, Rhia remember, and it is her claim that this cleaner spilt files as she rushed out of Mr Richardson's office."

Mother was not giving up–

"Evidently suspicion has been growing that personal files were being rummaged."

Up to now Savvy had sat quietly while Mother relayed the details, drinking her coffee and appraising the pair of us. I forced my face to wear a shocked expression.

"That is terrible. I do hope she kept away from ours"

Time for our guest to speak–

"She cared nothing for yours. Her search was further back."

Mother threw a quick glance to the woman seated in the chair. I tutted.

Coffee was disappearing faster than I could make it, the two women nattering away like hens in a farmyard – I know, rather a disparaging connection.

"Yes," Savvy unexpectedly added. "She had dropped files from the sixties onto the floor."

Need to sound surprised.

"Wow, would she be searching for an ancestor?"

Crass? No doubt, what else could I have said?

Four eyes scanned my flustered form, standing by the window wafting my hands up and down trying to cool myself down.

"This Fiona says she returned the files, and Mr Richardson agrees with her."

Savvy nodded as Mother took up the tale.

"On behalf of your father I am going to visit the bank next Wednesday and thank her."

Blast, why that day?

"Great," I lie for a second time. "I will come with you."

Mother smiles, suggests 'Afternoon tea' as I complain that I left my phone in the bedroom. Once there, the door closed, I hug Jimmy's guitar, and send Fiona another text –

'Mother accompanying me to bank next week. Make your story watertight.'

Wednesday July 11th

Whoever wrote the paraphrase that 'One lie leads to another' should be given a medal. It is not only the most profound quote stated but, fits this woman as a hand fits a glove.

To be honest, if someone had told me when I was younger that 'lies' would follow my every footstep, I would have dismissed them as crazy troublemakers, and certainly not to be trusted. Now, I know different. Day to day I wallow under the combination of lies and pretence. I am lying to my mother because my partner, housed up somewhere with my father in the search for a painting which I hope they never find, has told me not to trust her.

All I can add is he better have a good reason to say these things – Father too.

I am lying to my father's colleague, who whether I like it or not, has more than an insight into this snooping game; consistently lying to that mausoleum of a bank, whom I have not set foot into for work in the past seven months. The worst scenario – I am lying to myself, due to Hans's unceasing attention, and Jimmy's continuous absence.

Yesterday was an example–

Hans rang to make sure Mother and myself were 'back on track' after the fiasco relating to his aunt's ball. I complained bitterly over the painting he had shown me: practically seethed down the phone for him to discard it, refusing to listen when he reminded me that painting was a gift from his uncle to his aunt.

The word 'argue' is by far too mild for the stipulation I gave him, that he sneaks that vulgar painting from his aunt's house and meets me to burn it, or I would never speak to him again. I would not heed his remonstration that it was an impossible task. I swore to find the bona fide painting on my own. His words "I will be in touch" filled me with hope, yet at the same time, filled me with dread.

I must ask – What am I becoming?

Regardless of my griping yesterday, this morning Mother has taken on the human form of a ferret, sniffing continuously into things beyond her understanding, such as 'why the cleaner at the bank was unearthing files she could not possibly comprehend', and running into corners (obstacles) trying to find out why. My anxiety grew as she jumped from the bed, grabbed her dressing gown, and announced she was going to prepare breakfast–

"We must look the part, Rhia. Our social standing depends on it."

–all before the clock struck six. I wanted to laugh and cry together, enlighten her that the girl at the bank she was thanking on behalf of my father was the culprit herself. The remaining three hours until our taxi arrived was hectic – Suit with smart shoes, hair immaculate, makeup just so. If I hear these words one more time I shall scream.

As the clock ticked my apprehension mounted. What if Fiona gives herself away? What if she lets me down? What if the world, at this precise moment stops turning? Yes please.

--

The bank is bubbling: a pot on a high fired stove. Noisy, busy, excitable energy coursing around this drab sanctum. A timepiece somewhere in town strikes ten o' clock as Mother and I walk into the building to be greeted by an obsequious Mr Richardson.

"Welcome, Mrs Bryant. This is an honour"

I could not help but think 'Honour be damned. This whole meeting is a farce' Old Richardson gazed my way with an 'Oh, it's you' kind of attitude–

"You too, Miss Bryant"

If only this pretentious man knew.

Mother smiled, graciously, edging further into the ring of assistants gathered by the reception desk. Fiona stood in the middle, the largest grin covering her heavily painted face I had ever seen. I glared, she nodded, I craved to be anywhere but here.

"Miss Grubb, step forward"

Richardson's command rattled above the excess noise from curious customers entering and leaving the bank.

"This girl, Mrs Bryant, is our hero today."

My concentration leapt back to the circle. Hero? Silly man, that girl is my spy.

Mother reached out with her gloved hand, shook Fiona's, thanked her profusely. I swear the daft kid curtsied. Looking around me the whole bank had erupted into applauding this bobbing fabricator. Ten minutes, with my ear drums ringing at the commotion and it was over. Mother was being escorted toward Mr Richardson's office, the customers and assistants heading back to their business, and Fiona Grubb and I facing one another as enemies on a battlefield. Unlike many a warrior I conceded, plumped myself down into the nearest chair. Fiona stood next to me.

"That was cool don't you think? We got away with it."

I sighed. If I could take her outside and fasten her to the lamp post, all and sundry could pretend it was a medieval stock.

"What happens when other files are disturbed?"

Bending down on the pretext of rubbing her foot Fiona murmured –

"I am most careful. I put back what I find. Before you say anything about the cleaning woman, it was that woman who spoke to you the last time you visited, that made sure her suspicions were heard. I forgot to close Richardson's drawer."

My gulp of breath resounded in my ears.

"These silly women think I am knocking him off – counts me out."

This kid has got nerve.

"That is not funny" I slammed in her direction "What about that poor cleaner?"

Whisper I may, yet penitent I was not.

Fiona exhumed a small cackle, which sounded more like the snarl of a tiger.

"The cleaner? As I said, it was her or us. If you wish me to give myself up, fair play, but you, Miss Bryant, take the fall with me."

That was nothing short of blackmail – Payback.

Flapping her arms as the sails of a small boat in a crosswind the girl asks sweetly–

"Coffee, Miss Bryant?"

At this point the woman displaying the wiggling backside trotted towards us.

"Have you even asked Miss Bryant if she would care for a drink?"

"I have" Fiona retorted, head in air.

"So…" the woman thundered.

Fiona tossed her head higher, marched stealthily toward a door by the exchange counter and disappeared.

"I will apologise for her, Miss. An act I forever perform. She has got to be the silliest girl in creation, and, if you do not mind my saying, hovers about yourself as a fly buzzing around a spider's web"

The woman held out her long nails, admiring the cherry red she had painted them.

I felt the chill of her statement rise through me: a reversal of Mother's meaning to her favourite poem. Not once had I questioned what these random meetings conveyed to these women. Forcing a smile that belied the aggravation I felt, I refused to digest all the malicious tittle-tattle this woman was spurting. I heard 'Fiona hides in Richardson's office' and 'We can all imagine what is happening', plus 'The girl is brazen', and 'It is time she left'. Bringing my eyes to hold the cold stare from this termagant before me my lips formed the question.

"Is that customer waiting?"

Her head swung sideways, annoyance mounting as she spotted the crying child pulling on the young woman's skirt by the reception desk. Huffing, she spat a quick 'Sorry', then swaggered across in her three-inch heels.

No sooner had my mind eased from that viper's prattle than Fiona was badgering me with a mug in her hand.

"No cup and saucers left, so I thought a mug would do. No coffee, which is a bloody nuisance, you have tea. Pretend to drink it and listen."

I will think 'pardon', mean 'what the hell'. Even so, from spider to fly, or whatever modus operandi suits best.

"I have overheard (not again) that this Detdy character has another address.

Up your nose Richardson (manners) was communicating over the phone to someone. Me, I was in his cupboard (of course), and before you smile, like the majority (big word for this girl) of the women here, I was dusting."

I must admit, Miss Fiona Grubb is always in the 'right' place when needed. I sipped the disgusting excuse for tea, trying hard to keep my intrigue hidden.

"Well?" was all I could think to say.

"I have nothing else to report. If I find this out Miss Bryant, that will be it.

I am honestly finished – Done."

The determination in her voice communicates this time she means it.

What is the saying – 'Accept when a journey has run a course''. Ignoring whether that woman at the desk is watching us I turn to Fiona.

"Yes" I whisper.

"Good," she returns.

"What will you do?" I ask, at that moment genuinely interested.

Fiona smiles. "My aunt will sort everything out."

"That's great," I state, wondering who this fairy godmother may be.

"I can't say no more," she tweets. "Secret" she taps her nose, silly girl.

Hearing a commotion emanating from the corridor near Richardson's office told me Mother was on her way. The need to quickly establish when and how Fiona would pass any information she might gather I questioned –

"If you find that second address?"

"I will text you" she answered, fleeing before the entourage came to my side.

--

Evening

I am pleased this day is nearly over, and the gathering at the bank shuffled as a pack of cards, with the naughty knave still stalking the shadows, and grateful queen consigned to wait in the wings. If I speak the truth it exhausted me, worrying about the cleaning woman, plus fretting over the Grubb girl. While Mother could not praise the girl enough, demanding her instant promotion, Richardson revoked this by saying this heroine of the moment will be moving to Wales within the next two months. On Mother's telling I express astonishment, genuine may I say, for not one word of this news had passed Fiona's lips. Fair enough, she mentioned her aunt, of which I took little notice, especially when she was not forthcoming over the woman. Even so, you would have thought, with our kind of relationship, the girl could have least mentioned it. I will presume this is Fiona's wish to move that far. Anywhere really, that moves her away from me. Can you believe that? Never mind, that is life, full of ungrateful Fiona Grubbs. Mother, however, was elated over the news. She believed this young girl was due something good, if only as a backhand 'Thank you' for her brilliant discovery. Should I fall in line, say 'I could not agree more', then hide behind my hand with a smirk.

Around eight o' clock Mother announced she would savour the luxuriant waters of a perfumed bath, and headed, with her recently purchased silky pyjamas into the steam filled room. Now, while the sense of my mother's renewal from the beginning of the year is marvellous to see, her 'die hard' shopping habits, and relaxing 'without father' attitude convinces me further, as each new day dawns, that her charade was possibly staged for me. Please, do not ask why I perceive this so, for many things pass through our minds, and for no reason at all our subconscious deems it true. I must write, Diary, with a shaking hand and a heavy heart – Will my Jimmy be correct, and can my father and mother be conspiring with Savannah D' Mill? Are they combining tactics to throw me from the scent of something far darker? Something from my father's past that will add to my heartache. By the same token, can that past include Etta Detdy?

Breath forces itself from my body as for a split second my mind settles on Emery Dreyer. 'Why this man?' I muse. 'Could he be the spider mother continually reiterates in her poem, and if so, how can I untangle myself from their game?'

I grip the glass in my hand, watch as the smooth red wine invites me to drink.

Friday July 20th

Small entry today as the weather is playing 'ping, pong', or table tennis, with my body. One moment the sun is high in the sky, raring to go, overheating the populations under exercised forms as burgers sizzle on barbeques. The next it is raining, slashing it down with the ferocity of a hungry lion. At this precise hour, eleven o' clock in the morning, Mother is draining the last dregs of coffee, while my eyes scan the street below and I think 'what next'. Hearing my mobile ring, I wander into the bedroom, pick it up, and note the unknown number.

"Hello" the sound hardly passes my lips.

A faint sound crackles into my ear–

"Hi, Hans here, why are you whispering?"

"The number, it is not your own."

"Correct," he breathes deep. "I am at my aunt's house."

"Your aunt's house?"

"Correct again, she is not here."

"Right. I do not understand."

"She is with the Count in Germany."

"Still?"

I can hear the surprise rise from my throat.

"Yes Rhia, still. I have the painting."

"Right."

"I will bring it to you."

Can this be true?

"Right – No" – Lord, this is hard work.

Mother pops her head around the bedroom door.

"It is Hans" I say

"Yes" she replies.

"Say 'Hello'," I mumble.

"Hello" she calls.

He calls back, I nod, she recedes.

"Gone," I gasp.

I try to chat in a normal fashion, hit what many would call 'a blank wall'. Exasperated I hiss – "We had better meet. Is something wrong?"

I hear movement, feet on a wooden floor.

"I am walking through the kitchen area toward the garden, passing the cleaners. I must be careful," he speaks to someone. "She will be told I was here, plus I left in a hurry."

He must be joking.

"Are you living there?"

"No."

'Whatever' was my main thought. If this attempt at deception was to fool his aunt, then it was farcical, a child could achieve more. Wishing to bring the conversation to a quick end I said– "Must go. Where shall we meet, and when?"

Ball in your court, Hans.

He was muttering and mumbling. Laughable really, almost arguing with himself.

"Next Thursday, say Greenwich Palace, now the Old Naval College – Midday?"

"Right" I answer for the fifth time.

I close the phone call down, before I say something I will regret, and he blabbers on further. I take my position by the window once more, view the mobility in the street below. People rushing, cars queuing to turn the corner, red, blue, green, and white – slow down – My eyes focus on the white car, lazily waiting in line, indication to turn left. It was not quite the same white sports car that had sat on this street night after night, but similar, and it did send a shiver through me. I recoiled with that fear that has gripped me throughout this process. My mind flies back to Hans, and his act of self-reproach that he never finished in that garden. Was it guilt he portrayed? Would he have given me a hint toward all this 'car following'; explained why it was occurring, and maybe 'who' was behind it. Both Savvy and his aunt could stand in line for this, the former for 'protection', the latter – I am unsure. How can Mother or I be tangled up with a regime she followed – Never. Our problem is Father and that painting.

Questions, questions, a darkness begins to forge through my mind: those habitual rantings of confusion and disbelief. There must be someone that I can talk to without emotion coming into play, an open mind that will help me uncover this secret my father has striven to keep from me. I close my eyes in the way of a child wishing for an unobtainable present, see the vision rising before me: the white hair, the small white beard, those piercing eyes. Content with my manifestation I head back to the window, spot drops of rain on the pavement and road below, groan as the heavens darken, and the raging lion of thunder growls louder.

Thursday 26th July

The Old Royal Naval College (formally Greenwich Palace)

Hans had arranged to meet where the old 'Palace of Placentia' had once stood on the banks of the river Thames. This past building had been built by Humphrey, Duke of Gloucester in 1443, regent during the reign of Henry VI. He fell out of favour with Henry's queen Margaret of Anjou, who a few historians believe instigated the war at that time. She later imprisoned him in the Tower of London for high treason, and according to history, this is where he died. The Palace was enlarged under the reign Henry VII in time for his wife Elizabeth of York to give birth to their second child Henry VIII, whose monarchy overlooked the redesign into a dwelling of opulence. Both Henry VIII's daughters, Mary Tudor, and Elizabeth I, were born here. Later this grand Palace became the backdrop to moments of sinister malevolent, such as the arrest of Henry's second wife, Anne Boleyn, on claims of treason and adultery, and the disastrous marriage to his fourth wife, Anne of Cleves. During James I and Charles I's reign what became known as the Queen's rooms were built, but by the period of the English Civil War in August 1642-September 1651 Oliver Cromwell used the Palace for a hospital or a camp for prisoners. Afterwards the building fell into disrepair. In the year 1660, under Charles II's rule certain parts were demolished; replaced by a new building that forty years later became known as the Greenwich Hospital, leading to the present day where it stands as The Old Royal Naval College.

--

My excitement was growing. Hour by hour, moment by moment, I had watched the hands of that contemporary clock hanging on my wall move round. It may have been the most fashionable depiction of how to incorporate coloured balls into a household item, yet that certainly gave no leeway into why those hands were moving at a snail pace. Today that vile painting would be burnt, and it mattered not where Hans and I put it under the match, just that we witnessed its demise. Fair enough, the painting Father and Jimmy sought was still out there, my nude form moulded across those names of evil intent, but with luck it will not be found, and my father will reprieve me where Mother is concerned. Dressing I had quickly found a new pair of jeans (bought to suit my growing weight problem), and a loose shirt hanging in the wardrobe, waiting patiently among my other items of clothing for its non-ironed friends to join it. Matching these perfectly with a long-sleeved jumper I threw around my shoulders, I counted the time in comparison with my restlessness. As that clock edged nearer eleven o' clock I grasped the telescopic umbrella offered by Mother, pushed my feet into a pair of black ankle boots (I know, it is summer), snatched my small shoulder bag, and ran out the door.

--

Striding down the pathway in the direction Hans said to meet, I was glad of the breeze from the river. The number eleven bus (top marks if you have acknowledged the number eleven follows my story as an uninvited guest) had been crowded, full of shoppers and tourists out to revel in the warm weather, armed with a bag or a picnic basket. Scanning the crowd my eyes fell on the person I was looking for, smart in his casual trousers and shirt, holding a parcel close to his chest. Noticing how his dark, almost black sunglasses skimmed left and right, I waved. His hand moved from his side, not to wave, but to point, in a roundabout way, toward a crowd standing a little to his left.

Initial thought: 'Another meeting with Hans and there lurks a tail.'

Subsequent reaction: 'This cannot be true.'

My thoughts swinging in and out of practical control, I leapt as a hand yanked mine–

"Act normal, walk this way."

Negotiating our way through the crowds my companion stepped into a group of day trippers on a guided tour of this huge building.

"Who?" I began.

"We must deviate," was his sharp retort.

Nearing the main entrance to the college he indicated we lower our body to appear smaller. Once through the main door he swiftly pulled me from the group, and into a passageway. We stood there, the shadow of a doorway helping our plight.

"Not again," I moaned.

Hans inclined his head "Story of my life, and yours at the moment."

This was not funny.

"Who?"

He frowned "First guess, that sacked gardener."

"The Jimmy lookalike?"

"That's the guy."

"Why?"

"Who knows. The painting?"

I was shocked "You told me no-one else had seen it."

His hand squeezed mine–

"So, I thought but…" his voice was husky. "I now believe his argument with my aunt concerned his failed attempt to steal the painting."

I could not stop myself from trembling.

Not waiting for me to reply we slipped from the passageway to move back into the main hallway. Suddenly, he whispered in my ear–

"What if…" he paused, breathed deep. "What if, this painting is that original.

Apart from anything else, Jules Dragner is worth a fortune, hence…"

Is it possible for a heart to stop, then restart?

"Original?" the sound jerked from my throat.

"Shhh," his finger flew to his lips. "My aunt is unaware her painting has gone."

He looked troubled, "And yes, this parcel could be the painting with the names – Dragner's hidden masterpiece."

His implication was clear.

I stared at Hans's face, picking out the small contortions he was trying to hide. Remembering the scene in the garden on the day of the Summer Ball, I knew besides the gardener at that scene the third person was the 'slob' from Berlin. Was Hans's aunt being hoodwinked or not?

"Stasi?" falls from my mouth.

“Exactly, Rhia.”

Hans held my hand tighter as we moved forward. I shuddered as the ‘Ohhs and Ahhs’ from the tourists encased us in their wonder.

Slotting ourselves into another group of tourists we moved slowly through the magnificent hallway toward this building’s inner rooms.

“Is it possible your uncle may have contacts?” I mumbled.

Hans body stiffens.

“My uncle?”

He disengages himself from me.

“Yes, it was he who sent the painting.”

“As a gift,” he croaked, more surprised than angry. “He would have no knowledge.”

I felt bad, and maybe I was clutching at straws, yet someone was not sincere. Hans clutched the parcel closer to him.

“I am sorry, Rhia.”

I could feel the sweat in his palm.

“Who can we trust?” he panted, searching the crowd for the shadow.

I thought of Jimmy, then just as quickly said–

“I know a man we can.”

Before we could discuss anymore Hans pointed towards another group–

“We must mingle. Our lives may count on it.”

We eased our way into the throng of another passing group, keeping one eye to the whereabouts of the person, or persons tracking us, and headed for the Painted Hall.

--

The Painted Hall

Designed by Nicholas Hawksmoor, the Painted Hall, formally a dining room, is separated by archways into different sections with walls and ceilings depicting mythological, allegorical, historical, and contemporary characters, entwined with the royal arms of monarchy and gilded signs of the zodiac. Painted by Sir James Thornhill 1706–1726, they represent, as the word allegorical informs us – a moral story represented symbolically.

For instance: the ceiling in The Lower Hall was painted around 1708–1714, celebrating 'Triumph of Peace and Liberty over Tyranny'. Seated in the middle of this painting are King William 1662–1702 and Queen Mary 1662–1694 in all their majesty; the King resting his foot on a man, depicted in the historical summary as the veiled figure of King Louis XIV of France. The French King, at war with England, considered to be an aggressor, whose advancement into territory that was not his own looked upon as tyranny.

Within the smaller Upper Hall figures of Queen Anne 1702-1714, and her husband Prince George of Denmark, a marriage looked upon as advantageous to the English people, are surrounded by mythical figures, and statements to the four seasons.

On the North Wall stands the imprint of King George I, 1714–1727, the first monarch from the house of Hanover, and ancestor to Queen Victoria 1837–1901. It was here that Lord Nelson, Admiral of the Fleet, lay in state for three days before his funeral.

--

Wandering in a group that every now and then stopped to praise these wonderful paintings and forcing ourselves to join in with the small pockets of discussions (what we could understand) we became lost in what my father would dub 'the moment', not realising how near we were to the final hall. Emerging into the sunlight Hans walked in the direction of an ice cream van, bought two cones, and proceeded to find an empty bench, impressing me how important it was to act normal, yet not taking his eyes from the crowd pouring from that vast building. Ice cream in hand I sat, bit into the large minty swirl, and tried to relax.

"Have we lost whoever is following us?" I queried.

Hans nodded, plunging the creamy delight into his mouth. Swallowing, he said–

"Never be that sure. We must get this parcel into the hands of an expert."

I stopped eating.

"I suggest Count Reinbach, although how I will survive the humiliation."

Hans eyes never moved from the crowd.

"Really good choice. He often examines many pieces of art, whilst ignoring their subject matter."

"So, Jimmy's advice was correct, he can be trusted?"

"Jimmy?" Hans muttered in a low tone, then, "If only Rhia."

I caught my dripping ice cream just in time, felt the pleasure of the cool mint taste as I swirled it onto my tongue.

The last crunch of our treat devoured, Hans pulled me to my feet–

"We must move."

A slight indication of his head took my glance to the small group of tourists standing outside the doors we had previously exited. A pair of men stretching their necks to search the surrounding crowds could be seen above the rest. Hans began to walk as quickly as he could along the river edge, dragging me behind him, twisting his neck every few seconds to see how far the distance between us and them had become.

"Do not look. They may detect us," I sounded scared.

"They have seen us," he shouts. "Run."

We began to run, weaving in and out of the crowd. Experiencing pain in my side I stopped.

"You carry on. I will hide, somewhere. Say where you wish to meet me."

Breath was leaving my body with large pants and groans. Hans looked at me, back toward the moving crowds.

"That is impossible. They want the painting."

"I know," was all I could gasp.

"Hell, Rhia, please."

I could feel his anxiety.

"I cannot go further. The pain…" I stumbled to a bush. "I will hide behind this."

Hans's eyes said it all, bewilderment, annoyance, the fact that I was refusing to run.

Thrusting me behind a bush, he clawed in his pocket for his phone, spoke with hushed tones, while wedging the parcel beneath my arm. Finishing his call, he returned the phone to his pocket, grasped me close, kissed my forehead, and spat in my ear–

"Take this. Go to a café not far from here called 'The Brambles'*, the Count will meet you there. I will divert those thugs."

He was not happy.

"How?" I wince, the pain stabbing my side.

"Ways and means," he gushed. "I must go, wish me luck."

Luck, he requires a miracle. A second later Hans runs, leaving me with the bulky parcel, a griping belly, and the squeal of a female voice drumming my ears. Shifting my bottom to the bush's edge I gingerly peek around the perimeter. I see people staring at a man running, a red headed woman hanging onto his hand for 'dear life' (never understood this saying, yet it fits), and men in overcoats sprinting behind them.

I sit back, stretching my legs before me, trying hard to grasp what I have just observed. I consider the parcel in my arms. If this is *the* 'painting' then my father and Jimmy need to be told. I need to phone them, explain what has happened, and tell them 'whom' and 'where' I delivered it. They will be ecstatic. A little peeved, knowing I had beaten them to the winning post, but 'hey' that is life. The main point in all this will be they will not see this vile painting. Jimmy will be none the wiser over how intimate Kurt and I were. Yet, if everything stops here, how will I find Etta Detdy?

The buzz around me continues as I decide the 'coast should be clear'. Rubbing my stomach hard I struggle to stand, feel the pain generally known as 'stitch' reduce with height. I must get to the 'Brambles' café to pass this painting into the safe hands of the Count. I move from the bush and onto the pathway. Wishing Hans beside me thoughts focus on the red hair girl.

'How did he know her?' 'Could they be work colleagues?' by that I mean Savvy's team. Maybe she had been following us too. Does it matter. Should I care?

My answer tore from my throat–

"Yes, it bloody does" I snarl in-between gasps of threatening tears.

--

'The Brambles'*

It had taken me the best part of an hour to walk to the café. Although the 'stitch' pain in my side had disappeared my feet were hot and sore, my head was aching, and this bulky parcel was becoming cumbersome by the minute. Still uncertain into Hans's whereabouts, or exactly 'who' that flaming red head was, I realised I needed to do something with this painting to at least remove it from sight. Now, it is known, especially by those who followed my last adventure, that my ideas are not always wise. Therefore, when I write, dear Diary, about this one, many will either hold their stomachs in mock disbelief, or laugh so much they will end up crying. I decided as my new jeans were a fraction, and I mean a fraction, on the large side, the painting could do no harm pushed down them. How was I to gather this would concede to others thinking I was pregnant, and to the mess I found myself in?

The café was crowded with tourists of every nationality and culture. Tired, I found a small bench propped against a wall outside. Shielding my eyes from the sun I watched, fascinated, as a group of young 'bikers' argued and laughed over who would draw the short straw to fetch the burger buns and pop they had decided to buy. Loosening the jumper flung around my shoulders earlier in the day I let it slip to the ground. Forgetting the painting edged down the front of my jeans I leant forward to pick it up, muttered a groan, and raised my head to come face to face with the grin of a young lad, clad in a black leather jacket, and ears pierced with the largest hoops I had ever seen.

"Sorry," I moaned. "It is too hot for this thing," holding the dusty jumper up in the air.

"That's okay, lady," the grin grew larger. "In your condition who can blame ye."

His broad Scottish accent was hard to decipher, especially when he came back with

"Me mam is the same."

Whatever does he mean?

He stood up, hailed his 'mates' and shouted –

"Pregnant lady, someone get her a drink."

What was that? Did he say pregnant – Impossible.

I went to stand up, felt myself eased back down by a pair of tattooed hands.

"Sit ye down. We will fetch the drink – Pop?"

I had no choice but to nod, follow the black leathered female with her short spiky cropped hair and numerous nose rings slouch into the café in a way that determined her objection. The boy, eighteen if a day, stood over me with the concern of a sentry on guard.

"When?" his query was flung at me.

"When?" I responded.

"The bairn?" a scowl appeared.

"I..."

The boy cut off any explanation I was about to give, mumbling on in that broad accent–

"My mam has this problem. She forgets."

He turned towards his mates and laughed. I was being sucked beneath a river I had not created. The girl swaggered out the café door, shoved the pop before me, then swaggered away to stand with her pals. The kid, still standing over me, demanded–

"Drink."

I drank.

The noise from passing traffic and pedestrians swam around us as the heat of the day rose to its pinnacle, the skin of my stomach chaffing from the painting. I searched among the bodies approaching the café, wishing with every mouthful of pop, or the need to 'burp' that Count Reinbach would appear; Hans had said he would be here. The leather clad kid, who had moved to where his mates stood, had finally come to an agreement over the burgers and pop. keeping his eye concentrated in my direction. The short straw, fallen to the girl who had fetched my drink, slouched once more through the café entrance. The boy marched back my way –

"Do ye feel better?"

His accent vibrated around the space I had sprawled myself over.

I burped: an absolute need to release the wind gathering in my chest from the guzzled pop, while at the same time grasping my stomach as the folded stiff canvas impaled my flesh. The kid screamed to his mates –

"Lassie in labour – Quick – Phone for an ambulance."

Hell broke loose.

Leather jackets bounced before my eyes, long hair, spiked hair, dyed whatever colour was in vogue, ear and nose rings flashing in the sunlight, arms stretched out to my belching frame. I coughed, I sneezed, I squealed at the top of my voice; in the middle of this the girl had slouched her way back to the furore, carrying multiple burgers and bottles of pop.

Attention alert: phones were ringing all over the place. I panicked, thrashed out at any hand heading my way. It was then a solid grasp held my trembling fingers, pinning them still within the firm hold. How – I am still unsure, but my body moved from the bench, inching my way through the clamorous melee. Swift, as the bird flies, I found myself seated in a car, straining my eyes to the commotion I had left behind. Beside me sat Count Reinbach.

--

We drove, in silence, stopping only as we came in sight of the corner shop that leads to my block of flats. Count Reinbach smiled–

"What was all that fuss about?"

The lilt of his accent soothed my overheated mind.

"Nothing really. Kids jumping to conclusions. Thank you for your help."

"It seemed very real to me."

I was met by an earnest disapproval.

"Anyway, you have a painting for me that I need to verify."

"Yes," I stumbled, trying to remove the canvas from my jeans in the most modest way possible.

The smile creasing his lips reminded me that the thought alone to hide such a bulky item in my jeans was foolish. I wriggled, turned sideways, wrenched at a speed anyone wiser may have considered dangerous, to the painting that is, and finally felt the rough depiction of myself 'twang' pass my waistband.

"Please, do not think bad of me. This vile portrayal comes from the mind of a man practicing evil intent."

Count Reinbach's face was impassive, not a flicker of emotion or surprise ruffled his features. The long slim hands took hold of the painting, placed it, with a reverence known only to those lovers of art, on the back seat of the car. Returning his attention to me he said –

"Rhia, my dear girl, I would never think bad of you. In your hands lies the key to my world."

What an eccentric this man is, such a gentleman.

I open the car door, slip a foot onto the pavement.

"Do not forget you can confide in me," he said. "If I can help I will."

His solemn expression informed me he was sincere; a friend when life's water became too murky.

"The painting – Hans's aunt?" I sighed.

"No fear, I have got it. Is that not the saying?"

"Among others."

I smile at his poor attempt at a joke.

"Trust me," he was saying.

Pulling my weary body from the seat I absently answer–

"Jimmy says the same."

"Wise man," I hear.

Ducking my head low, I thank him again.

The Count smiles, re-ignites the car engine, mutters–

"A plan is only a plan when the mind is open to all possibilities."

I raise my hand as the white car pulls away from the kerb, think 'How odd', then head for home.

--

Entering the flat I find Mother listening to the strains of Mozart, curlers in her hair, and her usual green mask daubed across her face. There was no light, only the flicker of a single candle burning in a jar, balanced on a slate coaster on the coffee table. The darkness made me blink. My eyes, already heavy from this day's events noticed the glare held in her gaze.

"Where have you been? Hans has phoned. Left a message to say do not worry, he will call you tomorrow."

I make my way toward the bedroom, collect my pyjamas, and move quickly toward the bathroom.

"Rhia," Mother repeated. "Did you hear me?"

Did you hear me? Seriously, this has got to be her new record.

"Yes, Mother, thank you, I need a shower."

I could see from the small slither of light highlighting the contours of her stiffened features that curiosity was raging: an unleashed giant bearing down on the boy who dare discover the bully's castle without its knowledge.

I move my head, flounder in my answer–

"We had an argument. I, I walked home."

The green mask cracked in astonishment.

"Oh, that is why Hans told me you were being brought home."

I will kill him.

"Er, yes I forgot, the Count dropped me off. Not important."

This time Mother's face was incredulous.

"You forgot?"

"Yes," I snapped. "I was more worried about Hans. He, he was sick."

"So, Count Reinbach appeared 'Out of the Blue."

Mother knew this phrase would catch me out.

"Yes, that was it."

I moved nearer the bathroom door.

"You sound tired. Was it busy?"

For pity's sake, how many more?

"Very."

"Probably why Hans told me he phoned the Count to collect you."

What!

Mother swung past me, intimating she must wash her face. I stood there, wondering exactly what Hans had told her. Fresh faced she swung back out–

"Funny what an argument can do to the brain."

Heading towards the bedroom, probably to add the precious emollient, she laughed–

"Rhia my sweet, if you must lie, then please do it with style."

Persistence fits this woman like a new shoe that is tight to the foot. No room for manoeuvre.

Friday July 27th

How could I know this day would become pivotal in the search for Etta Detdy?

Mother fired no more questions my way, neither did she press me with her need for information over Hans's 'illness', or the Count's sudden appearance. I concluded she had either lost interest or realised the game she was playing had become tiring, at least for the time being. I had spent so long in the shower the previous evening that Mother, through aggravation and impatience, rewashed her face over the kitchen sink (yuk), as in her grievance toward me had left small patches of mask here and there. She then pretended to be sleeping by the time this woman crept into bed. This morning, as I write, my world is back to being systematic, if you can label 'wary and distrust' as orderly.

Mother rising from bed.

Mother noticing her hair was stiff from over-applied mask.

Mother rushing to the bathroom and dousing her whole head under the shower.

First laugh of the day.

By lunchtime Hans decided to ring. I took his call in the bedroom. He was upbeat, happy, and almost pressing himself down the phone to ask how my meeting with Count Reinbach went. My explanation covered everything from the moment he ran, to when I stepped out the Count's car. He laughed, or to be more precise, he roared over the leather clad kids.

I must be sarcastic and add 'Glad he found that episode so funny'.

There came a lull within the conversation when I could wait no longer to ask

"Who was the red head?"

Hans sniggered, evaded my query to his best ability, then succumbed with a quick–

"No idea."

"Pardon?"

"No idea," he restated. "She was just 'there'."

"You grabbed a stranger's hand and put her in danger?"

My voice quivered with disbelief.

"Danger? Those overcoats could not run to save their life. Further down the road I let her go, made my apology, and kissed her cheek."

"Bet she appreciated that."

My emotions were swinging.

"Yes, she did. Gave me her phone number."

"Tart," I whispered.

I could sense Hans was enjoying baiting me, so his sudden leap to more 'serious' business surprised me–

"I will let you know as soon as the Count rings me with the verdict."

Glad as I was to say 'Goodbye' to the cocotte, I knew, from the tone my friend was using that something was troubling him. Those small, yet important words 'act cool' bounced around my head.

"Please do," I ventured to his last statement, leaving a quiet moment for him to share what was on his mind.

"I have uncovered an article in a newspaper I found at my aunt's, date 1960s."

His voice rose.

"A paragraph about a young woman escaping from East Germany."

He wheezed through his teeth, reminding me how Jimmy always used this diversion when angry and worried.

"She was assisted by an English agent. Could this be the secret Etta Detdy?"

I fell silent.

"Rhia," the voice was low. "Is it possible her name may be on that painting?"

My throat was closing over; that sensation of darkness held me in its grip.

I sat staring at Jimmy's guitar, listening to Mother tuning the radio, the strains of a voice reading the news, the volume rising and falling to the movement of her fingers.

"You mean she was Stasi?"

"I don't. It was a guess."

Reality: my mind refused to function.

Surreal: my tongue had grown too large for my mouth.

What had she to do with my father?

Hans spoke first –

"The authorities are afraid this woman will be discovered, their agent. The name Etta Detdy must be false."

I knew that – Fiona's discovered paper. That was the hidden piece – Etta Detdy's real name. My whole body was shaking. Could she be Stasi? Could my father not only be her contact, but the agent who brought her to England?

I hear a 'whirring' in the background. Call to Mother –

"Are you baking cakes?"

Should have known her answer before she called back–

"Cakes? Not I, dear girl. If you would like me to pop to the shop I can."

Pleasantries – What plan is she scheming now? I quickly probe Hans –

"Is that 'whirring' sound coming from your end?"

He laughed "I am not baking cakes either."

Fine, but the sound continues.

"Rhia, we must investigate more – Etta Detdy I mean."

Hans's plea rings in my ears.

"Why?" I prompt, need to know his train of thought.

He sounds bewildered. "You first introduced the name to me."

"I did?"

Annoyance was growing "You know you did. What is the matter?"

"Nothing."

I could still hear the 'whirring', the catch in his voice–

"Look, when you sort out whatever is wrong give me a call. Obviously, some fact is testing you, and I am tired of saying the trust word."

Click–

The whirring stopped. I gazed longingly at Jimmy's guitar–

"Please come home soon. I am unable to stop these crazy thoughts. I need you."

Imagining his guitar was replying 'I am surplus to your needs. You and Hans?' I cry–

"Never. You have been my love forever."

The guitar slips against the wall. I bend to straighten it, raise it to my lips, replace it gently, take hold of my diary. Taking an invisible marker from my drawer, I write -

Dearest Diary,

This is for your eyes only,

How can I stop the torrent that is Hans Parker from drowning me?

Plus, what do you do when your own father is involved with a Stasi spy?

August 2001

Sunday August 5th

The month of August has begun with our old friend rain falling from the sky in drafts of repeated showers. We had enjoyed a July with temperatures soaring to the heady records of 22-25 Celsius. Without acknowledging that I am being derisive, my moans cover everything from forgoing summer clothes to Mother's request for igniting the fire.

Today I am swathed once more in jeans and a lightweight jumper: dark colours in my fight against my soaring weight. To be honest the four or five pounds causing my waistband to tighten. This green eyed, red headed Rubenesque female has eaten salad and yoghurt for one whole week. Embraced the joys of yoga under Mother's fastidious eye; practising the 'Downward Dog' and 'Body Rolls' until I was so fatigued that I sneaked a small muffin. I will blame this lapse from willpower upon my entanglement within my mind. Hans's explosive revelation that Etta Detdy could possibly belong with those hidden names from an abandoned regime. His insinuation that my father was further involved than I wished to believe, led me to questioning my mother over my father's younger years, rummaging through what I could see were painful memories, only to receive her answer–

"Speak to your grandmother. She knows everything."

That was it – 'The End', not one clue that would give me an insight into where Etta Detdy may fit in.

It is Sunday, and the usual visit from Savannah D' Mill as always runs my mother 'ragged' with the cushions and coffee. These past few weeks have seen our intelligencer arrive later and depart earlier. According to Mother this 'agent of the state' has a workload as high as a mountain. I have tried to contact my father and Jimmy, who have now been away for eight long months. Every night I have phoned the number Jimmy had given me, let it ring until his voice demanded I leave a message, by which time the words fly into the receiver totally different to my original heart to heart. On Savvy's last visit I broached this subject, mentioned how strange not to hear from Father at all. Her answer–

"No need to worry, Hal knows exactly what he is doing."

On Jimmy's part she gave me the same reply, and I can expect no better news today.

Breaking News!!!

I must report Fiona Grubb (I still giggle over the name) has contacted me.

It astounds me how this girl is always in the right place at the right time. Yes, the kid irritates me beyond measure. Yes, her cheek needs curbing to those who know better than her (Me). Yet, when it comes to scoring points this dithering teenage snoop hits the jackpot running. For that I give her resented admiration.

Her text last Friday caused my spirit to take flight. That, dear Diary, is no exaggeration.

She typed in a second address – A second address for the Detdy woman.

I was over the moon.

True, the whole text sounded as though she was reciting from a fairy story, but what did I care? This was another lead. She continued with an explanation of where she had found this address, evidently in the archives of that cupboard she constantly finds herself in, and how lucky she had been to not get caught. To my way of thinking this girl was not just lucky, she was downright blessed. The sweet, fairy book address settles itself within the pages of my mind, preserved there for future reference.

The Rose Cottage,

Stoneleigh*

Consulting the map on my phone Stoneleigh is on the outskirts of Coventry, another county I have no idea how to find. I will need to seek help.

It was not until I searched through my underwear drawer this morning, I uncovered the document that Fiona had sent me back in April. Those presumed names given to Father, Savvy and Etta Detdy, which are mainstream now, but false to their real identity. I twist the names of Guy Billington and Helena Crevelle through my fumbling mind, withstanding an urge to shout "Rhia Billington", and grasp at the next problem that raises itself. *If* the Count discovers names underneath that vile painting, and writes them down, Etta Detdy will not be there, for she will be identified in her former name. Again, *if,* and the adroit mastery of this small word could lead us anywhere, this female belonged to the

Dreyer family, this game that was playing out would change radically. I gasp – Is it possible that I am missing the clue that is staring at me, tormenting me, waiting for my own entrapment?

The doorbell rings. Savvy has arrived. Another endless afternoon of what I label 'chatting, drinking, and non-progression'.

Tuesday August 14th

What a day!

How can I explain, apart from writing that whoever invented the mobile phone really needs to be locked away in a cave; the subtle discovery into the word 'peace'.

It began with a call for Mother from Mr Richardson at the bank. A moan, of sorts, complaining, in the most discreet, yet pompous manner, that our monthly draft had fallen 'again' into the red. That is, we, she, us, her, had overspent. Most customers that use the bank receive letters in strong, but diplomatic wording requesting that person visit A.S.A.P; but let us be honest, Mother is not an ordinary client, nor would she stoop to being commanded by a man who has sneaked into her husband's position. How she managed to sweet talk him I will never know, for he backed down, agreed on 'another' quick deal, and fled with what my grandmother would giggle was 'his tail between his legs'

Following that call, which lasted the total sum of fifteen minutes, Savvy rang. Mother answered. I could hear – 'Hello', 'Savvy', 'What is wrong', 'Oh no', and this form of dialogue continued until Mother returned the phone, before collapsing onto the sofa in an overplay of aggrieved frustration. Watching in awe the performance before me she spouted "He has gone".

"Who has gone?"

My query hung between us in the way a hovering bird levitates above the trembling victim.

"Your Father"

"Father?"

"Yes, Savvy says all contact has been lost."

"Is that definite?"

Her eyes rolled toward the heavens, "If Savannah says so, yes."

"What will they do?"

"How should I know?" she wailed, following it on with, "We must leave."

The Bhutan screech once more!

Comfort can be hard, especially when you blame the missing person for delivering this interloper to your door, and as harsh as it may sound, my mother has completely taken over my life.

"We must go nowhere, Mother, until Father has been found."

I will not speak what was really on my mind until I have discovered the truth.

"You have no notion of his disappearance," she continues screeching.

"True," muttering to myself. "You do, that I am sure."

"So, how do we proceed from here?"

"We wait, Mother, just wait" I say.

It would have been no surprise for this exchange to continue for longer, if (I do hate this pesky conjunction) my phone had not intervened.

I forced my tone to be joyful, "Hi."

Hans's smooth sound lifted the concern I had refused to show Mother.

"Tired of waiting for you to call – Result," he spluttered.

"Right," I deliberately expressed, sensing Mother had pricked up her ears.

"Company?" he asked.

"True," I replied.

"I will be quick. Count Reinbach has given me the green light and asks we meet him on the 24th at ten o' clock inside the 'Tatters' building. If you cannot make that day or time he will have to leave it until September."

"Right."

"Does that mean yes?"

"Yes."

"Good. I think we have hit the jackpot, Rhia."

"Great, enjoy your day."

"What? Oh, okay, miss you."

"Miss…"

I stopped myself and replaced the phone. Mother was grinning –

"Hans?"

I stared in disbelief, wondered 'how', and grinned back.

Within an hour of each other during the afternoon, Mother's neighbour Mrs Smith rang with news about another neighbour across the street. This woman's husband had absconded with his secretary, leaving her with the house, the bills, and two small children. The street had collected a few things for the girls, leaving them at her door, so the need to talk was void. Evidently it was paramount this neighbour did not think they were gossiping: the latter which I refused to believe, for Mrs Smith was doing just that by phoning Mother. Finishing one conversation the phone fell silent, only to ring for a second time to complete her story of the husband's whereabouts in a remote village down South. Mother placed astonishment and intrigue in all the correct places, insisting that her husband was away on business to stop the tongues wagging. Completing the 'gossip' marathon she decided to 'take a bath', leaving me to resume the role of 'cook', a post, as you know, that I hate.

I daub the worktops with ingredients for my Spaghetti Bolognese, silently cursing as flour spills around me. This is my only cooking skill, and after Mother's disaster, I am not looking forward to this meal. So, you can imagine my horror when that sonorous trembling sound fills me with dread as I watch my mobile phone clattering across the worktop where I had laid it.

"Who now?" I shout into the quiet space, not recognising the number, or wishing to be disturbed.

"Hello," the voice tetchy.

"Hi girl"

I stop what I am doing, forget the pan I have just sat over a flame.

"Jimmy, is that you?"

"It is."

"This is not your phone."

"I lost mine. This is new."

"Please go nowhere, I just need to sort this dish."

He laughs "You're cooking – Wow."

I throw the spaghetti in the boiling pan, gather the mince, sprinkle spices and onions into another.

"I miss you."

Jimmy clicks his teeth. "I bet you do."

Waiting for his assurance that he misses me too I turn the mince flame down.

"How is my father?" I gabble.

"Fine," he says casual, edged with agitation.

"Is he there?" I stress.

"Yes, why would he not be?"

Oh Lord, he sounds annoyed.

Say something and I put Savvy on a collision course with father for lying to me, say nothing and I fall into what has become known as the Gordian Knot: a problem that deepens by the minute. Dithering, I choose the knot.

"Oh, nothing really."

Poor try.

"Rhia, what have you heard?"

Intolerance joins his ill humour. Inside myself the demons were fighting. I surrender to the drawn sword.

"Father…" an exaggerated sigh. "He has vanished."

What am I? – Undeniably a grass.

Jimmy was laughing, that noise that pours contempt on someone's idea. I stirred the pan on the stove, grabbed it as it began to spit, replaced it gurgling on a lower gas light.

"Your father is with me," the voice was harsh.

"May I speak to him?" I whimper.

I heard a shuffle. "Sorry, sweetheart, he signals 'no'. He is busy."

You can imagine my exasperation. I sniff the scent of smouldering mince, snatch the pan, curse to myself, and push the blackening contents to the back of the stove. My retaliation is swift–

"He is never anything else but busy."

Jimmy wheezes "Ohhh, temper."

"Tell him we need him home," I splutter. "You too."

"I want this mess finished too."

The catch in Jimmy's voice pulls at my heartstrings. How disloyal I have been to him. Not once stopping to think how hard he works. Shame on me.

I hear Jimmy move, snap at whoever is in the background. No doubt my father being bossy.

"Yes, yes, I will ask her."

Shuffling follows the growl.

"What is that noise, and what is the query?" my voice moved up an octave.

Jimmy stamps his foot–

"Bloody foxes, they are scavenging. Your father is demanding you do this task."

I struggle for breath, cannot believe his words. What has happened to the father I knew; his transmission from gentle father to domineering spy relays itself through my partner's tone. I scowl at the pan before me. Like Mother, I am playing cat and mouse with my spaghetti concoction. I slam it aside.

"Me?" I snarl, determined to creep out of whatever task awaits me.

"Yes, you" the sound is that of monotonous boredom.

"An address is written on a piece of paper at the bank. We need it A.S.A.P. for us to find the painting. Can you help us?"

My heart jumps.

"An address you say, for whom?"

Jimmy clicks his teeth. From the heavy breathing to the ridiculous habit with his teeth I knew this man was climbing that hill of fury, even more so when the waspish answer reverberated down the phone–

"I do not know, Rhia," he appeared to shake his handset. "When will you f.... Sorry – grasp the fact that this show is run by your father."

I forgot to stir.

I had never heard Jimmy be so churlish; the pressure from this search must be taking its own toll. How can I tell him?

"I am not working there without father." I say feebly.

"That has got to be your joke?" he thundered.

"No," the voice has grown weaker.

"You, you..."

I swished the sticking pasta, almost tippled it from the stove. Now, while I cannot explain his anger, I will overlook his aggression. Put it down to the stress of his situation: consider informing him that Hans and I may have found his blasted painting. Will he be pleased? Think again–

"I will try," was my response.

"Do," his voice quivered. "I have been told that address may have something to do with a woman. Tell no-one. They cannot be trusted."

"Has father said?"

"Yes," he growls. "Why are you such a numpty?"

That word.

"I am no numpty. By the way Hans..."

"Sod Hans," he shouted. "I must go. These foxes are troubling me."

The purr from the phone carried the words I whispered "I love you" towards his retreating mouth.

In my hand lays the phone where, but a moment ago, this woman was asked to uncover an address. That address I have within my possession already. If you have not heard the phrase 'Caught between the Devil and the Deep Blue Sea' you will not know how I feel.

On the stove sits a burnt saucepan; a dilemma that spells out quite clearly my problems of great magnitude. Why should my father choose me to reveal this address? He must know explanations are called for. That I need answers.

I ponder– my mind expanding to a thought creeping upon me. Wait, what if it was not father who called for Savvy's aid, but mother? I reflect on her continuous repetition of that poem – 'Come into my parlour said the spider to the fly'.

I think of Fiona Grubb, Alys Parker, Savannah D' Mill, Jimmy, Hans, Father, Mother, and lastly Count Reinbach, everything I have seen. My head spins. Is this a caveat I should take heed? I hear a sizzle, call–

"Mother, dinner is served – Spaghetti with salad."

–as I snatch the pan from the heat. Know my Bolognese lays cremated, and my honesty is dead.

Friday August 24th

The Tatters*

I had sent Hans a text to meet at 'The Tatters' around nine thirty: a chance for us to calm each other's nerves. From his reply I could tell he was equally as excited at the forthcoming news. I had tried to look 'good', applying concealer to my tired eyes, and a perky pink lipstick that at least matched the summer blouse overflowing my jeans. The night past was better forgotten, if possible, for I tossed and turned as a boat on a stormy sea. Jimmy's words haunted me, played cruel games throughout those dark hours. What troubled me the most was father's express wish for me to retrieve this address. Surely the man was not thinking straight. I knew nothing of his former life, not until Savvy and mother informed me. Even so, the person known as Etta Detdy was not mentioned. I had discovered her; Fiona really, by rummaging under my strict orders. The more I think about it the stronger my belief that apart from Hans and the Count I could trust no-one, Jimmy being exempt, and father – goodness knows what I should write. I had told Hans he must not trust anyone, gave him a quick rundown of Jimmy's call, and admitted I trusted him beyond measure (funny saying) not to tell anyone else. Therefore, if he has… I will…", no need for me to summarize my thoughts.

I stand looking around this small museum, hardly daring to think how boring it would be to work there when a presence behind me said softly–

"Penny for your thoughts?"

He twirled me round and kissed me full on the lips. I did not struggle.

"Hans, I did not see you."

"I know," he said that familiar closeness enveloping our minds.

Proximity overruled any concerns troubling me, as I felt the warmth of his hand grip mine; encountered a desire to lead him away from this place, pretend my life was normal. I could tell by his eyes he felt the same. A shudder swept through me. Hans went to speak as the catch in my memory of Jimmy's voice broke the spell. I was hurtled back to sanity as a tornado rips a tree from the ground. I moved apart, heard the feet approaching us, cast my gaze to the man heading our way.

Count Reinbach looked from myself to Hans, smiled in the knowledge held by those who maintain conspiratorial information.

"Rhia, Hans, it is wonderful to see you both."

That soothing voice draws us to his side, "Come, let us sit and talk."

He leads the way to a table surrounded by three leather backed chairs, asks us to sit. Making ourselves comfortable the Count moves to speak to a woman near the entrance. On his return he says–

"I have kindly asked for coffee."

'Must be serious' I thought, for coffee heeds news that will surprise, yet stimulate.

From an inner pocket of his jacket the Count extracts a notebook, causing my mind to recall images of a television sleuth. I smile. He sets me with those penetrating eyes, allowing his own smile to wash over me.

"Your painting is what is known in the art world as a hidden painting. In other words, it is Dragner's 'Crux' concealed by a nude."

My lips tremor.

Pausing as the woman the Count had spoken with sets large steaming mugs down in front of us, I lower my eyes. The admission alone of that nude tore the ground from beneath my feet. This man, whom for an unknown reason I find calming, and reassuring has looked upon that foul creation. He picks up on my mood.

"I have seen many artists' nudes, and I swear this one has been dismissed. Please, do not distress yourself."

"Vulgar," I whimper.

"Astonishingly beautiful," he corrects. "Yet, best forgotten."

I would have been foolish if I concealed a hope this man would not discern the figure sprawled on the bed.

"Names?" Hans rapidly asks.

"Names," the Count repeats, raising his coffee cup to his lips.

The look that passes between the Count and myself holds a silent 'thank you' on my part, a gratification of artistry on his.

"Many?" Hans asks, his brows knitting together.

"Enough," the Count flips his pages.

We wait, swallowing the steaming liquid in our agitation. Finally, the names pour out–

"Major Emery Dreyer, Kurt Dreyer, Ametti Dreyer, and epithets of various others. Pseudonyms of those soldiers are etched below their names. The German authorities will be pleased."

He took another sip of his coffee–

"May I ask to be trusted to forward this painting to them?"

I recoiled at the thought.

The Count surveyed my face, squeezed his fingers in an act of supplication–

"I have stripped the top painting away. I must admit the 'Crux' beneath is magnificent. The man is a master: a new age Constable with an eye for detail."

Hans, still scowling, asks–

"What about the authorities in this country, they need to be told."

Not waiting for the Count to reply he gabbles –

"The museum – they will inform Jimmy. He can come home, Rhia."

The Count picked up on the confusion running through my eyes, replaced the dredged coffee cup and suggested –

"Let us not rush things, for this painting needs far more scrutiny than mine, especially as I found a name this painter had written in brackets, Alina Dreyer, any ideas?"

The sensation of my heart skipped a beat. We both shook our heads.

"I have heard stories," the Count surmised. "A conjecture that roams on story teller's lips. There was a Stasi spy, younger sister of Major Dreyer. At the time of the Cold War, she fell in love – a British agent I believe. Anyhow, this girl knew things the regime deemed 'classified', and Dreyer decided to lock her away, break the love pact up. She killed a man, flew to her lover and he spirited her away to England. Secrets were prised from her. Could this be her?"

I swallowed hard. What do the wise women quote about a 'jigsaw' falling into place.

Count Reinbach leaned back in his seat. Hans copied. I sat there, searching my mind for the next move.

"Wow, that is some tale."

Hans flung a sideway glance in my direction.

"It may be just that – a tale," the Count laughed.

My friend swung his hand in the air, beckoned to the woman who had delivered our coffee.

"More coffee?" he questioned.

I nod, the Count refuses–

"I must go. Busy schedule. May I keep the painting and pass it on later?

It demands more in-depth research."

Hans casts another hurried glance my way–

"Fine, thank you for your help. My aunt and uncle?"

The Count stands.

"Do not worry on their part. I will explain. Alys will no sooner be told than she will phone you to give her support I am sure."

Bowing low towards me he whispers–

"Rhia, there is little room for movement within this game you play. Take care."

What did he mean?

Noting Hans confusion within himself I say–

"Out with it. Even a child could tell words are tumbling over your bottom lip."

He bites the lip, almost as if he would force the words to disappear.

"Well?" my curiosity grows.

"Etta Detdy," he ventures. "Do you think this girl may be her?"

I knew it.

"Maybe," I say nonchalantly, calm being the last action on my mind.

What could I say – 'Yes, they have got to be connected?'

Hans words are now stumbling from his mouth. "Do you know what this means?"

I do not answer.

"That if Alina Dreyer is Etta Detdy, then this woman is related to me. We must find her."

I feel the sting in his admission.

"We will find out" I say, trying hard to mollify his anguish.

--

Around midday we decide to end our meeting, neither in the mood for idle chat, minds running amok over the information gathered. Hans kissed my forehead, vowed he would be 'in touch', then slipped away leaving me dawdling at the crossroad of indecision. Without thinking, almost at the verge of distraction; what Mother would call 'not thinking straight' and my grandmother would name 'dotty' (her expressions fit her Bohemian lifestyle), I pressed the phone numbers to Fiona Grubb.

Yes, Diary, Fiona Grubb.

"Hello," the voice was timid.

"Fiona," I gush. "Please you must help me."

"No," she replied.

"Please," I beg, "I am in a quandary."

"Where's that?" she moaned.

Ridiculous girl.

"Nowhere," my voice was harsh. "I need you to uncover a truth for me."

"I leave in two weeks," she throws at me.

"Please," I beg further, "I need to know the background of Etta Detdy."

What was I asking?

"Aw, come on," she splutters. "Richardson will have my guts."

"Not if you make up to him."

Silence, probably gone too far.

"Fiona?" I gush, praying she has not stormed off the phone.

This silence was not golden.

I wait, count the people beginning to file through the small museum's doors, move my coffee cup around the table, think 'I must trim my nails'. Then–

"I am sorry," I whisper, hating the fact I am backing down, "I need your help."

The phone hums, I realise the girl is struggling in herself.

“I will help you, Miss Bryant, but let me say this firmly – It is the last.”

I release the breath I had been holding.

“Thank you,” I smirk, wait for her reply – Nothing.

Pushing the phone into my bag I move from the table, nod in the direction of the woman by the door, and head out into the busy day. It was evident why the Count loved the ‘Tatters’. In the way historians find their excitement into the past, his love for art knew no bounds: a banner proclaiming an unspoken depth of scholarship. It was this juxtaposition that caused me to wonder why the man tallied Dragner to Constable, an English landscape painter? Why not with a German painter such as Paul Kayser 1869-1942?

Please do not think this woman has finally succumbed to being ‘arty’. I only know this German name through a painting catching my eye as I left the building.

I begin my walk home.

Monday August 27th

Bank Holiday.

It is true to say this little island of ours has various bank holidays where we celebrate this or that in tune with a restful day for certain workers, or a flaming good ‘knees up’. Mother and I had decided on the former, lounging around and generally doing nothing, not even reading a book. For myself I had sworn my brain would rest, no matter what the Count had told us, and Mother, if she ever worries about anything other than social, appears to be doing the same. Phones have been switched off, that is apart from the house phone, which I have removed one part from another, dangling down the wall as a worm looking for earth. Both have a drink in our hand, and both sprawl as lions basking in the sun. We shall remain like this for the best part of the day, before thinking about our yoga moves. Impossible my brain shouts due to the drink. Who cares, I add, if the downward dog resembles a cat waiting to pounce on a mouse, or the tree, swaying to keep its branches steady wobbles unceremoniously. We will laugh our way through those moves, then drink to celebrate our achievement. This is the life. Shame that father and Jimmy are not here – Then again maybe not.

Friday August 31st

Still getting over my headache from bank holiday, and *her* text late last night. By *her* I mean Miss Fiona Grubb, my juvenile busybody who believes this woman must run to her bidding.

Explain next entry. I need a dark room.

September 2001

Saturday September 8th

Can you believe this – Miss Fiona Grubb (my take for' -'Who the hell does she think she is') has instructed me to meet up with her at the same bench in Postman's Park on the 8th at midday. The text, that came late Thursday night, was garnished with a small box beneath her text asking for a 'Yes' or 'No' reply– Please 'tick' was her wording, written in fancy text format, and sounding like a military sergeant major.

My thought never changes – 'Bloody cheek'.

Three times – I will repeat – three times, I tried to send her a new text. Guess what, her phone refused its entry; heaven alone knew how the kid had immobilized my answers. I tried to call her – again the line was busy. No matter how many times I pushed those dratted buttons, that squeaky mouse voice did not say 'Hello', leaving me with one option, to text 'yes'.

So, here I sit, waiting for the regal presence that is Fiona Grubb.

Sucking on the straw of a 'take out' orange juice my eyes catch the willowy outline belonging to this pompous young girl walking toward me. Collapsing at my side, the ruby mouth mutters "Hi". I continue to suck my drink, determined it would not be her that ran this meeting. She threw my re-buff aside.

"Thanks for coming at short notice, but it was today or not at all. I vacate (showing off) London tomorrow."

'Really' runs through my mind.

"I have your information," she carries on. "You will not like my documentation, big word hey, but you wanted the lot."

I finally stop sucking.

"Remember that paper I gave you with three names and their pseudonyms?"

I nod.

"Well, they are more connected than you thought."

It had fled my memory that this girl had also seen my father's alias. I watched as the satisfaction settled across her face.

"Evidently," she laughed. "Great word for me don't you think?"

If she does not come to the point – my imagination scrambled with the images of medieval stocks.

She picked up where she had left off–

"Evidently (deliberately re-said) your father and that woman Etta were lovers. She was pregnant."

Implication?

Tardy kid, she is trying to kick back at me.

"Is this your way of paying me back?"

Spiteful little cow.

The ruby mouth twitched, broke into half a smile, then settled in a downward dip.

"No, it is the truth as I have heard."

"Heard from whom?"

My tongue reminds me of a viper's sting.

"Miss D' Mill."

Shall I laugh? If the kid thinks she has shocked me, then she can think again. I will not show her the whirlpool in my head.

"Savannah D' Mill?" I grunted. "And how did *you* meet her?"

Fiona sighed, inspected her 'hacked' nails.

"I didn't. She was in Richardson's office. They forgot I was in the cupboard (please) due to the door being nearly closed. They were discussing Etta Detdy. I overheard."

She wore that silly grin. My hand crumpled into a ball. Deep within my mind I could hear the scream.

Today, it was extra busy in this park. A good job really, for believe me, Diary, I will take this kid by the hair, and string her from the nearest tree.

"The baby?" I snarl under my breath.

"Dunno, that's for you to find out. I'm done," she concludes in a haughty manner.

DONE? How dare she even think of stepping away? I will ruin her.

Plan B – pretend to cry.

I rubbed my eyes on the sleeve of my jumper; the morning had been chilly, unlike now, felt the sting of tears, then forced them to run down my cheek. The mouth puckered, I counted to ten. Fiona's eyes welled up–

"Please, do not cry, Miss Bryant. I am sure this can be sorted."

I sniffled –

"It can, but I need your help. Please do not leave me in this mess."

The lips tutted, her eyes softened, Fiona Grubb was caught in that web of deceit.

"What can I do?" came the query.

If the people within this park would not think me mad, I would get up and dance.

How exceptional I am at this game; honestly, who could possibly have the accomplishment to better me?

"Please, have one last 'root' in that cupboard. My father must have left a clue, a sign to the child?"

The girl paused, twisted her hands, eyed me as you would peruse a shoe for dog mess, responded in a downcast tone–

"I have a small chance late this afternoon. Old Richardson has arranged a small 'Goodbye' do. I do not know why, for they dislike me. I will nosy beforehand. Will that do?"

I stop pretending to cry. The kid stood, cast a look of disgust my way, and left. Sad in a way, for I wished her to hear my next request into which of the two addresses she had found were the real hide-out of Etta Detdy,

Never mind, it will be my job to find out, and I could not complain. I had been triumphant.

Wednesday September 12th

Today I write with sadness–

As the world spins on its axis, humans also work from their core; sense, smell, thought and perception. Our mind triggers certain apprehensions or convictions that either lead us to the truth or bury us in what generations past call 'deep water'. September 11th will be recorded in history as a dark day: a day when those core values were put to the test. Yesterday, in the state of New York, within the United States of America, two planes flew into those symbols of world trade known as 'The Twin Towers'. It was not an engineering failure, or a pilot error, but what this twenty-first century has come to designate terrorism.

Not only did those two landmarks of international communication topple to the ground, killing hundreds of people, but another plane was steered across the Potomac river from Washington DC toward the five-sided building of the Pentagon Headquarters of the U.S. Department of Defence in Arlington County, Virginia, where 189 were killed, and many injured. To compound these horrors, a fourth plane was flown toward Washington DC, but where all passengers aboard the former three aircraft were killed, the passengers on this flight overpowered their captors, and crashed the plane toward a field in Stony Creek, near Shanksville, Pennsylvania, saving lives.

Question "Why?"

Answer "Ideology."

An act to bring about a certain belief, however wrong, whatever the cost.

In history an instant occurrence that changes the perception of the world, or the lives of those who witness it, may be classified as an epiphany. Often noted as a revelation of joy, such as the honouring of the Christ child by the Three Wise Men, still celebrated two thousand years later throughout the world.

On a more sinister note, and we should thank the heavens this is rare, darkness can rise to challenge this oracle, bringing with it an aftermath of change.

For example: the belching of Mount Versuvius in 79 A.D. which obliterated the city of Pompeii. In a similar vein, September 11th 2001, in America will stand in history as a 'dark' revelation: that instant moment when an act of evil brought a change to the world forever.

As the headcount for casualties grows the miracle that is human strength and resilience also grows. Stories of bravery and honour cover the papers. As countries around the world find themselves embroiled, the joining together can be seen in an act of unity.

Friday September 21st

The world is still reeling from the horror of September 11th. Papers reporting the good and bad stories accompanying these prodigious events relate voices from around the world; journalism has gone crazy. In my own world I can report that neither Jimmy nor Father have phoned; of which surprised me. Under circumstances such as these myself and my father would sit around that coffee table discussing every political view, and every layman's attitude.

Strange really, for those actions alone should have raised my intrigue.

These last few days my mind had wandered to my upcoming birthday. Now, withstanding that every year marks a higher figure to celebrate, Jimmy and I performed what we called 'the ritual': a celebratory dinner, and a fun packed evening (if you know what I mean). As no-one gets in contact unless they wish me to report or spy into things around me, I have decided to cancel birthdays for this year. That said, far more pressing anxieties are looming before me.

Such as my message from Fiona – at last. It took the kid thirteen days to connect with me. Days I wished I could 'hang her out to dry'; days when I more than overworked my phone.

'Hid in cupboard, made an excuse to Richardson that I must finish tidying.
Get this, he completely agreed. Ring later'

Ring later – Shall I scream now?

Of late Mother has been 'loitering' around me. That is the best way I can write she has been spying over my shoulder when I am reading my phone. It is due to my nimble fingers that I closed my text box before she has a chance to read. I am sure that woman knows 'something' is afoot, especially as I have not told her about Jimmy's call. Yesterday she left early to meet an old friend. Not willing to say 'who' this friend was, presumption overtook my inquisitive brain, and I came down on the side of a neighbour, then a socialite from her circle. They all think the same snooty things. However, upon her return two hours later, her face held nothing but consternation. Can her 'up your nose' society pals be drifting away?

"What is wrong?" I ask.

"Nothing," she returns.

"Who did you meet?"

Catch question. Clever girl, Rhia.

"No-one."

She walks into the kitchen.

"Did you enjoy your meeting?"

No response. I admit defeat.

My summary returns to today –

Morning edged into a showery afternoon, and I was beginning to feel edgy over Fiona's absent phone call. By now the silly girl should have rung, told me her find, and bowed to my decision whether to release her from our collaboration, or not. Mother's mood, still reeling from yesterday, had progressively darkened, and by three o' clock her announcement that she was retiring to the bedroom to read caught me by surprise. Whatever had happened had pushed Mother to the limit of her patience. I grasp my mobile, twist it within my hands in the temptation to call Fiona. They say the spirit is strong, but the flesh is weak, and that is exactly how I feel as the gadget rings.

"About time," I scoff, raising it to my ear.

The clicking of teeth halts the tirade ready to fall from my mouth.

"Hello, Rhia, Jimmy here."

Not Fiona.

"It's you," I breathe deep.

"Yes."

"I thought…"

The teeth clenching continued.

"Forget it. I only called in the hope you had discovered that paper we mentioned last time we spoke. That address in-case you forgot."

This was derision.

I told myself Jimmy was under a great deal of pressure searching for that painting Hans and myself had found. I must say something.

"The painting," I begin. "What would *he* paint over the Crux?"

"Do you mean Dragner?" Jimmy sounded tired.

"Yes," my voice quivered.

"Something of no consequence."

No consequence? If only my partner knew.

"Address, Rhia?" Jimmy implores.

"Yes, but this painting, we…" I try to stress.

"Leave the painting," he storms.

Round and round in my head – My Jimmy will be forced to look upon that vile work of art.

"That painting," I try to continue–

"Rhia" the rasping sound cuts through the hysteria building in my mind. "Get a grip."

The clenching of the teeth grows louder–

"Address."

"What?" the word spurts out.

"Hell, you have not found it. Great. Your father will not be pleased."

"Sorry," my mind was spinning.

"Don't bother."

Suddenly his question made sense. Father and Jimmy would have Etta Detdy moved before harm could befall her.

"That address," I gabbled. "It is…"

Jimmy had rung off, and when I recalled on the number that had shown I heard only buzzing.

--

Late Evening

There comes a time, Diary, when not even you can ease the tension gathering inside me. Jimmy had upset the equilibrium of the day, bouncing off the phone, rude to say the least: mix this with Mother's secret meeting, and this orb I call my world looks bleak. It was becoming a fact that no-one was interested in my torment. It had been a case of tell her about the past, then let her 'get on with it'; the handling being neither tactful nor sensitive. Sitting here, by the window, on my own, I can reveal the street is deserted. No white car. No cars at all for a change, just an odd passer-by that is mindful on getting to their destination, be it the shop or home. I blink, the thoughts of my conversation with Jimmy troubling me. Without a doubt I should have given him at least one address for Etta Detdy. Forget the Grubb kid, forget my pride. Yet, each time my mind insists I do this, I fail miserably. Let me be more specific – It is quite transparent that girl is trouble, with a capital 'T', and quite transparent that if she were caught, I would be compromised also.

Nevertheless, why the stubborn hesitation when Jimmy asked?

My mind veers from this problem to settle with father. I would have thought he would remember where he had housed his agent, if that is what she was. The man is supposedly her contact.

Spiralling thoughts, around and around.

Back to the Grubb girl.

As you know dear, Diary, I do believe Fiona Grubb is silly, but she was adamant that move was for the Detdy woman. Swore she heard Savvy and smarmy Richardson discussing a move. There can be no reason for her to dupe me, this girl knows which side her 'bread is buttered'. My brain accepts that, yet I still cannot answer my own conundrum – Surely father being her handler – I pause within that thought – Would he not have to sign her movements off?

I move from the window, feel the slight chill of a creeping Autumn.

I have received no call from Fiona, although she promised. That worries me, especially as the girl uses the text as a platform to practise her delight in different fonts, and her phone as a conduit to surround me with messages of gloom. I will give her an hour, then I have not a clue what to do.

Wait for the fallout I suppose.

--

Midnight

The witching hour, and still gazing into the street, marking each body that runs here and there trying their best to sidestep the puddles forming on the pavement. The last half an hour has been spent in devising a plan to extract myself from whatever mess Fiona has got me into. Deep in thought I did not, at first, notice the throb of the phone which I had converted to silence. Realising this instrument was jumping around on the table behind me the rush to pick it up was nothing short of hilarious. Spotting the number dancing across the screen I let out a sigh of relief–

"Late," I spit, first word to fly through my mind.

"Yep, I am (hic)" the girl belched. "Oops, sorry."

I felt that familiar annoyance creeping over me.

"Have you been drinking?"

Silly question.

"Yep," another hiccup.

I could wait no longer. I gushed–

"Tell me you found something out."

A burp to blow my ears.

"Whoops, sorry, too much drink… Out, found, What, who, where?"

Is the girl dancing to her own inanity?

Believe me when I write this kid is wearing, could she not understand that I had waited too long for this call for her to mess it up.

"Fiona," I bark. "Where have you been?"

"Naughty Miss Bryant," she gasped. "Me? Let me think (hic) Where can I be?"

I am going to breathe fire down this damned phone.

"Fuck's sake, where?" I holler down the phone, willing Mother not to hear.

"Ah, you…" she dribbled. "You (I can imagine her finger swirling in my face) a sweary word – Ahhhhh."

Swear? I will more than swear. This fool of a girl had been plied so much drink she would not even know what day it was.

Try another tactic.

"Did your colleagues give you a good send off?" I asked, keeping my voice low.

"Yep, lots and lots of wine (hic)," another dribble, an extra hiccup. "I am in Wales, and out with my mates"

What a surprise.

Inside, this woman was pleased she had not been discovered, but annoyed that she had not rung me sooner. Now, the girl was in that category that is known as 'legless'; too much to drink, and not enough food. I must contend with the profanity of alcohol dimming her senses. Tread carefully–

"My task, did you succeed?" the voice light, my attitude kept in check.

"Task? Task? I wouldn't spit a task (hic)," she began to sing.

Frustration is getting the better of me. The need to shake her in the customary act of a dog with a rag toy shunning the sensible thoughts in my head.

"Fiona," the name rebounds along the line. "My bloody task?"

She continues that ridiculous singing, nothing making sense, words a complete jumble.

"SHUT UP," I say in the most demanding tone possible. "You will wake the world."

"Ah, that is where I must be," the silly girl dribbles.

From her end I hear the scraping of metal on metal, a door open and shut.

"Is that you?"

More silence, then–

"Off with me shoes. Off with me coat – Home… yeah."

The hiccups that followed were accompanied by further giggles and burps.

I can feel tiredness overcoming me.

"You walked home?" I enquired, anything to get her unruly mind back on track.

"Yep," she whelped.

"Alone?"

She laughed aloud.

"Would you (hic) with your men (hic)?"

What is she suggesting? What has she been told at that catacomb of a bank? I change the subject–

"Do you feel alright?"

She lets out a howl –

"My head is fuzzy (hic), my belly sore."

My wish to say 'good' died on my lips, instead I sweetly pushed–

"Did you find anything," pause, quickly adding, "in the cupboard?"

I will play along, any bloody thing to get my answer.

This time she was humming.

"This is not…" the sentence stopped by the rage building within me.

"Yes, you, something, I think," she spouted.

This was ridiculous.

I am having a moment when these hands desire to slip down a phone and grab the silly kid by the hair. Thinking 'calm down' I hear a rustle and know that must be her slipping from her coat.

"You think what?" my voice quivers.

"Yep, this…"

I do believe tipsy or not she was messing.

"And…" I could hear the vexation rising again from my throat.

"Pr – pre – (hic) Oh Lor, you not going to like…(hic)"

What is this kid on – Hot air?

She now started what I presumed was dancing, probably more kicking out from what I could hear. Then the singing began again, loud, squealing at the top of her voice. A male voice demanded she be quiet. The voice subdues, a croaking continues –

"Dad" she splutters.

Now, If I were not a good person, this woman would demand Fiona Grubb be subject to what is known as a Scold's Bridle. This was a form of humiliation mainly focused upon women thought to be witches and shrews in the sixteenth century. An iron muzzle within an iron framework placed around the head. The bridle part, or curb plate of two inches long and one inch broad, is placed into the mouth and pressed down onto the tongue, making speaking impossible. This cruel, and devastating harmful object of torture was outlawed, and either destroyed or put into museums – shame?

I sensed Fiona had moved from wherever she had been standing into the bathroom. I could hear running water, pleaded with the heavens that she would be kept from 'throwing up' until I had my answer.

"Fiona, tell me what you found, and I promise you will not be troubled again."

She giggled, a habit I know well from insobriety.

"Oh, I do not feel good, and your p-p-promises-sss are sh…"

She was unable to finish her sentence as the retching kicked in. She coughed, made the noise that follows retching.

"I know. Tell me, please," I beg.

"Pl… pl… pl-lease," she copies.

A huge burp, more giggling. This girl really needs a slap.

"The baby…" Fiona's tone wobbles, "the baby you."

Her hiccups are louder. She gushes more water.

"What?"

Incomprehension comes to mind. The girl is babbling. Has not a clue what she has said.

"I feel ill. The baby is you – YOU."

Is she so drunk her mind has blown?

"I must go, Miss Whatsit, going to be…"

Stupid, stupid drunken girl.

"Go," I holler. "Good riddance."

The sound of vomiting and screams drowns out my words. I throw the phone across the room.

Part Four

Deep Within East Germany

The man shivered, his thin shirt and trousers no protection against the cold biting wind blowing around this building. He had left behind the warmth of late summer, arriving within the walls of this forsaken prison six weeks ago, where passageways were dark, the guards foreboding, and the outlook bleak. It reminded him of that place he had tried to forget – Housewachen: the haunt of the betrayed, where every cry pierced his mind, and every stand for resistance lead to interrogation and death.

What did all this mean?

The man knew he was a catalyst for enticement. They wanted his father, and the son was merely the 'means to an end', or so they thought. He had heard the guards as they marched him to his cell complain of how low the temperature dropped in this part of Germany. Their inhuman laugh as they told him he would be 'lucky' to survive. Yet, survive he must. He was needed to complete this plan, his father's revenge.

He ploughed his foot into the leg of the strong iron cot, yelping as his thin boot connected with the post. This cell, no larger than his last, was far damper, with icicles twisting around the bars at his window, illuminating the frost laden moon the moment darkness spread across their frozen bodies. The straw mattress, rougher than his previous one, gave no comfort to his weakened frame; the cough now hacking his chest at regular intervals. The portable latrine, barely emptied once a week, reeked from the smell of disinfectant used to cover the putrid odour of human excrement. His eyes watered, the miasma from his bucket causing him to wretch. He coughed, spats of blood falling from his lips onto his open hand. How dare he be left like this, a master painter, well known in circles these fools could only dream about. Surely, as their boots or fists connect with his body, they must know what outcome they will eventually receive. They are but walking corpses – names in his father's black book.

He moves to the crack in the wall they have the cheek to call a window, breathes deep, feels the biting air. From the dirty glass he could see no yard, no prisoners snaking one behind another to the varied orders and whistle from a guard. No visitors filing through the steel plated gates. How could men – Rats, such as himself be worthy of visitors.

"Speak to the walls" those sententious guards had laughed.

"Speak to my father's fist" the man had spat back to the butt of a rifle, or the cap of a boot. He was alone, enjoying (satirical scorn) the pleasure of the violent criminals he had heard crying expletives into the night air. Men, with a far more dubious past than his, their thirst for blood a stain on his country's past. His gaze sought the ground below, a sheer drop. Again, the cough racks his body, this time his hand closes on a small clot, and his heart sinks. His lungs are dissolving as a painting fades with the years.

He flapped his arms around himself, trying to reclaim a heat that was never present. Could those who ran this place not see this building was stuck in a time warp? It belonged to an era long gone, when the Barons of a former age wore thicker clothing and ate better food, not the muck earlier thrown into his cell. He sent the tin plate skimming across the floor, tumbling the scraps of blackened bread and watery stewed vegetables onto the stone tiles. He would have fared better if the Berlin authorities had shipped him to an island and left him to die. Throwing himself down onto the prickly mattress he grabbed hold of the thin, stinking blanket they had thrown into his cell. He cursed. How could this threadbare coverlet keep him warm? His torso, ravished with scars and bruises from rough handling, his skin yellowing, and his hair losing the fair colour due to filth and illness. Shackled, he had been kept within this cell; all credit to his former life disposed. He was no famous painter here. He was no Major's son. His father, looked upon as a nefarious outlaw, defiled and laughed over; his name spoken and defamed every time those guards passed his cell. Punching the mattress, he began to wheeze, spasms ripping through his chest in waves of convoluted coughing.

How could he survive?

His mind fell into that quagmire of depression where light was not allowed.

The end story– He would die here. Not knowing if his plan had succeeded. Not knowing if the tyrant of his father's plot had suffered. His life now hung between two worlds; one being the dark, isolated existence within these walls, another the sphere where this debacle began. Both, he feared, and both embedded him in dread.

--

"Kurt."

The sound was low, almost a whisper, floating through the night air, tickling his ear in the process to wake him. The man's limbs convulsed, shook with pain, as the strong smell of vodka fanned across his face.

'Guards,' he thought. 'Playing their stupid night games.'

Often, in the dark hours between dusk and dawn, they would creep into his cell and torment him, raising him from the apology they labelled sleep, to taunt him.

"Dragner, Dragner," spat with the contempt they deigned fit, misused how they wished – Bastards.

This time he will spit back in their faces. Try to fold his fist into their mocking mouths.

Turning onto his side, lips pursed in the formation of a tiger ready to pounce, he tried and failed to fold his hands into a tight-fisted ball. Pain stabbed through him. Pain as he had never experienced, making him judder, causing him to scream out. He felt wetness suddenly spurt down his leg, wetting his trousers, leaving his weak bladder in the form of a running stream.

"Kurt."

Louder, insistent.

He tried to move, tried to twist his head. His name – his real name had been spoken. These fools had never called him that.

"Kurt."

A command. This call did not have the stamp of an insult, nor that usual number of '1989' (the night of the Berlin Wall, and the fall of the Stasi regime) those guards took pleasure in voicing. This call was different. There was someone leaning above him, willing him to focus. The man knew whatever move he made, he must not 'eyeball' this person. To do so, especially if it turned out to be those guards, his night would be drenched in further pain and sorrow. He squinted through half closed eyes, waited for the voice to steal through his haze.

"Kurt" a harsher command, this time saliva dropping onto his face.

A hand gently shakes him, then stops. Reaching through the blur of pain his own hand shot upwards, touched features swaying above him, strong, wilful, unrelenting in the need to rouse him. Who?

He must clear his rheumy eyes, must push through this odious pain.

Think, man, think. Uncertainty flooded his mind. That guard, the mad one with the bulbous eyes and large belly, he would act like this, kind, congenial, before scraping him from the bed and pummelling him into a bruised mess.

"Please," he croaked. "Do not hurt me."

Damn – He had forgotten to speak in German. Hallucinatory thoughts were beginning to grip him, images crowding in on him. Somehow, he must fight. These crows cannot win. Fight fire with fire. He grasped the figures coat, his bony fingers slipping downward to lay once more beside his shaking form.

"Hund," he mumbled. "Hund."

The word 'dog' had evidently taken the figure by surprise. Good, until an expletive "ScheiBe" (shit) raged in fierce contempt. The man recoiled. That word had always preceded a beating. He rolled closer to the wall, crouching in fear, waiting for the pounding to begin.

Someone was moving, nearer, nearer. The man winced, set his mind for the thumps that would follow. A hand was moving closer. He began to flay around the bed, legs jumping in his fight for escape.

Then, "Son" filled his ear.

What? A caress in the voice.

The pleas of 'Don't hurt me' in German burst in rapid succession from his trembling mouth.

"Shh," the voice was comforting. "Speak in English so *they* will not, understand."

Slowly the man stirred from his position by the wall. Impossible, it could not be–

"Father?"

Gently the figure eased the man upward, cradling his body. Tears that had collected behind the man's eyelids coursed down his cheeks, his hand flying to his mouth, suppressing the cough that threatened to consume him.

He had not undressed, he never did, not in this climate. Night always brought a dip in temperature. On a good night 15 Celsius below freezing, on a bad night 20 Celsius, to consider undressing would be foolish. Struggling to sit up, an involuntary shiver ran through his emancipated body as he collapsed into the waiting arms. This deliverer from hell had called him 'son' which meant his command was inviolable.

He must stand.

"Father, it is you." The cry was low.

Staggering unsteadily onto his feet he felt the warmth of a thick sheepskin coat envelope his shoulders.

"What have these pigs done to you?" his rescuer raged. "We must hurry."

Grasping the course material of a uniform under his fingers the man felt himself conveyed through the cell door. Moving stealthily down the passageway they met another two figures, who saluted, then took over the support of his body.

"My son was locked in a cell with an overflowing latrine for company. Someone will pay." the voice seethed.

In the man's confused mind anger was becoming counterpart to revenge as they moved down the dark passageway. He felt his body sag between the strong arms upholding him, dragging him, compelling him to move. He could not hear a sound, apart from the heavy snoring emanating from the cells they passed. What had happened?

Rounding a corner, a glint of stars before them, the man heard boots, voices shouting as they ran. From behind a whistle blared, a gun fired, catching the soldier to his left in the shoulder. Inside him a tumult of emotion was building. The snoring had been a trick; someone had betrayed his father.

"Father, leave me" he gasped "Go, do not get yourself captured or killed."

Through the mist of tears never far from the man's eyes, he detects those running toward him, and those pouring through the open door toward his father. The man sinks to the ground.

"Take care with him," the fiery voice flings. "Make him go. However, I do not care. Just get him out of this rat hole. I have business to finish."

The man pleaded–

"Father, please."

He heard the cry of battle leave the throat of his liberator as the soldier on his right side let him go and made ready to follow his commander. The wounded soldier lifted the man's sagging body, began pulling him toward the door as a low swift order shot their way–

"Go – The plan is in motion, the painting, the girl, the traitor. Take him, now."

His head ached, his eyes were failing him: behind him, running feet, harsh voices, screams of pain… Gunfire.

October 2001

I have moved into the month of October in a mood that would allow me to cast upon myself the gracious title 'Wine God'. Please do not feel burdened under my scratchy pen for all will be speedily explained. Travelling back in history to the duration known as the Roman Age, the month of October was a celebration to the gods Jupiter and Juno. Feasts were held where wine was consumed in abundance. My imagination, like those belonging to many a film director, portrays this era in the lavish abandoned festivities of wealthy Roman officials, forgetting the many poor collecting in alleyways or hovels that were designated as houses. My main point within this history of the month that in old English was called 'Winterfylleth' meaning Winter Full Moon, as this woman has drunk far too much wine to ease the pain of Fiona Grubb's findings. For the past nine days I have been mulling her words over.

The Baby Is You

Unable to digest the meaning of those words, or rather unwilling to do so, I have turned to the tranquilizing effect of fermented red grapes.

Believe me, this is wrong.

Mother has pleaded with me to share my worry, of which I have been brutal and inconsiderate, telling her to leave me alone. Savvy commented I was 'drowning' my dissatisfaction through a bottle. I have no time for these women, they are not to be trusted: at least I do not keep secrets that can break a heart in two.

I sip from the glass in my hand.

The most important decision made throughout these days is my wish to phone Hans, and demand (I know it sounds rude) he takes me to Coventry. It is vital I seek out this Etta Detdy. Find out exactly what is behind Fiona's pronouncement. At this precise moment I need someone to put my trust in. If

Jimmy were here my wine drenched thoughts would not be turning elsewhere – But, we know the old saying:

'A drowning man will clutch at a straw' (Sir Thomas More 1478-1535) *

--

Monday October 1st

I waited for Mother to go shopping; that Monday jaunt, regular as clockwork, buying nonsense for the fridge, and nonsense for the wardrobe. She had begged me to go, mainly due to the blazing row we had the previous evening where I lampooned her disgracefully, plus swore to tell my woes to Hans's aunt.

How did we step into this minefield?

Easy –

Two women making poor little me the point of their joke. Harmless or otherwise my brain was in no mood for their nuances, especially Savvy, and Mother's campaign to stay gripped to her side. To begin with, that butterfly of intelligence (supposedly), had flown in and out of the flat within the space of an hour, moaning over how much I was drinking and complaining that she had not long received a call from a colleague stating something important had occurred abroad. Now that important bit did not concern me, but the drinking bit certainly did. I rounded on her, bubbling over with innuendos and unforgivable digs at her past, to the point that Mother told me to 'zip it'. Hands up – or pen in this instant, she spoke in a rather more polite term, if still rude, than I have written.

I had never heard my mother utter anything uncultured, until now. I was furious. Not stopping to think I bounded every item I believed would sting, every remark I knew would hurt, and any dash of dirt relating to my father I could think about in her direction. My only salvation – I left Etta Detdy alone. The last throw of the dice was my hint at running to Han's aunt for comfort. Savvy tried to speak, halted by my course tongue in the mode of a thrashing piranha. A look at Mother, then she left, my befuddled brain causing my mouth into what I now would call a 'runaway train'.

"You lie to me," I shout at Mother's enraged face.

"Not true," Mother retaliated.

"You do," even louder.

"Such as?" she cries.

"Me," I rasped.

"You?" the tone severe.

"Tell me you do not lie to me."

Her eyes filled with the tears she had refused to spill.

"Not intentionally," she whispered.

I stood, staring at the quivering frame before me – No pity. Mother edged her way toward the bedroom, slammed the door as the sobbing began.

--

This morning I think back on that argument in shame. Only twice during the previous evening did Mother vacate that room. Once for the bathroom, another for a glass of water. She neither spoke, nor ate. However, I gorged myself silly, and fell asleep in the chair. On waking, the pain in my neck and shoulders spoke volumes, not only of the night flown, but my sad disposition in this whole mess. I could hear Mother in the kitchen, knew she had risen at some ungodly hour, and was trying to plaster over the enormous crack I had created between us by preparing breakfast. Slowly I pulled myself up from the chair, flinching at every ache presenting itself. The walk, or rather crawl, to the kitchen table was certainly no mean feat. I looked how I felt, crumpled, mucky, head bouncing away with every step I took.

"Breakfast?"

Mother's face said it all. I eased myself onto a chair, gulped my tea, wished I taken more care, then quickly ran (hobbled) to the bathroom.

Emerging I noticed Mother had put her coat on, not that she will need it, for October has begun on an exceedingly warm note.

"Going somewhere?" I asked sarcastically.

"It is Monday," she replied, twisting her gloves onto hot hands. "Shopping."

"Yes, I forgot."

"Are you coming?" a speck of intensity in her tone.

"Like this?" I pointed to my frenzied hair and pale face "No – Thank you."

"Please," she whimpered.

I shook my head.

"Will you stay in?"

Ah, crunch of the matter.

"Yes."

"Sure?" she pressed.

"Yes," I slammed her way,

Without another word she kissed the top of my head, and left without a word, dignified as ever.

Stomping around the flat, a cushion thrown here, a shoe kicked there, peeved beyond words that Mother would not share her own and Savvy's secrets, full of pent-up anger that my life was a charade. Brushing aside how bad I handled yesterday's meeting: barging in, nostrils flaring, mouth moving with the petulance known only to the recalcitrant child, it is a sure fact that Etta Detdy has predominately overtaken my life. Turned it upside down and threw trust 'out of the window' as my grandmother would say. I need someone who is willing to help me discover whatever lays beneath my father's past. Someone who knows their way around the art world enough to provide me with an answer into why that disgusting (there can be no other word) painting, along with Etta Detdy, form the basis of this turbulent year. I stand for a moment staring at the cars slowly moving along the street, smile to myself, and ring Hans.

"Hi," his voice is cheery.

"Hi to you," I retaliate.

A conversational pause–

"Rhia, what is wrong?"

I mumble, "I need your help."

"Fine," he says. "Anytime."

"I demand you take me to Coventry and set up a meeting with Count Reinbach."

No answer.

I swear a long sigh drifts across the gulf between us.

"Hans, are you still there?"

"Yes."

"What is the matter? Do you not wish to help me?"

"Yes, but…"

"But what?"

As always of late my temper is teetering on the brink of explosion. I can hear a strain in his voice–

"I do work for Savannah D' Mill. I should bring her in on this."

I catch sight of a couple having an argument in the street below, yelling at each other.

"You must not do that," I plead. "Please."

Again frustration.

"Rhia, I will do anything for you…"

I refuse to listen to his excuses.

"Do this."

I sounded as I felt, hot, tired, losing my grip on this year.

"You win," his voice was low, almost a whisper.

"Thanks, when?"

"Why the rush?"

"I need answers."

"Answers?"

"Yes, Etta Detdy."

I felt he paused a moment too long.

"Hans, we need to concentrate solely on this woman, and that vile painting. They are linked somehow."

The more I voiced this remark, the more my belief in this connection grew.

The moment that passed could easily have been a lifetime. Finally…

"I know, I will sort it."

"Great, as soon as possible," I enthused.

"Then what?" he sounded sad.

"I will be forever grateful, so will Jimmy."

The second catch in his voice surprised me.

"Will he? I doubt it."

I truly have no notion as to why this man should say that. If he knew Jimmy as I do, he would perceive how grateful my partner can be. He will not only be pleased my Jimmy will reciprocate the deed in kind.

"We must say nothing to Mother or Savvy. Their actions concern me."

"Likewise, should ours," his intonation conveyed annoyance.

Let me write this conversation ended on that statement.

Why? Tired of being told to re-consider my plans and movements.

Pause…

Oh, Diary, I like Hans. I do believe he has become that special friend, but even he carries that aura which causes me to be wary.

Complicated.

Sunday October 7th

Savvy ran into the flat as a chicken being pursued by a fox. Never, in all these months of knowing her have I beheld such a spectacle.

"It has happened," she spouts, catching her breath as she holds fast to the back of the sofa. Mother and I swap curious glances, waiting for the 'follow up' story to pour from those pink shaded lips.

"Dragner," she hesitated. "He was sprung from the prison in East Germany."

"When?" I threw her way. "By whom?"

"Late September by his Father," she retaliated.

By now the small jacket she was wearing atop her white blouse and jeans was adorning the wooden floor where she had removed it and let it fall. Her fury resembled that often photographed by wildlife presenters for television as they followed ferocious animals in the hunt.

"I cannot believe those guards did not throw away the key, then no-one, not even that creep that calls himself a father, could have saved his heinous offspring."

I was astonished at the level of Savvy's contempt. Trying hard to subdue her ranting I asked–

"Do you know where they are?"

"Know where they are?" she punched the back of the sofa.

"If I knew exactly where those rats were hiding, I would personally deal with them myself."

Mother walked to her side. Brave woman, for I would have be-decked myself in armour.

I watched as Mother soothed, in her way, Savannah's rabid actions–

"Sit, have you no lead at all?"

Savvy refused to sit, eyeing the sofa as if Mother had asked her to walk across hot coal.

"I do. They are in England."

Mother's eyebrows shot up.

"Yes," Savvy declared. "In England."

"Where?" I intervened, thinking this simple question a mitigation in the path of hostility.

She let out a laugh, some would call it a cackle, a noise that thundered around the flat lounge–

"I have no bloody idea. My colleagues have certain information that they boarded a ship for England, and nothing more."

"Oh," was all my mother said.

"Exactly," Savvy shrieked. "Oh, bloody oh."

The usually controlled woman punched the back of the sofa for a second time.

Wallowing in the luxury of this woman's torment I heard myself ask in a self-satisfied manner–

"Why could your colleagues not follow them?"

Savvy glared, a pain I had never detected before, emanating from her eyes.

"You are asking me," she raved. "Would it not be better asking them, those fools who were supposedly tracking that devil of a Major?"

I receded into the background, waited for the tension to subside. Listening to Savvy's continuous rants I proposed that most English of all cures.

"Tea," I suggest.

"Tea?" the vitriolic mouth spurted. "I could do with a stronger drink."

I glanced at Mother who nodded, motioned her head toward the kitchen, then seemingly waited for me to move from the room before speaking.

The moment I stepped into the kitchen the voices began. Pretending to move around the cupboards by slamming my hand against this door or slapping a worktop, I put my ear to that opening betwixt the door and frame.

"This is serious, Savannah" – Mother.

"Do you think I do not know that?" – Savvy.

"What can we do?" – Mother.

"Heaven alone knows." – Savvy.

"Rhia?" – fear in Mother's tone

"I have promised you Mena." – Savvy.

"But…" – Mother.

"No buts. We must see this through. If we do not there will never be peace for any of us." – Savvy.

"We have kept her safe all these years." – Mother.

"True, but this plan has been festering for years."– Savvy.

"His son?"

"Yes… wait, quiet, I cannot hear glasses tinkling, change subject" – Savvy.

Quickly I moved to the cupboards, open them, clink a glass or two, pretend to cough. and return to where Savvy and Mother were now sitting.

Will you believe me when I write that Savannah D' Mill's rage began to peter out by her second glass of wine. With no knowledge that Hans and I had already found a painting, the discussion continued into how Emery Dreyer can be captured. I would have loved to confront them with my plan, for not only will this 'supposed' first class spy be deposed by my clever investigation, but with the help of the brilliant Count Reinbach, we can discover more. How wonderful to face both these women in the knowledge I will find my own way into Father's dark world; uncover their secret past, and mine, while being made to understand that when it comes to deception – I am Queen.

Tuesday October 16th

Hans's text had 'bleeped' its way onto my phone precisely one minute to midnight last evening. Mother, snoring away (she would hate this diary if she knew what I was writing), did not stir, not one small muscle twitched as I pushed the 'read' button. His text was short, to the point, and riddled with upper and low case writing, almost as if the man is in a hurry, or it was being sent whilst he was walking. Goodness knows what he was doing at this hour for his message to be so disjointed.

> ' RHia, mEEt me aT thE 'RESpite from LiFE' baR on BraCKen StREET* at 2pm On TUESday 16th. LovE,,, HaNs x '

Was the man drunk?

I knew it was Hans's phone, his being the only other number beside Jimmy with a heart by it logged into my own. I will not try and explain 'why' this guy has been allowed this intimate status; sufficient to write 'my choice'.

As to the text, could he be messing around with 'mates', as men often do, or as suggested, he has drunk a considerable quantity of alcohol (in company with the Grubb kid!)? Anyway, I had heard of this bar. Jimmy had mentioned it, and not always in a good light. According to my partner, the bar owner had political leanings, and certainly did not think twice when preaching them. In that case, why in the world would Hans take a man of such sensitive tastes as Count Reinbach to this backstreet hovel? Tired as I felt, I believed it was my duty to voice my doubts over such a place. Trying to be as quiet as possible my fingers shot across the keys, expressing how unsuitable this bar sounds, and if he was drunk already to text as he had. You can imagine my indignation when the silly phone rejected my complaint. I tried for an hour, silently screaming at the tiny screen as each time my words sat there laughing at me. Weary and sore fingered this woman finally caved into what now had become plainly inevitable – Whatever phone Hans was using blocked any return texts. With a groan my fist alone could stifle, I buried my head in the pillow, gritted my teeth, and fell to sleep.

--

'Respite from Life' Bar *
Bracken Street*

Leaving the flat at midday armed with a bevy of books under my arm I set out in the direction of Bracken Street. I had told Mother I needed a rest from hunting through art galleries and shops, unearthing similar paintings to that elusive 'Crux', and considered a trip to the library. In other words, I needed liberating. Odd though it may seem, Mother readily agreed, even offered to join me. At this point I shook my head, pleaded the necessity for my own company, and hurried into the bedroom to consult our local map. Mentally digesting which route must be taken for the library and the bar, I slipped my feet into a pair of cosy boots and grabbed my raincoat from the coat hook (no promise given with our weather), a congenial covering for my long flowing skirt and jumper. Resisting Mother's plea for a hat, I flipped the pulled back ponytail, and swept through the door.

It took me two hours to pop into the library, renew the books I carried, chat to the librarian (Mother may visit another day and ask about me), and slip out unseen. Enquiring from a passing policeman the definite way to 'Bracken Street' I follow his instructions and arrive at two pm sharp – The black gloss painted doors stood open, displaying the heavy purple velvet curtain looped against the inner wall. Walking through the doors it was not hard to convince myself this building was at one time a funeral parlour with its button backed sofas pushed along a grey emulsion wall, and a thick black carpet. The lighting was so dim it was a miracle that the loudspeakers, dotted around the walls, were not playing music noted for a requiem. Adjusting my eyes to the gloom I notice the few clientele occupying these sofas were so laid back in attitude, you would consider them in a queue for embalming. Round glass tables placed in front of these seats had battery lights beneath them, highlighting the slouched figures. At the far side of the elongated room a large window looked out onto what many would call a courtyard garden cluttered with boxes of all shapes and sizes, which was a pity as this window was the only source of light. Allowing my gaze to run along the black painted bar, the word 'undertaker' came to mind. Black suited staff with high stiff white collared shirts were mixing cocktails with weird names – 'The Coffin Lid', 'The Rasping Grave' – and so forth. The wreaths hung around the walls not only made my skin creep, but surely upset the drinking joy of their 'phlegmatic' customers.

Edging nearer to the bar I came face to face with the blondest, blue eyed character I had seen for a long time, his outfit a replication of his staff.

"Good afternoon," his eyes full of mockery. "You must be Rhia."

Surprised he knew my name I nodded.

"The gentlemen are waiting in the back room. By the way, the description fits you perfectly."

Smiling, his head inclined toward another black painted door to his left, his gleaming white teeth resembling the hunting jaws of a shark. I walk toward the door, push it open, and enter a room matching the former in its gloomy décor, with one monumental difference. Around the walls hung pictures of 'The Berlin Wall', 'Checkpoint Charlie', and 'The Brandenburg Gate'. Underneath each picture the words 'Schild und Schwert der Parter' (Shield and Sword of the Party), glared at customers gathering to drink.

Jimmy had been right – This bar is politically motivated.

Catching sight of two heads bowed, deep in conversation. I stomp towards their table.

"What shall I say? 'Welcome to the worst bar in town' my dear Count."

Count Reinbach stands, bows his head a fraction, before saying–

"Fascinating place, Rhia, do you not think?"

I smirk, a repugnant answer hovering on my lips–

"That is a kind assumption. I would call it a disused graveyard, a political throwback. The man should be locked up."

This time the Count laughed out loud.

"Quite right, Rhia. All has moved forward."

I felt the tingle rush through my body as his eyes caressed mine, Hans finding my hand to pull me down onto the bench beside him.

A waiter balancing a tray of long cool drinks swayed his way into the room, the black kohl (which I had obviously ignored on entering) around his eyes giving him that air of a zombie. I moved awkwardly in my seat as this waiter, no older than twenty, yet exemplifying death and beyond, leant across my shoulder.

"Madam's drink," he spluttered, lowering the dark juice onto the table.

He presented Hans and Count Reinbach's drinks in the same manner before exiting the room in the fashion he had entered.

"What a place," I retorted. "What is this?"

"Curdled Blood it is called…" Hans took a large sip. "Blackcurrant juice."

"Yuk, I am sorry, Count Reinbach, you deserve better."

The white head shook –

"Do not worry, my dear, I will not forget this fancy dress party."

Fancy dress? The last fancy dress I walked into was full of slobs and political agitators. I leant toward the man opposite me, sipping his drink in comparative calm.

"This bar is not worthy of you. Hans was wrong if he thought it would be a laugh, or he was extremely drunk."

Thinking of the text I considered it the latter.

I could feel Hans's leg by mine; realisation filtering through my mind that he was shaking. Placing my hand upon his thigh I hoped the warmth could steady his ague.

"You wished to speak to me, Rhia?" the Count asked, his voice soft.

"Yes," I mumbled, holding onto Hans's leg tighter than I need.

"When Hans phoned me, I readily agreed." Those blue eyes shining.

"That is kind," I gush.

He sat back on the worn bench seat, an embodiment of caring and patience.

"I need help in my search for someone." I babble.

The Count smiled, "I thought it was that painting?"

"Well, yes, but I need to find someone."

The Count leant across to Hans, asked for coffee. Hans stood, letting my hand slip back onto my own lap, and walked from the room.

"That is better," the Count sighed. "The information I have found I wish you 'alone' to hear"

I looked surprised.

"Information? I have not told you anything yet."

The man leant further my way–

"Hans mentioned a name to me."

I was piqued. "Did he?"

"Please do not be cross. It was my fault. I tormented him into sharing the secret. I thought it was about you two…" pause, "I was wrong."

He looked contrite.

Whether it was the creepiness of this place, the regret etching its way through the man's eyes across from me, or the sheer frustration I was feeling, the name uppermost on my lips spilt over.

"Etta Detdy," I gasped.

Silence.

Everything had paused, from the music (my polite designation of 'tripe') to our own communication. He opened his hand; an encouragement for me to place mine within it – I did.

"Yes" he whispered. "That was the name Hans imparted."

I searched his eyes pleadingly.

"I researched the name, Rhia. Please say you do not mind."

"And…" I whimpered.

He exhaled heavily.

"In conjunction with the painter Dragner I found nothing" he lowered his eyes–

"Later I spoke to colleagues in the art world, gave them his name, pleading help.

Naturally, they emerged with his background and that of his father's rank in the Stasi regime," he shuddered. "Sorry, I have memories."

The Count gathered his breath–

"I took his father's name to the German archives. There was a sister, Alina Dreyer, young, beautiful, totally disobedient to the cause. Escaping from East Germany with her lover she gave secrets. I discovered she was having a baby."

"A baby?" the sound was uncontrollable.

Count Reinbach frowned.

The heat of this depressing bar was encompassing me; more so as the Count's tone grew softer, and those dulcet words embraced my aching heart.

"According to my research the child was born in England. I searched your birth records in this country. What I found was no child was born to a Philomena Bryant, certainly not within the dates I looked at, but an Etta Detdy did give birth, a girl, now in their thirties."

I felt the slam of his words. Did this mean the Grubb kid was right? Count Reinbach was waiting for a response. My throat constricted, I swallowed hard–

"It is so good of you to bother yourself with this problem, especially as your visit to this country was for art. I knew, from the moment we met your knowledge within that world could be my answer to discovering the darker secret to that disgusting painting."

The Count flashed a smile – "It is my privilege to help you, Rhia, and please do not think the Crux is the end. I believe Hans has already mentioned there may be two paintings with names German intelligence crave for. Good Luck to them I say. Many a hidden painting holds the key to deeper secrets."

I could not help but admire this man; his accent thrilled me, his knowledge astounding, even though I do not remember telling another human being of Mother's name.

"How did you know my mother's full name?"

"Hans must have mentioned it in passing," he waved his hand. "Here he comes now."

Hans came swaggering through the door, followed by the same freakish waiter, carrying a tray of tall coffin shaped mugs steaming with coffee.

"Thank you, Herbert."

My companion acknowledged the young man with a nod and a grin, who slowly trailed his way back through the door.

"Herbert?" I giggled, my humour re-appearing after all the drama.

"So, he says."

Hans sat, a quick glance toward the man opposite, before clasping the hand again laying on my lap.

"Original," the older man pointed to the mugs.

We laughed, tension easing.

"I have two addresses for Etta Detdy," I announce.

Both men stare.

"One at a block of flats in Coventry, another at Stoneleigh."

"Two," the Count whistles. "Lucky you."

Hans squeezes my hand, the pressure making me feel warm, almost arrogant in the handling of this situation.

"Yes, I have demanded Hans take me to Coventry."

The Count laughs out loud, "Good for you."

Nothing more was discussed over the Detdy addresses. We drank our coffee, scrutinized the bar's overhaul appearance, taking care to avoid the pictures and words hanging on the walls. As the dusk of autumn crept through glass panels set high under the roof in this room Hans and I bid the Count 'Goodbye'. Offering me his hands I pull away from Hans to clasp the inviting hold of this enigmatic man. Realising the Count wished to speak with the guy who ran this bar, probably to complain, Hans and I headed for the door. Leaving that depressing building it is difficult to remove the spider and fly poem from my head, also the question–

When did I confide Mother's full name to Hans?

Wednesday October 17th.

Quick entry in the diary today as I have decided to begin my diet in earnest and will soon be heading out for a two-mile jog, walk, creep, and sit in-between. Just needed to write that Hans confirmed he knew nothing of the Philomena name – Strange. Maybe Mother told Alys, which means she really likes Hans's aunt, and that was how he knew it. I need also to confide that Hans kissed me 'Goodnight' on arriving at the flat, after walking me home. If I let my pen do the talking it does not feel disloyal. It was only that hurried peck people share when standing outside a door, not knowing what to do next. I am sure the kiss was an innocent parting gesture. Either way, my heart feels this man is stepping into shoes he should not.

Hitherto, saying anymore would be rather erroneous.

Speak soon.

Thursday October 25th

I woke this morning aching in every limb, struggling to right myself in a position of human authority (stand up straight), and Mother mumbling her way through breakfast.

These two problems have no connection but speak volumes for my poor mixed up mind. The first state can be blamed on my strict diet and exercise regime. I have run, walked, hobbled so may miles that my legs and arms think they are nothing short of spare parts to a raging clockwork toy. How much longer I can keep this up, who knows?

The second has been ongoing since Hans called to suggest a date for the visit to Coventry. I had replaced the phone and said, without any bluster –

"Invitation from Hans to visit a church in Coventry."

Mother's face lit up.

"That is kind of him. What shall I wear?"

"Only me Mother, a twosome"

Her face darkened.

"A twosome, I am not invited?"

"No."

"I see."

I had not the heart to tell her it was my suggestion for Hans and I to travel to Coventry on our own, or the reason for our visit. I let her believe this day was a date.

Hence the continuous mumbling.

Today her moans increased. Among the milk and porridge came the 'parent' implication, then Jimmy's name was floated among the cinnamon bun, and lastly 'Father would not be pleased'. I did not utter a word, instead I demolished my porridge (all this exercise makes me hungry), nibbled my bun, and made ready to leave. Although today was thankfully dry, and seemingly warm after the previous rain deluge of the past days, I still decided to wrap myself in a raincoat and boots. Hans's suggestion included travelling to this city by train, which delighted me, and at the same time irritated me, for these journeys were forever overcrowded. Calling to Mother not to wait up for me the guilt I was beginning to suffer was more down to her–

"Goodbye, my child."

–than leaving her behind. Not giving another thought to the still moaning woman I sped out the flat and made my way to the bus that would drop me at the station where Hans would be waiting.

--

Our journey to Coventry lasted around an hour due to stopping at several stations collecting crowds of tourists heading to Coventry to view its Cathedral.

My first reaction as I stepped from the train was to discard the raincoat, roll it up as tiny as possible, then stuff it into the holdall I had crammed with various food boxes. Hans had laughed at my preparations for a day of investigation, asking if it was a picnic I craved for information. Sweating from my choice to wear jeans and a jumper it was best I waved his sarcasm away, noting how my friend's summer attire suited the day far better than mine. Predicting the weather this year has become a game within itself, for even those who receive pay to do this job had not a clue. The weather, the year, even the congregation of migrating birds cannot specify the 'seesaw' that is 2001.

Taking my hand Hans leads me down the street away from the railway station. We turn the corner into a long uphill road. Nodding towards a long white plaque with bold black letters he says –

"Warwick Road, this way Ma-am."

We laugh as we climb up the hill. Suddenly Hans stops, points across the road to a large red brick building.

"Impressive don't you think? That building across the road was my school – King Henry VIII*"

With pride he continues to enlighten me with the history of this sixteenth century construction.

"The school was founded in 1545 by John Hales; a commission set down by King Henry VIII upon purchasing former monastery land around the city. The first lessons began in the church choir stalls belonging to Whitefriars Monastery.

In 1558 the school moved from these premises to yet another John Hales property, at the hospital of Saint John the Baptist, now the Grammar School in Hales Street. The school remained there for three hundred years. After Henry's death when Elizabeth 1st became Queen, she visited the school in 1565, also James 1st in 1617. During 1885 the school moved from its premises to this huge building it is now, and in 1975 the school opened its doors to females."

As I let my eyes fall across this magnificent red structure it was easy to share his emotion.

The pavement levelled out as moving onward we halted at a division where a sign directed us to Leamington Road on my right, and Kenilworth Road on my left. Immediately across from this fork of directions stood a huge green belt Hans told me was Coventry Memorial Park, housing the war memorial designed by an architect known only as Mr Tickner, and built by John Gray in 1927. This memorial commemorates the fallen military of World War I, World War II, and wars until the present day. The scroll, named 'The Roll of Honour' is complimented by trees scattered around the park, also dedicated to the fallen. Surveying the flats on either side of these roads Hans held his hands behind his back and told me to choose–

"Right or Left?"

My startled eyes surprised him.

"Not playing?" he questioned.

I relaxed, let the tension slide from me.

"Left," I said, knowing it would save crossing the road.

"Left it is."

Hans held my shoulders and marched me toward the flats, our laughter ringing about us.

The flats that greeted us were 'non comparable' to those within a city. I always considered my flat grand, but these – they were swanky. The three storey buildings epitomized grandeur, with their huge glass windows, and long iron balustrade balconies, draped with hanging baskets of flowers, and small fruit trees. The outside brickwork was painted white, highlighted by the soot black windowsills and doors.

"This way."

Hans guided me to the first block, entrance door in the middle, three flats either side. Searching the list of flats and names he shook his head.

"We need the third block as numbers are single."

"This is Provost Gardens*?" I ask.

"So, the plaque says."

We left the first building, almost ran to the third block, and ran our fingers down the list of residents.

"Her name," Hans said with a smug smile. "Miss E Detdy."

"Come on."

I gripped his arm as we walked to the far door on the ground floor.

Knocking, I wait with a fluttering heart – No answer – Knock again, ring the bell, start to move from foot to foot. Hans looks tense – No answer. From across the spacious hallway comes the ringing tones of a woman's voice –

"If you wish to visit Miss Detdy, she has gone."

We twirl, stare hard at the middle-aged woman standing outside the flat across from the stairs. Hand on hips, her brown permed hair brushed to imitate the models on a glossy magazine. She heaved a long sigh–

"As I told the man yesterday when he banged on my door Miss Detdy has gone."

"Gone?" I repeat. "Gone where?"

Her grey/green eyes flicked over me, turned their attention to Hans as her refined voice echoed around the empty stairwell–

"Heaven alone knows. As I informed that horrible man who called yesterday Miss Detdy has vanished – Gone 'puff.'"

She formed a blowing sound through her lips.

I begin to stammer "When – where – how long – with whom?"

The woman shook her head –

"I have not one small clue, my dear, friends all these years, then gone, during the night I would say. No goodbye, no forwarding address, nothing."

Her soft laugh filled the brick painted hallway, resounded around the hollow stairwell.

Hans linked his arm in mine. Was he worried?

"The man who came was he…" he took a deep breath. "Was he English?"

The woman's eyes that had held a decree of sadness, now held fear.

"No, a German accent, average height, bulbous in form, salivating over his words. Has she committed a crime?"

Ice chilled my veins.

"The slob," I whispered.

Hans's expression was that of annoyance.

"I am sorry for all this disturbance. No crime. We wished to surprise her. Family."

"Family?" the woman's eyes widened. "She never had family visit her. Told me she had no children, that her relatives were dead. War I believe. Etta is, was a lovely person. Apart from the visit every six months from this pompous woman, no-one came. Thought she was posh, red hair just so, spoke with a plum in her mouth."

"Not alone," I heard Hans's whisper.

"Come to think of it that woman has not visited this year."

At this point I thought my head would burst. I thanked her, and quickly left.

Hans followed me, begging me to slow down.

The day was growing warmer, and if the month did not keep popping up on my phone each time I looked, it would not be hard to believe it was March more than October. I stomp around, cursing the day, bemoaning the woman we have just spoken with–

"Stuck up cow, you know who she was talking about?"

Hans draws me to him, kisses the top of my head, takes a long breath before saying–

"Your mother."

"Yes," I explode.

"Don't worry. Maybe you are not meant to find this woman."

I pull away, scowl at the sympathetic face near to mine.

"Give up you mean?" I scathingly throw into that face.

"Well…" he begins, stopping as I hurl,

"Never."

I can hear my resolve, hear the scorn as I say–

"I am beginning to realise why Mother wishes us to travel to Mattie. She has been involved in this mess from the beginning. What lies she has told me, and now you."

"It is not like that, Rhia, believe me. I…I find myself…"

"Enough," the sound bounced around us. "I need to find this woman. Discover my past."

"Your past?" he laughed "The past has a way of controlling our future if we do not control it first. Maybe your mother is thinking of you, and her way of helping is kindness."

I was stunned–

"Kindness? Are you mad? My mother is a social climber. Everything she does is for her own advantage."

I pull away from him.

Looking back at the flats I want to scream, swear, anything that will relieve my cluttered mind. Hans mirrored my movements.

"The second address," I demand.

Hans looks warily at my pleading face.

"Not today, Rhia, too far."

I show my indignation, "Too far, for whom, you?"

"That is not fair. Before you go anywhere you need to sort this conflict with your mother. It may not be what you think. Besides, our safety is uppermost."

I sneered "Do not worry, the woman will probably not be there."

"But if she is, Rhia, will that man the lady mentioned also find it?"

The scream left my throat as a musket from a cannon. Hans scowled. This was getting ridiculous. All I wanted was to find one solitary woman and ask her how this secret engaged with me. My companion began to guide my shaking body slowly back the way we had earlier walked, past his old school, the red brick walls glinting in the sunlight, downward toward the station. As we came to the corner where we turn, Hans stood still–

"Are you willing to let me show you a real treasure?"

My despondency growing, I was not in the mood to be homeward bound.

"Yes," I snapped.

"Good," he said.

Smiling, he grabbed my hand, and with a slight pull drew me toward the town centre.

--

Passing through the city centre we stood gazing at that iconic statue that is Lady Godiva, sitting atop her steer, naked as the day she was born. Hans told me this fine lady had ridden through the city, be it unclothed, or without her jewels (historical argument), for the people's unpaid taxes. The figure, overlooked by a representation of the head of 'Peeping Tom', the man who broke the rules not to look upon the lady, generates impressive viewing.

"They gauged his eyes out according to history," my friend announced, unaware how queasy this statement gripped me.

A few yards away from the statue we pass the Holy Trinity Church. I will call it the book cover to the wonderful cathedral that stands at the back of it, and as many books during World War II were destroyed by the idolism of an enemy, this one survived. Throughout the Luftwaffe's raid of the city on 14th November 1940, this old building stood whilst those buildings around it, including the old Cathedral of St Michaels, were shattered, and burned. This was partly due to an incumbent vicar named the Reverend Clitheroe, plus a few others who slept inside the church with ladders and hydrants, dousing any flames that took hold.

Hans walked on, ignoring my eager quizzing of where he was taking me. A gentle "Wait and see," slipped from his mouth as we passed a small garden area known as 'Lady Herbert's Garden'. Following the pathway under the bypass to the park he called the 'Swanswell', we reached a church on the corner of Upper Bird Street and Stoney Stanton Road, along the side of the park. This old building, now an annexe of the Coventry and Warwickshire Hospital, was once the church of Saint Marks. Slipping through the doors at the side of the church into what used to be the community centre, now changed into an out-patients reception area, Hans approached the young girl at the desk, who quickly spoke to an older man. Signalling for us to follow him he led the way through doors at the side of the desk, and into the vast space that in a former life had been the body of the church, where the man unlocked a door at the foot of what was once the nave. He beckoned us to follow.

Switching on a light the man quietly took a step back, ushering us forward. Hans pointed to 'his treasure'. A painted mural on what would have been the Eastern wall of the church.

"This painting was commissioned for this East wall after it was re-built after the window was damaged in the war. Entitled 'Christ in Glory'* this magnificent depiction of Christ rising to heaven surrounded by angels and suffering humanity, is a guarded secret of the church."

I could sense his emotion.

"Who painted it?" I asked, shocked at my intensity to its theme.

Hans smiled, under no misapprehension to 'whom' I was alluding.

"From the brush of a Jewish artist, Hans Feibusch. Born in Germany, and trained in Berlin and Italy, fleeing from the Nazis in 1933 to England. He was taken under the patronage of George Bell, who was the Bishop of Colchester. He engaged the young painter to design a mural on the wall of Dudley Town Hall, Birmingham. This remains the only other work by this man in the West Midlands. If you strain your eye you can see his signature in the right corner"

"Beautiful," I gasp.

"A secret," he mumbles. "Again one day to be revealed without searching."

Without diverting my scrutiny from this wonderful wall of art I breathed, long and hard–

"Meaning?" I asked.

"Whatever you wish," he sighed.

I knew he was conveying an undercurrent in our own search. Without thinking I moved nearer to him. Entwining my fingers in his, as we made our way out the small door and down through the waiting patients.

--

It is midnight as I write this final entry of the day.

I am so tired, disappointed yet fulfilled in different ways. If a soothsayer had told me how this day would pan out at its beginning, I would not have believed them. The curious disappearance of Etta Detdy played constantly on my mind. It was impossible not to think 'where, with whom, and 'why?', whilst enjoying the day with Hans and his historic journey around his childhood haunts. We had laughed, talked; pretended there was no agenda to this outing, closing out the need to set a date for the Stoneleigh visit, which even a person without the need I have, would concede Hans was conspicuously against, whatever he says. By late afternoon, the dusk creeping across the balmy October sky, we headed toward a small bistro my companion promised to be both good food and a fair price. Here we had stayed for the next three hours, relaxing within its intimate atmosphere, content within each other's company, and locked every now and then within our own thoughts.

The train that brought us home had been noisy, and surprisingly busy. Hans looked uncomfortable, moving us from seat to seat as if the ticket collector demanded a game of musical chairs. Twice, maybe three times I had queried his motive, receiving no specific answer, only the view may be better, or the seats softer. This caused me to laugh as the sky had already turned an inky black so my inspection of the passing countryside was limited, if anything at all, and whoever finds train seats comfortable must surely bring a cushion. A station from our stop he jumped to his feet, grabbing my hand, and pulling me into the corridor. As my mouth formed the question 'why' for an umpteenth time his lips covered mine. The pressure forced me backwards against the rolling rhythm of the moving train. Angered, yet excited, I held onto him until he lifted his face to search the throng of people gathering around us.

Surprised at the congregating crowd I realised the train was drawing close to the station. Stuttering to a halt, the doors automatically opened, and the crowd poured out onto the platform, pushing us with them. Hans again grasped my hand and began to speed walk toward the stairs that led to the station's exit, continuously looking over his shoulder. Once we had climbed the stairs and out into a buzzing city his 'cloak and dagger' antics left him. Hailing a taxi Hans opens the door and thrust me in. The driver smiled, no doubt deducing our evening had been spent 'well', winking at Hans in that 'man to man' attitude. Settling down for the short journey to my flat he muses–

"Good day?"

"Yes, in a way."

"Try and stay positive, Rhia."

"Explain," I emit a long audible breath.

"We both must assess what the next move will be."

I reply without thinking–

"I shall. Stoneleigh next."

The stern look prompted me to 'dig my heels in' further–

"As a matter of thought, what was all that diving and dashing about on the train?"

Hans frowned.

The taxi swung around the corner of my street, jarred on its brakes, and stopped outside the set of flats where I lived.

"Secrets," I murmured, moving nearer the door.

His hand sought mine–

"I thought someone was following us."

"Who?"

He shrugged his shoulders–

"Nobody I suppose, just people acting strange."

"Which people?"

My friend swallowed hard, leant toward me, kissed my cheek–

"You would laugh if I said Jimmy."

"Jimmy?"

The wonderment in my voice rung in my ears, "Please say that is you being sarcastic?"

"Yes," he muttered under his breath.

He kissed my cheek for a second time, gently pushing me from the seat.

"Goodnight, Rhia," and the taxi sped away.

I cannot explain my emotions. Part of me wishes to run after that taxi, grab Hans and entice, I care not how, an explanation from those lips. My other part is pleading to rest. I turn the key, listen for Mother's movements, sigh as stillness wraps around me. Taking a guess that Mother is asleep I tiptoe through the lounge to the kitchen, seek my diary that I hide at the back of the freezer, and quietly sit and write.

Friday October 26th

Mother is flying from room to room in a panic of 'what to wear'. She has been summoned to the bank by Mr Richardson to evidently 'talk' over affairs. It seemed, at least to me, that these 'affairs' were ongoing, this annoying man taking his incumbency too far. However, the letter stated ten o' clock, and the wording related 'utmost attention', so Mother refused to dismiss it. Curious as I was, my mind had 'other' pressing factors to solve. Making the flimsy excuse that 'I was tired' Mother left for her appointment in a huff (this being my polite word for the slang term of 'arsy'). Waiting half an hour to make sure this was not another scheme herself and Savvy had thought up to 'rein' me in, I dialled, pressed the numbers, phoned (whatever appellation this action is given) Jimmy's number. The voice that answered was sluggish.

"Hello,"

"Jimmy?"

"Rhia."

"You sound tired."

"I am. This search never ends."

"Like following me?"

I can hear his astonishment.

"What are you talking about?"

"Are you saying you have not followed me?"

"No, why would I?"

"Not sure, yesterday, in Coventry?"

The teeth rattling began.

"Fuck," he groaned. "I have not got time to trail round the streets after you.

Your father wants to get home, therefore you not finding the address he needed is impeding us."

Sluggish had turned to vexation.

"Is my father there?"

A louder groan.

"Not again. NO…" the throb in his voice hammered down the phone.

"Where is he this time?"

I could not let go.

"Bloody chasing clues you have not given him."

This Jimmy was nigh apoplectic.

I took a deep breath, resigned myself that my once loving partner was incensed at the continuous search for a painting (one of two) I had already found. My resolve weakened–

"Jimmy, do not be cross, but one painting has already been discovered."

Silence that signifies a turbulent mind.

"Jimmy?" I say weakly.

The roar spills down the phone as a mud slide down a mountain.

"How the fuck do you know?"

"I, with Hans Parker found it."

"You…" he shouts louder. "You, and him. Why have we not been told?"

"No-one knows," I mutter. "We gave it to Count Reinbach"

"Who?" his anger slows.

"The art connoisseur. He found names."

"Ah, Reinbach. What names did he find?"

His lowered tone took an edge from his temper.

"Stasi names," I mumble.

"Great," (sarcasm). "Who else knows?"

"Nobody."

"Keep it that way."

I waited for him to continue, dreading his question on the painting's disguise. How can I tell him?

"You say two paintings exist?"

"Yes."

"How do you know this?"

"Hans suggested it."

I will not mention the family link.

"Hans knows this, of course."

The slight mockery in his tone disturbed me. Was he jealous?

"He believes Dragner would do this. The man admires you."

"Really," he drawled.

This was getting boring.

"I believe you Jimmy do not appreciate the help that man is giving me."

I giggled, anything to ease the rigidity of this phone call.

"I can imagine *his* help."

"What?"

The imputation in his remark was all too clear.

Inside, guilt was growing. My Jimmy was struggling to complete the task the museum had set for him, my father also, and here I stood, arguing, cajoling him to be sweeter tempered. It was not coaxing he needed, but hard facts.

"I have that address father asked for," I preened, pleased with myself.

"Good," my partner bellowed. "About bloody time."

I felt the pang of 'hurt' sear through my chest.

"You do not need to be rude."

Jimmy sighed.

"Sorry, I just want this mess to end."

His climb down had got to be guided by my father.

I could have said 'Me too', but instead I flicked the pages of my diary where Fiona Grubb's addresses were written, read them, asked myself 'why' I felt so reluctant to share, then in the most gabbled manner spouted–

"Rose Cottage, Stoneleigh"

"At fucking last."

The raw quality in his retort stung me, seeping into my response.

"I hope you get more manners by the time you come home. I never wish to live this year again."

The voice from Jimmy's end of the phone was low, not his, but reminiscent of a teacher's authority. Jimmy's mood changed–

"Rhia, I did…"

"Forget it," I cried. "Pass the address to father. We may all meet there."

The line was quiet. Jimmy evidently ashamed.

"I must go."

A command. Surely my father in charge, if only…

"Let us both pray all this will soon end." I moan.

"It will," he declared. "Trust me, it will".

Tuesday October 30th

Four days had passed since that phone call, and my heart still felt heavy. Never had I heard Jimmy so stressed out. I realise his position at the museum relies on his finding the painting. I have also come to realise that if Hans discovers it first those fusty men on the board will not look upon it in a favourable light. Even so, there was no specific reason for him to be mad at me. I may have been a little withdrawn when it came to sharing the Detdy woman's address, perhaps because my mind told me Father should know it by heart; after all, as previously stated, he was her main contact. True, my excitement in beating Jimmy to the 'end line' was important for reasons I could not explain, and my earlier submission to Hans's advances, which my partner had no concept about, was a drawback, but otherwise he was still 'my Jimmy'.

Mother, arriving home from the bank, had shown a concern I had not experienced before. Explaining how Richardson was able to raise our money in lieu of the festive season made my heart drop as a stone drops into a pond; the man was not expecting Father home soon. It appeared that this meeting had given her ammunition to suggest for the hundredth time (tedious), that we pack and visit Mattie. Apart from my ears being sick of hearing this plea, I was beginning to wonder the 'real' reason into her rush to travel to a country she had never intimated was her choice of location, let alone that my grandmother may question her motives. Plus, there is Savannah D' Mill.

No, dear Diary, their little plot is unravelling!

--

Around two thirty I received a call from Hans.

"Quick call" came the rushed voice "Halloween tomorrow, would you like to party?"

Party? That would give relief from this situation.

"Sounds good," I gush.

"Great, meet me at the 'Respite from Life', say eight o' clock?"

"Mother?" I ask.

"I believe Mena is meeting Savannah."

"She has not told me."

"Oops," and he rung off.

Diary, If I write that pub is an ideal place for a Halloween would you laugh?

By seven o' clock I had ran out of humour, or at least trying to track down that side of my character. Mother had not mentioned her jaunt with Savvy tomorrow, not even skimmed across the topic of Halloween. Patience, as you know, is not my strong point, consequently by the seventh clang of the church chimes I spat out my annoyed curiosity.

"Mother, are you meeting Savvy tomorrow?"

Her eyes widened, her head cocked to the side, lips pursed, eyes flashing–

"Whoever told you that?"

"Hans," was my one symbol word.

She hesitated.

"Is it true?" I persevered.

Nodding her head in the most ridiculous fashion she muttered, "Yes."

"And me?" I query.

"Savannah knew Hans was interested in a party."

I took a deep breath–

"Did she now."

In a roundabout way I felt cheated.

Mother fell silent. I switched the television on, switched it off.

"Mother, what is going on?"

The smart red head shot upward, the masque of pretence falling from those factious eyes.

"Why do you question everything, Rhia?"

"Why have you been lying to me?"

Her chest heaves a deep sigh–

"Is it always impossible to leave something alone?"

How many questions to the truth? I think of Jimmy's dismissal of her honesty.

"You knew Savvy in her younger days?"

"Yes."

"Did you know anyone else?"

Mother threw herself back on the sofa, "Yes."

"Who?"

"Lots of people."

This was infuriating. Shall I confront her with *that* name – Etta Detdy.

Those ten letters that spelt that name fell into the silent room as an unwanted guest would crash into a party. Mother stared–

"Who?"

I gave her no chance to wriggle from her hole.

"Father secured her release from Germany, the Cold War, behind the wall."

Mother's mouth had dropped open. I resumed my attack–

"This woman is a Stasi spy who defected to the West."

"No, Rhia, whoever told you that. She is an informant."

I could not believe Mother's outcry–

"You do know her?" an accusation, not a question.

Her eyes fell across my puce face, the shadow of sorrow hid in their depth.

"She was a young girl…" she began. "Trying to break free from those cruel people you mention. Your father and Savannah helped her escape. They,"

another pause. "They helped her the only way they could."

"Which was?"

Mother shook her hands, let them fall into her lap–

"No more, Rhia. Savannah will be cross with me for sharing this amount of undisclosed information. She needs your naivety."

Silence more like!

It is said when a bull rages it stampedes. This woman has every reason to rage–

"Why?" my arrow was barbed straight at its victim.

Mother refused to speak.

"What a deceitful pair," I rant. "Jimmy was right, all of you have lied to me."

Her intake of breath shook me; her eyes narrowed–

"Jimmy?" her shock was flagrant. "He knows nothing."

"So, say you."

"So, says your father."

"You have spoken to him?"

"No, but I know his mind."

If anyone had asked me how I felt at that precise moment I would have screamed as I did at the woman cowering on the sofa in front of me–

"I do not believe you, Mother. This plot between yourself, Savvy, and Father is to save that traitor. Heaven knows where Richardson comes into it."

"Plot? No, you are wrong."

"Am I? We will see. I am determined to find the truth, and I have help."

Her pleading eyes settled on mine–

"Please, Rhia, do not do this."

"Plead all you want, Mother. You, and that so called 'agent' cannot stop me."

The cry that left her throat was that of a wounded animal. I had never seen mother beg, never seen this socially climbing freeloader (more than savage) in such a state. I stand above her, towering as the mythological God of war-

"From now on I will trust nobody but Hans, Jimmy, and Count Reinbach"

I fling, marching from the room.

Wednesday October 31st

Halloween

How fast this day is flying.

Hearing the church bells chime this morning I had risen from my bed to find Mother dressed, and ready for her meeting with Savvy. From what I could gather, which appeared minuscule, no sooner had I flounced from the lounge last night and cried myself to sleep, than Mother curled up on the sofa. More fool her I say. I can assure her she will feel as if she has stepped from a boxing ring: that unprepared person that believes they can spar professionally; aching limbs, and an unmovable back. Scanning the paper Mother had placed on the table I groan. News, if that is what a polite person would call it, is dismal, to the point that I swear the world is spinning out of orbit. It is while reading the gloom of world news that Mother decides to recite her favourite poem. I glare at her. Grateful eventually, she takes the hint and stops. All year those words have spooked me.

Today is Halloween: a day where magic comes to the foremost, or even spookier, a day to commemorate the dead. The word is a contraction of 'All Hallows Eve', and always falls on the day before 'All Saints Day', where the church celebrates the lives of their Saints. Halloween, in many cultures, begins three days of festivities dedicated to remembering the dead. These traditions are believed to stem from Celtic harvest festivals in this country, such as the Gaelic celebration of 'Samhain', otherwise known as the 'Thinning Wall', when the living can contact those who have passed from this life. It also is a celebration of darkness, or the forthcoming months of winter. Within these rituals it is often recognised that the festivals of Christianity and Paganism can overlap. An example being how the Druids worshipped the Lord of Darkness, albeit referred to as the Lord of the Dead, and the church encouraged the tradition of Soul Cakes; continued until the 1930s, where children knocked on doors for cakes that had been blessed by the church, as representing the souls of those who had died. Given to the poor and their offspring, the church pressed these children to enjoy the sweets it supplied, which became the precursor of the modern day 'Trick or Treat'. The most famous festival around the end of October, which today I can write introduces pockets of warmth among the scattering of showers, is the Mexican festival of 'Dia de los Muerlos – Day of the Dead'. Lasting for several days, festivities include dressing up, singing, dancing, the wearing of masks – the most recognised being the skull of Calavera Catrina, from the lithographs of Jose Guadalupe Posada.

Halloween in Britain and the United States of America has long become associated with a night of 'spooky' magic where witches weave their webs. While both countries dress up, decorate houses, and throw lavish parties, our celebrations last one night, and the 'party' tends to be less excessive.

At eleven o' clock mother says 'Goodbye', trepidation in her voice as her eyes work their way across my sullen features. Apart from 'yes please' and 'no thank you', neither of us has spoken. There had been no discussion of my paroxysm the previous evening, or a further explanation on Mother's behalf. It was almost as if the woman had run out of words; that snobbish blabbering well had dried up. The moment I was alone I ran into the bedroom, threw open the wardrobe doors and scavenged around my old clothes from my youth. I had a black net skirt, a tight bodice with sleeves, and a pair of thick black tights. If I cover my hands with hair gel, run them through my long hair, whiten my face with cream, and darken my eyes, it will complete my look. I will spend this afternoon emphasising my transformation. I could even stand outside the door of my nosy neighbour, then 'boo' her when she opened it.

Cool, game set, and matched – Ready to go.

--

Respite from Life'*

I walk through the streets this evening pleased with how my mutation from *'sensible'* human to way out zombie has been created. Through highlighting the word sensible I know it becomes a query within my own mind, spraying doubt over everything I do, yet still I cast those apprehensions aside–

Oh Diary,

I have prepared slowly for tonight, taking extra care with my hair, my clothes, and my make-up. This I do with more than a little consideration, my overall intent to really impress my companion. 'Why?' I imagine your query and must write 'My mind is not sure'. This mess that is my brain is holding fast to the perception that tonight may be what many identify as a 'game changer', a critical moment in my life. My eyes, which I have defined to shine like precious emeralds may captivate where my collective bulges let me down. This is important for I need the fizz that accompanies perspicacity, or in layman's terms – I need to be downright shrewd when seducing Hans to set the date for Stoneleigh.

Here I go –

Opening the door to the bar I pause for breath. Exhausted due to rushing, but also due to me tightening my bodice to such a degree that my ribs hurt, and my breasts feel pinched, this woman is pleased to have reached her destination in one piece. By this I mean the foolish 'honking' of an odd car horn, or the whistle of a passing kid. The streets had been full of ghouls and ghosts creeping along the windows and doors of houses, accompanied by screaming children and over excited adults, clothed in various forms of Halloween dress, munching bags of coloured goodies handed out by just as excited onlookers. I had literally zoomed around the corner into the street where this weird bar could be found. That was on top of that insult from the woman who lived down my passageway, which could be determined as my own fault. I had knocked on her door, ready to blow raspberries, or something as inane toward her, only to be halted by the most amazing witch outfit money could buy. She had smiled, gave me a packet of sweets (did she think I was a child), and cackled at me.

Slowly making my way past the surprisingly busy bar it reminded me not only of the Mexican 'Day of the Dead', but also a party from hell. Those customers that I had relegated as 'phlegmatic' on my last visit were now among those thronging around, dressed in their costumes from the underworld: black suits, black capes, red horns, long white teeth, and makeup.

I shuddered.

"Rhia," a voice calls, the hand blackened by dirt raised my way.

Pushing through the drinking 'devils' I feel a hand on my back, or an arm try to loop mine. I create my coldest stare, they withdraw. Reaching the room at the far end of the bar I throw myself into the waiting arms of a bandaged mummy, praying it is the person I seek.

"You're late," his concern enfolded me with warmth.

"Hans, thank goodness it is you. What is it in there, a party from hell?"

He grimaced.

"A uniformed party I would say, although what army?"

We both laughed.

Leading me towards a table he suddenly covered my eyes –

"Guess who is here?"

Mother, Savvy, Father and Jimmy – they all passed across my mind.

The sensation of being propelled forward and eased onto a seat, made my heart skip a beat. If for one moment I had known that anyone but Hans and myself were meeting here I would have dressed in an appropriate manner – Maybe.

Releasing his grip Hans bumped down onto what I gathered was the chair beside me.

"These bandages are so tight I cannot move," he moaned.

I slowly opened my eyes.

"Welcome, Rhia, we do look a sight."

Count Reinbach raised a glass in my direction. The 'devil' costume matched those worn by the customers propping the bar up in the other room. By his side sat Alys Parker, her 'fallen angel' outfit moulded to her frame as if she had stepped from a costumier's window. She too raised her glass my way, smiling as she mouthed–

"Welcome."

Immediately my inner self relaxed, and a silent 'Thank you' was sent to whoever had an insight not to let it be the four names that had rushed through my mind.

Hans nudged a drink my way, the clear swirling liquid teasing me to drink. I took a large gulp, hoping it would numb the pain ambushing my ribs.

"You look – different," Alys pronounced. "Maybe you have heard good news?"

I grinned, striving to referee the fight between my breasts and ribs into which would succeed into maiming me.

"I have concluded that I need to sort my life out," my voice building above the loud music.

"Good," she smiled. "Sometimes we need to discover the truth about ourselves."

I detected the taste of aniseed on my tongue from the drink I had finished.

"Exactly my mission," I declared.

"What about your partner your mother mentioned at my ball?"

Typical mother.

"He has other things on his mind, and I do not seem to be that important at the moment."

Alys looked sad.

"Never mind, you have Hans."

I breathed deep, waited for the pain to pass, let her words comfort me.

The Count began to throw his body into the spasm of the beating music, pulling at my arm he said–

"Let us dance," and he guided me onto the floor.

I was surprised at his rhythmic moves, his limbs in perfect co-ordination to the beat throbbing around the room. Not considering 'where', or 'who' I was dancing with I allowed the pulsating vibes to overtake me; hips in one direction, shoulders in another, my breath oozing from my open mouth, an odd groan escaping as the tightened bodice grew tighter. The Count laughed, I laughed, we were forging trust. Just as quickly the music changed, a slow sentimental sound, far from the crazy pounding of the former dance. Hans trundled to my side, gave a quick nod to a heavy breathing Count before clasping me within his arms. We moved at a decelerated speed, the measured notes a sweet release from the prior cavorting.

"You look enticing," Hans purred in my ear.

I sunk further into his body, pleased my plan had worked.

"You look in agony," I chuckled.

"I am, maybe…you and I…"

He stopped speaking as his lips found mine. Out the corner of my eye I could see Alys pointing our way and smiling, the Count nodding his approval. Hans lifted his head.

"Somewhere quiet," he suggested. "They will be happy now they have seen you."

"You mean they asked to come?"

"Yes, they were adamant. They like you, Rhia, as do I."

What is it about dimly lit rooms, soft music, and the knowledge that you have admirers?

The music stopped as a vibrating noise filtered into the room from the bar, the sound of fists pounding on wooden tops; any wooden top where flesh met surface. The cry of 'Schild und Schwert der Parter' grew louder with each thump. Hans glanced toward the table where the Count had risen to his feet, anger spreading across those constant unruffled features. We began to move slowly toward a door at the back of the room, winding our way through the pounding voices. Hans, using the force of his body, slammed the door until it opened, and we tumbled out into what appeared was a small courtyard garden. Still holding onto me he began to wriggle from the stream of bandages wrapped around his form.

"Don't look alarmed, I have shorts and a t-shirt underneath."

He struggled, I giggled gasping–

"What was that all about?"

He shook his head–

"I have not a clue, but Reinbach was ready to say something."

"Oops," I ventured, head spinning from *that* drink.

"Never mind, I know a place we can discuss Stoneleigh."

Stoneleigh – Stoneleigh, yes, that is my object – object – Blast the word, I must go there. I stumbled over my next query-

"The Count and Alys. They will think us rude?"

"Forget them," he mutters. "They agreed."

Throwing off those constrictive swathes he leads me to a gate where we slip into the street.

Heading away from the bar, we found ourselves sucked into the frivolity of the night: children scampering between doors, their pleas of "Trick or Treat" rendering house occupants to share bags of sweets or pay a penny. Gate-crashing onto this scene we meander from house to house, laughing, jesting, falling prey to the odd sweet or two. By the time the church clock struck eleven thirty we had wandered onto a street of small houses. Leaning my head on Hans's shoulder I realised he was unlocking a door. Suddenly I was inside, the door closed, and his inviting lips on mine. The pain my ribs had experienced throughout the night was turning to a dull ache, and my breasts felt free as the tight bodice was untied. My struggle between loyalty and deceit was ebbing away, and the latter was winning.

--

Early Morning

It is dark,

Dawn has not broken, the sky no chink of light.

I feel movement next to me, the soft touch of a hand on my clammy neck, a finger running across the tattoo that girds my arm. I move, slide nearer to the edge of what I realise to be a bed; sense the body beside me move into the crutch of my back, kiss my shoulder. Guilt floods my being. Memory, whilst a good commodity for learning and storage, brings ruination on a conscience-stricken mind. I think of Jimmy. Scream silently in sorrow.

"I do love you," I hear the voice mumble.

I do not answer, reach for my clothes. My phone buzzes. I take it from the skirt pocket I am fumbling with, turn onto my back, catch the tumble of dark hair caressing my pillow, feel the hand stroking my leg. I pull away, turn sideways once more, push the button that opens my text boxes – read–

'Where are you, Rhia?'

Ten in all, frantic in their urgency.

I throw my feet to the ground, grasp what clothes I can find, start to dress.

Hans, moving slowly from the bed reaches out, enfolds my body within his arms–

"It is dark, my love. What is the rush?"

Holding onto my phone I shudder in the cool of the night as I look at the time–

"It is three o' clock, Mother will worry."

He kisses my hair, my eyes, my lips.

"It is early. Do not worry. Your mother is being possessive."

Not true sears through my mind. Snobby – Always – Possessive – Never. I continue to dress, struggling with the ties of the bodice.

"Let me do that for you."

Hans laughs, instantly undoing the few ties I had managed to fasten.

"I must go," I repeat,

Further kisses covered my face.

"Remember Stoneleigh."

An uncertainty races through my body causing him to hold me tighter.

Remember he said – this woman could remember nothing; my only blurred thought, if I must think, was that aniseed drink.

"I do not remember an agreement," I bleat into the darkened room.

Hans soothed my hair from my face.

"We came to an agreement last night. We would go to Stoneleigh today."

"Today?"

"Yes," he mumbled. "Have you changed your mind?"

It was one of those moments when a brain searches for the recognition of a deed or agreement granted. Mine was lost.

"I have no clothes to wear." I gabbled, anything to help blunt my anxiety.

"Do not worry. It is all sorted. I have clothes here."

"How?"

"My aunt, before she lost weight."

"Your aunt?"

My disbelief was evident.

"Yes, she was not always slim."

Should I not ask what his aunt's clothes were doing here?

I make an extra effort to squeeze my heated body into the clothes scattered on the floor, fall foul of the hands removing them in succession. If truth be told I was losing this battle, his warmth was beginning to closet me.

"Today is your truth day," he whispers.

I think of Mother's text, think how she will react when she realises her daughter intends to pursue her plans. I feel nothing in this intoxicated state of gratification, as I cruelly decide the woman has no place within my thoughts. It is within that step from where I stand to that yawning bed, I know this journey has called me throughout life. Whatever I find, the truth is waiting. Hans gentle platitude settled around me–

"Come, soon we will be on our way, but first– "

Like the fly invited to the spider's parlour, I follow.

November 2001

Thursday November 1st
All Saints Day

Known in past times as All Hallows Day, or Hallowmas, this day is a celebration of every saint recorded, and is historically linked to November 2nd known as All Souls Day. To certain cultures around the world, the unification of these days held strong belief that spiritual bonds existed between the living and the dead, overlooked by those Saints in heaven.

We dress in silence; the thin cream polo necked jumper and dark pleat fronted trousers a perfect fit, a contrast to the grey jeans and black open necked shirt worn by my lover. This morning heralded that situation where two minds embedded within their own contemplations struggled for answers that neither person seemed to know. It was not hard for me accepting I had overstepped that boundary of propriety, where guilt with each thought of Jimmy, haunted me. I tried to fool myself into believing there had been purpose to my action. Oh Diary, you know I lie, if truth be told, this woman is incapable of facing facts. I could blame the drink at the party, or the fear on hearing that Stasi motto chanted. Both maybe correct, yet they would also be a lie. At least, with you, this pen must write the truth, trembling or not. I, Rhia Bryant had received exactly what she had wished for no matter how I proclaim otherwise. The complication–

How could I explain to Jimmy about last night, and *how* could I persuade him to forget my actions for a second time, to continue as if nothing had happened, and even more to the point – believe nothing happened?

From the bedroom we moved to the kitchen, still in silence, still deep in thought. Slamming the kettle onto the stove (no modern appliances here) Hans reached into the cupboard bringing out a packet of cereal. Pouring it into dishes he retrieved from another cupboard he looked upon my downcast face.

"Sorry," he shakes his head in confusion.

"Sorry?" I quiz, letting my eyes flutter downward.

"For last night."

My head shakes from side to side "It was just a passing fancy then?"

The cereal packet fell from his hand–

"No, whatever happens I do love you, plus I will take the blame when a certain person finds out."

My eyes fly upwards, search the face before me.

"Jimmy?"

He nods.

"Who says I will tell him?"

Scooping up the mess in front of him Hans let a swift smile run across his lips.

"Whether you do, whether you do not, he will guess."

"How?"

His eyes misted over with that personal wisdom another party is not parry too.

"He will."

I let the conversation drop.

Another period of silence followed while we drank the tea Hans brewed, and munched our way through overfilled bowls of cereal. Clearing away we tried hard to step around each other without success: the passing of a hand, the stretching of an arm; small details of contact that thrill the senses. Walking to the main door, checking the clock on the kitchen wall, Hans makes a remark that baffles me–

"Three o' clock, our appointment."

I look puzzled, "Appointment?"

That look that says I am not about to find out–

"Apologies, I am thinking aloud. It is the time we should reach Rose Cottage…"

He begins to hum.

"Stoneleigh?" I say in a hurried tone.

"As we agreed," an enforcement in his voice.

I still cannot remember any agreement. Now, that must be the drink!

Stepping from the house into the hectic morning traffic we head toward a sleek black car. I show surprise.

"My aunt's," he says as he opens the door for me.

Running around to the driver's door he slides in, fastens his seat belt, and turns the ignition key. Smiling Hans eases away from the kerb, using the driver's mirror to check any cars behind him. Throwing a quick glance over my shoulder I gasp – Pulling out from the kerb opposite is that all too familiar white car.

--

Two o' clock.

The journey to Coventry had been pleasant, all awkwardness of the previous evening disappearing as the miles sped past, the day warming up as we travelled. Between snippets of 'road signs', 'maps', 'lunch breaks', and 'scenery', I checked my phone for further texts, and tried to keep an eye to that pursuing white car. Since Mother's texts last night no-one had bothered me, generating a presumption that Savvy had guessed, and told her about my excursion. I could only imagine how annoyed she would be, clacking around like that mother hen she had become, frightened her deception was going to be revealed, worried any control she wavered over me had gone. Too busy keeping an eye to the trailing car I was pleased, although surprised, when speeding past the road sign for Coventry or Warwick I noticed our tail had swerved onto the road leading to Warwick. Confused into 'why?', I soon put it to the back of my mind and settled down for the rest of the journey.

We entered Coventry, travelling through streets that were alien to me. Skirting the perimeter of Baginton, Hans saluting the placard indicating his childhood home, we followed a sign that read – A46 to Stoneleigh.

"This is it," a perturbed look passed across Hans's handsome features.

"Pretty," I return.

"Soon your curiosity will be solved," he tried to laugh.

"Yes," I whispered, before suddenly saying. "I am scared Hans."

Turning a corner, he slowed down–

"Do you still wish to do this, Rhia?"

I fold my hands into my lap, will myself to be brave–

"I must. Something is pulling me forward. You will be there?"

"Of course," he says in a low voice.

We drive on, enter this village in a hushed tone.

The pretty village of Stoneleigh is nestled within the county of Warwick and is accessible along the road to the village of Kenilworth. This small rural idyllic draws tourists to the historical abbey and its vast park. Founded in 1154 by the Cistercian Monks, the abbey dominates the village, likewise the park, where the yearly 'Town and Country Festival' occurs, on or around the 30th/31st August. According to my companion this huge festival of animals, farm equipment, vintage cars, food, and various genre of craft and art is a massive success. Overlooking this activity, and the village in general stands the Norman built church of Saint Mary the Virgin, a red sandstone building whose walls glinted in the early evening light. This afternoon everywhere was quiet, sinister almost. There was hardly a car moving; apart from a couple heading outbound, away from the village. The people that live here were either recuperating from last night's activities, or out shopping at the nearest town. It made me think it was an omen.

O – odd silence

M – mysterious

E – eerie elements

N – nigh on empty

I shivered, moved uncomfortably in my seat as we searched for the address.

Pulling the car up by an overgrown hedge Hans pointed to a cottage standing on its own down an un-weeded gravel drive.

"Could that be the house we are looking for?"

He looked at his watch, let out a sigh of relief.

"Rose Cottage?" I queried, not hiding that touch of disquiet.

"That's it," he shuffled in his seat, switching the purring engine to 'off'.

"You sound sure?" the butterflies in my stomach were rising.

"Yes, look closely at that hedge where a sign is just about visible. The word 'Rose.'"

I strain my neck, trail my eyes along its wild growth and spot the board popping out.

"Lucky guess on your part?"

Hans nods. I cannot stop that growing concern.

Here diary, I must pause –

I have planned for this moment all year, yet deep within my stomach apprehension I cannot explain mounts. Looking down this overgrown drive my mind cannot help but measure up how orderly this moment had fallen into my lap.

Number one – That horrific painting appeared from nowhere.

Number two – Fiona Grubb found information needed comparatively easy.

Number three – Mother's insistence for us to travel to Bhutan, and Savvy's endeavour to twist my plans her way.

Number four - Jimmy's cool approach, and Hans's penetration of my heart.

I shudder, push these gathering details far from my thoughts, for if I do not these legs will jump from this car and run as far from this moment as possible.

Walking down the drive the trembling throughout my body grows. What will I find inside that cottage? Will my questions be solved? Hans slipped his arm around my shoulder–

"Are you okay Rhia? We could turn back."

I shook my head, captured a moment of longing in his eyes, as we continued down the drive. Nearing the door my heart takes another dive. Every curtain and blind are closed; an indication that the house will be empty. Feeling Hans move slightly away from me, my hand stretches toward the rusty knocker leaning against the weather-beaten door. I search my companion's face, step away from lifting this gargoyle head implying–

"No-one here, shall we go?"

Hans, standing straight, bites back–

"You wished to come. Now you are running away?"

I focus my eyes on his illegible features–

"I am unsure," I mumble.

"Unsure?" a tempest spouting from that rigid mouth.

"This woman, my father, my mother, do I really want to know?"

"Yes."

This man had changed his standpoint from a few seconds ago.

Passing over that tongue protruding gargoyle I look for a doorbell, find an old iron chain dangling from an iron bell. I venture toward it, felt the gentle push as Hans moved my hand away.

"Let us bang the door, yes?"

He checked his watch, three o' clock, gave a quick nod of the head my way, then knocked on the door, the sound of knuckles on wood echoing around us. It was in that moment my heart and stomach joined in unison to create the see-sawing action that traps many a frightened mind. I sense panic rising; the flight or fight sensation psychologists talk about. Remain/Stay runs through my head as a dog chasing its tail.

Hans knocked again, a nervous laugh issuing from his mouth as the rasping sound rippled through the still afternoon.

"I think the cottage stands empty," I say for a second time.

"Not so," my companion said as the door slowly opened.

A figure stood in the doorway. My mind reeled–

"Count Reinbach?"

"Rhia, my dear, come in."

--

Stepping through the door into a hallway I sensed my heart restrict; a daunting sensation, many try to explain, consistently fail, and end up calling it a premonition. Hans closed the door as we followed the Count into a large room at the back of this sombre cottage. I was unsettling to see how sparse it was. From the solitary sofa by a side wall, to one chair positioned in the middle of the room, these two being its only furniture. It appeared to me that Miss Etta Detdy was comfortable with nothing. Confused as to 'why' the Count should be here I instantly launched into a barrage of questions–

"I did not expect to meet you here, Count Reinbach."

His lips allowed a tiny smile to flutter across them–

"A little surprise my dear."

It certainly was that.

"Hans and I did not agree to tracking this address down until last night. Surprise you say, absolutely right."

I said it accusingly, then paused, telling myself that my proclamation was rude. This dedicated art lover had aided me well in my search. He had been nothing if not inspirational.

"I am sorry, that was rude."

The Count frowned.

"Did Hans not inform you that when I search it is with an outcome that I will unearth the problem? It was my insistence that brought you here today."

He sounded annoyed.

"Oh," I groaned. "It appears no-one tells me anything.

Overcome by embarrassment, yet trepidation I headed toward the lone sofa, flopped down upon it, and allowed my gaze to be drawn to the large glass doors that led to a garden. At least these doors were not shuttered, as I noted a sprawling pathway, twisting through flowers and greenery, hedged at the perimeter by medium sized hedges that divided this cottage from the rolling countryside. Not overlooked, therefore Miss Detdy had not bothered with covering of any kind. I sat, as those spectators involved in a game where two people walk up and down, studying the Count as he paced up and down this bleak room, his feet pounding on the bare floorboards, speaking with an officious air–

"Make yourself comfortable, my dear. This day will be long."

On past encounters I had found this man alluring – still feel that in a strange way, however, I wish he would drop the 'my dear', it was becoming creepy. I look around, fumbling for something to say. At last, I choose what is obvious–

"Is Miss Detdy at home?" I ask, considering the Count would know being the first to arrive.

"All in good time," he growls.

I threw Hans a glance, pleading for him to join me, remove his body from his static position by the door. He neither moved nor spoke.

"I will be but a moment."

The deep tone of the Count's accent rang in my ears as he leaves the room.

Not willing just to sit while Hans, the statue he has become, waits by the door, I walk to the window. Outside, a sinking afternoon sun glints on the few pots shielding their sleeping plants. My eyes move down the pathway, my heart somersaulting as I catch sight of the white car parked beyond a gate to conceal it from the driveway.

"Have you seen this Hans?" I call, frustration gathering when he does not reply.

I turn to where my companion is still rooted to his spot.

"Hans," I repeat.

Tired, from last night's lack of sleep, and troubled by this turn of events I splutter, mainly to myself, yet still expecting Hans to reply.

"Whose flaming car is it anyway?"

An answer is given, not my companion, but a drawl, a slurred mutter, gripping my heart in its vice– "Why, mine of course."

I twirl round to confront that overbearing 'slob' from my youth, easing himself through the glass doors.

"Miss Bryant," his tongue whipping in and out of his mouth, wetting his fat bulbous lips; a reptile hunting for food "We meet again."

I hurry back to my seat.

I glare toward the disgusting figure by the window, remember 'that' party, his slobbering acts of seduction. I shiver, my head twisting quickly as I hear the Count re-enter the room. The 'slob' salutes, I wish to laugh.

"I have seen a white car in the driveway, his," I nod my head toward the lout by those doors.

"Ah Ottmar, you have met our dear Rhia, but there again a whisper has told me, you both have met before today?"

The laggard yawned, turned, and moved his untidy body into another straight-backed saluting position, or something to that effect.

"Yes, Sir," the man said in an ambiguous manner.

Sir? Where does the fool think he is? The Count smiled, made his way to where *that* man was craning his piggy eyes into the garden. Slowly Count Reinbach removes the overcoat he greeted us in, revealing a dark grey uniform adorned by a row of 'pips' along his shoulder epaulettes. Running my gaze down his lean body I realised the figure standing by the window, from his uncreased jacket and trousers to the high polished shine on his knee length boots, was military. Ottmar, that is what the Count called him, presented a cap he had been holding behind his back. The Count accepted it, placed it upon his head, and the picture was complete.

This time my breath catches in my throat as realisation hits me. Dismissing 'Ottmar' from the room, Count Reinbach looked my way. His eyes were hard, no longer those gentle compassionate monitors that had held my trust, but ice blue steel, almost as if the man's absence from the room had afforded him time to remove any contact lenses he had used. In that moment terror wrapped its arms around my heart; terror as I have never known before. My brain screamed 'interrogator' and a flashback of a man's voice filled my ears. 1989 and I was overhearing an argument, a command: the bullying re-enactment of a time forgotten.

What had I done?

"I trusted you," was all that would leave my mouth.

The Count – this man – walked to where I was sitting–

"My dear, allow me to introduce myself, Major Emery Dreyer at your service."

I look at Hans, no sound from the motionless figure by the door.

Dismissing the 'slob' with an order to have water brought to me, the Count (what else do I call him: to let that evil name garnish my lips would be treachery) commanded Hans to remove himself, and change–

"Uniform man, show to this woman who you really are."

A quick glance my way and Hans left his 'post'.

I trembled, hearing the 'clomping' of leather soles on a wooden floor. A woman appeared, but not the woman I wished to meet. This was Alys, clothed head to foot in the same grey uniform, a glass of water in her hand.

"Drink," her voice was low as she passed the tumbler into my hand.

Sipping the drink my eyes fixated on Han's uniformed figure, straight backed by the doorframe, welcoming his aunt too warmly, kiss him on each cheek in a loving greeting. Resentment growing, I jumped up, spilling the water, screaming at the top of my voice–

"What the hell is going on?"

"Sit bitch," Alys flung at me, her immaculate English hidden under her Germanic accent.

"Hans?" I cried, pleading with his immobile form.

No movement, no support. My frustration grew–

'Swine, I hate you…I," I began as Alys swept across the room and brought her hand down across my face.

The Count grasped her arm–

"Can you get our guest another drink?" he requested.

Alys saluted and marched from the room. Holding my cheek, I decided to demand an answer.

Faster than I could form my gnawing question a woman was being dragged into the room. Forced to her knees, she was roughly pushed to lay at my feet. The intensity of body slamming against floorboards was chilling. The grey uniform who had manhandled her gurgled and gnarled as a rabid dog. From his lank blonde hair to her frightened eyes, I could see the resemblance. The woman was sobbing, the man almost foaming at the mouth. Hatred and pity, together, locked as one. The greying hair, intermingled with patches of strawberry blonde, was strapped back into a tidy bun, accentuating a red swollen face. Bruised lips moved to mumble "Get out", whispered with an urgent intensity. I flinched backwards, searched for any trust I had once felt from those within this room – nothing. Pulling the woman's head back the soldier spat- "Mother meet daughter – Daughter meet your real mother…"

I screamed, an involuntary sound bouncing around the room "No."

"Yes," the voice wailed in-between the coughing fits.

From the corner of my eye, I noticed Ottmar, who had slipped quietly back into the room, perform his malicious grin, creasing his repulsive mouth until I thought it would snap.

Alys, holding another glass of water, thrust it in my direction, not caring how many drops escaped to fall on the wounded woman's head. I grasped the dripping glass, placed it by the side of my previous one resting by my feet. Raising my head with a curse I caught the panting greeting escaping the soldier's lips–

"Hello, Rhia"

The ashen faced soldier who had thrust the woman at my feet laughed and coughed simultaneously. I looked into the sunken eyes, the pinched nose, the thinly stretched lips, felt my stomach sink as I yelped–

"Kurt."

--

I have often heard it said that a person can experience that moment when 'one stands outside their own body'. For me, this was it. This play, charade, farce, whatever handle could be put upon it was unveiling itself without a script. These actors, I use this term loosely for the sake of not wishing to smear this fraternity, move swiftly before me with precise action; their stratagem turning my world upside down.

Pushing the woman, whom I have now decided to be Etta Detdy aside, Reinbach grabbed my arm. Casually, I saw Hans move, then stop as Alys's hand interrupted his gesture. Pulling me to my feet I was catapulted into the arms of Kurt.

"Hold her," he commanded. "This play belongs to her; she will endure the happy end."

My former lover locked his arm around my waist, eased me into the cocoon of his gaunt body. I could hear the wheezing of his chest, feel the heat from his lips dribbling across my neck as he whispered–

"At last, you will soon learn what loyalty is."

With every movement of Reinbach's hand levelling itself across the pleading woman's cheek I felt a desire to struggle free. Whoever she was she does not deserve this brutal treatment, and with every beating the word "Verrater" accompanied the slap. Kicking the legs behind me I felt the grip of Kurt's hands slip away as he cried out in pain. The emaciated body fell to the ground, holding his legs in pain, coughing from the depths of his lungs. I ran to the woman groping on the floor, held out my hand, only to wince from the stamp of a boot.

Reinbach hauled me to my feet with the force of a raging bull, dragged me toward the waiting Ottmar –

"Control her, or do I have to do everything myself?"

Ottmar pulled me backwards, bent my arms behind me, as I squealed–

"You are the traitor, you are the liar, I hate…"

Reinbach clutched my face in his hand, ceasing the stream of outrage pouring from my mouth. "Enough Rhia, or I will mask the mouth that squawks– "

He turned his back on my trembling body as Ottmar pressed his hand across my mouth. I could smell sweat on his hand, discern the flabby form restraining me. I moved, felt more pressure, seized an opportunity to bite those stinking fingers. I bit, he whelped. This time he flung me to the floor, his boot connecting with my legs; the litany of German fouling the air. Alys marched across to me, grasping a chunk of my hair, pulling me to stumble across the floor to where Kurt was now standing, rope in hand, ready to tie my hands and feet.

"Keep her there," she hissed and moved to Hans's side once more.

Reinbach was striding around the room, the word 'Traitor' constantly flung at the woman who had crawled onto the sofa.

"Tell her," he pointed my way, "how her treacherous father lured you away from your loving family."

Etta Detdy cast her eyes to where Kurt had clasped his legs over my own, bearing down on the rope grinding into my skin.

"Your father helped me," she spluttered, blood oozing from her torn lips.

"Liar," her accuser shouts.

"My younger brother pleaded with him to save me," the faint cry carried the pain of memory and assault.

"Liar," he screamed, this time banging his foot on the floor, anger mounting as he spoke. He pulled the woman to her feet, held her suspended before him.

"Tell the truth, you witch, we need to hear it– every bit."

The dim light from the dying day highlighted the furnace raging within his steely eyes.

She wriggled "Henry was my f– friend," she groans.

Throwing her back onto the sofa, his steel shoulder pips glinting, he raised his hand once more–

"I will beat it from you. Admit, you betrayed us, and what for, a child you rejected–

Yes, Rhia, rejected, and a man who left you. You betrayed us twice, broke hearts, and hid. Do you know how long I have been searching? How many people have suffered because of you? It is time to pay Alina, Etta, whichever name you favour. Think carefully please (spoken through gritted teeth) for that moment is upon us."

Outside the light was beginning to fade, covering the room in chilling shadows. Reinbach, stood tall against the shrunken form of the bleating woman.

My hands were numb from the tight pull of the rope, my legs sore. I wanted to cry "Stop" as Reinbach and Etta Detdy parred; one in the dominant position of abuser, one beleaguered by the mouth above her. Daring not to move, yet desperate to break free I began to wriggle, side to side, forcing my paining legs to swing outwards. It was not until I felt the weight bear down on me that I suspected my 'gaoler' to have changed. Grasping my wriggling form between his flabby thighs Ottmar pressed hard, a wrestler's move to hold his opponent down. Moving was difficult, breathing even more so, leaving me gulping for air, as I trailed Kurt mimicking his father's silhouette. There was an oppression gathering in the room, a sinking feeling that I was witnessing only the beginning of something I could not understand; could not quite grasp as Kurt switched on the light, a single bulb dangling from a socket above that empty chair, every now and again glaring in my direction with a hostility he was unwilling to vent. Bringing Hans into my eyeline I sniggered. He had not moved: his inflexible stance not changed.

Alys had caught my snigger, hurried to my side, and literally 'boxed' my ears–

"Take that you, stupid woman. Did you really believe Hans liked you?"

Tears stung my eyes as the pain reverberated through my head. She marched over to where the Count was standing, still glaring at Etta Detdy, still getting himself ready to deliver another beating.

"Emery," Alys said. "What about…"

The Count reeled on her, a nocuous fire leaving what I once thought a gentle mouth–

“Major,” he roared at the top of his voice.

Alys jumped back, saluted, and returned to where she was standing with Hans. A terrifying fear squeezed my stomach. Emery Dreyer, the sadistic Stasi officer, the man Savvy warned us about. I let out a whimper – how can I think of her, or Mother at this moment? What had begun at the beginning of the year as a stand against conventionalism and order, was now turning into a terrifying ordeal. I had thought my insight into the world of deception would bolster my pathway. Purveying this man in all his savagery I knew I was wrong. This deceiver has herself been deceived.

Reinbach was shouting–

“This woman, my once devoted sister,” he brushed Etta Detdy on the cheek. “Is a fool,” he paused. “She left the family, sold out her country,” the rancour in his tone growing. “Her name is Alina Dreyer,” he bent nearer to the grovelling form on the sofa, “Alina Dreyer” he fell silent, then – “Do you hear?”

She shrunk back.

Ottmar’s position changed. He freed my gasping body, knelt behind me, his sweating hands roaming across my face, the taunts of his remarks whispered in my smarting ears. I cringed.

“Take your hands away from her,” Hans grunted.

The slob laughed, “Oh dear, you have travelled there.”

The Major boomed, “Be quiet”, his cold eyes glazing over as he commanded “Give the order.”

Alys saluted, Kurt saluted. Both marched from the room. I tried to twist my face from Ottmar’s grip, sought Hans’s fixated glare. The spluttering lips behind me began to mutter “Rache, Rache”, his excitement on the ‘revenge’ word growing. I moaned from the pain spiralling through my legs; winced as Reinbach slapped Ottmar’s hands from my throat wrenching me upwards–

“Get up, this is my retribution. I have waited so long.”

He yanked me harder, ordered the ropes be removed, motivating me by my hair to where that lonely chair shone beneath the light. Ottmar saluted, obeyed his master’s demand, and cut the ropes. Glancing at the woman crouched on the sofa I recognised she was saying the word “Run” over and over under her breath. Suddenly a scream left her mouth from the backhand blow, catapulting her head backwards, stilling the begging mouth.

“Ruhig,” came the boom in his native tongue.

The woman dribbled from the blood soaking her lips, curled up further, and hid her face. I knew he had told her to be quiet. Pulling me to stand behind the chair his hand took a tighter hold of my hair, twisting the long red coils within his grasp. His sneer was poison, as through the door marched Alys with a younger soldier and a man.

That man was my father.

--

My screams pulsated around the room. The harder I screamed, the tighter the Count held onto my hair. The young soldier, his face hidden under the huge cap he wore, stood back as Alys gripped the diminished frame to push it to the chair. Once there she tied his hands together, winding the course rope she was holding down around his legs. Slouched before me, his shoulders drooping, his tired eyes drained of any emotion was the man known as Henry Bryant.

"Ah," the Count spat. "My quarry."

His hold tightened on the hair knotted through his fingers, tugging at my scalp. I whispered–

"Count, what have you done?"

"Done?" the Count roared. "Exactly what this spy deserved, and I am Major Dreyer, never forget that. Say it – Say it" his voice penetrated the stillness of the room.

"Major," I whimpered, felt the aggressive yank of my hair. "Major Dreyer."

"Good, do not forget it, for every-time you do, he…" he spat at my father, "will pay."

I tried to touch the slouched body to the side of me, stretched, and was yanked back by the fierceness of my captor's hand. Tears spilling down my cheeks invaded my mouth, causing me to splutter.

"What– what gives you the right Major Dreyer to hurt him?"

Never in my life had I seen features twisted with such hatred and anger– Seizing my father's hair with his spare hand he pulled it backward, whilst pushing mine forward.

"Meet Guy Billington," he spat. "The felon who stole my sister."

He thrust, wrenched, clashed our heads together. I tried to cry out, to touch the sagging form collapsed on that chair.

The roar that left the mouth of Emery Dreyer was accompanied by a 'thud' as Etta Detdy hurled herself at her brother's feet.

"Emery," she pleaded, her hands gripping the glossy boots. "Please, I will do anything for you."

He kicked her aside.

"Anything? How can the past be wiped out? This, my dear little sister is a double-edged sword. In the words of an abused soul – it is payback time."

He threw his hands up in the air, releasing his hold on his prisoner and myself. Falling to the ground I searched the room, saw the faceless, speechless fools, and despised what they stood for. I turned my attention back to the Major, whose furious voice was lambasting into the pleading woman sprawled at his feet. He had knelt beside her, pulling her chin within an inch of his own face, before bundling her from the ground, shaking her shoulders with such rage that she bounced within his grasp as a toy of an enraged dog. No one moved. They had all become suppressed at the fury raging through the room. This time Dreyer dropped the sobbing woman onto the sofa with a warning of his next move to my father if she moved or spoke. No-one moved. Hans, a frozen incarnation of a bygone trooper stared, igniting further the revulsion building inside me.

It was the marching that dragged me from that black abyss I was sinking into. Kurt and this soldier, his face still shadowed by his cap, up and down, until finally standing to face my father's chair they saluted. I snarled, could not help myself–

"Who do you think you are, parade ground combatants waiting for a word from this man?"

The major curled his lips, let that heinous laugh spurt into the room, saluted back, moving his head in my direction. Kurt moved my way, grasped my arms, pushing me to kneel in front of this unknown soldier–

"This is loyalty, Rhia, look."

He was shouting, laughing like the madman I am sure he had merged into. I heard clapping reverberating across the room. Slowly, with an intention of carving this moment forever within my mind the soldier removed his cap.

Diary – how does this pen write the word 'frozen' without sounding overdramatic. I will use 'Anachronistic', hoping it delivers what it means- removing me to a period other than this story portrays.

I stared, experienced that same nausea that in the past had reduced me to embarrass myself. I went to speak, to seek any strength left in my stumbling body, to strike the mocking mouth that greeted me.

"Hello, Girl."

--

I emerge from the swell of the tenebrous hole I had fallen into with the disbelief of one who had faced her worst possible nightmare. Slowly opening my eyes, with the hope that the face before me had disappeared, I look around. Nothing had changed. Father was still strapped to that chair, the Major still stood behind him in threatening stance, his self-possessed reasoning a deadly threat. Etta Detdy still crouched on the sofa, quietly sobbing, cowing from her brother's anger. Kurt was talking to his father, and Hans, heaven forgive me for spitting on his name, was still standing by the door, accompanied by Alys, the refined woman having metamorphosed into a monster, also deep in conversation with the slob Ottmar. So, will someone confirm that the young soldier that had laughed in my face was not Jimmy – my Jimmy?

From my position on the floorboards, I gaze deep into his brown eyes glowering down at me. I say the name that I can hardly push past my lips–

"Jimmy?"

There was no love, no concern. His over-riding emotion, that of dislike–

"Yes, it is me."

My eyes ran over the grey uniform, the mirror polished boots, the cropped haircut.

"Why?" I felt the pain follow the word.

His hand shot out, wavered in front of me. I clasped it, pulled myself (as best as I could) into a standing position, never taking my gaze from those pools of recrimination.

"What is this game you are playing, Jimmy?"

"Game?" he questioned in a mocking tone. "I am playing no game. I serve the person you trusted. Unlike him (spoken with loathing toward my father) who thought he knew better than the greatest intelligence officer that lived, he swayed that stupid fool (his head nodding in the direction of the woman on the sofa) to run away with him, betraying her country, and her beloved family."

I inhale, cramming my lungs with as much air as possible–

“Are you mad? These fools are sick. Full of a hatred they do not understand.” Jimmy tossed his head in the direction of Kurt.

The sudden movement of reducing me to my knees once more caused the racking cough to pummel Kurt’s chest, the simplest of words produced in spurts-

“We may be mad – breathe – in your opinion, Rhia, – wheeze – but I will serve – gasp – this man to my death.”

I grovelled on my father’s lap, found his mangled hands, stroked the drooping head, wiped the bloodstained lips with my fingers. A sudden jerk, and my father’s head was forced upwards. The sob that left my mouth was one filled with pity. I could see how swollen his lips were, how bruised his eye sockets from constant slapping, and the red weal from pressing on his neck. His half-closed eyes were haunted.

“You bastards,” I choked. “Why, WHY?”

Jimmy, who had knelt with me, held my head close to his cheek, much to Kurt’s aggrievance.

“This swine,” he spat, the saliva trickling its way down my cheek, “is about to receive the lesson of his life. You were needed as the main witness if you like, to an end of a feud, a thirty-year deception that the Major calls the double-edged sword.”

A cold hatred seized my heart. If anybody else mentions that evil man’s quote – I will scream. Jimmy, not releasing my shoulders from his arm wiped my falling tears–

“Crying will not help, Rhia.”

“Mother?” I gulped, the bile from disgust filling my mouth.

“I taunted you with your mother. She was not lying. You are easy to mislead.”

He went to sneer, that contemptuous laugh that seems party to today’s events. I raised my hand, felt the welt of pressure drag it down. I watched as father struggled to form the words ‘I love you’, cried as I knew it was painful for him to speak. Why had he not spoken of his past? Would it have made a difference?

“I hate you all,” I shouted.

“Good,” Jimmy declared. “It will make my duty easier.”

I began to struggle, felt the slap of his hand across my head, plunging it downward into my father’s lap.

“Stay there, you pompous clown. Deceiver you call yourself – Ahhh.”

He placed his knee in the small of my back. I gasped, felt once more the yank of my head.

"Look, at this man's defeat, Look– "

In what appeared to me was Jimmy's frustration he slipped his arm around my neck, prised my throat across his arm. I tried to squeal, to plead with my one-time partner, accepted its futility, then let my mind loose within its own thoughts.

There was movement by the doorway. I heard Hans's voice–

"Leave her."

Immediately Kurt responded–

"Oh dear," he coughs, "little brother, you want more?"

Tension was growing: a classification of importance. I realised the Major had stepped back from the chair, had let go of my father's head and was strutting up and down the room, speaking in an inaudible voice to the slobbering Ottmar, who ran from the room, and returned with more whispers. A clock struck 'two', and the thought of 2nd of November ran through my mind. I prayed for help. The woman on the sofa had ceased her crying. My heart registers no sentiment. If this woman is my mother, as all here agree, I was just the main catapult for her escape from East Germany, and not the precious child that Mena thought of me. My hands travelled for the hundredth time on the man in the chair. I feel my head sag as Jimmy's clutch eases, and it falls forward onto my father's chest – A slight movement in the fatigued body, defiance I will say. His message of hope, seen many times in the past when dark days troubled him. Only not this time father – We have lost.

Friday November 2nd.

All Souls Day

The third day of what used to be called 'All Hallows Festival' – a day when the souls of the departed are believed to be in communication with the living.

The cobwebs of the gathering night hung in this room like predators waiting to scavenge the bodies of their prey. No-one, apart from the Major, had moved, his only traverse was to step into the hallway to take what Ottmar had called 'an important message'. This had been greeted with indignation into 'why' this slob of a man could not 'deal with it', relenting to the sufferance to deal with the call himself. I had spent this respite with my head on my father's lap, my mind clouded by remorse. Whatever was going to happen to us at least we will be together. The strutting, whispering, rivalry between the younger men had continued throughout those dark menacing hours, with no bathroom relief or exercise for myself or Etta Detdy. Father had slumped over, only to wince in pain as the Major, returning from his call, had jerked him upward.

"No time for messing. Our escape plan is on green. We must conclude."

I had never felt so scared. My anger, I could see, was distressing my father, that was when he had any energy to lift his limp head. Emerged in my own thoughts I jumped as Kurt slid onto the floor at my side. Running a hand across my hair, my face, and around my neck asked –

"Did you like my portrait?"

His simpering lips disgusted me.

"I hated it, as I do you, and Jimmy – all of you," I cried.

He laughed, "Oh dear, little Rhia is cross. Whatever shall we do?"

The breakdown into a coughing fit caused him to gasp for breath, holding his stomach from what I could only gather were the pains attacking him.

Alys rushed to his side, helped the choking figure to stand, easing his breathing and helping to relieve his cough.

Ottmar took his place, squatting on the now cold floorboards, his bulbous form hiding my view of the spluttering man.

"That figure," Ottmar licked his lips. "A man's pleasure, wouldn't you say?"

"The seductive minx," Jimmy hissed scathingly.

"The colours," Hans said, no doubt hiding his ridiculous face.

"The blatant hussy," Alys threw at them as she coaxed Kurt to drink.

The Major was losing patience–

"Enough," came the growl. "We must deal with the job in hand."

They stood to attention in a pattern that reminded me of the wooden soldiers children position outside their toy forts. Towering above my slumping father, the Major demanded another chair be brought to the room. Alys ran to collect one, brought it to his side, before saluting, and marching away. He placed it behind my father's chair. Sitting, he slipped his arm around the sagging man's neck, tightened his grip until my father's mouth dropped open, then squeezed harder.

"No," I squealed, hurling myself upwards.

"I am tired of waiting. Tell him to admit he stole her."

He glared at my ashen face, "Tell him – NOW."

The hatred exhuming from the Major's eyes frightened me. I gently took hold of my father's hands, rubbed them slowly, and whispered –

"Please tell him, please."

My father shook his head, as Dreyer reinforced his grip, the tiny squeak that signifies pain escaping from the formers bruised lips.

Panic was growing inside me, thoughts of losing this beloved man rampaging through my mind. From my periphery gaze I saw a form grasp the arm around my father's neck.

"Let him go, Emery, let him go, I beg you."

The Major pushed her away.

"Get back to your seat. Can no-one control this slut of a woman?"

He glared at Alys. She instantly ran over and hit Etta Detdy hard. The Major continued–

"I have waited many years for this moment, and you_" he glanced at the woman rolled in a ball on the sofa. "You are no longer my sister," he paused. "For I am the avenging angel. My sword is drawn, and whichever side it will fall, I will have revenge."

His voice was thick with anger. The hold tightened around my father's neck. Within me hysteria gathered, ploughing its way through any sensible thought I may have. I began to scream every expletive that fell onto my tongue, those words that as a young girl my father would decry. I did not care. Anything to stop this vengeful act of slaughter. It was not until the feel of cold steel connected with my cheek that my head shot round to stare down the barrel of a gun. I stop screaming, face my antagonist, cannot believe the smirk slithering across his mouth.

My breathing is stilted–

"Jimmy?"

He presses the gun harder to my cheek.

"Yes, Rhia, I have played the game well. Brought your father to justice. Now, it is my turn to reap the revenge I was promised."

His dark eyes bore deep into mine.

A church bell rang, struck the hour of four. I dare not move, for the gun resting on my cheek was moving in the trembling hand. The light above my father's head was casting shadows, out into the garden, beyond the boundary hedge. My head buzzed from the panting exuding from my father's throat as each breath got harder to find. Inside fear was rising, that black hole where the mind is drawn to the recriminations of its past. All those silly spiteful events that end sometimes in the most undesirable moment they could wish for. This was mine.

Before me: three men I have loved, not loved, and never pretended otherwise.

Behind me: Mother, Savvy, Fiona Grubb, and anyone whom I considered worthy of using to my own advantage.

All these were now crowding in on my fearful mind.

I sensed other feet behind Jimmy, cocking a gun ready for use. Heard the simple request–

"Let her go."

Jimmy sneered, pushing the gun harder into my cheek.

"Feel sorry for her," he tormented Hans.

Placing himself by my father's shoulder I noticed how he kept looking toward the window, counting under his breath. Dreyer snarled–

"Move, you cankerous dog. Every time my eyes set upon yours, I see him – if it was not for my sister, I would kill you."

I heard Father wheeze, gasp for breath as the arm around his throat strengthened. Hans held steadfast. Jimmy's eyes are flashing, the hand holding the gun shaking.

"Now is the time," he said.

I wait for that explosion of fire, that hesitation between this life and the next.

"No," Hans cries out.

A tsunami breaks loose–

A scream from the sofa, followed by a slap and an expletive from Aly's lips.

Kurt, gun in hand, raises it to Hans's head.

"Little brother, how dare you take what was mine."

I notice Hans counting for a second time. Another look to the garden, then–

shots rebound around the room; shouts of agony; death curdling noises fill my ears – shattering glass – black figures pour into the room – shadows of a darker existence break from the night outside. Feeling the gun fall away from my face I bury my head in my father's lap, hear a woman's voice–

"Emery."

"Helena."

"Let him go."

"Never."

"For me?"

"If only..."

Father gagged, I heard the scream, felt my father slump in the chair as the piercing shot rang out, before darkness engulfed me.

--

"Rhia," a voice penetrated my closeted mind.

I could feel myself move, senses struggling to wake from the sweet oblivion I had fallen into.

"Rhia," an undertone of concern in the calling.

Leave me, I have my feet on Bhutan soil.

--

Opening my eyes, I recollect I know this person; run to meet that moment between confusion and reality that swamps the brain on gaining consciousness.

"Savvy, is that you? What – Where? – Oh Lord, what happened?"

The face before me grimaced, her eyes moving from me to scan the room.

"What should have happened years ago, but with a few mishaps along the way."

She summoned a colleague to help me to my feet. I wobbled, experienced that sensation where this body had expelled vast amounts of energy for another reason beyond my remembrance, leaving a decimated control of the limbs. Suddenly that 'other' reason fired across my mind.

"Savvy, my father. Where is my father?"

My head was turning in the manner of a submarine periscope.

"Where?" I began to panic, holding onto her arm as I viewed the chaotic room.

Between the clasp of my supporter, and a determined effort on her part, they managed to guide me to the now empty sofa. Savvy sat beside me.

Scattered around the room I could see various sheets covering what I guessed, yet wished to dismiss from my mind, bodies. Her 'team' were labelling and removing each one by order. These men and women, still clothed in their tenebrous clothing, moved with rapid efficiency.

"Please, Savvy, my father?"

She managed a tiny smile–

"Henry has been taken to hospital. Your mother informed. Let me say," her voice broke. "My team arrived just in time."

"You mean... he is not dead?" I could not stop my heart from surging.

A sigh left the pale lips–

"No, he is not dead, but I must warn you, he is seriously injured."

I jumped up from the sofa "I must go to him." – realised the rashness of my deed and grasped at the hand offered my way.

"Please, Rhia, sit. He is in good hands."

"What happened to him?"

The thought of her answer chilled my heart.

"The shattering of the window caused my old adversary to twist. As he did so, he pulled your father's neck with him. The pressure shattered the spine, leaving Henry unconscious"

The hot stinging tears that had gathered and spilt earlier were now flowing down my cheeks as a river.

"What hope?"

Savvy squeezed my hand "Every hope," she sighs. "Every hope."

I sit back down, accepting the dizziness in my head would allow me to go nowhere, not yet.

"That bastard that called himself a Count?" I shot at her.

"Emery is dead," was her simple statement.

"Good," I said, scared at the rancour I felt.

Rubbing my hands together I looked in her eyes–

"Jimmy?" I muttered, hot tears hovering beneath my eyelids.

"Your father had suspected Jimmy's connection to Dreyer's organisation for a few months. His need was to prove it."

"So, he walked into his own trap?"

"Yes, but he knew to catch the larger fish he would need your help, and Etta."

"Our trap too."

Savanah D' Mill's face held the same wistful look she had begun our conversation with, her voice more accusing–

"Not really yours or Etta's trap. Henry took the fall while trusting me."

"Yes, I…" my voice petered out in shame.

I scrutinized the covered bodies.

Following my inspection Savvy patted my knee–

"I will explain."

Her tone was practical: many would call it professional reserve.

"First, I must give you a message from Etta."

"Etta?" I said the name without feeling, the realisation of any biological connection belonging to another life, not mine.

"She has gone, Rhia, her request was to leave things as they were, but she wishes you well."

"Well?"

"Yes," Savvy's voice was low, almost as if she knew my confusion, yet would not dwell on it. "Mena sends love."

I nod and turn my head away, unable to stem those crushing tears.

"Dragner," her voice rang out, "the name Kurt Dreyer prefers to be known by, and Jimmy Grant have been taken away for questioning. Ottmar Wilner or, 'the slob' in your estimation," a quick fleeting smile, "sadly evaded us."

She saw my despair.

"How?" I choked.

"Not sure, but I will find out, and I will find him."

She gave her 'team' another order.

The question hovering on my lips spilled out–

"Hans?" I hesitantly asked.

Her face was expressionless–

"I am sorry. He was shot."

"Shot?" my expostulating voice echoed round the room.

For the first time since we began this conversation her features softened–

"His brother shot him. It was instant," she hastened to add.

I was visibly shaking, those stinging tears destroying what small amount of composure I had–

"Why?" my rage was plain.

"Jealousy," she said simply. "That green eyed monster that can plague us all."

Now the sobbing began, the gushing tears of a heart torn apart with the events of the past day. I hated the world, myself, the hypocrisy that spelt Rhia Bryant.

"I should hate him," I groaned.

Savannah D' Mill took my hand–

"He was a brave man. Hans never once faltered from the job Hal demanded of him," another smile lifted her face, "apart from you."

I stiffened.

"Alys?" I queried, not wishing the previous conversation to continue.

"Shot by Dragner, trying to save her child," came the rapid reply.

Savvy brushed my arm, rose to walk around the room, still directing the removal of the bodies.

Unable to control the emotion sweeping through me I counted each body as they were carried from the room, knowing one was Hans. Felt a twist inside myself I had never experienced before. I thought of Jimmy, the Berlin Wall, the lies he had told me; my ravaged mind asking the question all deceived lovers ask–

'Had I really loved him, or was he that friend I had to keep near, a prop for my shallow life?'

I sank to the floor as Savvy negotiated her way through toppled chairs and broken glass: a blood splattered floor and the reek of cordite. It was barely two hours since her invasion, yet my world had changed forever. The yowl trapped inside my chest beat against my breastbone, crying to be free; free as the tears rolling down my face. I needed to do something desperate, to mark this day as *my* epiphany, *my* own horrid whirlwind. I called to her–

"Tell me Savvy, was there really a painting of the Crux, or was that heinous art a decoy for me?"

She looks surprised–

"The Crux is very real; a masterpiece the world of art is waiting to claim. Dragner *had* written important names beneath his original painting including his own. They had been written for future reference when those soldiers could try to re-group. Yet, the main aim was to paint over it as an integral part of the plan.

Revenge may take years, but it eats at the soul."

I detected a tinge of sadness hidden among the determination. Savannah walked away. A young officer came to my side- spoke softly in my ear–

"Miss Bryant, Miss D' Mill has directed me to show you to her car. She will join you in a moment, drive you to where your father has been taken. They will check you too. This way please."

Still sobbing I let him guide me to a car, stay with me until Savannah D' Mill appeared. Then, upon accepting new orders he returned to the cottage. Both drenched in our own thoughts, we headed toward the motorway.

--

St Matthews Spinal Hospital*

Late Evening

The car pulled into the sprawling grounds of St Matthews private hospital on the outskirts of London as the clock tower rung ten o' clock. The journey had been a disturbed one for me, whilst Savvy, thinking or not, had hummed a calming tune. Constantly my mind played out the past events: repeatedly showing me first one face, then another. I lived again those moments in Hans's arms, his eagerness to share those moments with me, my unwillingness to cooperate fully in his joy. I had allowed my desire to carry me, no consideration for his emotions, my bloodied mindedness to walk the pathway of deception uppermost in my mind. My head ached, and although Savannah had checked my hair, my face, she was unable to do the medical necessities. As the wheels roared down that motorway, I wished for that impossible dream, to turn this year backward. If that had been possible, the world would not be grieving, yet my father's plan would never have been finalised.

It is with a heavy heart I write– here this woman stands at that crossroad of indecision.

I get ready to leave the car as Savvy rests her hand on my arm –

"Prepare yourself, Rhia, the news may not be what you wish to hear."

I say nothing, climb from the car, and run into the building. The reception area is huge. A desk manned by a smart dressed woman whose age would be hard to determine due to her dark hair being pulled back from her face with the severity of old-fashioned tidiness. Nurses, in their crisp white uniforms, pleated white caps, dark tights, and strong sensible shoes, are knocking on doors, waiting for a call, and disappearing in a flash. I lean forward to the desk asking for 'Mr Bryant'. The woman peers above her spectacles edged on the end of her nose and asks my concern.

"Are you family?" she queries, snooty voice ringing out loud.

"It is alright, Patricia. This lady is with me," Savvy intervened.

Patricia, suits her, smiles weakly and carries on with whatever she was doing.

"This way"

Savvy led the way to a lift, pushed a button, waited for the doors to open, and stepped inside. I followed. The lift hurled upwards, coming to rest at the sixth floor.

"This part of the hospital is secured for us," my escort stated with pride.

I nod, emerge from the cloistered lift to an airy, pristine white, corridor. On each side were a set of three doors that led to huge emergency rooms, and various small, but comfortable single cubicles, room for a patient, bed, bedside cupboard, and two armchairs for visitors. Each had its own nurse, contrasting in a dark blue uniform to those nurse's downstairs, and a private television and telephone. Outside the far door my mother stood with her arms open wide. I ran, threw myself into those waiting arms and let the tears I had finally managed to stem in the car fall once more.

Mother held me tight, the strength of her arms wrapping around me.

"Thank God, Rhia, you are safe."

Her voice trembled as her emotion fraught body clenched me harder.

"I am sorry," my cries tumbled from my mouth, spilling over themselves.

"No need," she was saying. "Your father's plan worked."

How could she be so calm?

I stood back, monitored the pain in her eyes as she quietly uttered those words.

"Worked? The man nearly got himself killed."

She shook her head, "He was always in control. It was me who panicked."

My gaze moved to the door behind her, white shutters closed tight, the gentle sounds of machines bleeping away.

"Father," I urge. "How is he?"

The sobs she had been trying to suppress left her throat in a flurry of whimpers –

"He…" sob. "He is…" sob, "paralysed."

The emotion of self-sorrow that a few minutes earlier I had been ready to collapse beneath ebbed away. This man, who had shown himself to be my guide when I was younger, my mentor in later life, my stalwart from mother's foibles, lay paralysed in a hospital bed due to the likes of Jimmy and Dragner. Justice must be served.

I had never seen my mother cry, certainly not in genuine circumstances. Usually it was over something petty, or her need to gain that expensive new dress and shoes she wanted. Generally, it was the main event for her 'own way'. I turned round to search for Savvy, caught her emerging from another door –

"Those devils must pay," I screamed. "Father is paralysed."

Savvy's face was unreadable, not one small movement gave any sign of anger, her pain had been disguised into action.

"They will," she murmured, then with a louder intonation she said –

"I have just arranged a room for you both. You will find facilities to shower and eat."

Between sobs Mother thanked her, before disappearing through the door she had stood by. Holding my hands out I walked to Savvy's side. She took the extended hand, grasped it within her own and squeezed it tight.

"Take care, Rhia. I will pop in from time to time. Stay as long as you wish."

The gratitude I felt was beyond words. The distrust and impatience on my part had gone, replaced by a deep debt of respect.

"I will never forget your actions today. Thank you for his life."

For a moment that fleeting smile I had come to know so well swept across her face before fading, and the professional person took over. Slowly I walked toward the room that housed my father, depressed the handle, and crept inside.

Intelligence Headquarters – London

Sunday November 4th.

Savannah D' Mill walked into the room accompanied by a tall imposing man. Against the dark maroon of her tailored suit, his tatty blue jeans and white shirt signified a contrast that could not be ignored. From the precise way she had sat down at the table in the centre of the room, to the jaunty way the man slouched in his chair, an onlooker would ascertain that the woman was in charge, and the man her threatening sidekick. The prisoner, cuffed to his steel seat, an armed guard directly behind him, sat with the look of one who held all the cards, arrogant, defiant, and ready for conflict at the least erroneous move; an intransigent resolution he had been taught. He had been stripped of the grey uniform worn at his arrest into clothing thought more suitable; a white jumpsuit that hid nothing but his body and the red marks on his upper arms from the struggle he had put up as he was led from the place of arrest to a waiting car. Before him on the table rested a plastic cup filled with water, untouched.

The woman opened the folder she had placed on the table while her companion stared at the prisoner, his gaze boring deep into the captive's eyes.

"Your name for the record," he sniffed with contempt.

Savannah D' Mill leant forward to where a recording machine sat, switched it on, heard the purr, then repeated the question.

"Your name for the record please."

The prisoner said nothing.

She smiled, looked toward her companion, then repeated her question.

"For this record I am asking the detainee for a third time his name. State whether you are James Grant please."

The prisoner sighs, "Yes."

Flitting through her papers she produces two photographs. Pressing them before the man she asks.

"Do you know these people?"

He snatches a quick glance, skimming over the distinct profiles of Major Emery Dreyer, and his son Kurt, the renowned painter Jules Dragner.

He nods.

"Can you name them?"

This time no affirmation.

Her companion wheezed through his teeth–

"It is better for you to start talking."

An iron undertone rippled through his voice upholding the fire flashing in those penetrating eyes. The prisoner made the sound that denotes boredom. Savannah D' Mill looked from one man to the other, instantly returning to her calm undisturbed manner.

"Jimmy, may I call you that?"

The prisoner nodded.

"Jimmy, how did you get involved with these people?"

No sound.

"You do not belong," she prevailed. "Yet, I know you had known Kurt Dreyer, or Jules Dragner, as he is better known, for quite some time. Yes?"

No sound.

Her companion moved, anger etching his chiselled features. Banging his fist down hard on the table.

"Look, you crazy misled fool, they do not care one jot about you. Own up. Of course, you know this piece of dung, whatever bloody name he calls himself."

Completely ignoring this outburst Jimmy lifted his eyes in Savannah D' Mill's direction.

"We met at university."

His eyes found those of the man opposite, lifted his chin, and gave him that contemptuous grin.

The sergeant, code name Bret, slammed the table once more. Savannah D' Mill placed her hand on his, a signal for quiet.

"You agreed with his politics?" she said, laying her finger on Dreyer's picture.

Jimmy stared hard at the face radiating from that black and white snapshot.

"Obvious I would say," he murmured.

Bret took a deep breath – a bull ready to charge.

"Cocky Bastard," he yelled moving nearer the edge of his seat.

Savannah shook her head and smiled, "Why?"

Why? Jimmy groaned silently, his mind unsheathing this adverb every time he questioned his motives.

The cuff around the chair grated against the steel of the leg, causing the prisoner to move now and again in discomfort. The guard moving forward, pressed the prisoner's shoulder in a bid to suppress him, moving back to where he was standing once he was satisfied the prisoner would not create a problem. Eyeing the two people opposite him Jimmy returned to the un-flexible position taught by his mentor. He knew this man across the table would willingly hit him. The guy had that look – the look Major Dreyer sought in his soldiers. How this sergeant would have risen in their ranks. Jimmy watched as the man swept his hand through his ginger hair. Lord, he had everything: the vibrant looks, the short temper, the willingness to take his prisoner down – Impatience. How Major Dreyer would have noted this man to become the most brilliant soldier. One of those who drill the information from a person, or kill the prisoner trying.

He switched his attention to the woman. Now, she was altogether something different. Calmer, quieter, a predator who waits. Impressive. She knew the Major. 'Helena' he called her… History?

Savannah D' Mill was repeating that 'Why?' word. It resounded in his head.

"Jimmy, you have spent the last few years as Rhia Bryant's friend, closer at times. You became part of that family, almost to being considered a son. So, I ask again – Why?"

Bret stood up, moved around the room.

"Rhia?" Jimmy whispered, determined not to give in.

"Rhia Bryant," Bret spat close to his detainee's ear. "Mother F…" he stopped himself, controlled the expletive ready to jump from his mouth–

"Are you really that embroiled in their ways that a charge of treason carries no worry for you?"

Jimmy realised he was getting under the man's skin. A gambit he had been taught before relenting slowly and pleading he was threatened.

Bret bent low to his senior officer's ear.

"He is playing us."

"I know," she replied.

"Let me have him for half an hour."

"Not yet, how about coffee?"

"Coffee?"

"Yes, Sergeant"

Bret stomped from the room with disgust.

Switching the recorder off Savannah D' Mill sat back in her chair, stretched her arms, removed her jacket, and smiled.

"I went to see your parent's yesterday."

Jimmy's head shot up.

"I left after trying to comfort your mother. She had not set eyes on you for around a year. They hid their faces when I told them of your shame."

No movement from across the table.

"I tried to explain," she elaborated. "That it was possible that you were coerced. Is that true?"

Her plea made him laugh. Savannah moved her hand nearer to the machine. Jimmy uttered "Stop". The woman confronted his expression with one of satisfaction.

"*She* stuck by Kurt. *She* was fascinated by him, I tried to persuade her otherwise. No good. *She* thought I did not know what they were planning. *She* used me. So, if you cannot beat them, join them."

He sighed, removed his gaze from her face, looked toward the door.

"How long?" the woman urged.

"The Berlin Wall," came his reply.

"That long?" she mused.

"Yeah," said with sardonic meaning.

Bret re-entered the room.

"Bloody hot," he thundered.

The coffee, which he had spilt as he kicked the door closed, shook, its dark steaming liquid vibrating in their disposable cups.

"No milk," he moaned.

Savannah thanked him, returned to Jimmy.

"Split his guts, I presume," her sergeant indicated across the table.

That smile from his boss annoyed yet thrilled him. Savannah D' Mill pushed her coffee Jimmy's way.

"Here, it is not bad. Now, tell me why Rhia?"

This time Jimmy felt like screaming. He hated the 'why' word, he hated this room, he hated that smarmy idiot, strutting around in the fashion of an imperious Lord preening over his minions. Bret's eyes clouded–

"You joined an enemy intelligence group over a girl?"

The wonder in his voice made Jimmy sick.

"What do you know?" he hurled at the conceited man.

"I would say he is lying," Bret spluttered, trying to sip his coffee.

The room spun. If he, Jimmy, was not bolted to this chair, he would slap that man down.

Savvy waited a moment, then asked –

"Are you a liar, Jimmy?"

'Play the game' shot into his head.

"Maybe," he answered.

He could see he had won, with Bret anyway, he was fuming.

"I tell you what. Let me take this arrogant lump of shit to the hospital to see his master's handiwork, then I will treat him the same."

"Be quiet," Savannah ordered. "Please, Bret, find some milk."

"What?" the man began, read the message in her eyes, and for a second time left the room.

The moment the door closed Savannah D' Mill did not play cat and mouse. She was tired of that. Instead, she indicated to the arm guard to step forward, place his gun on the table, and step back.

"Jimmy, you have come to the crossroad. Whatever evasion tactics you have been advised to follow will get you nowhere. I want you to confess, agree to my offer, or I will reach for that damned gun, and shoot you myself."

Jimmy went to laugh.

Savannah's hand swept the coffee away from him, spilling its contents over the table and onto the floor.

"I am not in a joking mood. What your revengeful master did to my friend and colleague will not be overlooked. There will be no room for reprieve within your sentence, I will make sure that is so. Perhaps, on the other hand what I will offer, may just save your neck."

Sha sat back down, wiped the table with the cloth she was handed and spread out the papers before her prisoner. He was determined not to show his fear.

"An hour," she was saying. "An hour."

--

The Afternoon of the Same Day

Room A

Jimmy lay slumped on the bed, eyes fixated to the dark sky through the window in the ceiling. He had been given an hour to contemplate – Contemplate what?

Through his mind the day's activity tumbles over and over as a child frolicking over a village green. He had been offered a clause; that bated breath hiccup where those higher up this so-called intelligence ladder presumed they were showing mercy. For a reason he could not fathom he had found it hard not to split his sides laughing. Could they not see mercy had nothing to do with whether his acceptance was up for grabs or not, whatever prospects that fancy woman offered him. Those nights in Paris where he met with Major Dreyer and his followers had set what his parents would call the 'bar' high. Whatever that woman thought of him, he was no fool. From his very first meeting with the Major on that fateful night in Berlin his hatred was visible; his revenge for Henry Bryant incontestable. It was a hatred so dense that it left a taste in one's mouth that made you gasp for air. Over the months that followed he had signed up to his plan to seek revenge on what Major Dreyer promoted as insubordinate failure to follow orders on Henry Bryant's part, leading to the illegal removal of his faithful sister from the family, and severe pressure to convey intimate details of the regime.

He had never heard the name Savannah D' Mill mentioned, so the Major either did not know her by this appellation, or she was the secret past a heart can hide. His plan, on the other hand, was brilliantly devised to the last detail, its execution remarkable. Jimmy realised his part in the plan was regarded as important, especially when the major understood his closeness to the Bryant family. He was told to fall into line with the Major's son – the painter Jules Dragner – Kurt – not only his old rival, but his friend from university. Through one of Dragner's paintings, where this artist could not resist writing names (his own and Hans's included) they would draw their fly into the parlour. It was an easy decision to make Bryant's daughter, Rhia, the bait. From that point, when he took an oath, put his signature to paper, there was no return. He was trapped. Dreyer might be dead, others were not, which begs the question of choice.

"You can choose a life within your country's service, that of a double agent, or you can suffer life in prison."

This was his choice?

The dark sky had more on offer. Her choice would lead him from one bloody regime to another.

Then, there was his final request. That his parents visit him. An hour, maybe two, where he could explain his actions. He would try to make them understand his point of view. What had been that woman's answer –

"No."

She had told him, in no uncertain terms, that only prisoners who relent and agree to their generous offer, with prerequisites of course, had privileges. She had stood staring down at him, those red lips funnily inviting, and asked –

"What can you tell your parents, Jimmy Grant, that you cannot, and must tell us?" If only she knew.

No matter how this woman beguiled him, and that was her covert weapon, she could not make him break his oath. She reminded him of those Stasi renegades in Paris, they had longed for his soul too. Well, this he was certain of, this woman was not the Major. She had not saved him from himself. She had not comforted him that night in 1989. She had not listened…

Jimmy knew Kurt's aim, to lure his besotted friend to his will. He saw them slink away, lived the pain, felt the jealousy rising within him. The revellers had carried him across Checkpoint Charlie, unceremoniously dropping him when they reached the East. Lost in the swarming crowd he had wandered, crying for the love of his 'girl'. From nowhere he was dragged into a shed. His first thought was that he would be killed, his clothes stolen, and his body dumped. He was wrong. A man, still in his grey uniform had recognised him from pictures his son had sent home from England. He poured out his discontent, let his emotion run free. The man listened, gave the sympathy his poor wounded heart needed. This man, an officer of the Stasi, knew about the red headed girl and Kurt. His mission, to gleam knowledge concerning her family. I was bowled over, blind to his faults, angry with resentment and desire. I gave him my oath, and my future was settled.

Jimmy stared harder at the sky. It was true what Savannah D' Mill had told him. He was at a crossroad, with an hour before that key would turn, and his answer required. There was no running away, no pretending, it was the deal or nothing. Solitary confinement was not his choice. Tossing onto his side Jimmy knew whatever he chose the cards were stacked against him. He managed a smile thinking of Rhia's face when she found out that guitar in their bedroom had a 'bug' concealed inside it: a cleverly concealed transmitter, given to him in Paris from the Major's own hand. What knowledge he had gained. What a lesson his so called 'partner' had learned. Now, his jealousy and anger had dissolved he knew he had loved her, in his way, always would. Oh hell, the silence of this room grated on him in this hour of resolve. He thought of his parents, their mistrust and shame, and sat bolt upright, snatched a quick glance toward the door, closed his eyes tight and mumbled "Hilf mir – Help me."

--

Room B

The dark thoughts hurtling themselves around Kurt's mind matched perfectly with the dark room he had been flung into. He had been refused a lightbulb by that arrogant man that at first introduced himself as a sergeant, but after an hour had begun to sound more like a childhood nightmare. He was a bully, for he knew exactly what a bully was.

He must stop there – He ran to the corner of the room, sank down onto the floor.

Shadows of the past floated before him, creating their own theatre to perform the horror plays instigated by the realms of his imagination. It did not matter how many times he blinked his eyes commanding them to 'go', they would still act out their spectacle of barbarity, throwing his cadaverous body into tremors and sweats. Squirming further into the corner his agitated thoughts now sought those 'kinder' shadows he had suppressed when daylight had filtered through the small window in his roof. He called upon their presence, challenging these ectoplasms of his mind to show themselves. He needed their willpower to fight the demons that tormented his days as they inflamed his nights. Their defiance to his nightly dreams always came late; always allowed those cacodemons to win.

Covering his head, blocking out the smallest star twinkling through his window, he let the sadness of loss wash over him. These people had no sympathy for him. They cared not how that bond, strong between father and son, had been severed. How the main stay of his life had been blown away by one bullet. How that woman, 'Helena' he had called her, had snapped his father's life as a branch from a tree. He had stared, pulled the trigger of his gun, witnessed his father's and Hans's fall, discerned the pain at the back of his head, and his own plummet to the ground. Kurt stuffed his fist into his mouth. He must not cry – He must not let that ginger haired swine think for one moment he had the upper hand. No-oo, for those demons will smite him. especially when his father's body along with his aunt, must be flown back to the country of their birth, not in honour, but in the guise of traitors. He let the sad depiction of his mother and her shame, wash over him. How she would howl at Hans's death, her favoured child. Suddenly he sniggered, wiped the spittle from his lips, and settled for always being 'second best'.

Noise – Outside the door. He could hear voices. Scrambling around in the corner he pressed himself nearer to the floor, pushing his ear onto the cold concrete. What could he hear? Feet – Living demons moving nearer – They must not take him, they must not… Wait, his father was speaking–

"Be brave son, we will face them together."

There was a racetrack in his head. One set of cars pushing another set aside; the figures crammed inside them squealing at him–

"Do not face that man, that creature of the Intelligence Corps."

Kurt nodded his head, agreed with them. His ghosts had also gathered how insensitive that man was to his, Kurt Dreyer's bravery. Whatever words that overbearing man had used, and his expletives were many, *he* had not given in. He was Kurt Dreyer, the magnificent painter, Jules Dragner – he laughed, silently at first to himself, then louder, filling the room with the sound of hell.

Be quiet – He was not going to let the voices outside hear him. He curled into a ball. That way he, that ginger headed fiend would not see him. They, the shadows, would hide him. Stifle the coughing, his balled fist rammed further into his mouth, the dark of the room would protect him.

The voices grew louder.

"Shhhhh," he places a finger over his mouth. "They must not hear him, those parasites outside the door. They are waiting for him to break – Never."

He scrambles from his corner and crawls to the door. He can hear the name 'Ottmar'. Hear the reply of his father's batman, this man he thought escaped.

Wait, they are taking him for interrogation. What will they ask? What will he say?

Kurt feels the choking sensation gathering in his chest, squeezes his throat, muffles the sound.

"Shhhhh," he mumbles again. "The enemy is at the door."

He sits with his back to the door, searching the room for implements of war. That man, that dog who barked to the woman's command had held 'extradition' over his head. Fool, he had thought, as if that would scare him. He knew, where his capture would lead him, back to that place his father had released him from, and whatever happened *he* would not go back there. The shadows would take him first. It was just a case of choosing: the nightmares or the dreams.

He snorted, pushed his fist further into his mouth.

"There," he whispered to no-one in particular. "I have quietened myself."

He began to cough, the sensation of his lungs ready to burst.

A bang at the door, a key, a push that moves him along the floor. Men, one, two, three rush into his room, drop to their knees, ease him forward. Pulling him to his feet they help him to the bed, sit him down, try to inject his arm. He fights, scratching at the sheets, screaming amongst the coughing. Focusing on the man in the white coat he gabbles–

"Tell me your name. Do as Major Dreyer is asking."

Silence.

Monday November 5th

Kurt's eyes flicker open, the weak winter sun pouring through his window lights the walls a creamy white. Glancing around the room he notices nothing has changed. Yet, wait, this is not his room. His bed is higher, and a white gown is covering his body, also crisp white sheets tuck him in tight. Slowly he turns his head to glare at the bedposts behind him. They have straps with wrist holds. Quickly his gaze lowers to the bed itself. Along the edges of the bed, he can see more straps. His gut feeling tells him they are to restrain him. Hell, these tools of constraint were commonplace within the walls of the old Stasi prison – Hohenschonhausen.

How many times had he strapped a prisoner's body to a bed so they could not escape? How many times had hands been forced into manacles such as these?

He knew their use.

Agitated, he notices the nurse hovering outside the half glass door. She was a vision of white. A sure sign they had confined him to a military bolt hole. He was more than a prisoner – he was a project.

His shadows told him so.

It was they who told him he had been sedated, they who assured him that it would be the only way he would have gone quietly. After all he was the son of Major Emery Dreyer. Knowing this, how dare those dogs pump opioid into him.

They had tried to part him from his shadows, fools that they are, separation is impossible, these silhouettes are part of him.

His eyes fall on a red button. Trying to move his arm and realising it was attached to a drip he swung himself onto his side, reached with his free hand, and pushed as hard as he could. In they rushed, the nurse in white, the burly muscled porter, the thin mouthed bespectacled doctor.

"Mr Dreyer," the thin mouth spoke first. "How do you feel?"

Mr? Lieutenant to you, his mind shrieked, the free hand spinning outwards catching the porter on the cheek.

"I need to get dressed. Where is my uniform?"

The porter grabs the flaying hand, looks at the doctor.

"You need to rest," he says.

Kurt whispers to his shadows, they have no reason to 'rest' him.

The doctor moves forward, his black rimmed glasses hide smiling eyes.

"Mr Dreyer, I will give you something to help."

Rolling backwards into the bed Kurt gasps for breath –

"What hell hole is this?"

The nurse looks at the doctor, who reaches for the needle balancing in the tray at the bottom of the bed.

"Mr Dreyer, this is a hospital. You had a spasm and could not breath."

Kurt spotted the needle, spoke in the low tone that indicates action, thrashing around the bed.

Leaning across their patient the porter grabs Kurt's arm, at the same time the doctor and nurse plunge toward him.

Kurt thought diversion tactics, he knew them all.

"We need you to relax," the nurse said sweetly.

Lies.

The bespectacled man was gaining an advantage, and the porter placed an arm around his shoulders and eased him upward. Gently he forced a cup between the patient's lips, then tipped it – Diversion tactics.

"A drink as the doctor told you."

More lies.

His shadows were gathering, telling him to resist. The fuzz in his head was in command, helping him with the little strength he could muster. Writhing and screaming he freed himself from the porter's hold. The cup crashed to the floor. The man lost his footing. Kurt, waving his arms in the air, pulled the drip from his arm, swung his legs from the bed, and collapsed onto the floor.

Instantly he heard scrambling, doors banging, more feet, more voices. Feeling his way around the legs of the bed, he kicked and hit any contact that came near to him. He laughed at the whelps, cooed at the orders given, concealed himself under the bed. Here he was safe, hidden from the prying eyes, the babbling tongue. His shadows were whispering in his ear, controlling his thoughts, making him answer back.

Faces peered at him, coaxing, luring him with whatever they considered his downfall. They were crazy. He shouted at them, words they could not understand, his native dialect uppermost. Once, twice he stopped to consult with those in the shadows, calling them whatever name they deserved. Hans ridiculed him; he who stole the red-haired minx. His aunt threatened him, pleading with him not to hurt her child: her child indeed, silly woman. His father was commanding him to face his foe, those 'stinkers' that oppose his every move, gathering around his bed as if it were a fox hole, bleating for him to 'come out'.

His family gather in their bid to command. He 'shoos' them away, all but his father. He began to cough, the brutal force slamming through his chest, winding him as he gasped for breath. It reminded him of a tornado, that whirling wind that spirals in the sky. Suddenly, the pain that ricocheted through his back caught him unaware: ripping along his spine in the form of a knife cutting him open. Kurt screams, kicks his legs outward, demanding himself to roll over and over down the length of the bed, his hand grasping the front of his nightgown, pulling at it as a cat claws a cushion. He must be free. Light appears as he feels the bed move from above him. His enemies are closing in. They grab him, seize an arm. The prick is quick, making his arm throb as the tranquillizer shoots up his vein.

Darkness has fallen as Kurt moves his head to search for the voice he can hear.

"Father," he whispers, obeying his mentor's command to speak English.

The shadow steps forward.

"My son."

Kurt could see plainly the pride within his father's eyes. He had not given in, even when his enemies outnumbered him. Fingering the smooth sheet beneath his hands he resisted the straps they had enclosed him with. Movement was constricted, his legs equally locked down. Trying to raise his head he could see they had moved him. He no longer had a private room, but he was behind a glass panelled cubicle. There were people crowding together, looking through the panel as they would at a zoo. Was he the main attraction?

His dreams troubled him. The dark rooms where pain and stench drew him to their door. The bodies, no matter the gender or weight, lying prostrate on the floor. The commands, one after another, pouring into his mind like water from the jug in his clenched hand, gushing through his ears, until he buries his head in shame. What did they mean?

He began to cough, dragging spasms where breathing was an impossibility, pain swirling around his lungs, making him gag for air. The doctor rushes to his side loosening the straps that bind him, trying to place an oxygen mask over his nose.

Kurt struggles, pulls at the mask that will comfort him.

"No," he gasps. "No more."

Breathing was non sustainable. His energy was ebbing away.

"Father," he mumbles, "I am here" the blue eyes closing.

He senses hands on his chest, the pummelling of his heart, takes hold of his father's hand, and steps to his side.

Part Five

Tuesday November 27th

The snow has been gently falling all night, and now, eleven o' clock in the morning it has accumulated to at least three inches, making it difficult to walk in the shoes Mother and myself found ourselves wearing on our journey home to the flat. The past three weeks have flown past, many of the days spent in a haze of not knowing what we were doing, or where we should be. The uncertainty felt after my father's operation was our only concern. Filled with a sense of shame, guilt, and loss I had refused to leave that hospital room every time my mother suggested it. We had every facility needed, so apart from clothing, of which Savvy commissioned a woman officer to collect, there was no haste to leave. Mother and I spent each day reading, talking, sitting by father's bedside, before separately leaving his side to shower and eat. Sleep was taken in snatches. Those 'forty winks' often spoken about as an older person snoozes in the day. Neither felt we could leave him alone. If truth be known, we dare not. It was a superstition that if one or the other was not at hand he would not survive. Silly really, for his nurses were highly trained, and his doctor was always at hand. Our actions highlighted the question in the daily paper I was reading whilst nibbling my breakfast this morning – Do You Need Therapy?

I would say we do.

Today, we have decided to come home (my flat) under pressure, to have a discussion with Savvy before she heads off somewhere warmer. To say she is lucky is no jealous talk – Well, it is to be honest, for if father had recovered, and I had the chance, this woman would run to the farthest corner of the earth, ignoring the eyebrows raised, and the biting mouths murmuring "Jumping ship". I would run and run, until I found myself in those loving arms of my grandmother. Anyway, (written with that sigh notifying a need to shut this mind down), we chose the flat and not a room at the hospital for two reasons.

One, coercion from 'Miss D' Mill, and Mother's wish to check the post. Evidently, she had written to Mr Richardson (take note, I did not call him old Richardson) to make an appointment to work out Father's assets.

Two, we both craved for a bath. Those trendy hospital showers are fine, but our own 'bubble' bath is heaven sent. Also, the flat is extra private; no nurses, doctors, or Savvy's staff bustling in and out.

So, here we find ourselves, trudging home wearing inadequate shoes, not bothering to call a taxi, just ambling and happy with each other's company.

Mother, hands plunged into her duffle coat pockets smiles at me –

"Change your life, Rhia."

I turn my head, feel the briskness of the wind on my cheeks, invite that same wind to blow my unkept hair in any direction it chooses.

"Change my life?" I query, tasting the microscopic ice droplets as they float onto my lips.

"Yes," she shivers. "Travel, treat yourself to a different look. Life is very precarious."

I wish to laugh, a luxury I have not allowed myself these past weeks.

"What precisely do you intend to do?"

She smiles, a glorious, wonderful gesture for a woman who cries silently to herself every night.

"Ah, that is what I wish to discuss with you today."

More secrets. Will they never end?

Father, who had been in an induced coma since that awful day was due to be woken anytime soon, and I had a feeling he was at the bottom of Mother's suggestion. Bowing our head against the wind we said no more, trudged onward, until finally we turned the corner into our street.

Funny how old habits die hard, I automatically glanced up and down, scanning for a white car.

--

Statement – The flat is cold, or I think it is.

Rushing to scan the dial that records the temperature within these walls I notice it is high, at least 24c. I should be boiling, stripping off my coat, and walking around in a t shirt and shorts. Mother has complied to this rule, flinging her coat across the sofa, and grabbing a dressing gown, before heading instantly for the bathroom. Hearing the water running into the bath I head for the bedroom, sink down on the bed, and study Jimmy's guitar. There it stood, propped up by the wall, claiming its stance within my bedroom as a certainty. The round sound hole placed in the middle of its refined body called to mind an eye, watching my every move. Taking in its superior position among my other clutter, such as books, and toys, plus the odd pair of shoes, I try to weigh its importance against Jimmy's presence. His last words on the night before he left were to joke how his guitar would keep me company. At least I thought he was joking, yet this instrument had stood by this wall as a constant reminder that my lover had gone. I hated it through those long months, and I hate it now. Snatching it up I swing it onto the bed, reach for a pair of scissors in the drawer, then in a frenzy that howls 'heart wrenching pain' I cut each string as if they represented those words he whispered in my ears.

Cutting the last string a 'ping' sound oozed from inside, followed by a 'whirr'. Foolishly I thought this piece of wood may have a mind of its own, before plunging my fingers into the gaping cavity, and sweeping them around. I feel a small device, hard, round, no larger than the head of a drawing pin. Not caring what damage befalls this 'precious' guitar I tug as hard as I can, finally retrieving the tiny gadget from its hidden nook. There, between my fingers rested what I presumed was a kind of hearing device, a spying commodity, a transmitter. Anger took hold of me, gripping my heart as a hand would squeeze a lemon. The stark truth dawned on me, my dearest friend, my companion of my emotional gratuity, had 'bugged' my room; heard every word Mother and I had spoken these past months. There is a saying–

'When truth hits you, it hits you hard'*

I, Rhia Bryant, or whatever my name should be, have allowed myself to flounder in the mire set by one I trusted.

The tears, never far from the surface these days spill down my cheeks. Holding tightly to the small device my other hand grasps the ruined guitar. Lifting it from the bed I place it on the floor, bringing my foot down upon its yawning face.

"I hate you – I hate you."

My screams reverberate around the room.

--

Afternoon

The wise minds of this world would agree with Mother's assumption that 'self-pity' gets a person nowhere.

I say – 'What do they know?'

It is my heart that is breaking, and my mind that reveals another 'faux pas' every time this woman tries to give reason to her past actions, such as acts that opposed my foolish imaginings of the truth.

It was my steadfast belief that I (alone) could find the painting of the Crux, discover those names, and allow this overwhelming disregard of others sensibility to impel me onwards with no consideration or caution for anyone.

I was blind to the facts presented to me.

How did Count Reinbach know where I would be that day in London?

How did the painting suddenly appear at Alys's ball?

How could I have believed that my father was too busy to talk to me?

Sitting here, waiting for Savvy's arrival, Jimmy's mutilated guitar searing itself through my mind, I knew I had been duped. Jimmy, Kurt, Count Reinbach, Alys, and Hans (which for a reason I cannot understand) had played their part with conviction.

Mother smiled across the coffee table. She had discovered me sobbing, fragments of the guitar strewn across the bedroom floor. Nothing passed her lips, not 'Do not worry' or 'It will pass'; nothing to declare she had known better. She had carefully guided me to the bathroom, filled the bath with the most alluring perfume, before leaving me to wallow in that luxury. I could not believe how caring she had been. Refreshed, I emerged from the bathroom to find no trace of the guitar. That part of Jimmy had been obliterated, if only by my mother's quick actions. Dressing, I found myself concentrating on that earlier conversation to 'change my life'. The last few weeks had made me realise nothing stays the same, and even a different hair cut has the power to lift a mood. Had I really entered that phase when my general outlook and attitude needed to be restructured? It certainly was tempting.

Savvy arrived around two, her furry hat and coat gleaming from a thin layer of snow.

"How cold," she remarked, spotting the roaring gas fire, and moving towards it as if it were a beacon calling her home.

Mother took her coat and hat enabling the woman swamped in an overlarge bright pink jumper to sit as near to the flames as one dare. The maroon of her trousers, strapped to her legs in the sixties fashion of drainpipes, glimmered in the red and orange heat. Sliding a hand through her damp hair she looked my way –

"How is life treating you Rhia?" she asks.

"Not that well," Mother throws back.

Savvy let out a sigh, nodded in Mother's direction, either for her comment, or the 'T' sign she was exhibiting with her fingers.

"You must acknowledge that what happened was not your fault. It would have occurred anyway," she said partly to me, partly toward the kitchen.

I felt a partial warmth wash over me, but however these people tried to create a 'get out clause' for me, the truth is I fell into the trap of my own constructing, and knew to my cost that as deception sews, so it can reap.

Tray in hand, Mother walked from the kitchen, placed her load onto the table, then sat with an aspiration threefold her usual demeanour. Casting her eyes my way she says with a tinge of yearning–

"Savvy is leaving us tomorrow. She will be taking a belated holiday."

"Yes, a journey I have promised myself for a number of years."

"Travelling across Asia," Mother continued.

Savvy smiled.

"Alone?" I queried, surprised at my own forwardness.

This elegant woman's smile grew.

"I will fly to South Asia first to visit a dear friend. From her I will receive the many jewels of wisdom she will give, then onto Japan, and another friend recovering from an injury"

There was something about this declaration that left me wishing for further revelation.

As you know, dear Diary, curiosity is my downfall, so there will be no surprise when I ask–

"Do we know your colleague?"

Mother cast me that castigating look that says 'Do not meddle' I apologise–

"I am sorry, it is not my business."

Savvy laughed, shook her head –

"Do not fret, it is someone who needs my help."

I quickly realised I would not be told more.

Drinking tea, conversation centres around how the bizarre weather of the past year has treated us poor mortals. We laugh, an activity which was rare to us at this moment. We joked, another activity which if honesty is the given act, no-one within this conversation had found the time, let alone the will to take part. Lowering her mug to the tray on the table Savvy pulled a folder from her bag-

"For you," she pushed the buffed folder my way.

I stared at the hand that held this wallet closed.

"It is a statement of what occurred in Germany in the sixties. How your father and I became embroiled with the Dreyer family, and the part of history within the events of the present day. It explains everything."

Savvy held it tight, not once taking her eyes from my face–

"What you must realise, Rhia, is everything that happened was to keep you, and your family safe," her hand slipped from the document. "One more thing–

I must extract a promise from you, please do not read it until a time within your life when your mind is settled."

Letting my eyes trail over the buff folder I inclined my head, "I promise."

I move without haste to the bedroom and enclose the folder in a suitcase on top of the wardrobe, tempted to look, but determined to keep my promise.

Change must start somewhere – Is that not right, Diary?

I had noticed the dark stamp across the buff cover. The words 'SECRET' and "THE RUFUS FILE" encasing the thick document inside, wondered if Savvy was risking her job in affording me clarification into my past.

--

Late Afternoon

Shadows of this winter day had begun to draw around us. From the ringing of the church clock to welcome the hour of four, to various lights springing into life up and down the street. In-between Mother's sandwiches and at least two more pots of tea, our conversation had covered every elementary topic a set of chattering females could span. Savvy did not utter one word or sentence referring to Hans, or any references to Kurt and Jimmy. I could not help but think 'why' – and knowing how much I dislike that word you will not be surprised how downright irritating it is when I find her lips sealed as a tomb. Did these women believe my mind, or heart when mentioning their names would have me running for my handkerchief?

I must state on this page–

I AM STRONGER THAN THAT.

The pen shakes in my hand, dribbles down the page

Outside the window I observe the snow falling onto the pavement below, no crunching feet, no loud voices. The scene may be part of a Christmas card, pure, white, silent as that print advocates. I shudder from my thoughts. Of late, evenings had become my adversary, thoughts rampaging through my head how I could have managed this past year differently; depressive thoughts raise their head as ghouls from a horror film.

Mother is the first to penetrate my thoughts–

"Rhia, come and join in our chatter. Soon we must leave, return to the hospital."

This is the moment I muse Mother has decided to share what these friends already know. I retake my place next to Savvy on the sofa, ready myself for more frustrating nonsense. Not so…

"Your mother has something of importance to tell you."

My heart beats faster.

"Your father and I will be moving to a clinic in Switzerland as soon as he is able. Savannah knows this treatment centre. It examines your father, and his walking ability in the future. Training and convalescence together."

I look horrified– "Me?" I cry.

Somewhere deep inside me that petulant child rises her head again. Mother lowers her eyes, Savvy's light up with indignation–

"Hal needs rest, encouragement, and the will to survive. You, my dear girl, need to discover your real self, not an inherited whim."

Whichever way I swallow that pill, her words stung.

I sink into that silence my heart has discovered to hide beneath, just as quickly rising above the dark arms of melancholy and ask in a sonorous tone–

"Shall I come too, two heads and all that?"

Both women glare, Savvy being the first to clip my wings–

"Impossible. Mena has enough to cope with. She cannot help at this time.

Besides arms are waiting to greet you."

Whatever can this resourceful spy mean?

I will agree that I – Rhia Bryant – the rich kid – the banker's daughter – who crushed aspirations and followed the path of deceit – could label her life a sham – even so, to be left paddling on the river alone – Bloody unfair!

I evoke the happiness of my days spent with my grandmother, in this flat. Mattie had lit up the days she had spent with me, made those hours count, and the months ring with happiness. My problem had been when she chose to stay in Bhutan, make her home there for however long she wished. I resented the company of Lotus, the friendship of the anchor mother. In plain fact I was jealous: green with envy as I had been with Kurt, with Jimmy, and Hans if I was being honest. I was the girl who had everything, yet nothing fitted. I stumbled over Savvy's words–

"You," I swallowed hard, my eyes tracing her defined features. "Will travel to Switzerland after your break?"

There was silence, before Mother answered soberly–

"No, Rhia, Savannah is retiring. Her entrance to that room, through those glass doors imbedded shards in her arms. Emery Dreyer was to become her last 'coup de grace' as the French would say."

I had not taken note, too wrapped up in my own sorrow.

It was time for my tired brain to grasp an excuse, however flimsy I do not care: an absolution to my jaundiced attitude.

Oh Diary, you will not believe what flowed from my mouth next–

"That's it," I jumped up, jigging around as a puppet on a string.

Mother and Savvy stopped talking, gaped at me, mouths ajar.

"I will sell this flat. Go to Mattie. Start anew."

A chorus of "What?" enveloped me.

"I will leave," my lips were saying, my mind unsure. If nothing else this suggestion will change Mother's mind about me going with her. So, whoever reads this will comprehend my shock when Mother says–

"Good idea." Savvy's lips break into a smile–

"When?" –

"How long for?" Mother asks. I was breathless.

Light was fading, along with the flicker of my plan. How could I go back on the suggestion I had offered as a way out of my floundering mind? Whether or not meant, I am stuck with it. Savvy inched her way from the sofa, took her coat, and slipped it on.

"I must go. I have a lot to complete before tomorrow's flight. Your resilience is inspiring, Rhia. Never have I met a person such as you – Never. Your idea sounds workable. Good luck."

I forced myself to laugh–

"Yes, it is a good idea. New Year here I come."

She laughed. Mother hugged her, allowing the word "Never" to resound around the room.

If only she knew how I really felt inside, scared, intrepid, a soul that has no anchor. Savvy was standing by the door waiting for my farewell. I held out my hand as this operative (for this is how I shall regard her from now on) pulled me to her. She winced, let her arms slip to her sides–

"I am glad your father messaged me. Together we won the fight. Remember nothing is ever what it seems."

Tipping her furry hat, she gave Mother a long stare; communication I would dub it, a silent acknowledgement that their path would cross again, in the long distance known as future, then left as a bird flies the nest. Left alone, Mother and I, locked in our own idiosyncratic musings, scampered round the flat washing cups and plates, dousing the fire, switching off lights, gathering fresh clothes. The snowy evening beckoned us, and the hospital waited for our return.

December 2001

Wednesday December 12th

My dearest diary,

Please do not scold me, my poor heart would crumble beneath your admonishment. Once more this woman has not written on your uniformed pages since November 27th; a total of sixteen days. It is my fault, dear friend, my only friend, the truth being this woman could not be bothered – to write, to think, or even to feel your embossed body within my hand, for less I spurt out the thoughts ravaging my head. I am a heart in limbo, thrashing in a body that can only feel loss and shame. I dread reading the news each day that passes, for all papers, and this hospital collects many, are full of such headlines as–

'Painter Died', 'Art Exhibition in Memory of Jules Dragner',

'Sorrow Fills The Art World.'

'His death from a heart attack (of which you and I know differently), has soared his paintings to an exorbitant price.'

Funny how life works out.

What I really need to say, dear diary, is that this woman is back, pen in hand, and a determination to end this year as I started it, imparting to your sealed lips every thought and deed that drove me forward. If I am to be honest, and what else can I be with you, I have missed you. Not that I would own up to such a thing, for I am now a thirty something woman looking out at the world, and not inward to myself. I have changed, and whilst you may mutter, if diaries can mutter, 'Here we go again', I must do something to get this life back on track.

I have had my hair cut short into a short backed, longer sided bob; very modern, easier to manage. The sleek red style has changed my features overnight. My face has taken on a more 'sophisticated' (Mother's term) look. She believes it matches my slimmer body – I have not eaten chocolate for three and a half weeks, and it shows, not a lot, but a teeny bit (I believe). I have begun to laugh more, hiding the pain that is never far from my eyes.

I will pause here, gather my breath, wait a few moments before I share with you my punchline – I have decided to give you a name – 'The Crux of the Matter'.

I hope you can appreciate my joke.

My indisputable good news is that my father is sitting up, propped up really, but however this report is viewed it is a fantastic step in the right direction. While Mother has been making all the preparations for their journey to Switzerland I have been chatting and hugging (gently) with this hero in my life. Whilst we do not speak in-depth about those days in November, or Father's treatment at the hands of my friend and partner, we do cover his reasons for not telling me about the past. I must admit his fear of detection was greater than my need. Also, I have gradually realised that in rare circumstances, and it must be 'rare', deception can be given credit. He was pleased to hear I had written to Mattie with a plea to join her, and that she had replied with eager anticipation; a date set for me to travel on January 2nd.

Whatever my reason for this new chapter in my life dear friend, you will travel with me.

Saturday December 22nd

Gosh it is warm for December. Any flutters of snow that fell our way soon melted and disappeared completely. The country is moaning, complaining that Christmas will not be the same without a cooler temperature, plus a threat of those fluttering particles, or even the nip of old Jack Frost. For myself: it does not matter what the weather is doing for my mind is set on the future. I have gone forward with my plans to 'run away' as I call it, and to 'remodel' myself as Mother implies. The concierge downstairs has helped me to put the flat on the market, showing perspective buyers around, and helping me to choose those who would cherish and love it. The outcome was a young couple searching for their first home together. Their moving date was finalised for the 3rd of January 2002. On completion of papers the packing began, and all small items would be stored with one family member or another as my parent's house had been 'Let' with the prospect of selling. The larger furniture had been sold with the flat: or would be taken by the family on my day of departure.

Life was charging ahead at meticulous speed.

Much to our surprise Mother and I received invitations to the Christmas 'get together' at the bank. Signed by Richardson himself it is being held in the staff room this afternoon. Unsure whether we should accept father had pressed us on the matter, getting dispirited at our reluctance.

"For me," he would say each time we strived to bring up a point against it.

This continued until the nurse demanded we leave so Father may rest, and Mother phoned the bank to confirm our presence. Facing those red lipped, 'told you so', petty muckrakers would be a hill to climb, but Richardson's prattling at being promoted would push me overboard. All morning I had told myself to stay calm, to help mother clamber through the pain and embarrassment she would encounter.

Dear Diary, as always, this woman is wrong.

--

The Bank

Preparing ourselves for this occasion had been no mean feat. We had searched through our clothes, those that had not already been packed, to choose the most sensible, yet admired garment we could find. Due to father's access to the Swiss clinic being Saturday 29th of December, Mother's main wardrobe was hung or folded in travelling crates awaiting transportation, therefore her choice was limited. Ultimately, she chose the navy trouser suit that had been left aside for her journey, teamed it with red shoes and bag, before applying a dash of lipstick to match. I followed in her wake, down to the red shoes and bag: twins in everything but deportment and size.

The taxi we had ordered shunted through the busy streets. It appeared, to my way of thinking, that every household in our sprawling suburb had consigned at least three people to complete the Christmas shop as the pavements were congested, and the roads corresponding. Tail to tail honking and ridiculous parking was but a taster for the two days left before the red suited man's arrival. There was no zeal in my heart over the forthcoming celebrations however many shop windows displayed 'Merry Christmas' signs. Not even the happy faces of children pointing with glee to displays of books, toys, and animations of favourite characters flowing across an odd television screen could spark an intake of breath, or jubilant surge. The festive spirit had died that day in Stoneleigh, and I had not realised the levy on a troubled mind until today.

Pretence, Diary, can numb many a heart.

I lay my pen on the page, sit back, allowing myself to wallow in self-pity.

Enough–

Our slow journey to the bank took the route past the park where people were gathering to talk; raise a drink in honour of this occasion, and generally be merry. My eyes, following trees lit with vivid illumination glimpse the bodies of lovers clinging together beneath their leafless branches. I catch my breath, imagine what 'might have been'. Dragging my gaze from these carefree figures I concentrate on the grey asphalt as the taxi wheels near our destination.

Arriving at the bank we were greeted by the same decorations winding around the windows and doors casting their luminous colours across the dull, warm afternoon. I sighed, followed Mother out of the taxi, and commanded myself to act as normal as possible. They would all know the circumstances of my father's leaving, know the part I had played, and my downfall. Placing my feet on the first step I could not help but re-play my last visit here. Shuddering I grasped the steel handrail that guided us to the entrance, determined those gossips would not uncover my pain. Mother, whose nervous tension was plain in the continual way she had fidgeted in the taxi, floated through the doors with her head high and her red lips set in a tantalizing smile. Mr Richardson rushed to her side–

"My dear Mrs Bryant, how are you?"

Mother hesitated, offered her hand, and inclined her head stating–

"Fine, thank you," at the top of her voice.

"Good, good," he boomed, directing her toward the staff room door.

No small acknowledgement my way, not even that onerous smile he was flashing at Mother. I followed in their tread, noticing the hands of my former colleagues flying to their mouths to cover up the giggles.

Entering the room marked 'staff' I was surprised at the 'low key' decoration. The fairy lights had been kept to the minimum, and the paper hangings (at one time this country's main Christmas display) was located to the part of the room that housed the food, then only draping from the tables. A drink was instantly placed within my hand, the face before me the greatest surprise of the day – Fiona Grubb.

"I…" my stuttering voice made her smile.

"Hello, Rhia Bryant, welcome to the bank."

Not wishing to draw even more 'pleased you were brought down' glares than I was receiving I hedged my way into a corner.

"What the hell are you doing here? I thought you had left."

I swear I snarled, but Fiona chuckled–

"Why do you never see what is clear to everybody else?"

What? How dare she surprise me in this manner, then confuse me with her silly anecdotes. I shook the 'bob' that was now my hair.

"I can see you have cut your hair. Do you think that changes you?"

My mouth fell open as that small, but direct pain shooting through my mind once more.

"I do not know what you mean."

Fiona raised her glass to her lips, indicated for me to do the same.

"I think you do, Miss Bryant. I think you do."

She drank, I mimicked her action.

Fiona refurbished my glass, which in the end, I had thrown down my throat in humiliated haste.

"What you did," I seethe. "You have no room to judge me."

"Oh, but I do," she quipped. "All part of Savannah D' Mill's plan."

"What…"

The loud exclamation turned more than one head my way, as tongues wagged, and fingers pointed.

"I work for her intelligence team."

The kid said it with such flippancy I felt this girl had waited these months to deliberately embarrass me. I took a deep breath. Fiona wished another girl 'Merry Christmas' who brushed past us on her way to the food tables.

"All that pretence of secrecy and moans at getting caught were lies?"

She shrugged.

"All according to how you look at it. Savannah needed complete chicanery for both hers and your father's goal to work."

I pictured myself standing by a pit of fire, the tentacles inviting me to jump.

I could see mother in deep conversation with Richardson. The cashiers, now unleashed, were busy tittering over any segment of gossip they could find, whilst I was huddled in a corner facing this demon juvenile's truth pill.

"You wish me to believe you acted on behalf of Miss D' Mill?"

"That is up to you, but 'yes', I do. My brief was to make you believe me."

The wine was turning sour in my mouth.

“Oh, you did just that,” I cried. “I can see the whole game was full of deceit.”

This time it was her turn to shake her head–

“Not deceit, Rhia, but persuasive subtly.”

Her nauseating grin would have lit up Trafalgar Square.

If I could scream I would. This girl – No, this agent of deception had fooled me.

“Your kind are fooled easily,” Fiona (her real name?) said sipping the last dregs of her wine.

My kind – MY KIND. Does Savvy know how rude this kid can be? That is if she is a kid at all.

“Tell me, does Mr Richardson know what game you were playing?”

Another glass drained down that ridiculous throat.

“He knew, he positively agreed, and he kept your mother informed.”

“My mother?”

Fiona screwed up her nose, accepted more wine from a passing colleague.

“Funny that, all accept your mother, who was scared for your safety, was a hundred per cent behind your father. It was obvious Dreyer must be stopped.”

I remember the times Mother had begged me to visit Mattie. Now, I know why.

“At my expense.”

Fiona grabbed the glass from my hand, her eyes were burning–

“Get over yourself. If anyone needs pity it is your father. Those monsters were prepared to kill him.”

Without another word I recall Dreyer’s motto – Payback time. I face this kid with bilateral characters, whisper in her ear–

“With spies like you who needs weaponry?”

She smiled, that same ingratiating motion Savvy used–

“That is correct. Nice knowing you, Miss Bryant.”

She turned away from me to speak to a woman that had stopped by her side.

I move in Mother’s direction. Taking her aside I ask–

“Must we stay longer?”

She slipped her arm around my waist–

“Mr Richardson has been appointed to replace your father.”

This was no reply to my question.

“Oh good,” I lie. “Shall we go?”

Mother's scowled expression did nothing to relieve the emotion bubbling up inside me.

"Go? I have not eaten."

"Blast the food," I bellow.

"Rhia."

Mother's reprimand is swift.

"Sorry, my head is spinning."

I glance to where Fiona was standing, whimpered as she raised her glass.

Mother passed her own glass to a bewildered Mr Richardson, still looking pleased with himself, still wearing that 'I did it' mask. Moving away from the gloating fool she asked–

"Are you ill?"

Everything Fiona had said crushed down upon me, creating the tears that forced their way down my cheeks.

"I feel…"

I stumbled. Mother steadied me.

"Please phone for a taxi Mr Richardson. My daughter is unwell."

We headed toward the door, mother clutching me to her. I twisted my head to look for Fiona. She had disappeared: a sylph who had achieved what many before had attempted yet failed.

Tuesday December 25th
Christmas Day

How fast the hours fly when parting is upon us.

Christmas Day was spent with my father in the relative peace of his hospital room. Thanks to the staff, and especially one doctor who should have been a techno warrior instead of a medic, we connected with my grandmother. This emotionally charged broadcast between mother and son had us all in floods of tears, and that vacant space where my heart once resided fluttering slightly at the thought of those loving arms. Allowing Father to sit in a wheelchair for more than a few moments, he was pushed into the dining room for Christmas lunch, where tables decked with decoration and food stood in resplendence. There we sat, entertained by a small choir of nurses, whilst eating the food that had been carefully prepared. Clearing away gave space for a doctor to read out a special message from the agency father had worked for: an appreciation of Henry Bryant's work, and his and Savannah D' Mill's goal to bring a fearful interrogators reign to an end. As the doctor finished his eulogy, it crossed my mind that maybe, when Father's stay at the clinic, and my own rehabilitation, (which I have finally decided my visit to Bhutan must be called) ended we could talk this saga through. In conclusion to his short reprieve from bed my father held our hands as we listened to more carols.

I had decided to return to my flat this evening, prepare for my own journey, and not suffer the pain of further 'Goodbyes'. Hugging my parents, I realised what the phrase 'an empty heart' would feel like. With Mother's promise to phone me before they left, and when they arrived, I hurried from the room, but not before my father wearily passed me a book of poems with one title highlighted-

"Read this, it is for you, my precious girl."

I fled down the stairs, stopping by the main door to read–

Reflection*

In the bleak evening of a winter day
The birds will settle – the moon display,
Its gown of silver, its arms so cold -
The fervent whisper
Of a broken soul.

--

Turning the key in the door I stumble. Post scattered across the floor; Christmas cards neither Mother nor I had bothered to read, mingled amongst the bills waiting to be finalized. Switching on a light this almost empty flat was a reminder of the bleak days ahead. Pushing the envelopes aside with my feet I head for the fire, twist the button to six, and throw my coat across the sofa. This solitary item of furniture would be my seat, bed, and eating area for the remaining days before my flight. I had left everything else for the concierge, who had kindly disposed and sorted the boxes and furniture labelled 'To be sold' or 'To be burned'. Moving to the bedroom I warily open the door and peep inside. Everything gone. My clothes were packed in various sized suitcases, waiting as soldiers on parade by the window, their tags destined for Bhutan. I close the door, wander into the kitchen. Eyeing a mug and teabags by the kettle I decide one strong brew is called for. Not quite the festive tipple, but, in my case, far safer.

Carrying my hot tea back into the lounge I am tempted to gather those letters from the floor and read the messages unknowingly sent to Jimmy and myself, wishing us well, and how long before we tie that time – honoured knot. I gulp a large mouthful of tea, scoop up a few envelopes and head back to the sofa. One Christmas card after another is adorned with inuendoes of exactly my former notion. I sling these across the room, tearing up the flamboyant ones. Holding the last cream coloured sleeve within my hand I notice it has been typewritten, posted 17/12/2001, and franked 'Japan'. Instantly the name Savannah D' Mill enters my head. Excited, I almost rip it apart and yank out the single sheet of paper reading-

'I live – 'H''

Letting the paper fall to the floor I sense my body trembling, the letter 'H' whirling around my confused mind. As each day had passed my heart yearned to speak one more time to that presence that was no more, a manifestation of a man whose German roots, yet English upbringing, haunted my thoughts. I had not realised until it was too late how close we had grown, the blue-eyed agent and the amateur spy.

Twirling the creased envelope still laying on my lap over and over I try to suppress the gnawing fears.

Is someone playing a sickening joke?

Is this revenge for Dreyer?

Has that 'slob' emerged from wherever he flew?

So many questions – no direct answers.

I gripped the paper tighter, gulping more tea, forcing those frequent tears that hover behind my eyes not to fall. I feel fear, smell it almost, as I run to the light-switch, douse the light, praying no-one is watching the flat. Creeping back to the sofa my body sinks further into its crevices. Shall I ring Mother, demand her flight from the hospital to my side? Shall I lock myself in this flat until the day of my departure?

Every fibre within me was screaming.

This is Christmas day: a day when carols are sung, and families cling together, celebrating the birth of a child who designates peace. My father is broken, my mother his main support, I cannot tear them apart. Whoever wrote that note – I clear my throat, let sense crush my fear – take control of my fate.

Whoever wrote that note has indicated it came from Japan, Savvy's holiday hideout. Could it be possible…

I let my eyes roam around this darkened room. This flat held my adolescent dreams, my adult yearnings, and now, my broken heart. Each corner resembles the darkness I forced myself into. That girl, teenager, woman, whose pretentious attitude flouted the people she loved into deceit, yet from those ruthless acts of self-indulgence may I try and believe this woman is being shown clemency?

The church clock strikes midnight.

Monday December 31st

New Year Eve

The church bells peel out and singing could be heard blaring from the flats across the street; the evening was alive with excitement. I pause writing, think for a moment or two, let events of the past days pour over me.

I had received a call from Mother late Friday evening. It was the 29th, and their journey to Switzerland had succeeded smoothly. She told me Father was sleeping after a difficult day, and her heart jumped with joy to be settling into the apartment in the clinic grounds at last. We chatted, mainly about my own departure from this country, then a request I thought odd into whether Savannah had phoned or written. A quick 'no', before rushing into something else only appeared to aggravate her. Thinking it must be the long day I wished her 'goodnight' and 'stay safe', hung up the phone, then slapped a thickly cut cheese slice between two pieces of bread, and brought it back to my sanctum that was the sofa.

If asked, I could relay in a moment the hour or second of each day since Christmas I have left this flat – Twice. The first was Boxing Day to run to the corner shop, buy four loaves of bread, a huge block of cheese, lots of crisp packets, bars of nutty chocolate, a packet of rice crisps, milk, and wine. At this point the shopkeeper asked me whether I believed the country was set for ten-foot snow drifts. He thought he was funny. I thought he was rude. Surely customers can buy exactly what they wish. Storming out I hurried back to the flat and munched my way through a large bar of heaven (chocolate). Sod the diet.

The second was a hurried visit to the tourist company to verify all was in order with my flight. This was nothing short of a farce. The young girl, (please, what is it with me and young girls), her curly brown ponytail bobbing right and left as she walked, found my presence terribly intriguing; an easy conquest to earn her several brownie points. The scenario 'Here comes money on two legs' fits her comfortably. Asking me to sit, then ignoring my "No thank you" over the coffee question, she swamped her desk with brochures of Bhutan. Immediately my explanation of the facts such as my grandmother, the day of my flight, my need to verify times, set her on a route to jump across my 'need' and suggest her own 'upgrade'. Again, declining her offer I could see that nothing I was saying was being taken seriously.

Thinking back, I wonder if this girl was a relation to Fiona Grubb.

The next fifteen minutes was spent back and forth in an argument of wills – She, suggesting this 'upgrade–'

"Miss, this offer is more you."

Me, shrieking in her face that everything was fine.

Finally, I slam my fist on the desk, rant like the demented soul I feel, take what I need from the manager, then run home to the safety of my sofa, curl up once more with another large bar of chocolate – Help.

That letter, note, bulletin, whatever it should be labelled, still lay on the floor, staring at me comparable to Cyclop's* eye within Greek mythology. It had burned foolish hope in my heart, wound my mind to such ill humour, that the past few days have been filled with remorse, regret, and pity. I will blame my childhood, far easier an excuse that admitting I alone have chosen those weed covered paths in my mind. The damning spy thing – everything that was kept from me. How would life have differed if I had known?

I pause…

It would not – I was always that child with tantrums and cheek. I have no doubts that Father's secret would have been blown. I grasp the handwritten note, consistently turning it over and over. Is this Hans's writing? I cannot remember. I will raise my glass to it as I slop the wine in a plastic tumbler.

"Happy New Year," I say to the paper in my hand.

--

My head is nosediving, crashing to the floor in a flurry of nonsense, the note crushed in my closed hand. I stomp my way into the kitchen, my body heavy from what I have gorged.

Heat – The room is a furnace, the glow emitting from the cooker spreading around the kitchen walls.

Heck – When did I turn that on, and more importantly what for?

I know, to heat this flat through. Well, it has certainly complied. I sit on the floor, soak up the heat, stretch to turn the 'off' knob. I creep back to the lounge, squeal at the empty space. Stop, I believe the sofa is moving.

I reach out to touch – Nothing.

I shut my eyes, fold up my fists, hear vicious words dripping into the room. I belch, smell the foul air, roll over, watch as the slinky shadows from my mind play out their drama on the walls.

Mercy me, I can feel material upon material filling my hands – Baggy?

These pyjamas are not mine. I struggle with this, psychologically assault my mind for taunting me – repetition of an earlier era?

Wait – The mist is clearing. These pjs belong to Jimmy. That traitor… that… I try to yank the bottoms from my legs. I must be free. Cast them from me, burn them, never to be seen again. I start to roll.

Where am I?

Kicking my legs in the air I swear at the enveloping folds that are gobbling me, devouring my body until exhaustion pleads with me to cease moving.

Idea –

I will move faster, jump around, kick harder.

Where am I?

Roll, roll, roll – one big 'whoosh' and my legs are free. Joy beyond belief, then –

I can feel cold wrapping around my limbs, rushing at me, soft cushions beneath my bottom. I move my legs, the motion of falling engulfs my mind –

Down, down, slam.

The hardness of the boards, Swearing I begin to slither. This rejected moaning bag of wind slithering –

Where?

I clutch the note, spot the stains of red wine, grasp at the sofa. Nothing.

My head aches –

NOTHING.

2002

Extra pages in my Diary -
Tuesday January 1st

Diary, as you know I have come full circle. I wake this morning with a thick head and a heavy heart. I have drunk too much before, many a time, yet last night was different. Emotions in my body had sprung to life, releasing my mind from the stress it endured, while deciphering the changes I need to make. I say to those who will read my diary –

"Please, take my advice, do not walk this path."

I believe the saying is 'Think before you leap'.

Wise words.

Even so, my arrival at this moment was surely pre-ordained: a lesson this woman had no power to stop, yet the pathway chosen could have been smoother. My life has been a paradox of jumbled mishaps, falling in and out of love on a whim, no thought for those who cared for me, little tolerance with those who did not think as myself. I truly was that 'rich-bitch' once called, stepping from one delusion to another. Now, I can emphatically inform you that those who rush through this world with a care for no-one but themselves should stop to consider.

"If insight could be futuristic, humans would think twice," and pain would not be so brutal. I stand in solidarity with these words.

--

The weather this morning is sunny, yet chilly: a frost laden night emerging into the warmth of the day. Sometime during waking from my bed of sloth I switched the knob on the radio, my lone companion these past days. The woman's voice blabbering over its airwaves is on fire with holiday suggestions – the perfect month to travel, how much luggage a person may carry with them, what to wear, until I get to the point of slamming the perishing instrument off and humming my own music. Can she not understand that today I begin another period in my forsaken life; besides, I have eaten my last popcorns, drank my last milk, and threw away my last rubbish. By now I should be feeling free – I do not.

If only I knew what that note meant. I dare not phone Mother. Could you possibly imagine that woman's reaction? I do not know Savvy's phone number; evidently a spy changes their contact details frequently. I am alone, sailing upon this raging river.

Who cares?

Oops, must not say that in my new life.

Hearing the rap at the door I freeze, play a form of snap in my mind where the protagonist will be my enemy, slide onto the floor from the sofa, and creep to peep through the spy hole. I can see a woman: a woman whose make-up fills the small round glass outlook. Mind is careering through the many images of women's faces I have met and stops at number six. I open the door.

"Hello," a jovial face.

I run my eyes up and down her swan like frame, the bright red hair a match to my own.

NO – not true – This woman, my neighbour, creates this hair colour from a bottle.

"Hello," I answer.

"A going away present," she says, pushing a package into my hands.

I blink. Never been that friendly with her, always found her nosy, and funny.

"Thanks."

I swallow hard, then shut the door.

Back on my safe sofa I unwrap my gift. It is a knitted doll, rotunda like me, red knitted hair curling around the doll's face. Across the red knitted trousers and yellow top 'Good Luck' scream at me. Emotions, too poignant for my pen to write, shudder through my body. How cruel of me to dismiss her with such discourtesy. I rummage through the large travelling bag at my side, find the writing pad I am looking for, scribble a few lines of sincerity, then rip the page free, folding it into a tiny square to post in her letterbox downstairs. The horn of a taxi blares out, disturbing the peace that has descended on an intemperate society. I run to the window, acknowledge it is mine, grab my hand luggage, twirl my last 'Goodbye', then literally run down the stairs.

Wednesday January 2nd

Nepal Airport

Shrangri La, the name given to the beautiful mountains and valleys of the Himalayan Orogeny spreading before me, the snow-capped peaks glistening in the low winter sun. I smile, the excited voices of the tourists ahead of me fill the snow sprinkled tarmac with cries of delight; joining the wonderment of the many visitors before them that view these mountains for the first time. It had been a long journey, one where thoughts of my past mingled with anticipation for my future. Breathing in the fresh crisp air I scold myself into why it has taken so long for my feet to tread this soil. I will not accept my implausible arguments anymore, telling myself that planes only land at this airport once, maybe twice in a week during the winter. This is true but, it really is not an excuse to keep me away. Neither are the various intangible excuses about the weather. Yes, I know how snowy it can be, how many villages get drifts that make movement impossible. My grandmother has explained all this, yet still, to my remorse, this woman looked another way. How could I be so thoughtless as to ignore this beautiful snow-clad Eden?

Waving to the tiny band of tourists as they gather round their sheepskin swathed guide, I enter the welcoming warmth of the airport building. Nothing had really changed, apart from the desk attendant who was younger, and the music streaming was softer. I look at the clock, note the hour being midday, then walk to the desk. Introducing myself the young man smiles –

"Miss Bryant. I have message for you."

Surprised I take the paper offered my way, nod my thanks, and sit on the nearest seat. My grandmother had written to me before leaving England explaining how the pathways must be trekked with care; asking me to have patience and enjoy the warmth of the airport building while waiting for my guide. Glancing at the paper I realise the handwriting is not Mattie's own, it is…

What is this, another sick joke?

I read – '***See you soon, H***'

I scan the building, my heart pounding, my hand trembling. The terror that has haunted me grips every fibre of my body. I run to the desk.

"Who brought this message?" I ask, forgetting the 'nice' me of a moment ago.

The young man colours up, his flushed face staring at me as a child stares at an angry parent.

"I do not know, Miss. The... the paper was put... placed... left... on my desk in my absence," he stuttered.

"Absence?" the tell-tale voice of fury rose.

"Men's room," he whispered.

The anger deflated.

Sitting down, I listen to the strains of Beethoven's Moonlight Sonata streaming across the building, the wonderful poetic genius of this eighteenth century German composer, often considered the greatest composer in the world. Entranced with the swirling notes of tragedy and romance, I allow my own heart to conspire with the hypnotic chords.

The last euphonious note fading I turned in the direction of the desk.

'Why?' I would ask myself thereafter, for my heart literally jumped from my body.

Talking to the young receptionist, pointing in my direction, a tall, dark haired man, thinner than the last time I had seen him, had begun to head my way. Breath, only moments before that had assisted my sighing to the glorious music, was struggling to make its way between my lips. I rise, my face pallid in the bright winter sun.

How could this be? What did it mean?

"Rhia," an utterance of exasperated joy.

Emotion floods through me, that sweet agony of loss and discovery, as his left arm opens wide. Rushing into it I feel the sting of tears as my breath explodes with his name–

"Hans, I was told..."

"Thank God," he mutters.

His arm fell away, the exertion of energy draining the skeletal frame. Taking his right hand in mine I drew him toward the bench I had just vacated.

Settled, the questions began to tumble from my mouth; this orifice released at last from its captivity of fear.

"How? Why? I do not understand."

The drawn face before me managed a smile, held onto my hand tighter, raising my fingers to his cold lips.

"Savannah D' Mill's plan. She devised it down to the last detail."

I hesitate, ask in a quivering voice –

"Was I part of that plan?"

"Never," he weakly pronounced. "Not from the first moment I saw you."

Through my tears I could see the effort he was making, how honesty was wrestling with those secrets he could not tell. His voice shook –

"The plan was for me to hold back, pretend I was 'one of them', then as the shooting began to fall to the side. If I was lucky, and Kurt's bullet went astray, I would live, but to those within that room I had died."

"You look ill."

My statement, not meant to sound condemning, blasted into the void around us.

"I did not fall quick enough. Kurt's bullet hit my shoulder, destroying my clavicle. I lost a lot of blood, and the arm is dead."

The sadness in his voice caught my heart.

Lowering my eyes down his left side I noticed the strapping and the fear of reprisal seared through me.

"Who knows you live?" I whispered.

Again, the weak smile –

"Savannah, your father and mother, your grandmother, and you."

In my mind that was too many.

"I was brought here today. A promise from Savannah, to aid your healing."

"Mine?"

Hans fell back further into the seat, his eyes weary from the journey and his pain.

"Technically, Rhia, we are cousins, but your father and my mother, are not related. Please give me a chance."

My mind was still whirring –

"Your aunt?" I heard my intake of breath.

He shook his head –

"There was nothing I could do. She chose her path."

Startled at his manner my eyes sought the mountains outside the airport window.

"The Dreyers?" I mumbled.

Hans tried to laugh, stopped as the pain ripped through him.

"The Major. He hated me. I was his brother's son. The memory of his past deeds. For the record, throughout my childhood, and even into manhood I was afraid of him. Kurt followed his father."

His lips quivered.

I hesitate, speak the name that is haunting my mind-

"The 'slob' – Ottmar Wilner, what about him?"

Hans tried to smile, groaned from the pain, his voice quivering on the reply-

"He… he got away from what I have been told," sharp intake of breath – "the bureau cannot say where, although I have…" another gasp, "heard" – a deeper gasp "the guy promoted in Savannah's role…" – this time pain draws a tear to his eye, "her former sergeant, is trying to hunt him down…" – a whisper, "this game's for Jimmy no doubt."

I gaze at the man beside me, wonder if this is true, feel emotion tumbling from my heart in a torrent of confusion.

We sit, two figures lost in a moment of time, Hans hardly speaking, his pain visible, his fingers trailing through my shorter hair. Enveloped in our thoughts, I scan his face, thrill at the wonder of this miracle, hands clasped together as a ship-wrecked person clings to that solitary life raft. I hear the clanging of bells. Acknowledge the young man's wave from the desk. I move closer to Hans, catch the wince he tries to cover up, feel the cold lips pressed to my cheek.

"I promise, Rhia, not to let you down. As soon as I am well, I will seek you out."

I could feel the slow hot tears between our cheeks, turn my head, find that ice-cold mouth, and caress it with my own warm lips.

By the reception desk my guide is calling my name. Reluctantly I pull away, gather my travel bag, and walk toward him.

--

In the glow of the fire where my trekking party set camp for the night, we drink a little rice wine. Before me, the promise of my grandmother's wisdom. Behind me, the man who has turned my heart upside down.

Oh Reader, this story may be ending, but the conclusion is yet to be written.

Author's Note

As always at the ending of a book hovers that double sided emotion of relief and disappointment – my own double-edged sword.

Relief that the plot, or story has found its way onto paper, and disappointment that it now disconnects with me to find its own way into the world.

I believe that an author can act as a narrator to their story or share the journey of the protagonist within their pages. I enact a little of both, therefore allowing a clearer insight into history and its surroundings. So, it is with immense pride that part of the background to this book is connected to the city of my birth – Coventry, England.

With this in mind – I would like to thank the headmaster of Henry VIII School on Warwick Road Coventry for his permission for me to mention this wonderful building within my rhetoric (Page 223).

The painting of Christ in Glory by Hans Feibusch (Page 219) can be found within Saint Marks Church, on the corner of Bird Street, Coventry.

The Cathedral of Saint Michael positioned next to the bombed ruins of the Old Saint Michael Church, plus Holy Trinity Church, resides within the city centre, the former opposite Coventry University. Both are a tourist's delight and emotionally beautiful.

The Memorial Park lies at the top of Warwick Road, where the road forks to Kenilworth and Leamington Spa. Etta Detdy's flat is fictional (Page 224), to my knowledge no such address exists. Joining that fictitious address is Etta Detdy's Stoneleigh cottage, 'The Amour', 'The Brambles', 'The Tatters', the bar 'Respite from Life', and St Matthews Spinal Hospital; invented but nonetheless important.

The name Rufus, derived from Latin means 'red', or 'red haired'. Is Savannah D' Mill passing on a 'red' alert warning, or mentioning The Rufus File, or may it be a pet name for her sergeant?

Historical facts are as follows – Jakob Bartsch (1624) The Crux (Page11)

Lots' wife (Page 24) mentioned in the Bible at least four times in Genesis 19 – 15/16, again 26, and in Luke 17 – 32.

Mount Merapi, literally known as 'Fire Mountain', or 'Mountain of Fire' is an active volcano north of the city of Yogyakarta, Indonesia (Page 27)

Hall of Mirrors (Page 32) is based within the Palace of Versailles, France. Erected as a hunting lodge by King Louis XIII – Completed as a palace by his son Louis XIV.

The Workhouse (Page 32) were buildings constructed in past centuries where those suffering financial debt and homelessness were sent to work and live.

Mary Hewitt's poem 'The Spider and the Fly' is mentioned throughout the book, especially pages 34/58, as a precursor to someone who practices deceit.

The saying 'A stone that gathers no moss' on (Page 82) is a proverb credited to the Latin writer Publilius Syrus (83 – 43 B.C.).

Quote on (Page 212) belongs to Sir Thomas More (1478-1535)

The poem – 'Reflection', penned by Emily Edwards on (Page 280) was taken from her new poetry book – subject World War 2.

The saying "When truth hits you, it hits you hard" is penned by Emily Edwards.

Cyclops Eye (Page 282) refers to a large one eyed giant.

It is with grateful thanks to Sarah, that after I unknowingly lost the first edited manuscript of this book, she encouraged me to re-write this sequel. I will forever say 'Thank you'.